MATILDA examined her bruises; she was quite pleased with them. How William had tugged her hair. Had he admired it? He must have noticed how golden it was. When she allowed it to escape from its plaits, it hung round her like a cape. He must have been aware of it when he had pulled her from her horse by it.

What impertinence! She could not forget it. "I have made up my mind," she told her parents. "I will marry William, the Duke of Normandy."

"My dear child, the man maltreated you."

"I know, Father. He threw me into the gutter, he seized me by my hair. I believe he took great delight in ruining my gown and bruising my skin. But, Father, what a man he is. I wasn't afraid. I was just excited, excited because there is such a man in the world—a man who takes what he wants and is unafraid—and I am going to marry him."

Fawcett Crest Books
by Jean Plaidy:

THE CAPTIVE OF KENSINGTON PALACE

THE QUEEN AND LORD M

THE QUEEN'S HUSBAND

THE WIDOW OF WINDSOR

THE GOLDSMITH'S WIFE

LIGHT ON LUCREZIA

THE BASTARD KING

A NOVEL BY

Jean Plaidy

FAWCETT CREST • NEW YORK

THE BASTARD KING

THIS BOOK CONTAINS THE COMPLETE TEXT OF
THE ORIGINAL HARDCOVER EDITION.

Published by Fawcett Crest Books, a unit of CBS Publica-
tions, the Consumer Publishing Division of CBS Inc., by
arrangement with G.P. Putnam's Sons

ISBN: 0-449-24273-0

Printed in the United States of America

First Fawcett Crest Printing: March 1980

10 9 8 7 6 5 4 3 2 1

ROLLO

WILLIAM LONGSWORD

RICHARD THE FEARLESS

RICHARD II   EMMA m. ETHELRED m. CANUTE

RICHARD III   ROBERT The MAGNIFICENT   EDWARD The CONFESSOR   ALFRED   HARDICANUTE

WILLIAM THE CONQUEROR
m.
MATILDA OF FLANDERS

ROBERT   ADELISA   WILLIAM RUFUS   ADELA   HENRY

CECILY   RICHARD   CONSTANCE   GUNDRED

PART ONE

THE BASTARD

The Birth of the Bastard

On a hot summer's day in the year 1026, Robert, Viscount of Exmes, who was the brother of the reigning Duke of Normandy, saw a beautiful girl washing her family's linen in the River Ante which ran at the foot of the castle of Falaise, and his desire for her changed the course of history.

Robert, aged seventeen and the second son of Richard, Duke of Normandy, was of a nature to resent the fact that he had not been born the elder. That his brother—named Richard after their father—should have become the Duke when he, already known as Robert the Magnificent, should have to stand aside merely because he had had the misfortune to be born a year or so later, was unendurable. It was for this reason that he was endeavouring to take his brother's ducal crown from him, that he had captured the castle of Falaise, and was at that time in residence there.

It was certain that Richard would make an attempt to wrest it from him so the castle was well fortified and from the towers sentinels were on duty through the day and night, but Robert took time off to hunt the wild boar which abounded in the nearby forest; and it was as he was returning from such a hunt that the meeting took place.

Even during the first encounter Robert sensed the unusual qualities of the girl. She was undoubtedly beautiful but there were many beautiful girls in Normandy. She was young. Perhaps she had seen no more than fourteen winters. There was a pride about her and a dignity as she stood there, skirts above her knees exposing her white shapely legs while she stamped on her linen and

8

sang a song which Duke Rollo had brought with him from the Scandinavian countries whence he came to the land of France with his warriors in their long ships and so plagued the King of that country that he had been forced to concede to him that land now known as Normandy.

The girl's long hair fell cape-like about her shoulders; her blue eyes were soft as she sang but the pride and dignity of a Viking's daughter was evident.

Robert, who had had no compunction in taking the castle of Falaise, would certainly have let nothing stand in the way of the gratification of his senses, and he desired this girl as he never had another. So he commanded his followers to return to the castle and leave him. Alone he made his way to the edge of the river, but if she noticed him she did not appear to do so; she went on stamping her clothes and singing.

'Good morrow, maiden,' he called.

She lifted her head and, as she looked at him, his senses exulted in the pleasure to come; she was even more beautiful than he had realized.

'What do you do here?' he asked.

'I am washing your linen, good sir.'

'I like you well,' he said. 'Whence come you?'

'From the town,' she answered. 'My father is Fulbert, the tanner.'

'Come out of the river, daughter of Fulbert the tanner. Or shall I come to you?'

Her face flushed faintly. 'Neither,' she answered. 'For I have my work and you are too fine a gentleman to dally with me.'

If she were afraid, she did not show it. He could stride into the river and seize her. Who would dare question the action of the lord of Falaise? Her family? Nay, he would quickly show them to whom they owed allegiance if they attempted to curtail his pleasure. He would cut off the hand of any man who raised it against him. Aye, and nail it to the door of his dwelling as a lesson to others.

Yet he did nothing. The dignity of the girl disturbed him. Strangely enough he was content to wait. It would only be a postponement. He had now sensed that quality in her. It should not be a quick encounter on the turf. He would prefer it in a castle chamber.

So he was content to stand there looking at her, the sun on her golden hair, she, poised like a deer or a gazelle, wary

9

and by no means eager to obey the lord of the castle.

He lifted his shoulders and jumped on to his horse, and for a few moments remained looking down on her. She went on stamping the clothes. He hesitated. Should he seize her, teach her to show insolence to the lord to whom she owed allegiance, or should he bide his time? She was very young; perhaps she did not understand what he wanted of her. She was a virgin child—perhaps even younger than she appeared to be.

He rode on to the castle.

*   *   *

She looked up and saw his retreating figure.

She knew him of course. She had had a glimpse of him when he came riding into Falaise. Her grandmother and her father talked of him and his mighty family.

'Trouble there will be,' her father had said. 'For Robert is not the one to take a second place. And second he must be, for his elder brother is Duke Richard's heir and that's all to be said of it.'

He was also not the one to see a desirable girl and pass her by because she did not come to him when he beckoned—unless there were so many waiting for him at the castle.

She could not be indifferent to him, for he was powerful and goodly to look upon; and she, who loved so much to sit at the feet of her grandmother and listen to the stories of the great gods and heroes of the Northlands, believed that she had seen one of them by the river that day.

*   *   *

In the hall of the castle, Robert was restless. There was only one fire on this day as it was summer and over that, at one end of the hall, hung the great cauldrons in which the food was cooking. The scullions hovered over it, anxious to placate Robert's ill-humour; the smoke rose up to the vaulted roof and escaped through a louvre there. It was cool and dark in the hall for the thick walls which kept out the heat kept out the light as well; the windows were narrow slits open to the elements.

Robert was still thinking of the maiden in the stream and was angry with himself for not taking the girl and settling the matter there and then; when he was angry with himself he vented his wrath on others, and his servants were afraid to approach him.

Not so his squire. Osbern de Crépon, a young man of a dignity which matched his own, a friend whom he trusted. Osbern came to him and asked what had happened to put him into an ill-humour and before long Robert was telling him about the girl he had seen that afternoon.

'A maiden!' cried Osbern. 'When have you not known how to deal with a maiden?'

'She had an air ... unlike any I have seen before.'

Osbern laughed. 'What has happened to you? Was she a sorceress?'

'Of a kind,' answered Robert moodily.

'Come, we cannot have you sad. This is a simple matter. Send for her.'

'Would she come, think you?'

'Are you not lord of Falaise?'

'In truth I am and would have every man know it.'

'And woman too. What's stopping you? Who is the maid?'

'She is beautiful.'

'So you said. Thanks be to God there are many such in Normandy.'

'A true Norman. Hair like gold and a proud spirit. She is the daughter of one Fulbert, a tanner.'

'Ha, would you be so squeamish about a tanner's daughter!'

Robert laughed. 'Nay,' he cried. 'Send for her. Have her brought to me this night.'

* * *

The linen had dried well that day. She had brought it into the cottage and folded it. Her father—the finest tanner in the town of Falaise—watched her as she laid it aside and went to the pot which was boiling over the fire.

A fine girl, his Arlette; each day she grew more and more beautiful. He would have to find a husband for her; he wanted to see his grandsons before he died.

She was thoughtful today; silently she went about the cottage room. She could not get out of her mind the memory of the bold man who had stopped by the stream to look at her.

11

So clearly he had brought back to her mind the stories her grandmother told her of the great Duke Rollo who was so big that no horse was strong enough to carry him, of William Longsword and Richard the Fearless. These were his ancestors and they lived again in him. They were descendants of the men who had come in their long ships—the great men of the sea, the explorers, the conquerors. In their own land whence Rollo had come, they had worshipped the gods and heroes—Odin and Thor, Beowulf and Sigurd. They had been fearless, brave and bowed to no man.

She had seen one of their like today; and she knew that she would never forget him. So she was sad, thinking that ere long some man would speak for her; perhaps it would be one of her father's apprentices, and she would spend the rest of her life among the odour of skins; and something told her that she would never cease to remember the day when one of the heroes of the land had stopped briefly to admire her.

Darkness had fallen when the sound of horse's hoofs came near to the cottage. Someone was at the door. Could it be that he had returned?

Her father had stood up, shielding her. The man had stepped into the cottage. She began to tremble because she knew that it was a servant who had been sent from the castle.

'What do you wish?' asked the tanner and she could hear the tremor in his voice.

'You have a daughter,' was the answer.

Her father was silent, but she stepped before him and said: 'I am the daughter of Fulbert, the tanner.'

'I have a message for you. You are to come with me to the Castle.'

'Who sent you?'

'My seigneur.'

'Why does he send for me?'

She was aware of the smirk on the man's lips and her spirit was in sudden revolt. She rejoiced that he had not forgotten her, yet she knew what this meant. He had not come to her in person; he had sent his servant. She would be taken into the castle when it was dark and be returned to her father's cottage before sunrise. It had happened to others before. But it must not happen to her. This was different. Why had he ridden away after he had seen her?

She was sure that never before had he done such a thing. He had desired her; she was aware of that. And she had never been so deeply moved, bewildered and uncertain in the whole of her life. This was important to her; it must be important to him.

She would not be taken to his castle to be returned to her father's cottage and sent for again mayhap if he could find none better to amuse him. No. Some instinct commanded her.

She said: 'Go back to your master. Tell him that if he wishes me to come to his castle, I will do so—but not by stealth. I will not be taken in by some postern gate as a woman who is of no account. If he wishes me to come willingly I will come to him by daylight. He must lower the drawbridge and I will ride into the castle on a horse he will send for me. He will furnish me with an escort. That is the only manner in which I shall ride to your seigneur.'

The man laughed at her.

'The seigneur is in an evil mood,' he warned her.

'I have said my say,' she retorted.

He bowed and rode away.

The tanner looked at his daughter. 'What came over you?'

'I know not. It was as though something spoke for me.'

'I fear. I fear for you, and for myself.'

'He will not harm us, Father.'

The tanner shook his head.

He had seen many a hand nailed to a door. He looked down at his own which he stretched out before him. How could he carry on his work without it? Perhaps they could fly. To Rouen? They could be followed there. What of his trade? He was well known in Falaise ... the finest tanner in the town. What had come over Arlette? She might bear a bastard it was true, but it would be a noble bastard. The Dukes and their family were good to their women. But they did not care to be flouted. And Robert—he whom some called Robert the Devil—others Robert the Magnificent—was a proud man.

As for Arlette her moment of triumph had passed. She sat in a pile of skins in the corner of the room and thought of what she had done. Would he send for her? Would he take her by force? Would he burn down her father's cottage? Or would he ignore her. No, never that. He would surely not allow an insult to pass.

Through the night she did not sleep. Nor did her father. At every sound they started up.

And at last the sun rose and it was day again. They had lived through the night; but what would the day bring?

Throughout the morning none from the castle came near the tanner's cottage. But an hour after noon, a party of men rode up.

The tanner shut the door and drew the heavy bolt but Arlette cried: 'Do you think that will save us! Let us at least show good spirit.'

She opened the door and stood there, the sunlight gleaming on her golden braids, her tall figure erect, her blue eyes flashing.

The leader of the party had dismounted. He came towards her leading a richly caparisoned horse.

He bowed before her.

'My lady,' he said, 'we have come to escort you to the castle, over the drawbridge, in full light of day.'

She smiled; she had never known such triumphant joy.

She turned to her father who was cowering behind her in the cottage.

'Father,' she said, 'I go to the Seigneur with honour. This is a day to rejoice.'

She mounted the horse and surrounded by a fine array she rode across the drawbridge into the castle of Falaise.

* * *

They were well matched—the tanner's daughter and the descendant of the Dukes of Normandy. She had both beauty and spirit; she was Brunhilde to his Sigurd; and, in the weeks even before their child was conceived, they were aware of this.

There was an unusual dignity about her; it was as though she had spent all her life in castles; any slights which came her way, for many believed that her power over the seigneur was, by nature of their relationship, transient, were met by indifference and disdain. Robert was surprised by his own emotions. He delighted in her. He sought no other woman and it quickly became clear to the members of his household that it would go ill with them if they did not pay true respect to the Lady Arlette.

When she knew she was with child she was exultant.

'Now,' she told Robert, 'I shall always have someone to remind me of you.'

14

He passionately declared that she would need no reminder because he always intended to keep her at his side.

She shook her head for, although she believed then in his vows of lifelong fidelity, they lived in dangerous times; and Robert was not a peaceable man and was even now living precariously in a castle he had taken from his brother.

But for the first few weeks after their meeting there was nothing to disturb their love; and with each passing day the bond between them strengthened. Robert was to find a depth in Arlette which delighted him; as for Arlette, Robert was for her a figure of romance and legend. He had stepped straight out of one of those stories which her grandmother had told her; he was Rollo and Sigurd all in one.

Robert was indeed a colourful character. A man of great contrasts, he was capable of acts of devilish cruelty and considerate kindness. He was extravagant; he loved finery and he could be chivalrous. This side of his nature was brought out through his connection with Arlette. He was a strong man and there were many who fervently agreed that it was a tragedy for Normandy that his less spectacular brother Richard should have been their father's first-born. There mingled in him many characteristics of his sea-roving ancestors with a fervent desire to be a good Christian. Young—he was only seventeen years old at the time of his meeting with Arlette—he was tall, handsome, vital; he was not known as Robert the Magnificent for nothing.

When he knew that Arlette had conceived he was overcome with delight. He wanted a son in his own image.

He would in due course be obliged to marry, to get an heir who could well be the Duke of Normandy. Robert was certain that his feeble brother could not remain in possession of what should surely have been his by right of everything but the year of his birth.

So he rejoiced with Arlette.

One night Arlette had a strange dream. She awoke in terror calling out: 'No...it is a child I bear...not this great tree.'

Robert, awakened, soothed her tenderly and she lay against him telling him of her strange dream.

In this her time had come and the child was about to be born; eagerly she awaited to hear its cry. But instead of a child there came forth from her a great tree which spread its branches across the town of Falaise on to Rouen and it grew and grew until it covered the whole of Normandy and beyond.

'It is a sign,' said Robert. 'This child within you is no ordinary one. He will be a great man. As great as mighty Rollo perhaps.'

She was soothed, contented, and passionately she longed for the birth of her child.

She was sure it would be a boy and that Robert would do his duty by him. But would he in truth raise his bastard son to rule over Normandy? Of one thing she felt certain: he would if he could. If it were within his power the fruit of her body should stand side by side with the Dukes of Normandy.

* * *

Arlette often visited her father's cottage. There her old grandmother sat at the spinning wheel, as she had in the days when Arlette was a child. It was at her feet that Arlette had sat and listened to the stories of the past.

To her grandmother she went to tell her of her strange dream.

'The child within you will be a boy,' said the old woman. 'He will be born to greatness.'

'He will be a bastard,' said Arlette. 'Robert must needs marry. What of the sons he will have by his true wedded wife?'

'Our dukes have ever loved their mistresses more dearly than their wives. William Longsword was a bastard and have you forgotten the case of Richard the Fearless?'

'Tell me again,' said Arlette; and there she sat in the darkened cottage while the distaff was idle and her grandmother talked of the old days.

'And Richard the Fearless out hunting in the forest came to a cottage and there he saw a beautiful woman. He passionately desired her and though she was the wife of one of his foresters, he reminded the man of the *droit de Seigneur.*'

Arlette nodded. How many a young girl had been taken to the seigneur that he might deflower the virgin before her marriage.

'Now the forester's wife loved her husband dearly and she determined that no lord on earth should take his place. So she went to her sister Gunnor, as beautiful as herself,

16

and she said: 'When it is dark go you to the Duke's chamber and lie with him in my place, for you have no husband and will betray no man.' This Gunnor agreed to do; and by the time Richard at length discovered the deception he was so deeply enamoured of Gunnor that he laughed and bore no grudge against his forester's faithful wife.'

'But he married the daughter of the King of Paris.'

'And loved her not. She bore him no children and when she died he married Gunnor; and Gunnor bore many children and one of these was Richard, the second Duke of Normandy, who was the father of your own Robert.'

Arlette said: 'And this child I carry?'

'Who knows. He could one day be a Duke of Normandy.'

Arlette smiled. 'When Robert is not the Duke? When my child will be a bastard?'

'Hush. Have I not told you that many of our dukes were bastards? Is it not a fact that our men have loved their mistresses more dearly than their wives? Something tells me that 'ere long your Robert will be Duke of Normandy. If he is, and if he continues to love you . . . and if the child you bear should be a boy . . . a boy of spirit and courage, a true Norman, who can say?'

Thoughtfully Arlette went back to the castle.

* * *

In a few weeks' time the child would be born and Arlette had prepared her lying-in chamber; it was to be a room in the castle from which she could look down on the river Ante and remember the day when she had gone there to wash the family's linen.

That she was loved by Robert was something like a miracle; that she was to bear his child made her happiness complete.

She had prepared the child's garments and she could not wait to hold him in her arms.

On this day the hunters had brought home the deer—a fine large stag which was carried in by two bearers. The smell of cooking filled the hall; the cooks were bustling over the fire; a young boy, son of one of the foresters, was set to turning the spit; and soon they would be seated at the feast.

In her bower Arlette put on the velvet tunic with the long flowing sleeves which so became her and undid her braids so that her golden hair fell about her shoulders. That she

17

was large with her child detracted not a whit from her beauty.

Down in the hall, the floor had been strewn with fresh rushes, the board had been set up on trestles and the benches placed round it. At the top of the table was placed the only chair—that of honour—in which Robert always sat and on his right hand was Arlette's place. After the company had eaten drinking horns would be put on the table, and there would be singing and telling of tales.

Robert was in a merry mood. He was planning fresh conquests. He had stayed in Falaise so long because of Arlette but he would soon have to set a guard in Falaise and move on to Rouen. His eyes gleamed at the thought. Rouen was the first city of Normandy. When it was in his hands, then he could indeed rejoice.

The meat was carved; the Duke served first, then Arlette. She used an ornamental knife which had been given to her by Robert so that she did not have to use her hands as much as menials did. She was fast learning castle manners.

The stag meat was tender; they had eaten heartily and were drinking; one of the minstrels was about to give a song—an old sea song which the Vikings had sung as they roamed the seas in search of lands to plunder—when there was sound from without and a man came running into the hall to fling himself at Robert's feet.

This man's clothes were dirt-stained; he was gasping as he cried out: 'My lord, they are but a few miles away. They will attack at dawn.'

Robert immediately demanded that the man be seated and tell his story.

He was one of those, he said, who wished to see Robert, Duke of Normandy; he was an innkeeper and men had come to his house, taken his food and his daughters, and in their cups had talked. They were on their way to the castle of Falaise and planned a surprise attack.

Robert stood up.

'The feasting is over,' he said.

The messenger was refreshed and further questioned. Robert shouted orders, commanding his followers to get to the defences.

Then he looked at Arlette.

'You must not stay here. Who knows what could happen to you? You must leave at once for your father's cottage.'

18

She said: 'My place is with you.'

He smiled at her tenderly. ''Twould be so,' he replied, 'but for the child. Our first thoughts must be for him. I would not have him harmed for anything in the Dukedom.'

She saw the wisdom of this and allowed herself to be escorted back to her father's house.

*   *   *

From the castle came the sounds of battle. Duke Richard's men surrounded it; his soldiers were encamped on the grassy slopes, and the sickening sound of their shrieks could be heard through the town as boiling oil was poured down on them from the turrets. It was the sound of the battering ram for which Arlette listened. How was Robert faring from within? Could he hold the castle against his brother?

She longed for news of the battle though she was certain of the outcome. Robert must be victorious for it was not conceivable that he could be beaten. The people of Falaise were with him to a man; they had declared often enough that Normandy needed a strong man and Robert was the man.

But now the child was impatient to be born and she could think of nothing else. The grandmother was there with a woman to help her and together they delivered him. Lusty his lungs proclaimed him to be and it was necessary to neglect him while they looked to his mother.

'He can wait awhile,' declared the grandmother, 'but what think you our lord would say if aught befell Arlette?'

So the boy was laid on the straw and left to himself and when Arlette heard the whisper: 'A boy, a lusty boy!' she remembered the dream of a great tree which grew from her body and cast its shelter over the whole of Normandy and beyond.

When the women were assured that Arlette was no longer in danger they turned their attention to the child.

In his fingers was the straw he had caught up from the floor. 'Why look at this,' cried the grandmother. 'He has grasped the straw!'

His mother smiled. 'Already,' she said, 'he is grasping everything within his reach.'

19

'I never such power in a new-born babe,' murmured the grandmother.

So in the tanner's cottage, to the sounds of battle, the bastard was born. He was named William and his mother believed that he was born to great destiny.

The Duke of Normandy

THE stone walls of the castle rose above the town; from the turrets sentinels kept their watch; in the great hall the servants clustered about the fire and the smell of roasting venison filled the air. Above the hall in her boudoir the Lady Arlette sat with her women. Her daughter Adeliz sat at her feet playing with her embroidery silks, and as the women talked they listened for the sounds of arrival.

Now and then Arlette rose to go to the window cut in the thick stone walls, shading her eyes to look for the company of horsemen with Robert riding at the head of them. He would be eager, she knew, to be with her, to caress her, to swear his undying devotion which he had proved for the last six years; and his first words would be when he had done this: 'And where is the boy?'

She smiled and looked down at the courtyard now where he played with his companions—the sons of barons and counts whom Robert had decreed should be his companions. 'For, my love,' said Robert, 'he must be brought up among men. He must quickly learn to leave the shelter of his mother's skirts.'

He had learned that already. She watched him strut below—a leader if ever there was one. His short green tunic which reached to his knees became him well. His neck was bare, as were his arms and legs. Looking down on that group of boys none would have had any doubt to who was Robert's son. They played with sticks which in their minds were swords and already they were taking lessons in the art of chivalry which must be mastered by all well-born boys.

William was shouting: 'You will follow me. Come. Thor ayde. Thor ayde.'

Where did he learn such things? wondered Arlette. From the old women of the household who would never forget that they came from the land across the sea and would always sigh for the pine forests and the fiords.

William had dropped his stick suddenly; he had had enough of fighting; he wished to hunt and he had his new falcon to try out.

Should she call him? Should she say: 'William, your father may be here at any moment. You will hear them riding into the courtyard. Go and change your tunic. Comb your hair. Let your father be proud of you when he comes'? Or should she let him be seen as he was, his eyes alight with the triumph of his mock battle or with his sparrow hawk and his dogs and horses?

Robert did not want a boy in a clean tunic with his dark hair neatly combed; he wanted a son who would be a fighter, a leader. She knew that he intended that boy to follow him, to rule all Normandy when he was in his grave. It had been a prophecy—that dream of hers. The boy down there in the courtyard, in spite of the fact that he was Robert's illegitimate son, was destined to rule Normandy.

William was unaware of his mother's scrutiny. He must make the most of his play hour. Soon old Mauger would be sending his men for him. He would be reminded as he had been a hundred times: 'There are lessons to be learned from books, my young lord, as well as from games.'

William disliked Uncle Mauger; there was something sly about him which he sensed and, even though he was supposed to revere him because he was an Archbishop and a learned man, he never could do so. He much preferred Osbern the Seneschal who could be stern too but in a manner which inspired respect; but he liked even better the company of Gallet the Fool. Gallet amused him; he was full of strange tricks. It was said that his brain was addled, but William was not so sure. He had a way with dogs and knew how to train a falcon. Surely such a man could not be a complete fool? He adored William too—another reason for his good sense; there was nothing the Fool liked better than to do some task for the little master, as he called him.

Then there was his cousin Guy, who was being brought up with him, trained in the arts of chivalry, learning to sit his horse like a Norman, and to excel in the arts of war; and who must, much to his chagrin, share those tiresome hours in the schoolroom with sly Uncle Mauger, who was Guy's uncle too.

Guy gave him airs now and then because he was legitimate. William was not sure what this meant; all he knew was that Guy was proud of being so. Uncle Mauger, he whispered to William, might teach them and punish them when they were idle, but he was a bastard for all that; and they should not forget it.

William stood ecstatically sniffing the roasting venison. This was a special occasion. His father was coming. For this reason the foresters had brought in a fine stag of ten branches and everyone had marvelled at him. It was fitting that they should have brought in a stag like that for such an occasion.

He was hungry. He wished his father would come. He went into the hall and stood watching the sizzling meat.

'Stand clear, little master,' said one of the servants, 'or you'll be splashed.'

'Yes, little master, fine meat for a fine occasion.'

'My father will soon be here,' he said. 'He comes from Rouen.'

They did not answer him. They knew it well and he did not mean to tell them news but merely wished to talk to them.

They forgot him and went on with what they had been talking of before he arrived. He stood listening. He listened a good deal. He liked to hear people's talk, particularly when they seemed to be unaware of him. It was then that it became more interesting. Today they were not talking of his father's visit, though they might well have been, but of someone who lived near by and who, William believed, was in truth the Devil.

Often when they had been talking of Talvas of Bellême and he approached they would nudge each other and there would be a significant silence. For this very reason he had become greatly interested in the man. There was something quite shocking about him. He had heard old men warn boys of being on the road after dark. 'Talvas could get you,' they said; and there would be such a look of horror on their faces that William himself shuddered without quite knowing why.

Now he was certain that the cooks had been talking of Talvas by the manner in which they had stopped when he approached.

He went into a corner and sat down behind one of the benches and gave himself up to enjoying the delicious aroma of cooking venison and thinking of his father, whose

23

father had been Richard the Second, Duke of Normandy, whose father had been Richard the Fearless, the first of that name, and whose father in his turn was Duke William Longsword the son of great Rollo. For one thing he must learn first was of his ancestors and of the land of fiords, mountains and pine forests whence they came, and of the heroes of that land such as Ragnar and Sigurd who had become famous in history because of their courage.

Courage, bravery, to live without fear, that was the Norman code. He learned that from his father; it was above all things never to be forgotten. With Uncle Mauger it was a matter of poring over books, learning to read and write, a tiresome preoccupation when there were ponies to ride and falcons to be trained, sword-play to be mastered, archery to be practised.

He liked to be with his mother to hear of the magnificence of his father who according to her was the greatest Duke Normandy had known, even greater than Rollo and Richard the Fearless; she told him the stories of the heroes which her grandmother had told her. His grandfather Fulbert lived at the Palace and William loved him because he was different from anyone else he knew. He used to tell William how to skin a wolf and tan it and how the resulting leather was useful for so many things. Life was full of interest; he felt secure and well guarded for he was aware that when he rode out Osbern always kept close to him and he was never allowed out of the Seneschal's sight. He could not help being aware that he was to be especially cherished. It was not so much because he was a little boy whose mother loved him dearly and whose father was interested in him and who had so many friends in the castle; there was another reason. It was because his father was the Duke of Normandy and he was his only son.

Richard the Fearless must have felt this when his father William Longsword came to visit him—for fathers it seemed rarely lived in their castles with their families; they were always away on other business which invariably involved fighting. Now he, William, awaited a visit from his father, Robert the Magnificent. He wondered what they would call him when he was a man, William the ... ? What should it be? He would like William the Brave, he thought.

Now they had forgotten him and were whispering together. He heard the name Count Talvas de Bellême. Yes, they had gone back to the Devil.

'No one is safe on the roads. If you're found you'll be taken to the castle of Domfront Alençon. And there you will be thrust into a dungeon. And they say that he then asks his friends to a feast and when they have drunk their fill and beyond, the prisoners are brought up from the dungeons...'

'And then...what then?'

'Then they make sport with them.'

'They kill them?'

'It could come to that in time. But there's no hurry about it. 'Tis a slow matter. Nails are torn off, eyes put out...hands and feet cut off and made sport with.'

William put his hands to his eyes; he looked at his hands.

They went on whispering together; he wanted to stop his ears but he had to listen. He could see it all so clearly; the hall at Domfront Castle which would be like that at Falaise, the cowering prisoners—young men and old ones too who had been unwise enough to be caught by the Count of Bellême's men who prowled after dark in search of the unwary.

He could not bear it. He ran out crying: 'No, no. It is not true. It is wicked. Only traitors should be treated thus!'

The varlets stared at him; the face of the chief cook even redder than before.

'The little master!' he said.

One of the women came forward and said: 'What then, little master? Was it a bad dream then, a nightmare?'

He stood facing them, his grey eyes flashing. Did they think he was such a baby to be put off with tales of nightmares? Had he heard them, or had he not? He might be only five but he would remind them that, although five might be very young for some, it was a different matter with the son of the Duke of Normandy.

''Twas no nightmare,' he said. 'I heard you talking of Bellême.'

There was a gasp among the company. One of the women knelt down beside him. 'Listen to me, little master. We did talk, but you listened and to listen is sly, you know. The Lady Arlette would not be pleased to know that you hide in corners to spy.'

'I did not spy. I heard...'

'What you were not meant to hear! Now go out into the courtyard, go back to your play and forget what you heard here. For we did wrong to talk so, and you did wrong to hide

25

yourself and listen. And what's done and can't be mended is best forgot.'

He nodded slowly. There was wisdom in it.

He walked out into the courtyard but he could not get out of his mind the thought of the hall of Domfront Castle and the cruel things that were done to the innocent...such things which should only be done as punishment for great crimes such as disloyalty to one's sovereign Duke.

He would go to see his sparrow-hawk—always a heartening matter, but before he could cross the courtyard he heard the sound of horses' hoofs and the clatter of arrival.

William forgot everything but that his father had come. He did not stop running until he came to the porch. Across the drawbridge rode his father, a little ahead of his escort. He wore the purple robe which proclaimed his rank and on his head the velvet cap edged with ermine; William was aware of the sword in its ornamental scabbard at his side, the steel which covered his legs and feet. Jewels glittered in his cap and at his throat. He was indeed a magnificent sight!

William wanted to hold his stirrup while he alighted but he was not allowed to perform this important ceremony, but his father noted his attempt and was pleased by it.

Osbern was watching him, William knew. He must do what was expected of him. Otherwise he would suffer reproaches. But that was not so important as that he should shine in his father's eyes.

The Duke towered above the small boy. William knelt in homage to receive his blessing. The Duke muttered a prayer for he was a very religious man—though his actions did not always point to this.

He rose and the Duke picked him up and held him high above him.

'You've grown, boy,' he said.

'Yes, Father. I thought you would wish it.'

'And have learnt much, I trust?'

'Yes, Father.'

'We shall put you to the test.'

A look of apprehension crossed his face when he thought of what Uncle Mauger might report, but there was such love and pride in his father's face that he soon forgot that.

'Now, to your mother,' said the Duke.

And walking side by side they went into the castle.

Robert embraced Arlette and marvelled at her beauty once more as he did on every occasion after a separation.

'So you are well and happy,' he said.

'Now that you have come,' she answered.

He must kiss their little daughter, but Adeliz, for all her charm, could not delight him as the boy did.

It was good to be home with his family, for this was his family. He had married for form's sake Estrith, the sister of King Canute of England, but he had no children by her and had soon left her to be with Arlette.

They feasted in the hall and Robert would have his son beside him. A boy could not learn too soon, he said.

'He is but five,' Arlette reminded him.

'This is a boy who must shoulder responsibilities early.'

'Why so?' replied Arlette. 'You have many years to watch over his growing up.'

Robert did not answer and his silence made Arlette uneasy.

The company ate heartily of the venison; they drank freely; there was music and jesting and the telling of stories. Many times had little William heard how Ragnar slew the dragon and Sigurd passed through the ring of fire but it thrilled him afresh. However, soon he was asleep and his mother took him on to her lap and he knew no more until next morning when he awakened to find himself asleep on his bag of straw and remembered that his father was at the castle.

* * *

In the peace of their chamber Arlette and Robert talked into the night; and they talked of William.

'My heart rejoices in the boy,' said Robert. 'You have given me much and among that my great treasure, my son.'

'Who could but be proud of such a one?'

'He is advanced for his age. I can scarcely believe it is but five years since they brought the news to me of his birth.'

'He is all that we could have wished for, though Mauger complains of a lack of attention at his books.'

Robert laughed. 'I'd not have him otherwise. I want my son to be a duke, not a clerk.'

27

'That will be in the far future.'

Robert was silent and the fear returned to Arlette; she knew there was something he had to tell her and that he was putting it off, for he did not wish to spoil their first night together after their separation.

She said: 'Sometimes I wish that you were not the Duke. If your brother had lived...'

She should not have said that. She knew in her heart that he was not guiltless of his brother's death. She had believed often that his involvement in that death overshadowed him, lay like a burden on his mind—one which he could cast aside for a long period and suddenly find he was carrying it again. She sensed that he carried it now.

The battle for Falaise which had been going on at the time of William's birth had been inconclusive. Richard III had made a truce with Robert, but the friction remained; Robert could never take second place; he had been determined that nothing must stop his becoming the Duke and since he had had a son, he was more than ever determined.

Richard had sat down to a banquet one day and had never risen from the table; nor had those who sat down with him. There could only be one solution to such a happening. Someone had poisoned them. And who had everything to gain from Richard's death—who but his brother Robert? Robert had not been at the scene of the multiple deaths, but that fact did not exonerate him. At whose orders had the poison been administered? The answer to that question would point to the man responsible for the murder.

Fractricide? It was a deadly sin. Yet, Robert had often convinced himself, only good had come of it. Normandy now had a strong Duke where before it had had a weak one. The fate of Normandy was too important to Rollo's descendants to allow any squeamishness over a death or two.

This seemed to have been the conclusion the people came to, for although they deplored the method of removing Richard, they must applaud the accession of Robert known as the Devil or the Magnificent according to how one felt towards him.

He was a good ruler, a man dedicated to Normandy; a deeply religious man whenever it was not impossible to his interests to be so. He had no legitimate son but the little bastard at Falaise was good proof that he was capable of

28

begetting fine sons. So the manner of Richard's death was forgotten and Robert was accepted as the Duke.

Arlette had rejoiced because she believed that this would be an end to the fighting; but it seemed there was always some matter of danger to disturb the lives of such as Robert.

This reunion must be a happy one, but she could not resist trying to discover what was disturbing Robert.

They talked of William—a happy subject.

'I have made up my mind,' said Robert, 'that he shall follow me. He shall be my successor. Your son, my love, will be the next Duke of Normandy.'

'Will the people accept him?'

'If I command it.'

'We love him dearly. We know him to be the finest boy in Normandy. Remember, Robert, though, my humble birth. Can the daughter of a tanner give birth to a Duke of Normandy?'

'If she is the best and most beautiful woman in the Duchy, yes.'

'And he basely born as some would say?'

'Never use that word of him, Arlette. A bastard he is and we must accept this. But he was *my* bastard and that is better than being any other man's legitimate son.'

'You have many years to reign as Duke, my beloved.'

'I trust so, but who can say. Many of us are cut off in our prime.'

She heard the catch in his voice and she knew he was thinking of his brother. How could he help it? They had played together in the castles of Rouen and Falaise. They had slept on the same straw; they had sat at the same board. Brothers! And now one dead at the hands of the other.

If he had been as his ancestors had been perhaps he would have suffered less remorse. Odin, Thor, Freya, they would have understood. He had killed because he needs must, because for the good of Normandy a strong Duke must reign. But he was a Christian and Christians must expiate their sins.

At length he said: 'Arlette, most heavily does my sin hang over me.'

She said: 'You have given Normandy a strong Duke. Yourself.'

'I bear the Curse of Cain,' he said. 'Sometimes I fear that until I can cast off my sin I shall carry it with me.'

She held him tightly in her arms. 'For tonight,' she said, 'you are safe with me.'

He was silent for a while and then he said. 'Arlette, I have been thinking of what I could do. If I made a pilgrimage to the Holy Land and prostrated myself before a holy shrine I could obtain forgiveness for all my sins. Perhaps I should do this, Arlette.'

'You would leave us for so long?'

'But think, when I come back I shall be cleansed of my sins. My conscience will be free.'

'And while you are away what of Normandy?'

'I have good and faithful men here.'

'And will they remain good and faithful, deprived of their Duke?'

'They shall have their Duke.'

'But he will be far away.'

'I shall leave them ... William.'

'A child.'

'Others of our Dukes have taken on the ducal role at an early age.'

'But he is so young ... and a bastard.'

'Was not Richard the Fearless?'

'You must not go. You must stay here. God will forgive you more readily for looking after your son and your home than for making this pilgrimage.'

'I must go, Arlette. Something commands me.'

She knew well that it was useless to try to persuade him, so she said: 'And you would indeed make our son your heir?'

'It has ever been my intention.'

'How soon shall you go?'

'When my affairs are in order.'

'And one of these will be to make the barons swear fealty to your heir?'

'Yes. But there is much to be done,' he said.

'You will prepare the child?'

'Is he old enough to understand?'

'He must be old enough since you are forcing this burden on him.'

'I shall be back ere long.'

'And he will remain your heir?'

'Have I not said he shall follow me?'

'You must remember ...'

'That he is a bastard, yes! Perhaps he will be called William the Bastard but when he remembers who his parents were he will see no disgrace in that.'

'You love this boy as you could have loved a son born in wedlock if you had one.'

'I love him as I could never love another child. He is the son of his mother and just as I can love none other as I love her, so it is with her child.'

'So, because I went down to the stream to wash clothes one summer's day I am to be the mother of the next Duke of Normandy.'

'There, does the thought not give you pleasure?'

'None, for he could only be so by the death of his father. Stay with me, Robert.'

'Ask anything else of me. But let me purge my conscience. Let me return to you with this sin wiped from me. Then we shall know even greater happiness. And together we shall watch the boy grow into manhood.'

'Come back to me, Robert,' she said. 'Oh, come back to me.'

* * *

When the Duke was in the castle there was a subtle change. People talked in whispers; they hurried about their duties; the foresters hunted for the finest stags and the fiercest boars; there was continual feasting, for the Duke's vassals came from throughout the Duchy to pay homage to him.

Arlette became more beautiful, William noticed; watching his mother and father together he wished it could always be thus.

During the first hours he overcame his awe of his father. He liked to climb on to his great knee and sit solemnly watching his face while he talked and only now and then allowing the great jewelled brooch which held his cape in place to absorb his attention.

His father asked him many questions about his hunting, his archery, his sword-play. 'As yet,' said William, 'it is with sticks. May I not have a real sword?'

'All in good time, my son.'

'I should like a dagger too.'

'Wherefore my son should you wish for a dagger?'

'If I met someone . . . someone wicked. If I met the Count of Talvas . . .'

'What know you of the Count of Talvas?'

William grew scarlet with mortification, but he could not lie to his father. 'I listened to talk,' he said.

'You thought it good to hide yourself and listen to what was not meant for your ears?'

'I thought if I was to be like you, I should know everything.'

It was an answer which did not displease the Duke.

He never ceased to marvel at the intelligence of this boy, who was moreover strong and sturdy. He delighted in him.

'You did well,' he said. 'You have to learn more quickly than other boys. Did you know that?'

'Yes, Father.'

'Why must you?'

'Because you are my father and everything you have must be of the best.'

'A good answer, son. Can you shoot an arrow far?'

'Farther than Guy.'

'And you can ride faster?'

'Yes, Father.'

'And your lessons?'

William hesitated. 'Has Uncle Mauger spoken to you?' he asked.

The Duke laughed. 'Not yet,' he said. 'Am I to be disappointed in that field?'

'I like not to be within stone walls.'

'Nay, 'tis natural. But these things must be mastered, my son. You will have need of all you can learn. That you will understand as you grow older. You will need a strong arm to protect your mother.'

'You will do that.'

'But if I were not here.'

'But you will always be here.'

The Duke looked sadly at his son. 'If I should not be I should like to leave her in your charge. Will you swear to me always to protect her?'

'Father, I swear.'

'So you need a strong arm and a good head. The out of doors will give you one but for the other you need all you can learn from Uncle Mauger.'

'Then, Father, I will work hard at my books.'

'It will please me if you make as good progress with them as you do in aught else. Remember though, it is a good Norman's duty to defend his land at all costs.'

'I know it, Father.'

'Has Mauger taught of the history of Normandy?'

William's eyes shone. He talked of Rollo—great Rollo, the Giant Walker, the hero who must walk because no horse was strong enough to carry him.

'But a ship was,' cried William, 'and by God's grace he came to Normandy. He sailed his ship up the Seine as far as it would go, and the King of France sat shivering on his throne...'

The Duke laughed. 'So Mauger has told you that, has he?'

'My mother tells me. She sings the old Norse songs to me and so do many of the women.'

'Never forget, my son, that you belong to that great race who settled here and founded Normandy.'

'Never shall I!' declared William.

'You are of a tender age as yet, my son, but as you have learned you cannot dally long in childhood. A boy such as you must learn not only of his homeland but of those countries surrounding it. What know you of France, my son?'

'France?' said the boy puzzled. 'My mother told me that the King of France would have great Rollo kiss his foot and that this Rollo refused to do. So he bade one of his henchmen do it for him and this man, being a good Norman who kisses the feet of none but his Duke, lifted his foot so high that the King fell backwards.' William laughed. 'It was a goodly thing to do,' he added.

The Duke was silent. 'You must understand this, William. We are in a measure vassals of the King of France.'

'Could Normandy be the vassal of any?'

The Duke smiled. 'My son, I would you were five years older. This small head has much to learn.'

'It is a good head, Father, and eager to learn.'

'I doubt it not. The King of France is powerful. He granted us this land and it is well for us to live in good friendship with him. If he called on us to help him and his cause were just, we should do so.'

'But only if his cause were just.'

'And to the good of Normandy.'

'Yes, Father. I understand that.'

'King Robert of France is a good man but a good man is not always a good King, my son. Robert Capet is of fine mien; he is a scholar, a musician and he loves poetry, but

33

there is a weakness in him and he is at the mercy of his wife, Queen Constance. It is not good for a man to be ruled by women.'

'Why does he let her rule him?'

'Because he is a lover of peace.'

'It is good to love peace.'

'Only if it is a good peace. You must attend when your Uncle Mauger tells you of our neighbours. What know you of England, William?'

'England.' William wrinkled his brows. 'It is across the sea, is it not?'

'Is that all you know? You must know more because we have close ties with this land—stronger ones than those with France. Our Normans settled in that island even as they did in this land; and our friends are there, our own people, William. My father's sister, my Aunt Emma, married the King of England. He was Ethelred, and at the time of the marriage was engaged in war with the Danes. Emma took many of our Normans with her to England when she went and such a marriage brings countries closer together. There were two sons of this marriage—Edward and Alfred. They are your cousins and they are in Normandy now.'

'Why, Father?'

'They are in exile, but more of that later. You will meet them and I wish you to be their friend.'

'But I will, Father. I long to meet my English cousins.'

'Now you must listen carefully for this is not easy to understand. Ethelred had married before and had a son Edmund. The Danes meanwhile had driven Ethelred and Emma from their throne and Sweyn of Denmark took possession of it. Canute, Sweyn's son, reckoned he was King, but Edmund declared *he* was. There were battles and it was finally agreed to share the country between them; but when Edmund died Canute took his share and ruled as King of all England.'

William was bewildered but his father patted his shoulder.

'You are young yet, William,' he said. 'But you will remember much that I have told you. I do wish you to be on good terms with your cousins Edward and Alfred, for one of them or both may rule England one day, and the ties between us are strong since your Aunt Emma married into the country. I must tell you now that she was not one to lose

34

anything that she had won and she was determined to keep the English crown within her grasp, so when Ethelred died she married Canute. Now when she married him she made him swear that any child they had should inherit the throne. That excluded not only Canute's son Harold Harefoot but also Edward and Alfred.'

'But Edward and Alfred were her sons,' said the puzzled William.

The Duke drew William between his knees and looked searchingly into his face.

'The Danes were in control through Canute. Emma knew that her sons Edward and Alfred would not be accepted, so she turned her attention to her son by Canute and determined that Hardicanute should reign.'

'Would you and my mother love other sons better than me?'

The Duke drew his son into his arms and embraced him fiercely.

'Never, William,' he said. 'Never! Never.' Then he was tender suddenly. 'I would stuff too much into that young head of yours,' he said. 'Come, we will go into the courtyard and you shall show me some sword-play with your sticks and we'll go riding with our falcons and mayhap we will hunt the boar.'

The boy's eyes danced. He had momentarily forgotten the complicated family relationships which his father had attempted to make him understand.

In good time, the Duke promised himself, but I see I must wait awhile before I go on my pilgrimage.

*   *   *

The Duke's visit was interrupted by the news of the death of King Robert of France. This was important to him for, as he said to Arlette, the safety of Normandy was bound up in that of France, and the alliance between them which dated from Rollo's day must be kept firm.

The messenger who brought the news was refreshed and given shelter in the castle and he had much to impart as to what was happening at the court of France.

Ever since she had come to France from Aquitaine, the Queen had made the poor King's life a misery; she was so imperious, so malicious, and of such a governing nature that the meek King had been afraid of her. He never gave a gift to any of his servants without the admonition: 'Pray do not mention this to the Queen.' She was determined to have her way and her eldest son had never been her favourite.

The messenger's account proved to be accurate for it was not long before a fugitive arrived in Normandy: King Henry of France.

William was told little of this. He went on practising outdoor skills with the stern Thorold whom the Duke had designated to teach him and he did his bookwork under the eyes of the even sterner Mauger; but Arlette was anxious because she was well aware that this new development at the French Court could mean war.

She was right.

In their bedchamber Robert talked to her of the matter.

'Must there always be these wars?' she asked.

'There always have been,' answered Robert. 'I have given Henry sanctuary at the Abby of St Jumièges.'

'Where you keep all your exiles. The Athelings are there, are they not?'

'Yes, they are. I want William to meet his cousins. I shall go to Jumièges to see Henry and I think it would be well if the boy came with me. It is time that he began to understand what goes on.'

'You forget he is but five years old. You try to make a man of him before he is even a boy.'

'I feel within me that he must grow quickly to manhood. He will come with me to Jumièges and that means, my love, that you will come too.'

'And from there?'

'I must needs ride out against the Dowager Queen of France and her upstart son. We Dukes have sworn allegiance to the Capet Kings and I could not stand by and see the younger brother replace the elder.'

She looked at him strangely and he would not meet her eyes. The death of his elder brother hung heavily over him.

* * *

Thus it was that William met his Atheling cousins. He was immediately attracted by them for they were so different from everyone he knew. They were not young, being some thirty years of age—men, in William's eyes, older even than his father; but they did not appear to be so old because they were so gentle. They spoke softly; and they were so fair as to be almost white and they had the bluest eyes William had ever seen.

He was fascinated by those blue eyes. The brothers liked to read and write poetry, and they composed songs which they sang beautifully. Surprisingly to William, they found greater pleasure in these things than in sword-play and the hunt. They did not care for the hunt at all. William felt he should have despised them for this but how could he despise such noble-looking beings?

It seemed to him that in their presence some of his father's men seemed awkward and rough. Edward and Alfred wore beautiful clothes and there were jewels at their throats and on their fingers.

Beautiful blue-eyed Athelings! thought William; and he was sorry for them because they were in exile.

There would come a day, his father told him, when they could be kings of England, for indeed they had more right to the throne than Hardicanute who was younger than they and had been born of their mother's second marriage.

But at this time the Duke was more concerned with the rights of the exiled King of France than of the Atheling cousins.

*   *   *

It was an exciting day when the Duke rode out at the head of his army, the King of France beside him.

The Duke had told William on the previous night that he was going to set the King back on his throne. He was going to thwart the wicked Queen Constance, depose her young son and give back to King Henry what he had lost.

How thrilling it was to see the flag of Normandy flying in the breeze beside the golden lilies of France! And how excited William was to watch those gallant soldiers marching into battle, the knights wearing hauberks, their helmets and boots of shining steel flashing in the sun, their lances in their hands. The foot-soldiers too were well prepared with their feet bound in buckskins and hides about their bodies.

William danced madly round in his excitement.

His mother, standing beside him, seized his hand and held it very tightly. He looked up at her and saw how sad she was, and wondered how anyone could be sad to see such magnificence; and his father was the finest of them all.

37

He supposed she was sad because he was going away. He too would be sorry for that; but he was going to put the true King back on the throne and that was a good thing to do.

'When I am a man,' said William. 'I shall ride just like my father does at the head of my armies.'

*   *   *

It was silent in the castle. Everyone was thoughtful; each day his mother went to the highest turret and waited there a long time.

William forgot his father for long periods because there was so much to be done. He wanted to have excelled in archery, to beat Guy at everything they did together, so that he could boast to his father when he returned.

Every time he performed some feat with extra skill he would say: 'I will tell my father as soon as he comes home.'

The days passed quickly—except those hours with Uncle Mauger. Guy whispered that Uncle Mauger was not what he seemed, that although he was an Archbishop and supposed to be a Christian he worshipped the old gods, Odin and Thor, and that he practised sorcery.

'Then he is a wicked man,' whispered William.

'If your father knew he would never allow him to teach you,' said Guy.

'Then it cannot be true, for my father knows everything there is to know and he would not allow Uncle Mauger to teach me if it were true that he were not a Christian.'

But he did not like Uncle Mauger and he would watch him suspiciously during lessons and strange pictures would come into his mind. He wondered what one did in practising sorcery. He had a clearer vision of the Count of Talvas of whom he thought now and then. Sometimes he dreamed of the hall of Domfront and terrible things happening to those who had been unwary enough to be caught.

In due course Robert came back to the castle. His armies had been victorious; he had routed the Queen Mother of France and her upstart son and had set King Henry back on his throne.

*   *   *

There were the usual feastings and revelries to celebrate his return, but it was not long before he was considering a new project. He wished to do for the Athelings what he had done for the King of France.

William had an inkling of what was afoot. Since his talk with his father he had tried hard to discover all that he could of England. The country had a fascination for him, largely because it was the home of the beautiful Athelings. They had seemed oddly content with their seclusion at the Abbey of Jumièges. Robert visited them once more and William had been delighted to be in the company that went with him.

The cousins were a source of wonder to William. Their voices were soft; their hands white and beautifully shaped; their clothes were different from those of all others and William had an idea that they were transformed merely by being put on his cousins' graceful figures. His father had told him that they were Saxons and this was why they were different. They grew fond of William and they would tell him stories of England and they told them beautifully after the manner of the old Norse sagas; these were not so much of conquests and bloodshed, but of peace and the spread of learning. They enjoyed talking of their ancestor the great King Alfred who, although a peace-loving man, had done much to defy the Danes and so ensure a period of peace. He had cared passionately for the betterment of his people and spent his time not in feasting and debauchery but in discovering how best he could promote learning in his country. He made just laws and instituted a system of fines for offenders, for he knew that the most effective manner of punishing offenders was through their purses. If a man deprived another of a leg or an eye he was fined fifty shillings, which, explained Alfred, was a great sum of money. There was a grade of these fines. For cutting off the ears a fine of twelve shillings was imposed and the loss of a tooth or a middle finger would cost the man who inflicted such damage four shillings.

William thought again of Talvas and decided that if such a system existed in Normandy, Talvas could lose all his fine estates for the injuries he had inflicted on his victims.

Yes, Alfred was a great King.

'Yet a humble one,' said Edward, 'for with greatness comes humility.'

That was something William could not understand but he liked the story of how Alfred, when flying from the Danes, found shelter in a cowherd's cottage and while seated at the fire preparing his bows and arrows, the cakes which the cowherd's wife had set down to cook began to burn, whereupon the woman loudly abused the King—having no inkling of who he was—and cried out that he was too lazy to turn the cakes when he saw them burning but would be ready enough to eat them when they were done. And how had the great King behaved? He had sat still, humbly accepting the abuse and even asking for forgiveness, because, although he had brought wise rule to the country he governed, he had allowed the old woman's cakes to burn.

That was humility, explained Edward. And Alfred had been rather a saint than a king.

William remembered that his father had said that a saintly man was not necessarily a kingly one; but he was assured this did not apply to great King Alfred.

But Alfred had died and the good he had brought to his country had not in every case lived on after him. The Danes were a perpetual menace to peace, and how could any country survive without that? The English had lived through troublous times and in due course Ethelred had come to the throne, he who was known as the Unready because he was never prepared in time to meet the invader. And he had married Emma who for her beauty was known as the Flower of Normandy.

The result of this union were Edward and Alfred themselves.

But Ethelred could not stand against the mighty Danes and Sweyn of Denmark drove them from their thrones and into exile where Edward and Alfred had been ever since.

Nor were they sad to be in exile, William noted. They loved the life of the Abbey. Could it be possible, wondered William, that his Atheling cousins preferred the peaceful scholarly atmosphere of the Abbey to the warlike state of their own country? They had spoken with more reverence for their ancestor's preoccupation with learning than for his skill in driving the Danes from his country.

They were strange, these Atheling cousins, and they made a deep impression on him.

Soon William realized why his father had come to the Abbey. Robert had set the King of France on his throne and

40

now he was going to recover the throne of England for the Athelings.

He told William something of this when he said farewell to him.

'Those whom we help will be our friends,' he said.

'Will they remember, Father, that we have helped them?'

Robert tousled his son's hair affectionately. 'You have a point there, son. You will find that those we help are often ready—nay eager—to forget the service we have done. But there may be some grateful men in the world and we must hope those we choose to aid will remember.'

'The Athelings would remember, Father.'

'You have a fondness for these cousins, eh?'

'I like to look at them. I like to listen to them. They have such beautiful blue eyes.'

Robert laughed.

'Well, I am going to conquer the land which rightly belongs to them. I am going to give it back to them.'

'I think they would rather stay here, Father.'

Robert was silent but pleased with his son.

'You will come down to the coast with your mother to watch us sail. There you will see a truly marvellous sight. The ships of Normandy, my son. Remember always that we are men of the sea. We are great fighters. Our knights in armour are a worthy sight, are they not? But first we are seamen. We owe all we have to the sea. Our ancestors left their own lands in search of others and they came in the long ships. We are invincible on land. But the sea belongs to us.'

And indeed it was a goodly sight—those long ships with their prows painted to look like dragons breathing fire as they plunged through the waters! So had their ancestors ridden the waves—Harold Blue Tooth and Giant Rollo. They struck fear into the watchers on the shore as they approached. And so would it be in England—the native land of the beautiful Atheling cousins.

The fleet sailed to wage war on England and William returned with his mother to await his father's return.

* * *

That which William had believed impossible had happened. His father's enterprise had failed.

Could it really be that the long ships had been defeated?

41

Indeed it was so, though not defeated by another fleet, but by the elements.

As Robert's fleet had sailed towards the English coast a storm had arisen and the great ships had been scattered and Robert's own ship in which had sailed the Atheling cousins was washed up on the shores of the Island of Jersey.

What a sorry sight it must have been to witness the wreckage of those fine ships! Robert could only gloomily await the arrival of one of his captains whose ship was sufficiently seaworthy to carry himself and the Atheling cousins back to Normandy.

* * *

It was a sad homecoming. Robert was despondent. There was no feasting that night in the castle, for Robert had no taste for it. The songs of the minstrels could not charm him. He did not want to hear of the exploits of great Viking seamen when his own had failed so wretchedly.

In their chamber he buried his face in his hands.

'My ships lost,' he mourned. 'My enemies will be laughing at me this day.'

'It was the storm,' soothed Arlette. 'Who could stand against such?'

'It was defeat,' insisted Robert. Then he stood up and looked long into Arlette's face. 'God is displeased with me,' he said. 'He will never forgive me until I have expiated my sin.'

'A storm could arise at any time,' insisted Arlette. 'No seaman could withstand such a storm.'

'It happened to me,' said Robert.

His gloom continued. It hung over the castle. In the great hall the cooks stirred their cauldrons in silence. Nobody mentioned the enterprise, and for William it was a great discovery. His father could suffer defeat.

At least, he reminded himself, the Atheling cousins would not be sad. He was certain that they were delighted to be back into exile.

Robert came to a decision. He told Arlette first what he intended to do.

'I have committed many sins,' he said, 'and it is clear that God is displeased with me. I must show Him that I

42

intend to lead a good life and dedicate myself to my country.'

'He will know it,' replied Arlette.

'Yes, He will know it. But sins must be paid for. I shall go on a pilgrimage to the Holy Land. There my sins will fall from me like a wearisome burden. I shall feel free again. He has shown me clearly by sending this storm to destroy my ships that he is displeased with me.'

'How could you leave Normandy?'

'Only by leaving another in my place.'

'You would appoint one of the seneschals?'

'I would appoint my successor...our little Duke.'

'William!'

'Why not? I have decided that none but he shall follow me.'

'A child not yet seven years old!'

'A fine boy and old beyond his years. I will make a Duke of him. I will prepare all to accept him when I am gone.'

'Do not speak of such things. Are we not happy now together? Why should we wish for anything different?'

'You do not understand, my Arlette. I am heavy with my sins. I fear retribution if I do not seek forgiveness.'

'Then ask it here...ask it on your knees.'

'It is not enough. I must make sacrifices. I must leave what I love most...you and the boy and the girl. My home, my love, my little ones. I must leave you all and go to the Holy Land. I will be back, my love, purged of my sins.'

'I fear,' she said. 'I fear greatly.'

'It must be, Arlette.'

'What if you do not return?'

'You will have a son to protect you.'

'A little boy. Even William could not do that.'

'You shall have protectors, my love. But I must think on this. When I saw my broken ships I knew that this was a sign. I cannot pass it over.'

And Arlette was filled with great foreboding.

* * *

William had ridden out into the forest, Thorold beside him as ever. There was something going on in the castle, he knew. His father looked strange and remote and no more confidences were exchanged between them now, although sometimes he would find his father's eyes fixed upon him in a kind of wondering stare. His mother was silent too. Sometimes she would seize him and hold him tightly against her. He wanted to wriggle free but did not care to hurt her by doing so. They were both acting strangely and he believed it had something to do with the great defeat and the disintegration of the fleet. He wanted to remind them that at least the Athelings were happy. They did not want to go out and conquer England and regain the throne.

But all this could be forgotten in the fresh air and to ride through the green forest was a delight. Thorold had said he must give up ponies and master a real horse and this he had done after a while, although it had not been easy. There was so much to be learned; he must be a pupil in chivalry and the mastering of a horse however fiery must be quickly accomplished.

The bearers had carried the venison home. It was a fine beast. There would be rejoicing when it reached the great hall; but doubtless there would be the same solemnity at table as there had been since the return of his father.

They left the forest and rode into the town and as they did so a heavy, broad-shouldered man dismounted his horse and swaggered towards them.

There was something terrifying about this man; William had been aware that the few people he had seen had disappeared into their homes. The man was evil; there was no doubt of that. It was in those small lively eyes, that thin cruel mouth. On his face was the mark of a thousand dabaucheries and it was evident that those eyes had looked on sights from which all decent men should turn away.

Thorold had laid a hand on William's bridle so that their horses were still close together.

'Count Talvas,' said Thorold, 'I present to you the son of your Seigneur.'

William felt the colour in his face. This was the man of whom he had heard such tales. This was the most wicked, the most cruel man not only in Normandy but also in the whole of the world.

He knew that what he had heard had been only half of the atrocities this man had committed; he knew that he had strangled his own wife with his bare hands because she had begged him not to practise such cruelties; he knew that he had married another and at his wedding feast committed such odious and sickening torture on his victims

44

that he had shocked even those who followed in his footsteps.

To be unprepared for such a confrontation left him bewildered. He had dreamed of this man whose name was a byword. Grown up people and children lived in terror of being taken into his dungeons and submitted to the most nauseating and obscene torture.

What had his father said. 'If you fear look straight into the face of your fear. Then perhaps you will be less afraid.'

That was all he could do now.

For several seconds the man and the child looked into each other's faces; it was the man who dropped his eyes. He turned away, muttering to himself: 'A curse on you. You and yours will destroy my house.' He was clearly afraid to look into William's face.

Thorold was astounded.

'What happened to you?' he said.

'I merely looked at him and, Thorold, I was not afraid. It was he who feared me.'

It was astounding. It was like a miracle. What power had this child to subdue such a man?

When Arlette heard an account of what had happened, she said: 'It was the innocent goodness of the child against the wickedness of the man. It is a sign. Once before I had a sign when I dreamed that a great tree came from my body and covered the whole of Normandy and beyond. This is another sign. My son will soon be proclaimed a Duke of Normandy and he will be the greatest Duke that Normandy ever knew.'

*   *   *

Duke Robert sent for his son and when William arrived he drew him to the stone window-seat which was cut out of the thick wall of the castle, and putting his arm around him bade him look down on the land.

'Normandy,' said Robert. 'Our land, my son. Our dear, dear land.'

'Yes, Father.'

'You are nearly seven years old, William, but as I have told you before, you are old for your years. You are as advanced as any boy of ten in my dominions.'

William glowed with pride and his father went on: 'This pleases me, for I have something of great importance to say

45

to you. I am going on a pilgrimage to the Holy Land.'

'Shall I go with you?' asked William seeing himself smiting the Saracens, planting the Christian cross on lands where it had never been before.

'Nay, William. You will stay here and guard your mother and Normandy.'

'Can I do that?'

'You will do it because before I go I am going to name you my successor. You will be a Duke of Normandy and the knights and barons will swear fealty to you.'

'Would they do this?'

'They would do it if I commanded them.'

'Perhaps they would say I was over young.'

'They may say what they will as long as they obey.'

'Father, what must I do to be a Duke?'

'You must learn your lessons; you must become strong, ready to be a leader of men.'

'It seems no different from what I do now.'

'First you must be educated; you must learn with a new zest.'

'So it is to be still learning.'

'I want you to understand the importance of this. I shall be far away. I had promised myself that I would be here to watch over your upbringing, but it cannot be. Now, my son, you will understand that a boy of seven cannot alone govern a great domain. My good friend, Alain of Brittany, will be Regent in your absence.'

'*My* absence, Father?'

'You are to finish your education at the French Court and have as your guardian none other than the King.'

William was filled with dismay. 'Do you mean I am going away?'

'Only for the time that I am on my pilgrimage.'

'What of my mother?'

'She will be safe and happy here.'

'Safe and happy. Without you ... without me.'

Robert smiled. How could he tell this boy how he feared for *his* safety when he was not there to protect him? How could he tell Arlette that his journey was a dangerous one and it might well be that he would never come back to them?

He feared for them both; but his guilt was greater than his fear. He could not rest until he had expiated his sin and the only way he could do this was through this pilgrimage.

46

He would make every possible arrangement for his loved ones. He trusted Henry of France. Had he not been responsible for placing him back on the throne? Henry must needs respect his vows of friendship; he must have gratitude for the one who had been of such great use to him. He would care for the boy; he would recognize him as Duke; William would be safer at the Court of France than anywhere else in the world.

As for Arlette he had plans for her. She would need a man to care for her and he had already instructed Herlwin of Conteville, one of his most trusted knights, to marry her and care for her for the rest of her life if death should overtake him.

'Tomorrow we shall leave for Rouen and there the knights and barons will swear fealty to you. They will give their solemn oaths that they will accept you as their Duke. When this is done I shall go away content that all is well.'

* * *

To ride to Rouen beside his father, to see lying before him that great city of Normandy—this was an experience he would never forget.

There flowed the River Seine, silver in sunlight. The city was like an enormous castle shut in by its walls and the moat, its spires and roofs dominated by the square tower of the Cathedral of the keep-like edifice known as Rollo's Tower.

The Castle itself was bigger than that of Falaise and this was their destination. Never had he felt so proud as he did riding into Rouen with his father. The people came out of their cottages to see him pass and raise a cheer for him.

The Duke smiled his approval.

'Look, William,' he said, 'the people love you already. Always must a ruler cherish the love of his people.'

William was thinking: To go away, far from my mother, far from home. To the French Court. He tried to remember what the French King had looked like when he had ridden out to do battle for his throne; he could remember nothing of him. He thought: I shall have to leave my dogs, my horses, my falcon. I want to stay here.

He could have wept, but how could a Norman weep, especially one who had been told he had no time to dally in childhood?

His mother was subdued and sad; she did not wish his father to go to the Holy Land and her son to go to France.

*　*　*

In the great hall the knights and barons were assembled. His father led him to the throne which he alone used and bade him sit upon it.

Robert then addressed the assembly.

'Behold your Duke.'

There was a silence that seemed to go on for a long time. Then there broke out a murmuring. William's sharp ears caught the whisper: 'Bastard.'

It was like a dream such as those he had had of Domfront Castle and almost as frightening. He had noticed since he had come to Rouen that people looked at him strangely. They whispered and stopped when he approached. 'He is young,' they said, 'and a bastard.'

His cousin Guy, boasting of his legitimacy, had used the word as though it were something unpleasant; and now he had discovered that he was one.

His father's face was angry suddenly and when he looked so he had the power to silence any of his vassals; they were quiet as he explained that he was going on a pilgrimage and that he was leaving them their Duke—his own son William. He might have seen but seven winters but from this moment he was their Duke and they were all to swear fealty to him.

Again there arose that titter and once more William heard the ominous whisper: 'Bastard.'

'He is my son.' The words were like a clap of thunder. There stood Robert the Magnificent, Robert the Devil; and his words were a warning. 'It is my will that you accept this boy. He is my chosen successor. Bastard he may be, but he is mine. You will all swear fealty to him.'

Another silence then someone—it was Osbern de Crépon—cried: 'Long live Duke William.'

*　*　*

He stood before the altar in the great Cathedral while Archbishop Mauger, sterner than ever he was in the schoolroom, demanded of him: 'William, will you in the name of God and the people of Normandy be a good and true ruler and guard your people from their enemies? Will you maintain truth, punish evil and protect the Holy Church?'

'I will,' said William. 'So help me God.'

'Kiss the gospel book,' whispered the Archbishop, and this he did.

Two bishops then came forward and put about his shoulders the ducal cloak of red velvet edged with ermine. It was so heavy it was difficult for him to support it. A golden coronet was placed on his head. It was so big that it fell over his brow; a sword was placed in his hands and thus encumbered he must make his way to the throne.

Seated there, weighed down by these heavy accoutrements he received the oaths of allegiance from the knights and barons.

'Sire, I proclaim myself your vassal in word and deed. I swear loyalty to you and to preserve your laws as far as therein lies my power,' pronounced each of them in turn.

Robert looked on triumphantly while this was done and never before had he so delighted in his son.

Thus William became Duke of Normandy; and a few days after the ceremony Robert left with his son for Paris.

At the Court of France

FOR the first weeks at the Court of France William believed he would never cease to mourn for the past. His father had taken a tender farewell of him—and how different he looked in the garb of a pilgrim! Not Robert the Magnificent at all. The King of France was kind; he had sworn to Robert that he would care for William as he would his own son; but William, recently a Duke who had received the oath of fealty from his vassals, found it hard to accept the fact that he was a vassal of the King of France.

Before he left, his father spoke seriously to him. It had emerged that William was possessed of a hot temper. He would scarcely have been his father's son if he was not. But he must curb it. He must share his possessions. It had also been noted that there was a certain avaricious streak in his nature. All Norman failings. Duke Robert was condemning them now because his mind was occupied with spiritual matters. At one time he would have thought it not such a bad thing that a leader could grow suddenly fierce and that he should regard his possessions with some affection.

Avarice had brought him to this pass. Had he not coveted his brother's dukedom? If he had been content to take second place he would not be setting off on a pilgrimage now.

The King of France talked to William on the day his father left and told him that at his Court he would be instructed in the art of chivalry; he would hunt with his falcon; he would have his dogs and horses and he, the King of France, would do all in his power for the son of a man who had befriended him in his hour of need.

So Robert could ride away with a good conscience but William was sick with longing for his home. As a good Norman he must not show his grief but it was there none the less.

There were boys of noble birth to share his games and lessons, but they were French not Norman. Smaller in stature than the Norse giants, William despised them; he found their habits mincing; they ate their meat more daintily than he had been brought up to, and it was soon clear that he was not one of them.

The manner of his instruction was different from that he had received from Osbern de Crépon and his squires in Normandy. The French did not speak their minds with the frankness to which William was accustomed. Knightly instruction, which in Normandy was a matter of martial skill and chivalric behaviour, was in France a part of the religious training.

William, brought up to speak his mind, was scathing in his comments on this.

'Why,' he said, 'you French make monks of your chevaliers. In Normandy ours are warriors.'

The French page with the silky curls who liked to wear rings on his fingers laughed sneeringly. 'But do we not all know that Normandy is a land of pirates?' he asked of his companions.

William's hot temper was immediately evident. This pretty French boy was sneering at his ancestors! Great Rollo, William Longsword, Richard the Fearless would have quickly shown the Franks who were their masters.

'Rollo sailed up the Seine,' he cried. 'Rollo ravaged the land.'

'Pirates,' chanted the boys forming a circle round William.

The young Duke could not contain himself. He struck out right and left. Two of the pages fell to the ground; two more attempted to fell William, but without success. He would show them that one Norman was a match for four Frenchmen. Blood spurted from the nose of one of them. The other began to scream for the guards.

'The Norman has gone mad,' he cried.

William was seized by two men-at-arms.

'What's this, little savage?'

'I'll not have them speak ill of Normandy and Normans.'

The guards laughed. 'He has the devil's own temper, this

one. It's time he was put in chains and left there till he forgets his rough ways and learns good French manners.'

'Let me go,' screamed William, his face scarlet with passion. 'How dare you molest the Duke of Normandy!'

Such a clamour did he make, and so uncertain were the guards and the priests who had heard the clamour, as to what should be done to a young Duke whose father had left him in the King's care, that they decided there was nothing to do but to take him before the King himself.

Henry listened gravely to what had happened.

'You will have to forget your rough ways while you are at our Court,' he told William. 'You are to be instructed in the art of chivalry. That does not include indulging in brawls with those who are learning with you.'

'They insulted Normandy,' declared William. 'Would you stand aside if any insulted France?'

The King silently studied the boy. He was too precocious, he decided. He had been forced up too quickly. He was a fine boy, but too ready with his fists and his tongue.

'You will have a care how you address your suzerain,' he said. 'Methinks that because certain honours have been thrust upon you, you have grown beyond your stature.' Henry softened. He liked the boy. 'Now, William, your father has told me to curb your temper. He has asked me to punish you when you so deserve it. You deserve it now and I am going to punish you in a manner which I think will hurt you most. You will not ride for a week. You will remain for that time in your own chamber; you will not see your dogs or your falcons. Two of the priests will be with you and you will study during that time. Now go away and when you feel inclined to lose your temper next time, remember what it has cost you.'

William retired sorrowing. He wanted Falaise; he wanted Rouen; he wanted Normandy. And he wanted his mother.

* * *

With the passing of the months he grew reconciled. His speech softened a little; his manners became more gracious. A middle-aged squire had been allotted to him—a man of great skill who saw in William an apt pupil. It was a delight to teach him the use of warlike weapons. It was being said that of all the boys who were being brought up in the Court none could compare with William of Normandy. His use of the sword and spear was masterly; his arrows fell farther than those of the others; he was an expert with a javelin; and he quickly learned how to wear his armour. His skills delighted him and did much to alleviate his homesickness.

It was inevitable that he must learn certain facts about himself. He was soon enlightened as to his birth.

'How is it that your grandfather should be a tanner and your father a Duke?' asked one of his companions.

It was strange, he had to admit it; but not so strange when he realized the truth.

His father had never married his mother; a union between them would have been out of the question because she was the daughter of a tanner. But they had had a son—himself. He was a bastard.

The knowledge irked him. It was degrading in some way. He had even heard himself referred to not as William the Duke but as William the Bastard. He became more aggressive. He had to show them that if he were a bastard he could defend himself against the sneers. His manners brought him punishment and often he was eating his meals alone without wine or beer and working at his books instead of exercising his dogs and horses. It was folly, he knew; for while he was out of doors he could forget aught else but the joy of the chase. He must curb his temper. They were right—but his blood seemed to boil in his veins when he heard that whispered word Bastard.

* * *

A whole year passed. Although he still thought longingly of Normandy, his life no longer seemed strange. He was accustomed to the manners of the French—their fêtes and banquets; the carefree way in which they combined religion and pleasure; he was working hard, learning much. He was certain that he could ride into battle at the head of his armies if the need arose.

He remembered how his mother's eyes used to follow him wherever he went, and how eagerly interested she was in everything he did. Indeed he was still homesick now and then. Often he thought of his father and wondered how he fared. There were occasional messages. He had heard how Robert had visited Rome where he had been graciously received by the Pope. For all his desire to do penance, Robert could not forget that he was the Magnificent. He hated the shabby pilgrim's garb; it was alien to his nature to wear it, and he did not care that people whom he met on the way should mistake him for an ordinary pilgrim.

So he decided to discard his coarse robe and stick, and dress himself in magnificent clothes, and ride a fine horse so that all might know him for who he was. He would distribute alms as he went so that all might stand in awe of Robert Duke of Normandy.

William loved to hear news and often in his thoughts he was back in the great hall of Falaise listening to the scullions chatter as they hung over the steaming cauldrons.

One day, he promised himself, his father would come home; he would come to Paris and take him home.

* * *

He was growing up. He had been two years at the Court of France. He was no longer a child. He had learned much. He could beat other boys his age not only because he was more skilled than they but also because everything he did was done with a stern dedication. He believed that one day he would have a country to rule and he meant to rule it well.

He must excel all others not only because he was a Duke but because he was a bastard. He could reconcile himself to this fact temporarily. Had not many of the Dukes of Normandy been denied the blessing of having been born in wedlock? One only had to consider the history of his family. William Longsword, Rollo's own son, was a bastard. Richard the Fearless was another; Richard the Second was the baseborn son of Richard the Fearless by his mistress Gunnor. His own father was not illegitimate; but it seemed he was the only one. And with such a beautiful and good woman as Arlette for his mother, it seemed disloyal to wish she had been some Princess. But for all these thoughts he hated to hear that whispered word Bastard, and to see the look of amused scorn in the eyes of those who said it. When he saw it he wanted to make them tremble in their shoes and to assure them that even though he were a bastard he was a legitimate Duke of Normandy. His father had made him such and the knights and barons of his country had sworn to serve him.

54

One day the King sent for him and, when he looked into Henry's face, he knew that something terrible had happened.

'I have ill news for you,' said Henry gently.

'Is it my father, Sire?'

The King nodded.

'He is ill?'

'He is dead, William.'

'Dead. My father dead?'

'He died as a Christian.'

'But he is too young to die.'

'Death comes at all times and your father courted it.'

William could not listen to what the King was saying; he could only think of his father—gay and magnificently dressed, coming into the hall, sitting at the head of the table, walking with his arm through that of his mother. And now he was dead.

'My mother?' he asked.

'She is to marry as your father wished. He even chose the man for her.'

'I must go to her.'

'Nay, William, you must stay here.'

'She will need me.'

The King laid a hand on William's shoulder. 'This is a shock for you. Go to your chamber, rest awhile and pray to God for His help, for you will need it now more than you ever did. Just stay with your grief and do not make plans yet. What is to be will be. Let it take its course.'

William followed the King's advice. He lay on his bed and thought of what this would mean. One idea struck him. He was in truth the Duke of Normandy now and a Duke's place was with his people. Had his father not said he must grow up quickly? Had he had some premonition of what was to happen to him?

*   *   *

The French Court was in mourning for the Duke of Normandy. Those who tried to comfort William told him that at least his father had not died with all his sins upon him. He had actually been engaged on a holy pilgrimage when death had overtaken him.

It was a small comfort, but William wanted the old days which he now realized he would never know again. He

55

wanted to feel that excitement he had experienced when his father had come home and he had some tale to tell him of a newly acquired skill.

His mother. He thought of her often. He remembered how much more beautiful she was when his father came home, how her eyes would shine; and when he was away how she would go to the turret and shade her eyes as she looked for his return.

He learned what had happened to his father, how he had travelled through Provence and Lombardy to Rome where he had been so well received by the Pope; how he had discarded the brown sacking garment of the pilgrim for one worthy of his rank; how richly garbed he had ridden on a mule which was shod with gold; how when it shed a shoe the gold was left on the road and the mule re-shod in the same precious metal. No one could have been in any doubt that this exalted pilgrim was indeed Robert the Magnificent.

When the Emperor of Constantinople had received him, and in the reception hall of his palace there were no chairs, the Duke had spread his rich cloak on the floor and sat on it, commanding his followers to do likewise with theirs. When they departed they left their cloaks on the floor to show that they could not demean themselves by picking them up, for costly as they might appear to others in their own eyes they were trifles.

Such extravagance delighted the poor who seized on everything that was cast off by the rich and extravagant Duke.

When he had reached the Holy Land Robert had taken a sickness and was too feeble to be able to walk, so that a litter must be devised and four of the natives were engaged to carry it. Being met by a party of Norman pilgrims who stopped to parley with him, he was asked: 'What shall we tell your people when we return to Normandy?'

'Tell them,' answered the Duke, 'that you see their master being carried to Paradise by four devils.'

This had amused the pilgrims and they had returned to Normandy delighted to have news to impart of the Duke who they said had won the respect and awe of everyone by his magnificence and generosity. Because it was necessary to pay in gold to be allowed to enter Jerusalem many pilgrims were grief-stricken because they had not the money to pay for entry. It was discovered that Robert had

56

won their undying gratitude and respect by paying their fees for them. For this and his extravagant gifts, which he had scattered in all directions, blessings had rained upon his head.

William was glad of that. Whatever his father's sins they would surely have been forgiven for all he had done since setting out on his pilgrimage.

It was on his way home that he had died. There must have been poison in his wine cup, for both he and his friend, the Count d'Arques, who had been with him since the beginning of the pilgrimage and who drank with him, died too.

William pictured it all so clearly. His father having recovered from that sickness which had forced him temporarily to take to a litter, having made his pilgrimage, his mind at peace. He would have been thinking of Normandy, and Normandy for him was Arlette and his children. William knew that chiefly he would be thinking of his son, asking himself how he had grown in two years, what new attainments were his ... and then he had drunk the cup and that was the end.

It was sobering to think how many people were struck down in the prime of their lives—removed as one would remove a tiresome insect that plagued one.

Then the awful realization came to him that he would never see his father again.

* * *

He must see the King. He must talk to him. He must tell him that now it was imperative for him to go home.

The King listened gravely. 'I promised your father,' he told him, 'that I would care for you as long as he was not here to do so.'

'But I must go back to my Duchy now. I am the Duke.'

'You are a boy yet. You are ten years old. A boy of ten cannot govern a country. Your father set up able men to do that for you.' The King eyed him obliquely as though wondering what he might tell him. He hesitated. Nay, he was often misled into thinking the boy was a man. It would be cruel to burden him with the truth. How could he say to such a boy: 'Your dukedom is in revolt. It is naturally so. The lords of Normandy do not want a boy to govern them ... and that boy a bastard.'

57

William's eyes were fixed on the King's face, but the King said: 'You are young yet. You must stay here because I have my duty to discharge.'

'I must go back to Rouen,' insisted William. 'I *must* know what is happening there.'

'You will know fast enough,' said the King.

* * *

William was riding with his fellow pupils when he heard the cavalcade making its way into the courtyard. He hurried to the embattled porch and there he saw a party of men. He gave a cry of joy for among them he recognized his old friend Thorold and with him Osbern de Crépon.

'Osbern!' he cried. 'Thorold!'

They had seen him; they leaped from their horses and there on the stone they knelt to him. How proud he was! For the first time since he had come to the Court of France he felt indeed their Duke.

'Osbern, what means this? You have come to take me home?'

'We have come to persuade the King of France that it is necessary that you return.'

William was too full of joy to reply. Then he remembered that his father was dead and was ashamed that he could feel so.

'But I want to go home,' he cried. 'Oh, Osbern, Thorold. You cannot know how I have wanted to come home.'

The Dangerous Journey

It was a bitter-sweet journey home. How well we remembered riding this way before—but then his father had been with him. Nothing, however, could mar the relief and happiness he felt to see Normandy again.

'Why do our fields look more green?' he asked Osbern. 'Why do our forests seem more grand?'

'Because they are Norman fields and forests, my lord.'

Osbern riding beside him—fine handsome Osbern—had changed. He seemed less old than he had and the reason was that William himself was older. William liked to look at him and admire his strong Norman profile; he was more respectful to William than he had been in the past. The reason was clear. I am now their Duke in very truth, thought William.

On the other side of him rode Thorold, the mighty Norman who was his bodyguard. He also was respectful; he would not now laugh to scorn the boy who had groaned when he fell from his horse; he would not dare now to command him to ignore his bruises like a man and stop whimpering like a child, mount again and ride.

Behind him rode others of his vassals: Raoul de Vacé, the Counts de Beaumount, d'Eu, de Meulan and Pont-Audemer as well as Roger de Vielles—the most notable men of Normandy and all come to bring him back to his domain because they wished all to know that they were his loyal subjects.

Rouen! How beautiful it looked in the sunshine!

'Ha. I see Rollo's tower,' he cried. And how fine was the river with the spires and houses on both sides of it.

He said to Osbern: 'I'll warrant my mother is on the highest turret watching for me.'

Osbern looked at Thorold and he saw the nod which passed between them.

'The Lady Arlette is no longer at Rouen.'

'No longer there? Does she not know that I am coming?'

'She married as was the command of your father. He had chosen Sir Herlwin de Conteville as her husband and when we had news of the Duke's death this marriage immediately took place.'

His face puckered. He could not imagine it. His mother with another husband. Rouen, Falaise no longer her home.

These changes were hard to bear.

The people had come out of their houses.

'Long live Duke William,' they cried. 'Long live our little Duke!'

'How loyal are my people,' said William with emotion; and he did not notice the looks which Thorold and Osbern exchanged.

* * *

The castle seemed strange and empty without his mother. He had so eagerly looked forward to being with her. He had wanted to see Adeliz; he had looked forward to telling them of his life at the French Court. Those varlets who had often told him to get from under their feet now bowed low at his approach; no one would dare accuse him now of listening to what was not meant for his ears.

He had gone away a young boy; he had come back a reigning Duke.

There was perhaps some gratification in this. He felt a great pride when he went to the topmost turret and looked down over the town and across the country.

'This is mine,' he said aloud. 'Mine. All mine.' And he held out his hands to grasp it. Never, never would he let it go.

In the great hall of the castle the knights knelt before him, as they had done before and swore fealty to him. They would serve him with their lives and he promised to protect them with his.

He was indeed their Duke.

But when the ceremony was over lessons began again

60

and he was expected to go back to his books under the stern eye of Uncle Mauger.

He protested. 'Now that I am the Duke I shall have done with lessons.'

Mauger smiled in his unpleasant, sneering way.

'My lord is mistaken. The study of language, of history, of literature, is of as much importance to a Duke as how to wield a sword.'

'I think not,' said William haughtily. 'And I shall have my way.'

Mauger brought his unpleasant, secretive face close to William's. 'Take heed, young master,' he said. 'You will find less time for your pleasure than you ever did before. You have great responsibilities and such that fools could never shoulder.'

'Am I a fool then?'

'You may be if you neglect the priceless gift of learning.'

'It would seem to me that all that was good has gone and what is bad remains.'

'There is much that you have to learn, my lord Duke. Come, let us lose no more time in the discovering of it.'

So he sat at his books under the supercilious eye of Mauger.

But change was in the air.

He was summoned to the great hall and there he sat on the throne while Raoul de Vacé addressed him on behalf of the assembly.

In view of the troubled state of the Duchy it was thought advisable that the Duke should show himself to his people. He must therefore prepare for a tour through the important towns of Normandy.

William was excited. It would be a change from poring over Latin books with old Mauger. Moreover, they would pass through Conteville and he would be able to see his mother.

* * *

It was left to Osbern—who was closer to him than anyone else now that he had lost his father and could not see his mother—to tell him.

Osbern came into his chamber and sat on the stool there. 'There are many things you must understand, my lord,' said Osbern. 'And the first is that there is trouble within your dominion. Trouble from outside is a terrible threat to any land but when it comes from within that is more to be dreaded.'

'From within, Osbern? What means this?'

'Some of the barons are of the opinion that Normandy needs a strong Duke. You are but ten years old.'

'I will be a strong Duke and not always ten years old.'

'They are concerned with now, my lord, not eight years' time. I regret to tell you that Alain of Brittany was not what your father believed him to be.'

'A traitor!'

'Scarcely that—but ineffectual. There is murmuring throughout the Duchy. One cannot be absolutely sure whom one can trust.'

'I shall always trust you, Osbern.'

'Oh, there are a few of us. You can rely on Thorold.'

'I would to the death. Thorold and all the lords who swore fealty to me ...'

'You must learn not to be too trusting.'

'Osbern, I will not be kept in the dark.'

'I thought not, my young lord. Nor shall you. Many of those who owe you their fealty are restive. They are saying that you are too young and that ... others come before in the succession. They are saying ...'

William stood up, his fists clenched and his eyes flashed. 'They are saying that I am a bastard. Is that it, Osbern?'

Osbern lowered his eyes. 'They are saying that, my lord.'

'And if I am a bastard. Was not William Longsword a bastard? Was not Richard the Fearless one? And was not Richard's father murdered when he was but my age?'

''Tis true indeed and dangerous times had to be lived through. Thus it is with you, my lord. We must be wary. We will show you to your people and they will see that young in years though you may be, you are still their Duke.'

'I wish to meet the people. To tell them this. I want to find the traitors among them. I will kill them with my own hands ...'

'Calm your temper, my lord. Let us not waste time in wild dreams of what we would do to our enemies. Let us first find them. We shall be on guard at all times. I shall sleep across your door and, if the need should arise, in your room. Thorold will be close at hand. You understand the danger?'

'I understand,' said William.

'Then we will prepare for your journey and during it we must take extra care. Thorold and I will be at your side throughout.'

'When do we leave?'

'In a few days. First we shall go to Caen; and after that to Lisieux and Falaise.'

'Shall I see my mother?'

'We will visit her at Conteville.'

'There we need not fear traitors.'

'Nay, your mother and her husband will always be your true friends.'

'I should like to visit my Atheling cousins. I never forget them. I used to think of them often when I was in France because then I felt I was exiled from my country as they were from theirs ... Why, Osbern, what is wrong?'

'While you have been in France much has happened.'

'Indeed it has. My father has died and my mother has taken a husband and I am become the Duke of Normandy in more than name. I know that much has happened.'

'Beyond the seas,' said Osbern, 'there have been great happenings.'

'In England?' asked William.

'I know that your father told you much of that country. It was always his wish that he could return it to the rightful heirs. Once he sought to invade it but it is not an easy country to invade. Surrounded by sea as it is, a conqueror would always have the elements to consider.'

'The Danes did it and so did the Romans.'

'They did and your father believed that the Normans would. But they were defeated.'

'It was because of this that my father took his pilgrimage. He believed that the hand of God was against him because of his sins.'

'God rest his soul. He earned the forgiveness of his sins. Canute, the King of England, died while you were in France, and do you remember what your father told you? He had a son by a previous marriage to that with your ancestress Emma, called Harald, but Emma made him promise that the throne should go to the son she and Canute should have.'

'Yes, I do remember, and my cousins Edward and Alfred Atheling were the true heirs because they were the sons of King Ethelred and Emma and she only married Canute after his death.'

'I see you have this complicated family relationship clearly in your mind. You will know too that the son of Canute and Emma was Hardicanute. Well, when Canute died Hardicanute was in Denmark and Harald declared himself King. This made a division in the country, the North accepting Harald, the South insisting that Hardicanute should be king, even though he were absent. The country was split and half was governed by one and half by the other. This meant, however, that both kings of England were Danish, which did not please the Saxons.'

'A country divided is not a safe place,' said William.

'Ay, true enough. Moreover Queen Emma was most displeased. She became more so when Hardicanute refused to leave Denmark and Harald became King of all England. He had no love for her. Had she not persuaded Canute to disinherit him in favour of Hardicanute who cared so little for his inheritance that he would not take the trouble to come and claim it? She is not a woman to stand by calmly while what she has had is taken from her.'

'She is a Norman,' said William proudly.

'Ay, a Norman and what Norman likes to part with his possessions?'

"Why should he when he has won them? I will fight for every inch of Norman soil while there is life in me.'

'Let us hope there will be no need. I was about to tell you that Emma sent for her two sons by Ethelred, Edward and Alfred. They had a greater claim to the throne than Hardicanute. They should come and stake it.'

'I am glad. I felt tender towards those cousins, Osbern. I shall never forget their fair hair and their beautiful clear blue eyes. I have never seen eyes like theirs.'

Osbern shuddered and William looked at him in dismay.

'Osbern . . . *they* are not *dead*.'

'Hear me out,' said Osbern. 'There is a powerful man in England of whom you will doubtless hear more. His name is Earl Godwin. He is a very clever man for it is said that he began life as a cowherd.'

'Then how could he become an earl?'

'The story goes that during the war between Canute and Edmund Ironside, a captain of the Danish army was lost and asked the way of a young Saxon cowherd. When promised a reward if he would help this cowherd, Godwin, took the Danish captain to his father's cottage. The old man told the Captain that his son would be risking his life if he helped him and he was his family's main stay. They would starve without him. But if he took the Captain back to Canute's camp would he reward him by taking him into his army and giving him a good rank there? The Captain realizing that if he did not have the help of the young cowherd he would be taken by Ironside's army, agreed.'

'And did he save him and was he rewarded?'

'So well, and so clever was he, that he rose to very high rank and in time commanded the army. He was handsome as well as clever and the sister of Canute fell in love with him and married him. So not only did he become head of the army but a member of the royal family into the bargain.'

'He must indeed be a clever man.'

'He is indeed and in the absence of Hardicanute ruled for him.'

'So from cowherd he has become a king?'

'In all but name. But Hardincanute continued to refuse to return and Harald became King of the whole of England. He is not a Christian. He laughs at all that is holy. It was for this reason, we were led to understand, that Emma sent to Normandy for Edward and Alfred to return to England to claim their right to the throne.'

'And they went, Osbern?'

'Ay, they went. We gave Edward a fleet of forty ships. He landed and at Winchester was met by a fierce band of soldiers who drove him to go back whence he came. He saw at once that he was unwanted and by the Grace of God came back to Normandy.'

'He is safe here now, Osbern?'

'Edward is safe.'

'But...not Alfred?'

'You are very young to hear such tales. It was cruel. It was wicked. It was treachery of the worst kind. Alfred landed on the Kent coast and rode from Canterbury to Guildford. Six hundred Normans and Flemings accompanied him. They were treated to all honour. Godwin, who had now thrown in his fortunes with Harald since Harald had become King of all England, received him. There was a banquet and at night while they slept, Harald's men arrived. Alfred and his men were taken prisoner. One out of every ten became a slave; the rest were killed barbarically.'

'And Alfred?'

'They stripped him, and naked as he was, placed him on a donkey and tied his legs together beneath the animal's belly. And so they took him to Ely.'

William kept his eyes on Osbern's face. He dared not ask the question but Osbern answered as though he had spoken.

'Yes, they murdered him ... most cruelly they murdered him. They put out his eyes.'

'His beautiful eyes!' cried William.

'The knife pierced his brain. He did not live long afterwards.'

William clenched his fists. 'By God, if I am not revenged I shall be haunted all my life by those beautiful blue eyes. Tell me who did this foul deed? I will go to England. I will kill him.'

'My lord, you have your own battles to fight. We cannot be sure who killed him. I cannot believe that he was lured to death by his mother. The letter was said to come from her, but Harald or Godwin may have forged it. Who can say? I do not believe it was Emma, for she has now left England and has gone to Flanders.'

'And Edward. What of Edward?'

'I hear he has become more melancholy than ever. Sadly he mourns for his lost brother.'

'Oh, Osbern, how wicked men are!'

'Let us always remember it, my Duke. Let us take the greatest care that they never have an opportunity to practise their cruelty on you.

* * *

It was exciting travelling through the towns and villages. Everywhere it seemed the people came out of their houses to cheer him. They threw flowers in his path.

'Long live the Duke!' they cried.

High on his horse, sometimes in his ducal cloak, he felt as though, young as he was, he were indeed their father and they his children. He vowed that he would be remembered in the future as his ancestors were. His name would rank with those of Richard the Fearless and Great Rollo.

What a joy it was to arrive at Conteville and to see his mother. She was overjoyed and still as startlingly beautiful as he knew she would be.

She took him in her arms as she had when he was a little boy and she wept over him and told him how she had missed him during his stay in France.

'And I you, Mother,' he told her. 'I thought of you often.'

'And now you are our Duke. Oh, William, how proud I am of you.'

They talked of his father and were sad again. 'He was good to me, always,' his mother said. 'He even provided me with a husband to care for me when he was gone.'

'And your husband pleases you, Mother?'

'He is a good man. He is determined to obey the Duke's command and care for me.'

'So you are not unhappy then?'

'I'm as happy as it is possible to be without your father. He said to me before he went: "We must always live for the future. It is always what it is to come that is important, not what is past." Sometimes I think he knew that he was never coming back.'

'It is strange, Mother, not to have you at Rouen.'

'I would we could be together. But I must live in my husband's house and you are the Duke.'

She was content, he could see, and when she told him that she was expecting a child he rejoiced, for he knew that the children she would have from her new husband would stop her grieving for Robert and the boy, who because he was a Duke of Normandy, could not be brought up by his mother.

*   *   *

He could not stay at Conteville though he felt a great desire to do so. He liked his stepfather and it had been comforting to enjoy the tenderness which only his mother could give.

There was work to be done, Osbern told him. In spite of the good impression he had made on his subjects he had powerful enemies. Osbern had told him the names of some of those who had turned against him. Talvas of Bellême was one of them. He remembered that encounter long ago when he had looked into that evil face; he remembered the curse the man had uttered against him. He would never forget those terrible stories of the barbaric cruelties inflicted by Talvas on the innocent. What more diabolical sport he would wish to have with one whom he hated! Talvas was on the prowl, waiting to snatch him. For a moment he thought of running to his mother, begging her to keep him with her at Conteville. She would hide him there; she and his stepfather would do anything to protect him.

Then he despised himself. Was he not a Duke of Normandy of Rollo's line? Had Rollo ever thought of what might happen to him if his enemies captured him? Had Richard the Fearless? 'Please God, make me as great and as fearless as my ancestors,' he prayed.

Men of his own family were against him. His father's brothers—those who were illegitimate—had declared that if a bastard boy should be elected Duke why not men? He suspected that Mauger agreed with them. Those sly sneering looks he had received in the schoolroom were significant. Mauger was an evil man. It was said that he practised sorcery. Was he practising it now? Was he murmuring to his evil familiars, asking their help in delivering the Duke of Normandy into their hands? Was he invoking the aid of the Allfather Odin? Was he praying to Thor to lend him his Hammer? But the power of the Christian god was greater than that of those of the pagans. He was certain of it, and as certain of his destiny.

When the people cheered him he forgot his anxieties. The women smiled tenderly at him. 'God's blessings on our little Duke.' He charmed them because he was a handsome boy. He was their idea of what a Duke of Normandy should be. And because he was young the women loved him even as the men asked themselves: 'How can a child govern Normandy?' But his governors were good strong men and determined to carry out the wishes of the Duke Robert who had died in an aura of sanctity and would therefore have some influence in holy places.

It was inspiring to travel through his realm, to arrive at the houses of his loyal subjects, who felt themselves honoured to have him under their roofs.

It was such a night when they came to the house of one of his subjects and weary from the day's ride they feasted and went to their beds. Thorold and Osbern took it in turns to sleep in his room while the other watched at his door. They never varied from this routine and he realized in time that had they done so he would never have survived.

He was deep in sleep, for he was always tired out at the end of the day's ride, when he was aware of Thorold at his bedside.

'Wake up,' said Thorold.

He started up. 'What is it, Thorold?'

68

Thorold's answer was to pick him up and wrap him in a great cloak.

'Thorold, I cannot see. I am stifling.'

There was no answer. He was taken out of the house—he was slung across a saddle and Thorold was riding as though for his life—which he was of course, and that of the little Duke.

His heart was beating fast; he was in danger. Someone knew he had been in that house and had come to take him—or was coming. Perhaps they were there now searching for him. He could see the evil eyes of Talvas as he pricked the straw with his sword. 'Come out, you little bastard! *Bastard! Bastard!*' How he hated that word. If they had not been able to apply it to him, would he be riding through the night like this? But Alfred had not been a bastard and they had cut out his eyes . . . his beautiful eyes. He had died. Better to be dead than to live without one's eyes—a prisoner of cruel men!

The horse had stopped. He could hear voices.

Thorold had lifted him from the saddle; he was able to free his head and breathe the fresh night air.

'Are we safe?' said a voice.

'Nay. They could follow us. We must needs hide here until fresh horses can be found.'

'Into the hayloft,' said a voice.

'Thorold,' William said imperiously, 'who are our enemies this night?'

But Thorold ignored him. How like Thorold! He could be as respectful as William could ask when there was no danger but as soon as there was he made it clear that William was a boy and must obey his elders.

He was taken into the loft as though he were a bundle of straw and hay was piled up over him.

'Lie there. Not a sound. Don't move until I come.' It was Thorold who gave the orders now.

It seemed long that he waited in the loft, his ears straining for every sound that might mean his pursuers had discovered his hiding-place. He imagined Talvas at their head; he could picture his coming into the loft cruelly laughing, knowing that he had run his quarry to earth.

It was terrifying to think of the stories of that cruel man. And now he was chasing the Duke of Normandy as he had his other victims. And if he found him? William touched his eyes and thought of Alfred

69

Because he was trembling he tried to shut out the thought of Talvas and thought instead of his grandfather Richard the Fearless.

It was almost as though Richard lived again. Richard had been a bastard even as he had; Richard's father had died when he was a child; Richard had been taken as a hostage into France and his faithful squire Osmond (how like Osbern!) had one day put Richard into a sack and covered him with hay, told all who saw him that he was going to feed his horse and had ridden with Richard out of the castle, out of France and brought his little Duke safely back to Normandy.

So would it be with William. His faithful friend would save him even as Richard's had.

So he lay under the hay and listened for the sounds of horses' hoofs. Osbern lay in the hay with him waiting to spring on his enemies, ready to defend his little Duke to the death. And I will fight too, William promised himself. I would kill Talvas and all who come against me.

At length that long night was over. Thorold had found horses. They set off on their ride to safety and so they continued their tour of Normandy.

* * *

But their enemies were powerful and more dangerous still, secret.

William's friends saw now how dangerous it was for him to go openly among his people, for then his enemies would know where he slept each night and they would come by stealth.

They were everywhere, in quarters least expected. The Count d'Eu, one of William's most loyal supporters, was attacked while out riding; one by one the little Duke's supporters began to die.

They were hunting him, William knew. So must the wolf feel when the pack was after him. But he would always feel safe with Thorold and Osbern, those two giants who arranged that always one of them should be with him.

Then one day Thorold was no longer there.

Never had William felt so desolate as he did on the day they told him that he would never see Thorold again. This was worse than going to France, than leaving his mother, even than the death of his father, for when Robert died it

70

had been more than two years since they had seen each other.

And now Thorold, big powerful ever-watching Thorold, was dead...lost to him for ever.

No more would that rough voice bid him lie still or be silent. No more would that great protective body stand between him and his enemies.

Thorold was dead. They had poisoned him. These wicked cruel men who were determined that they would not be governed by a young bastard had killed Thorold.

William was no longer a child from that moment. A fierce hatred burned in his heart. He had loved Thorold. There had never been such a stong man, such a brave man as Thorold. He loved Osbern too but Osbern was gentler, a squire rather than a warrior. These two men had been to him what no one else had ever been since he had left for France. They had replaced his parents. And now Thorold was dead.

'So help me God,' said William. 'I will be avenged on those who killed Thorold.'

In the quiet of his bed at night he wept for Thorold. He hoped his ancestors did not see the tears. What would Rollo say of a Duke who wept? Had Richard the Fearless wept when he lost his father? Perhaps in secret and tears might be forgiven if no one saw them.

I wish I were a man, thought William, so that I could go forth and smite the murderers of Thorold—ay, and every man who dares call me bastard.

* * *

Osbern never left him now. He even slept in his bed. Osbern missed Thorold too.

Osbern talked to him often, not attempting now to hide the truth. 'We have many enemies,' he said, 'as you now know. But we have friends too. There are too many who wish to wear the ducal robes and they are suspicious of each other. In this lies our strength. We cannot go on like this. I heard that many of those who wish you well believe that you should go to your mother and stay with her. There you will be safe.'

'My enemies could come there for me.'

'Nay. We would have Conteville well fortified. You

71

would be among those who love you. Your stepfather is a man of some power and *he* has faithful friends. Your mother would make sure that everything was done to safeguard you. You would continue with lessons and live the life natural to a boy of your age.'

'I am the Duke, you forget.'

'I could not forget it—even if you would allow me to,' said Osbern with a smile. 'But we cannot go on like this. One day our enemies would catch us. You have to live...as a symbol. We have to get through these difficult years of your minority and when you are of age you can step into your rightful place. There are four or five years to be lived through but if we can keep you safe during those years and your loyal friends can keep your enemies at bay, then you can take over your duties when the time is ripe.'

'I am ready to fight them now. By God's splendour, Osbern, I long to go into battle.'

'A strong oath, my lord.'

'Strong men use strong oaths. I am done with childhood.'

Osbern shook his head. 'We can only enter manhood, my lord, when childhood has done with us. Let us face facts. You are too young to rule and you must be fitted to rule. You cannot be made so, roaming the country as a fugitive. This is what your loyal friends and advisers have decreed. Duke you are and Duke you must remain, but because of your tender years you must needs listen to those of maturer wisdom than your own.'

Osbern could always defeat him in argument. And in his heart he knew he was right. Even Richard the Fearless had had to accept the advice of his counsellors when he was a boy. He had not done with lessons yet.

* * *

They were on the way to Conteville, and stayed the night at the house of a man whom Osbern knew to be loyal. They supped and retired to the room which had been given to them. A large room full of shadows. Osbern went to the hangings, his knife in his hand as he always did—ready if any should be hiding there to despatch him without delay.

All was well.

They lay down to sleep, Osbern beside him, Osbern nearest to the door, to shield him: and so they slept.

72

Something had awakened William. It was dark in the room. He lay still listening. A footstep on the stair? The slow stealthy opening of a door. Nay, all was quiet.

He closed his eyes. He was mistaken again. It was always thus when he awakened in the night. He would think of Talvas entertaining his guests, of Alfred's beautiful eyes, of Thorold who was lost to him; and then reassured by the bulk of Osbern beside him he would fall asleep. He dozed and dreamed that someone came and stood over the bed. In his dream he heard a voice. 'Die...die, you bastard.'

Half waking he thought: A dream! Another evil dream. He could feel Osbern beside him and comforted, he slept again.

* * *

It was morning for a little light penetrated the narrow apertures.

'Osbern,' whispered William, 'it is morning.'

Osbern did not answer, and after a few minutes William rose from the bed.

'Osbern! Osbern!' he cried.

That was blood on the bed...the blood of Osbern!

'Oh, Osbern, my dear, dear friend. Wake up. Speak to me.'

But Osbern would never wake again. In the night he had been stabbed to death.

William heard that word ringing in his head, triumphantly, maliciously spoken: 'Bastard.' And he knew that Osbern had been killed in mistake for himself.

* * *

He was twelve years old and although still a child in years he had suffered the emotions of a man. Thorold dead. Osbern dead. He had loved these men. He wanted to go out and do battle with their slayers; he wanted to wreck a terrible vengeance on these murderers.

This could not be. But there were still men who remembered their oath to him and to his father. He was their Duke and they would serve him with their lives. They would wage war against his enemies but it was too dangerous to have him roaming the country. Narrowly he

73

had escaped assassination: both those brave men—Thorold and Osbern—had died in his service. He could not hope to escape every time.

It was explained to him. 'You are a figurehead. As yet you are too young to be the Duke in aught but name. You remember how important your father always thought it that you should be trained in every way to fit your position.'

He knew what that meant—going back to the schoolroom, studying the arts of war not in practice but with his teachers.

Of course they were right. He was but twelve years old. If only he had been born ten or even five years earlier. But what was the use of railing against that?

He agreed to go back to his mother.

The Seed Is Sown

SHE was at the top of the turret as he had known she would be. She told him this when he rode into the courtyard for by that time she was down there.

'My boy,' she cried. 'Thank God you have come home to me.'

She took him into her arms; she wept shamelessly. He feared that he too might show a womanish emotion. But how good it was to be home!

She had a warming stirrup-cup waiting for him; he was thin, she complained.

'William, my love, I am going to feed you. You have the best chamber in the castle. Come, I will show you. And then you will meet your sister Adeliz and your brothers. Odo cannot wait. I'll swear he is peeping out at you from one of the windows. He has heard such tales of you. Even little Robert knows. Herlwin, my husband, has sworn to serve you with his life and you know your father gave him a large estate that he might care for me and be your faithful vassal. On this estate everyone is for you ... every man, woman and child.'

Yes, it was comforting to enjoy the luxuries of Conteville. He could almost believe he was back in Falaise.

He embraced his sister Adeliz who had grown since he last saw her. He liked the children. Odo was a bright little fellow, who liked to stand at his side and gaze at him as though he were one of the heroes of his favourite legend, for his mother had told these stories to him as she had to William.

For a day he gave himself to the pleasure of being with

his mother, his stepfather and the children. They were his family on whom he could rely with as much certainty as he had on Thorold and Osbern! Having experienced the uncertainty of not knowing who was a friend, it was good to sink back on a couch of security.

There were dogs and horses and falcons at Conteville. 'Choose what you will,' said Herlwin. 'We get some good hunting here.'

He rode far from the castle with Herlwin. 'These people you see are loyal to a man,' said his stepfather. 'They depend for their livelihood on me and would not dare raise a hand against my stepson even if they wished to. But they do not. They are with you.' And it was true that people seeing them together called a loyal 'Long live the Duke'.

He began to sleep as he had not done since that terrible morning when he had awakened to find Osbern's bloody body beside him.

He would return to the castle tired but exalted from the hunt. There was feasting in the castle hall as there had been at Falaise with himself at the head of the table as his father used to sit, and his mother on his right hand, his stepfather on his left.

He would lie on the grass beside the moat with young Odo and tell him how they had struck down the stag with their arrows and what a fine big animal he was. He would carry his little half-brother on his shoulders and trot round the courtyard with him; he would take him out on his pony; the boy adored him.

But he was in little mood for merry-making after the feast; he did not wish to hear the ballads and stories of heroes because they reminded him of Thorold and Osbern. So he and Herlwin would sit together over a game of chess.

His mother looked on, smiling at them both. It was as it had been many years and even more adventures ago when his father had come home.

A few days after his arrival at the castle he returned from a ride with his stepfather to find his mother waiting for them in the hall.

She was smiling in a manner which told him that she had a surprise for him and that it would please him.

'There is someone to see you, William,' she said. 'He has come to beg to be taken back into your service.' She turned and called: 'Come, Gallet.'

76

And there was Gallet the Fool kneeling before him kissing his hands.

He must control his emotions. There must not be any foolish tears. Why should they come to his eyes at the sight of that slight figure kneeling there, and the rather vacant eyes looking up at him as though he were one of the gods or heroes of the Northlands?

'Gallet,' he said, 'you are welcome ... you old fool.'

Gallet understood in spite of the fact that he was such a fool.

'You'll have a fine sparrow-hawk for me to train, Master?' he asked.

'Welcome, Gallet,' said William. 'It pleases me to have you in my service.'

*   *   *

But days were not to be spent in sport and family pleasures. He was at peace here, but his realm was in turmoil. Loyal men were fighting for his inheritance. Although he could not join them he must do as they wished, which meant he must go back to the schoolroom as well as perfect himself in arms.

He must resume his studies under Uncle Mauger, which did not please him. But although he was no longer a child, he was not yet a man, and he must tolerate this cynical tutor who was reckoned to be one of the most learned men in the Duchy. Raoul de Vacé, the Constable and Regent of Normandy, was also his tutor, and William was expected to give as much attention to learning as he did to the study of arms. He would never be as good a scholar as he would be a man of action, that much was clear; but a leader could not be ignorant; as Mauger said, rulers must be acquainted with the past for then they would be aware of the mistakes of their predecessors and could profit from their knowledge, so avoiding the same errors themselves. There was wisdom in that and in spite of his dislike for his uncle, William had to admit that he was a wise man.

His stepfather's son by a previous marriage came to the castle as a companion for William. He was Raoul de Tancarville to whom William took an instant liking. It was pleasant to have a companion. His sister Adeliz, although he was fond of her, could clearly not join in his lessons and

77

pastimes as a member of his own sex could.

He had not been at Conteville a week when his cousin Guy arrived. What a joy it was to see him! Guy was the son of Duke Robert's sister and they were friends from the old days.

He said: 'I am to take lessons with you, cousin. It will be as it was at Falaise.'

William was delighted. He realized that was what he wanted, to get back to the happy days at Falaise, to forget the horror and misery he had witnessed, to sleep peacefully in his bed at night, his quarrels to be arguments with Guy and Raoul, his battles a round of fisticuffs about which they laughed afterwards.

There was one occasion when he bloodied Guy's nose. The incident followed one of those moments when William—as he did now and then—remembered that he was Duke and their master.

'Remember,' he said to Guy, 'that I am older than you.'

'By not much,' retorted Guy. 'Besides, I'm my mother's legitimate son. You are a bastard.'

That hated word! William's fiery temper, as easily aroused as it ever was in spite of his efforts to restrain it, flared up and Guy was sent sprawling on the cobbles of the courtyard.

Guy was on his feet, in a devilishly irritating mood, dancing round William, from a safe distance chanting: 'Bastard! Bastard! William the Bastard!'

He could have killed Guy, for in that moment he hated his cousin. He might have done so too if his stepfather had not parted them.

'Now, William! Now, Guy! What is this?'

William glared at Guy as though daring him to say that word which was the cause of the quarrel. Guy said nothing.

'Two boys who cannot guard their temper,' said Herlwin sadly. 'When will you grow into men?'

William was sorry he had lost his temper. Osbern and Thorold had always told him he must restrain it if he was to govern well.

Then Mauger came out to the courtyard and said that as a penance they should do an extra Latin exercise.

Side by side they sullenly sat in the schoolroom. Outside the sun was shining. They should have been practising their sword-play or archery or riding with the dogs at their

78

heels, any of which was preferable to struggling with this tiresome Latin.

Guy looked at William with that crinkling of his eyes which was rather beguiling.

'Idiot,' he said. 'Who cares if you are? I wouldn't mind being one if I were Duke of Normandy.'

William laughed. They were good friends again.

They compared exercises. They would help each other the sooner to get out into the fresh air.

*　*　*

These were happy years—boyish delights were enjoyable. Within the walls of the castle of Conteville what went on in the outside world seemed far away. Suffice it that his loyal supporters were holding their own against the rebels. Skirmishes there were and battles, defeats and victories; but those men who remained loyal to the wishes of Robert the Magnificent grew stronger. Their symbol was the boy who was growing up in safety at Conteville.

Arlette was almost as happy as she had been with Robert, and felt more secure. He, by nature of his position, was constantly leaving her; she had suffered constant fear when he was away from her, which may have compensated for the ecstatic joy they shared together. Now she had passed into a peaceful happiness. It was true she could not look too far ahead. There would come a time when William would go away, but for the next few years she had him with her; she had her daughter, Adeliz, and her little ones, Odo and Robert; she had her kind good husband; and in the wide estates of Conteville, William could ride out even alone without fear of the assassin's knife.

William had become a young boy again. He no longer awoke to feel for the blood-soaked body of Osbern beside him. His concern was trying to ride faster than Guy, shoot his arrows farther. This rivalry between them was something they both enjoyed, though there were occasional fights. Guy had learned that he only had to mouth the word 'bastard' to make William fly into a passion. So he would use the word slyly. 'Oh, the poor fellow's a bastard.' And then open his eyes in innocent astonishment when the red colour flamed into William's face. He could infuriate William but the rivalry between them gave a zest to life.

Herlwin encouraged William to mingle with the humble people on the estate. 'It is necessary that a ruler should understand all his people—humble or noble,' he said.

So often William would ride out with Guy and a party and they would call at the cottage of humble folk. Because they were near the coast many of these were fishermen and William would listen attentively when they talked to him of their catch. He could put them at their ease; he was able to talk to them far more easily than Guy ever could. Guy was too conscious of his rank, of being the legitimate son of a daughter of a Duke of Normandy. He could never forget that Richard the Fearless was his great-grandfather as well as William's.

Herlwin was pleased that William should be so liked by the humbler folk.

'It will stand you in good stead, William,' he told him.

When they were at the coast, if the day was very clear, they could see the outline of land.

'England,' said William. 'I remember well my Atheling cousins. Such beautiful young men! Poor Alfred. You know what became of Alfred?'

'They put out his eyes,' said Guy.

'He had the most beautiful eyes I ever saw. Except Edward's. They were beautiful too.'

'Beautiful eyes will not get them a throne.'

'Poor Alfred will never have a throne now. They killed him. They put out his beautiful eyes and the knife pierced his brain.'

''Twere better that he should die. I'd rather be dead than live without my eyes.'

'Edward is still in Normandy. I should like to see him again. My good cousin.'

'Mine also, William. They are the true heirs to England. They come before this Hardicanute. They are the true *legitimate* heirs.'

He cast a sly glance at William and went on boldly, 'They should come before the whims and...'

The colour had started to come into William's face; his jaw projected even more than usual, his lips had thinned. These were the danger signals.

Guy looked mischievous. No, he had better be careful. He continued: 'Before the whims and wishes of those who oust them, I think our old kinswoman Emma is something of a terror. What think you, William?'

'She is a woman who will fight to keep what she has won. She is a Norman.'

'Well, now she has her son Hardicanute on the throne—for I hear he has returned from Denmark and now governs that land over there. He has learned good drinking habits in Denmark and spends his time in drinking and feasting which may make our doughty Emma wish that she had not made her pact with Canute and her son Edward might be the King.'

They pulled up their horses and stood looking across the sea.

'How calm it is today,' said William. 'On such a day as this my father would have conquered it and Alfred would never have lost his eyes.'

'Who knows what will happen now,' said Guy. 'Mayhap Edward Atheling will go back there after all these years in Normandy. They say he would like better to live the monk's life he does here than to be a King on a throne. Yet it is right that he should be King, for he is the *legitimate* heir...'

He glanced at William and touched his horse's flanks. He was away, William in pursuit, out-distancing him, riding ahead, showing him as he did many times a day that a bastard can be a better man than one legitimately born.

So passed the years when William grew into his manhood.

* * *

'There is news from England,' said Herlwin as he came into William's chamber. 'Hardicanute is dead.'

'What will happen now?' replied William.

'We must needs wait and see.'

'It may be that this is Edward's chance,' said William. 'I would I could go to see my cousin.'

'Why, William, you imagine all men are as you. There are many who say that Edward Atheling has no wish for a crown.'

'It may be that he would be chary of going to England—remembering what happened to his brother.'

They talked awhile and together went down to the great hall where the roasted flesh of wild boar was awaiting them.

After they had eaten they talked of England and what would happen now.

Arlette mentioned that sad day when Robert had returned to Normandy—defeated by the storms which had suddenly arisen and destroyed his fleet. She always believed that if he had successfully conquered England he would never have gone on his pilgrimage. But she was philosophical now. She had a good husband, a charming daughter, her dear little boys and her wonderful son William was with her if but temporarily.

'It was a pity Hardicanute ever went back to England. He brought no good to that country,' said Herlwin.

'Yet he was greeted warmly enough,' said William, 'by both Danes and Saxons.'

'In truth he was,' put in Guy. 'For he came with sixty ships and men to defend his claim should any dispute it. I heard that his first act as King was to take revenge on his dead brother Harald, and that he had his body dug up, the head cut off and that with his body thrown into the River Thames.'

'Much good would that do him!' said William. 'He betrayed himself as a man of no account by such an act.'

'But it relieved his anger against Harald, so perhaps it *did* him some good.'

'He was a bad king and few will regret his death.'

'He taxed the people so that they cried out against him,' said Herlwin, 'and in Worcester where the people defied his tax-gatherers he laid the city to waste and had its inhabitants put to the sword.'

'That is no way to rule,' said William.

'Would you, cousin,' asked Guy, 'be such a ruler that you will allow your subjects to flout you?'

'None shall dare flout me,' declared William. 'But I will have justice in my domain. If people protest against taxes I shall examine their complaints.'

'It is easy to be a great ruler with one's mouth,' Guy reminded him. 'Ha, look at yon Fool Gallet drinking in the words of wisdom. He believes you, cousin.'

'Then he is no fool.'

'I'll warrant he understands not a word of what you say. That's so, Gallet, is it not?'

'Yes, master,' answered Gallet.

'There, William, you see, you are adored by those without understanding. You will not win such an easy victory over wise men.'

Herlwin said: 'Come, master Guy, we want no quarrels.

82

This matter is a serious one. What happens in the countries close to us can have its effect on us as our Duke is well aware.'

Constantly, Herlwin was thinking, he was having to remind Guy that William was his suzerain and although a little badinage was acceptable in the schoolroom it was not to be tolerated before servants.

William understood Herlwin's thoughts and smiled. He was quite capable of handling Guy.

He said: 'One day, Guy, you may discover what kind of ruler I will be. In view of the fact that that day will most likely come, a wiser man might see fit to guard his tongue.'

Guy was a little subdued for him but he quickly said: 'This Hardicanute is no more then and it would seem this is not a matter for deep regret.'

'The real ruler was Earl Godwin—he and Emma,' William said. 'Hardicanute was too fond of a life of pleasure to rule. All he cared for was the levying of taxes to pay for his pleasures—which were mainly eating and drinking.'

'I have heard,' said Herlwin, 'that he sat to table four times daily and on each occasion would sit for several hours so that there was very little time between these four gigantic meals and that the servants and cooks were cooking every minute of the day.'

'When they were not eating they were drinking. Never, it was said, had such consumption of food and drink been seen.'

'It is an old Danish custom,' said Herlwin. 'The Danes are big men and need constant supplies of food and drink. It is a wonder they ever had time for conquest.'

'And now,' said William, 'the people of England are heartily sick of Danish rule. Canute was a good king, but his son was far from that. I believe the Saxons and the Angles have had enough of them. They would welcome back Edward Atheling.'

'I wonder if he will go?'

'I have learned much of what takes place in England,' said William. 'My instructors are constantly telling me that I must study the affairs not only of Normandy but also of our neighbours. The Danes have been in the ascendancy too long; and they are the foreigners. They pay no taxes; they enter the houses of the Saxons who must needs feed them and treat them as guests as long as they wish to stay. Moreover the intruder becomes the master of that household so that the owner may not drink without his permission. If a Dane wished to take the wife or daughter of his Saxon host he would do so and if the Saxon avenged his honour he was punished. Many Saxons so took this revenge and then fled to the forest to become brigands, that being the only way in which they could live. They naturally sought to rob and murder their Danish masters. Such brigands were treated as though they were wolves, for a price was set on their heads as is the case with these animals and they were even known as Wolf's Heads.'

'William has done his lessons well,' said Guy lightly. 'Why, cousin, do you plan to make England part of your domain as well as Normandy?'

'The Duke is wise,' said Herlwin. 'These affairs can so easily be ours. It is true that this reign was a cruel one and I will stake my castle and lands on the return of Edward, for the people of England are in truth heartily wary of this submission to the Danes and they will back the Atheling.'

'Was he poisoned, this Hardicanute?' asked Guy.

'It could be so,' said Herlwin. 'He was at the marriage banquet of one of his Danish friends. You can picture the scene. The company had been eating for many hours and the feasting had gone far into the night. Hardicanute lifted a goblet to propose yet another toast. He drank, staggered forward and fell to the floor.'

'It may well have been poison,' said William.

'Which shows how careful rulers should be,' added Guy, laughing into William's face.

'They must constantly be on the watch for traitors,' agreed William. 'That, alas, is a lesson they learn at their mother's knees.'

It was a short while afterwards that they heard that Earl Godwin had thrown in his lot with Edward Atheling and that Edward was invited to return to England.

* * *

Before he sailed for England Edward Atheling came to Conteville to take leave of William.

He knelt at the Duke's feet and William said: 'Why, Edward, rise. You will soon be a king and I am but a duke.'

William was anxious to know how Edward felt about his recall. That he was apprehensive was clear. Naturally he would be remembering what had happened to Alfred.

'You know I wish you well,' said William.

'And I you. Never shall I forget the sanctuary that has been given me in your country.'

'Methinks you are loth to leave us.'

'I have grown accustomed to the monastic life.'

'If you are king you can live as you please.'

'Do you think any king may do that? One of the conditions of my return is that I marry Earl Godwin's daughter, Editha.'

'Marry that man's daughter? There have been rumours that he was involved in the murder of Alfred.'

Edward looked sad. 'He is the most powerful man in England.'

'He must be clever. He, a cowherd's son, to aspire so high. You must be watchful of him, Edward.'

'Ay, I must be watchful of so much.'

'I have often thought of England. I remember so well the stories you and your brother told me of King Alfred. Do you remember?'

'I do. He was a great King—one of our greatest.'

'It may be that you will be such another.'

'He had many children. I shall have none.'

'You must have heirs.'

'Nay, that I shall not. I have sworn a vow of celibacy to God and all his saints.'

'But you are to be married.'

'Only because Earl Godwin has made this condition.'

'Edward, could you not have refused to go?'

'I saw it as my duty. England needs a Saxon King. She is weary of the foreigners. If I did not agree some Danish claimant would have appeared. I must do my duty. I hope I shall always do that. But I will keep my vow of perpetual continence and nothing will make me break it.'

'You must have an heir to follow you to the throne.'

'William, why should *you* not follow me to the throne of England?'

'I, Edward!'

'Are you not the great-nephew of my mother Emma? It could be for me to name my successor.'

'England,' said William wonderingly. 'I have always felt an interest in that country ... far more so than I ever did in France which is closer to us.'

Edward smiled at him. 'I shall never forget, William, what I owe to Normandy. I must go to England because it is my duty. I must marry Editha, although it will be marriage in name only. But my heart will be here in Normandy and I shall take with me the customs of this land. There will always be a welcome for Normans in England while I am the King. One day you will visit me there.'

They took farewell of each other and William bade Edward godspeed.

He waited eagerly for news of his arrival and often feared that they might have betrayed Edward as they had Alfred and put out his beautiful blue eyes.

At length there was news. The English, heartily tired of Danish rule, had warmly welcomed Edward, who had married Editha and kept his vow not to consummate the marriage. The monks applauded this; they said he was a saint and he became known as Edward the Confessor throughout the land. And because twenty-seven years of his life had been spent in Normandy he was more Norman than Saxon. Although he had not been allowed to take a Norman entourage with him when he landed, Normans began to filter into England. Edward's first act had been to abolish the Danish taxes. This ensured his popularity and since he was so pious, he quickly became reverenced. There was no murmur from the people when Norman fashions were introduced into the country and it became fashionable to speak the Norman tongue as was done at Court.

William learned all he could of England. A new ambition had started to grow. Not only did he wish to be a great Duke of Normandy, to stand beside Rollo and Richard the Fearless. He wished to be a King of England.

The Traitor

IT was time he left Conteville. Rouen was the principal city and he moved there, taking with him his mother, his stepfather and their family. He was seventeen, still young but old enough now to take part in councils. His grasp of affairs astonished his ministers; yet he was cautious, never boastful, and his skill in military matters was outstanding. There was still conflict in the Duchy but his supporters were in the ascendancy now and as he grew older the complaint against his extreme youth must necessarily be modified.

Guy had not accompanied him to Rouen. He parted with his cousin with regret and, as a show of affection, presented him with the Castle of Brionne.

It was a sad farewell he took of him, and Guy, though making a show of being his jaunty self, was also moved.

'It will be strange without you,' said William.

'With whom will you wrestle now?'

'There'll be others.'

'It will be different, William. With them it will be an exercise. With me ... well, admit it, cousin, you could have killed me sometimes.'

William conceded this.

'It gave zest to our fights, did it not?'

'It will be tame without you.'

'Picture me in my castle of Brionne. At least I shall bow the knee to no one there. And very soon now you will be armed as a chevalier—then, my lord, you will be Duke in very truth and ruler of us all. The future lies rosy before you.'

'Still,' said William, 'I shall miss you.'

87

The King of France arrived at Rouen. He had come to take part in the most important ceremony William had yet known. This was to be his initiation; he was to show his people that he was worthy to be armed as a chevalier and prove he was skilled in all the arts expected of him.

Those arduous years of training had culminated in this and he meant to excel himself so that his people should have no doubt that he was indeed fitted to rule them.

Never far from his thoughts was that hateful word 'bastard'. Because of it, he must not only do what was expected of him—but more. Was that why Richard the Fearless had earned his name? Had he too felt this pressing need to wipe out the stain of his birth?

Henry arrived, suave and friendly; but William was wiser than he had been when under the King's guardianship. He was well aware now that Henry's friendship with him was a matter of expediency; he must not be charmed by honeyed words and affectionate manners. He must remember too that he needed the help of the King to subdue his rebellious subjects and restore order in the land.

There was feasting at Rouen and William himself stood behind the King's chair on these occasions and himself served him as a mark of respect and deference. The King knew and William knew that their friendship was uneasy. Only the preceding year the King had destroyed a fort on the frontiers between his kingdom and Normandy. The loyal Norman who guarded the fort had at first refused to pass it to the French but William and his advisers had decided that they could not take on a war with France and subdue their own rebels at the same time and had commanded the loyal Norman to hand over the fort which was destroyed by the French. 'Neither should have it,' said the King; but almost immediately he rebuilt another and placed a French garrison in charge of it. This had been too much for William. He was eighteen years old, of an age to lead his men into battle. To allow the French to remain would have given his enemies the chance they needed to declare him unfit to rule. He rode out with his men, attacked the fort and put the French to flight.

This incident seemed to have been forgotten, for the King was now in Rouen, and William was accepting him as his suzerain and paying him the homage of serving him at table.

The stage was set for the great ceremony.

The citizens of Rouen had assembled in the field in which William would perform his feats and win his golden spurs.

There was a silence as he rode out into the field. Seated on his horse, dressed in steel hauberk, his shining shield attached to his left arm, his lance on his right, he was a magnificent figure. Slender and tall, commanding, his face noble under his gleaming helmet, he looked as strong and defiant as the lions painted on his shield.

His primary test was to pierce a straw figure which had been set up on a pole; this had been dressed in the tunic worn by Normans going into war and which was made of mascles of steel. In addition to this tunic, a shield was affixed to the figure. William's task was to ride to the figure and pierce both shield and tunic without pausing in his gallop. To perform such a feat required years of practice and even so only great skill and precise timing could achieve it.

William's heart was beating wildly; if he did not succeed he would be dubbed for ever as unfit to rule. The old cry of 'Bastard' was in his ears as he heard the shouts of the people. He knew that the eyes of the King of France were on him, wary, veiled. Was he praying for William's success or failure? There was one present on whom he could rely with the utmost certainty—Arlette, his beloved and loving mother. He knew that as she sat in her enclosure strewn with grass and herbs, mint and roses, she was praying as fervently as she had ever prayed in her life, that he might succeed.

His half-brothers Odo and Robert were tense with excitement. His stepfather wished him well, as did all loyal lords. He wished that Guy were there. Guy should have been there. Why was he not? Too busy looking after affairs at Brionne doubtless. He could well imagine Guy's giving himself airs since he had become a seigneur.

This was more than winning his spurs. He was no ordinary pupil of chivalry. He was the Duke of Normandy with a far from stable country to control. So much hung on his ability to ride to that inanimate figure and at precisely the right second to send his lance through the steel.

He had practised it thousands of times. He was skilled. But was he skilled enough? What if his fears of failure betrayed him?

But he must not fail. This day he must take his golden spurs from the hands of the King of France.

The moment had come. He could see the figure on the pole. The sun was hot; the crowd tense.

There was the King seated in his box, inscrutable. How many of the nobles watching were his true friends? How many hoped for his success? How many prayed for failure?

The moment had come. 'Rollo, William of the Longsword, Richard the Fearless, Robert the Magnificent ... revered ancestors, do not let me fail,' he prayed. 'Let me take my place beside you as one of the great Dukes of Normandy.'

He was not sure whether the thudding he could hear came from his horse's hoof-beats or from his heart. Time seemed to be passing very slowly. The straw figure was far away. It seemed to take on a life of its own, mocking, malevolent, a sorcerer determined to defeat him. 'Bastard!' it seemed to say. 'Is a bastard worthy to be a Duke of Normandy?'

Anger swelled up in him. He quelled it. 'Your temper betrays you,' old Mauger had said. 'You must be calm to be ruthless.'

He was right upon the figure now. Up shot his lance, through the shield, through the mail it went. The figure hung for a second in mid-air and crashed to the ground; and he was still seated on his horse; he was riding round the field. He could hear the applause of the people.

He had won his golden spurs.

*　　*　　*

Rouen was en fête. Everywhere he went the people cheered him. He was indeed fitted to be their Duke. Never had they seen such equestrian skill as they had witnessed in that field.

His mother wept with joy.

'How I wish that your father could have seen this day! How proud he would have been! Never has any Duke of Normandy excelled as you did. Rollo would have seemed of no account beside you.'

He laughed at her. 'Nay, do not be disloyal to Rollo, Mother.'

And she was afraid because deep down in her heart although she was a Christian she still feared the old gods and heroes and Rollo was one of the latter. His name stood beside those of Sigurd and Ragnar. Had not Rollo given Normandy to the Normans?

He felt secure in her tenderness. They were happy days which followed. Odo and Robert clamoured for his attention. He could not help but revel in their adoration. His stepfather was delighted.

'I never l ard such cheers as those for you when the King of France gave you your spurs. The people are for you as they never were before.'

'We have our traitors still. Let us not forget that,' said William. 'But Henry has offered me help to subdue them. He wants a peaceful Normandy and good relations between us.'

'You trust him?'

'No. But I need his help. This state of anarchy has gone on too long. No one can say I am too young to rule now and I intend to do so.'

His stepfather agreed.

No, thought William, none can say I am too young but they can still call me Bastard.

'My first task now,' said William, 'will be to summon all the nobles together and they shall swear fresh oaths of fealty to me.'

'At Rouen?'

'At Bayeux, I think. If they swear the oath they will find it more difficult to rebel against me in the near future. So without delay...to Bayeux.'

He said good-bye to his half-brothers and his mother and sister. Arlette embraced him tenderly.

'My pride is so great I cannot begin to express it,' she told him.

'You express it in your eyes, Mother.'

'I knew you would do it. I know you will do everything you set your heart on. I shall never forget the dream I had before you were born. It was not a dream. It was a prophecy.'

'The dream of the great tree which grew from you and its branches spread over Normandy.'

91

'Ay, my son, and beyond. Out over the sea...'

'Out to England,' he said. 'Mother, did it spread over England?'

'It spread far and wide. I can tell you that.'

He kissed her hands. 'And I tell you this. There is no lady in the land that I would have had to bear me...but you.'

She laid her cheek against his hand. 'God prosper you, William...for ever.'

Her mood changed suddenly. She lifted her beautiful eyes to his face and said: 'William, you will have to marry now.'

He laughed. 'I have far too much to do.'

'Your duty is to get sons, William. Who will follow you? It must be your son.'

Marriage? He pondered the matter. There had been little time for women. But she was right, of course. He would have to marry.

When he had restored order to Normandy he would give the matter some thought.

* * *

He rode triumphantly into Bayeux amid the loyal shouts of his people. His eyes gleamed with pleasure to contemplate this fair city.

Mine, he said to himself. All mine!

He never ceased to be delighted when he contemplated his possessions.

He would see Guy in Bayeux, he promised himself, for naturally Guy must be among the company of nobles who must come to swear fealty. They would talk over old times, banter a bit as they used to; Guy would make sly comments about the Duke of Normandy and he would retaliate about a certain seigneur who had become very important since he had been in possession of the castles of Brionne and Vernon.

In the great hall the knights were assembled. He sat on his throne and surveyed them, remembering the scene so long ago when his father had taken him to Rouen and told the people he was their Duke.

One by one they came to him; they knelt, they kissed his hand, they swore their loyalty.

But where was Guy? Why did Guy not come?

Herlwin came to his chamber.

'You have something to tell me?' asked William.

Herlwin nodded.

'It is Guy. He is ill? By God he is not...dead!'

'Nay, William. Alive. Too much alive for our comfort.'

William rose, his hand on his sword.

'What means this?'

'He was always an arrogant young devil.'

'You mean he is conspiring against me?'

'He thinks he has a greater claim to the dukedom through his mother who was your father's sister.'

'By God's splendour, am I not my father's son?'

'And presented to us by him as our Duke. That is so and all those loyal to Robert the Magnificent are with you. But there are some...'

'More rebels...and Guy amongst them. Guy. My old friend and companion.'

'You were always sparring.'

'But it was not meant in rancour.'

'Not by you, William.'

'So Guy would set himself up as Duke?'

'He has some supporters. He says...' Herlwin hesitated.

'I know what he says,' cried William. 'He says: "What right has a bastard to the Dukedom?" That's it, is it not, Herlwin?'

'My lord Duke, that is what he says.'

The colour flamed into William's face. He said: 'I gave him Brionne, I gave him Vernon—two of my most beautiful castles. I could have kept them myself. God knows it hurt to part with them. But I gave them to Guy and with them the means of rebelling against me. Wait, Guy de Brionne, wait until I lay my hands on you.'

*   *   *

He was more shocked by the defection of Guy than he wished anyone to know. He wanted to get away to think.

Over the years at Conteville he had grown into the habit of riding out alone and incognito. In this manner he had learned a great deal about the humble people of whom most nobles knew little. He would tell them that he was the son of a family of traders which was true, for he was on his mother's side; he would thus discover their true feelings as to their conditions. It was a great advantage.

He had made up his mind that when he had brought his dukedom to a state of peace he would examine what could be done for the poor of his dominion.

On this particular occasion he could think of nothing but Guy. So, those bouts in the schoolroom had been deadly serious. When Guy fought him he had wanted to kill him. There had been no true cousinly feeling on Guy's part. His taunts of Bastard had hidden an irrepressible envy. Guy wished to be Duke of Normandy. William laughed at the thought. Frivolous Guy, who thought too much of his own pleasures! Proud, arrogant, jealous Guy, whose only virtue was his legitimacy!

And Guy to betray him!

In times of stress and difficulty William had begun to find comfort from the sea. Merely to look at it soothed him. His mother had said it was due to his Viking ancestors, and the coast of Normandy had taken on a special charm for him of late. Across the water was Edward's kingdom and whenever he could hear news of Edward he listened to it avidly. England fascinated him. Ever since Edward had put into his head that one day it could be his, it had been thus.

Edward had many years left to him but when he died ... who could say? What if Edward named him as his successor? Then he would go and take the land which was his.

Land! How beautiful it was and how proud he was to possess it. His mother had told him how when he was a baby he had clutched at the straw on the floor and clung to it. His first acquisition! His nurses had said that he liked to gather his possessions about him and guard them. He hated to part with even the meanest of his playthings.

And he had given Brionne and Vernon to his false cousin!

It was far to the sea. He could not reach it that night so he would put up at the inn, making sure that the innkeeper would have no idea that the Duke of Normandy was under his roof. He was wise enough to know that he could not go about his dukedom without an escort. But he would not give up these solitary journeys and his friends had grown accustomed to them now.

He was given a room. He paid for it and settled down for the night.

At such a time, with thoughts of Guy's treachery uppermost, there came back to his mind vividly the occasion when he had awakened to find Osbern's dead body beside him.

There was a faithful man—unlike his cousin Guy!

How could one be sure whom one could trust?

He took off his clothes and lay on the bag of straw naked, with his cloak covering him, and over and over in his mind went memories of Guy—Guy endeavouring to out-ride him, to throw him in their wrestling matches, to shoot his arrows farther, always ready to mock with that cry of 'Bastard'.

He was startled by a rapping on the door. He was out of bed in a moment; his eye on the heavy bolt which he had drawn as he had always done in strange places after the death of Osbern.

He put his ear to the wood.

'Master…master…'

He knew that voice, but it could not be!

'Who is there?'

'Gallet…Gallet, your fool.'

Then he was not mistaken. He drew the bolt and Gallet, mud-stained and dishevelled, came into the room.

'Gallet, what means this?'

'Fly, my lord. There is little time. They are on their way. They may be now not more than a mile from here.'

'Who, Gallet, who? Tell me who?'

'Please, master…'

William put on his shirt and seized his corselet.

'No time. They will be here. They are armed…many of them.'

'Who, Gallet, who?'

'Ranulfe of Bayeux, Néel of Coutances…many many of them. They support Guy of Brionne and they will be upon you in a matter of minutes. I heard them planning. They thought I was too foolish to understand. One of their men has followed you here to this inn. My lord, I beg of you if you will live…go…go now.'

'My blessing on you, Gallet,' said William, and half naked as he was, snatched up his cloak, wrapped it about him and ran down the stairs and out of the inn to the stables. He saddled his horse and was away.

The night air was cold on his insufficiently clad body and as he came along the road he heard the sound of galloping horses' hoofs. He turned his horse into a wood and waited there. He knew that the party, with murder in their hearts, were riding on to the inn.

* * *

He was never to forget that ride through the night; on he went, his bare legs and feet frozen, wondering what would happen to him if he came face to face with his enemies now—unarmed as he was, his horse wellnigh spent.

Good fortune was with him.

A man was riding towards him. How strange he must look. What would this fellow think?

'I believe I am on the road to Falaise,' he said. 'But I am unsure. I have urgent business there.'

Urgent business clad only in a shirt and a cloak!

With what joy did he hear the man's reply.

'My lord Duke, I am your loyal subject. Pray tell me what I may do for you.'

'First give me some warm food and clothes, then a horse.'

'Follow me, my lord.'

William learned that he had the good fortune to meet with Hubert de Rye, one of his loyal subjects. In a short time he was in warm clothing, was fed and a horse had been provided for him.

Hubert de Rye's three sons then rode with the Duke back to Falaise.

Another narrow escape.

Oh, Guy, thought William, so you would murder me then.

* * *

He could think of nothing but Guy. During his life he had known many traitors but none like Guy. There were times when he felt bitterly wounded and at others he was filled with a searing hatred. He was going to punish Guy. He was going to show him what it meant to betray the Bastard.

He would make war on Guy and the rebels.

At this time, true to his word, the King of France came to William's assistance. William had won his spurs; he had proved himself skilled in the arts of war; he was not without learning either; in fact he was capable of governing. The King, at this time, desired a peaceful neighbour and he thought that here was a good opportunity to show William that the matter of the frontier fort had not impaired their friendship. He offered to help the Duke rid himself of trouble-makers. He wanted a peaceful Normandy, for war was infectious; and it was not good that rulers should be overthrown by their rebellious subjects. It happened therefore that as William was preparing to go to war against Guy and his supporters, he was joined by Henry at the head of the company of French soldiers.

Now were William and Guy facing each other in earnest. Guy was not the only traitor but it was of Guy that he thought. The lust for battle was upon him; he was going to prove to himself and to all traitors that he was indeed the Duke of Normandy.

How right his teachers had been! All that he had learned over the years of training stood him in good stead. He knew no fear. It was as though Rollo rode beside him.

William was in the heart of the mêlée. How many died from his lance that day he did not know. All he knew was that with every thrust, every clash of steel he was showing his cousin Guy what it meant to go against the Duke of Normandy. In every man he killed he saw his cousin Guy.

The French acquitted themselves well; and the enemies of the Duke were no match for him and his allies.

His first victory! He had emerged with honour; moreover, he had taught his rebellious subjects a lesson.

His first thought was to send a message to his mother for he knew what her agonies would be.

'This day,' he wrote, 'I have shown the rebels who is Duke of Normandy.'

It was true; but as he stood with the King of France surveying the field of victory and listening to the groans of the wounded and the dying, he deplored the need for such action and fervently prayed that in time he would bring peace to Normandy.

'There is no profiting in wars,' he said. 'But traitors must be taught and how else can this be done but with blood?'

Guy had been there among his enemies. But where was he now. Somewhere among those bloody bodies?

He sent one of his men to find Guy de Brionne and bring him before him.

But Guy was not to be found. He had escaped, it was believed, and was taking refuge in that fortress which his Duke had given him.

'Does he think he will escape me there?' cried William. 'By God's splendour, he will learn that the castle I gave him will not give him refuge from my scorn and anger.'

*　*　*

The King of France left for his own country but William's task was not over.

Men were rallying to his banner after the victory and there were many who declared that Rollo and Richard the Fearless had been born again.

They should not be disappointed in him. They should know him for the stern just man he intended to be, and so should Guy.

What a beautiful castle was that of Brionne! Its grey walls rose seemingly impregnable, defiant, jaunty almost. Brionne, Guy's city, which went with the castle, was enclosed in its stone wall. From the ramparts arrows could be poured down on an invader.

Inside the castle Guy would be rubbing his hands with glee.

Brionne was impregnable, he believed. No one could take it. It was built to hold out against the invader.

William looked at it and saw that the advantage was with Brionne. How storm such a fortress?

In his mind he saw the sly face of his cousin and he knew that he was saying: 'The Bastard can never break us. He will give up the attempt and then we will go after him, and kill him. The attempt failed in the inn but we shall not fail again.'

Now was William's chance to prove himself. Was he going to give up? Was he going to let Guy laugh at him, let him say: 'There is your Duke. He is beaten. But what can you expect of a bastard?'

There must be a way, and William would find it.

He did. He built two towers on the banks of the river; thus he himself had a fortress to face that other. From these towers he bombarded the city and the castle and nothing was allowed in or out. The siege of Brionne had begun.

So they faced each other, he and Guy, and victory for one would be the end of ambition for the other.

Often William stood at the top of his tower and looked to that of the castle. Was Guy there watching, thinking of him? It was almost certainly so.

And when he and Guy met face to face what would he say to him? Would there be any necessity for words? What should he do, hang him from one of his own turrets? Or pierce his heart with his sword?

He shuddered. Commander of armies that he was, he did not care to kill. When a mad rage was on him he would kill without thought; but he regretted his rages and had always tried to curb them.

Guy must die. But he hoped not directly by his hand.

Guy was entrenched in his castle, well equipped for a long siege, and William saw that the only manner in which he could take Brionne was to starve those within its city walls.

The weeks began to pass. It was winter. William chafed against the delay. He was joined by more and more loyal supporters, for the knights of Normandy were realizing the power and strength of their Duke.

From his camp facing Brionne he often went hunting; it was his favourite sport and always had been. It kept his soldiers happy and whenever they supped from a fine boar or delicious venison William would think with grim satisfaction of what was happening within Brionne and how Guy and his supporters would smack their lips if they could smell the spoils of the hunt.

It was a time for brooding. His temper might be hasty but he was possessed of patience. It was a waiting game he must play with his cousin and as long as he realized that he could not fail. He talked now and then with those he trusted of what he intended to do for Normandy. Building fascinated him; even the construction of those two towers had given him a deep satisfaction. He wanted to make a good life for his people; he wanted to make rules which would give them justice.

'But first of all,' he would end, 'we must have peace. To be a Duke is not as my cousin Guy may think—receiving the homage of one's people, performing feats of equestrian skill, riding among them in magnificent robes. Nay! It is governing well, giving them good rules that they may live in peace and know the meaning of justice.'

The winter passed.

William said: 'We remain inactive here yet to remove

99

ourselves would be a victory for my treacherous cousin. I have a plan. I will leave a garrison here while I go off to regain that which was taken from me. There is Domfront which the Count of Anjou took from the Bellêmes and holds against me; there is Alençon. While we wait here I will regain these two towns.'

He began with Domfront which was unprepared for the siege and quickly gave in. He then turned his attention to Alençon. The speedy surrender of Domfront had not prepared him for a show of strong resistance at Alençon.

Moreover the citizens attempted to sneer at him. They had hung the walls with hides and as William approached made pretence to beat them with their lances.

'Hides, hides for the bastard tanner.'

William's calmness deserted him. He had been ready to show mercy to the Count of Anjou and had allowed him to escape when he took Domfront but now his temper was aroused. This was too much.

'By God's splendour,' he vowed, 'they shall regret this.'

He led a furious onslaught on the town. Burning pitch was thrown at the walls. Fury blazed within him no less violently than the walls of Alençon.

'They shall wear neither hands nor feet again when I have conquered them,' he vowed.

The battle was short and swift. Never before had the Duke of Normandy fought so furiously. He hated the people of Alençon as he had never hated enemies before.

How quickly they realized their mistake so to taunt the Duke of Normandy. Men might betray him, attempt to murder him, and be forgiven; but to sneer at him as Bastard was more than he would tolerate.

The prisoners were brought to him. He looked on while his orders were carried out. And when those people screamed for mercy he had none. They had committed the unforgivable. They had called him Bastard.

He looked on with grim satisfaction while their feet and hands were cut off and thrown over the walls of the city that all might see what befell those who dared to sneer at him.

* * *

He was alone. Would he ever forget the sight of those writhing bodies? Would he ever be able to shut from his

100

mind the memory of those eyes raised to his? He would dream of writhing bodies and bloody stumps of arms and legs—men who would never walk again, never work. Useless bodies! They would curse him for ever.

'But they called me Bastard,' he justified himself. 'They deserved death, but I was merciful, I took but their hands and feet.'

A ruler must be harsh at times. He was fighting for his life. They could not say that he was not a bold and courageous man. But they could say he was a bastard.

Men must learn what it cost them to speak thus against their Duke.

He must forget the men of Alençon.

* * *

Domfront and Alençon in his hands, he turned back to Brionne.

It was summer now. For many months now they had held the siege. Surely they could not last much longer?

One of his commanders met him as he rode to Brionne.

'The castle is on the point of surrender,' he was told. 'Several have already come over to us. They say they are dying of starvation.'

William smiled. His tactics had been correct. Guy would learn now with whom he had to deal. How easy it would have been to make a spectacular onslaught on the castle and to have been beaten.

He had done right to wait and to take Domfront and Alençon in the meanwhile. News might have been smuggled into Brionne as to what had happened to the men of Alençon. How were they feeling there now? Were they shivering in their fear? Were they studying their precious hands and feet?

He rode up to the castle and as he did so the drawbridge was lowered and a figure appeared, a wretched starving man who could scarcely walk.

Could that be Guy?

William approached him and looked at him.

'Cousin,' he said. 'My traitor cousin.'

Guy was on his knees before William.

William threw him from him. Poor abject cousin, the young arrogant cock of the schoolroom. Guy! What had he planned for him! He was not sure. Some dire punishment

101

which he would have to work out. But what could he feel for this poor abject creature but pity.

Guy raised his eyes to William's face, and for the moment they looked at each other.

Guy was too sick from lack of food to care what became of him. But oddly enough William cared.

He raised up Guy.

'You're a bag of bones, cousin,' he said.

'And you will kill me.'

'Kill you,' said William. 'That would mean I feared you. I fear none, cousin—not even a poor starveling such as you.'

'What will you do with me?'

Fleetingly William saw those footless and handless bodies; he saw the stricken looks of the watchers as the warm and bloody feet and hands were thrown among them.

'I shall take back your castles,' said William. 'They are fine castles and will now be mine. As for you, you may go where you will. But let me not see your face again.'

They said it was strange that one who had played him so false should escape while the citizens of Alençon for jeering at him had been so mutilated.

Victorious he came to Rouen; and when his mother embraced him, he remembered once more that she wanted him to take a wife.

A wife. He had not thought much of women. There had been little time in a life which had been so taken up with treachery and wars, sudden death and the need to learn to govern.

He thought of his father's returning to the castle and the joys of his reunion with Arlette. He thought of the children who delighted his mother and he remembered his father's joy in him.

He needed a wife who would love and teach him the comforts of homecoming. He needed sons who would follow him.

He wanted that. He wanted closer bonds with his own people.

He would marry and she whom he married must be a lady of high birth. That would be necessary for his son's sake. The child must be no bastard, nor must he be of merchant stock.

He talked to his mother. How she loved these cosy talks!

So he would marry. She had long wished for that. He would know the pleasures of the married state. She had long been amazed at the manner in which he dedicated himself to his duties. Now he should have some of the pleasures of life and the greatest of these was love, a home which was indeed a home whether it be castle or hut. He needed children—and most of all a son who would inherit his ducal crown.

'There is Matilda of Flanders,' said his mother. 'A lady of high rank, a princess no less. She is the one for you, William.'

'Matilda of Flanders! She is the daughter of Baldwin of Flanders, of noble birth, and very marriageable I have heard.'

'It is true,' said his mother. 'Herlwin decided she would suit you long ago.'

'Then, Mother, I will marry the lady.'

Arlette laughed.

'You had better begin your courtship first and without delay.'

And as William hated to waste time and the more he thought of marriage the more he liked it, he decided to do just that.

Encounter in a Street

In the tapestry chamber in the Castle of Lille two girls bent over their work. Expertly they plied their needles, holding back now and then to cast a critical eye over what they had done. They were both in their teens, and their costly gowns set them apart from their woman attendants who were at the other end of the room, some sorting out skeins of silk, others working tapestry.

Matilda, the younger of the girls, was the more beautiful. Her flaxen hair was dressed in a long plait that had she been standing would have reached to her knees. This thick rope of hair was caught in a snood which twinkled with a few jewels and her long blue gown with the hanging sleeves became her well.

Her sister Judith was handsome too. They were proud girls because their father, the Count of Flanders, a gentle, kindly man who had the good of his subjects at heart, indulged them, and their mother was the sister of the reigning King of France.

The Count clearly regretted the fact that his girls were becoming marriageable and if a match were made for them this would mean their leaving home. It was not so much that he wanted to keep them with him for his own pleasure as that he feared that they, who had had such a happy home, might not find the same contentment away from it.

At this time there was an air of excitement throughout the castle because the Ambassador of Edward the Confessor had suggested a bridegroom for Judith, and Judith was the focus of attention at the moment.

Matilda laid aside her tapestry and said: 'Shall you take him, Judith?'

It was an indication of the indulgence of their father that it should be a matter for Judith to decide.

Judith put her head on one side as though considering the matter.

'They are very handsome, these Saxons.'

'They have the clearest blue eyes I ever saw,' agreed Matilda. She was thinking of the ambassador Brihtric Meaw who was called 'Snow' because of his white skin, the most beautiful man she had ever seen. If Tostig were as handsome as Brihtric, then Judith should take him willingly.

'There is a gentleness about them.'

'Gentleness. Your future father-in-law must be far from that.'

'We cannot expect them to be all alike.'

'Then should you not learn more of Tostig?'

'I would I could,' said Judith.

'I would never marry a man I had not seen,' put in Matilda. She had always been the bold one, her father's favourite, the one he had delighted to indulge, who had amused him with her forthright opinions.

'It is a long way to England.'

'I should expect a man to woo me,' went on Matilda, 'and if it were too far for him to come to me, then it would be too far for me to go to him.'

'You are being childish.'

'I am saying what I feel. Is it childish to speak one's mind?'

'We are not village people whose marriages are of no concern to any but themselves.'

'My marriage shall be of concern to no one but myself.'

'What nonsense, Matilda. You know our marriages are arranged for us.'

Matilda smiled. She had never liked to be left out of anything and when marriage for Judith had been talked of she had immediately begun to think of it for herself. She had not had to look far. Her eyes had alighted on the beautiful form of Brihtric the Saxon. What grace! What beauty! Those blue, blue eyes! The gentle way he spoke! How harsh was the Flemish language compared with soft Saxon. She had decided she would like to learn Saxon and speak it all the time. She would like to go to Brihtric and tell him that she had chosen him and that he would no longer be a plain ambassador for she, the Princess, had chosen to

105

marry him. He would be transformed into a Prince and her father would give him estates. Her heart swelled with love for her beautiful Saxon. Poor Judith who had been offered Tostig—the son of the Earl of Godwin. She was sorry for her, for no one could be as handsome as Brihtric.

'Tostig,' she said. 'The son of a man who was a cowherd!'

'The Earl of Godwin is the most powerful man in England,' cried Judith indignantly. 'It is for this reason that his son is offered to me.'

'A cowherd's son!'

'How clever he must be.'

'Clever men often have foolish sons.'

'You are jealous, Matilda, because there is no husband for you.'

That made Matilda laugh. 'Never fear, Judith, I shall choose my husband. I admit I should like to go to England.'

'It is a country which people used to speak of a great deal. Now that it is ruled by the saintly Edward and all is peaceful there, we hear less of it.'

'I do not like what I hear of Edward. He must be rather a tiresome man I think. Imagine. He is married but the marriage has never been consummated. I wonder what Queen Editha feels about that?'

'Perhaps it is her wish.'

'Perhaps so, since she has such a husband.'

'He is a saint, they say.'

'Who wants a saint for a husband? I want a strong man, a man who will think he commands me. And I shall allow him to believe in that deception. I intend to have my way.'

'Because you have with Father do you think you will with a husband?'

'I think I shall,' smiled Matilda.

She was thinking of Brihtric. He was hardly the kind of man she had described. He was gentle, poetic, a true Saxon; yet there was a set to his jaw which told her that he could be a very determined man.

How beautiful are you, Brihtric, she thought. And how your blue eyes will shine when I tell you that I have decided to marry you!

She picked up a blue skein and began to stitch with it. It was the colour of his eyes; and his skin was white as snow. My dearest Snow, how happy you are going to be.

She would say to him: 'My dearest Brihtric, I have chosen you.' And he would reply: 'How I long to marry you

106

but you are a Princesss of Flanders and I am a humble servant of my King.' She would reassure him: 'I shall marry whom I wish. You may leave this to me. I will speak to my father.'

'What are you smiling at?' demanded Judith.

'I was thinking that if you marry this Tostig and I marry into England too, we shall not be parted.'

'I should like that, Matilda.'

'So should I,' said Matilda.

* * *

The Count of Flanders and his wife came in to see how the tapestry was progressing. Gracious Adelais, the Count's wife, never forgot that she was the daughter of a King of France; her husband Baldwin was proud of her; he was an indulgent husband as well as father and as he possessed many virtues and in spite of his gentle and kindly nature he was a good and just ruler, his country was almost as contented as his family.

Matilda's skill with her needle was something to be proud of. It was renowned throughout Flanders and beyond it seemed. It added to Matilda's marriageability, for not only was she most highly born but also particularly skilled in an art which was generally accepted to be an asset in a wife.

Matilda would record events in her tapestry. She had completed a work which proclaimed her ancestry. Baldwin and Adelais never tired of showing it to their visitors.

Matilda was descended not only from the royal house of France through her mother, but King Alfred the Great was also an ancestor of hers for his daughter Elstrith had married Baldwin II of Flanders. This wonderful work depicted the marriages of her family and how lovingly Adelais' eyes always dwelt on that portion which showed her bringing in the golden lilies of France.

There was also a connection with Normandy, for Eleanor of Normandy, Matilda's grandmother, was the aunt of the reigning Duke William.

Producing such a tapestry had increased Matilda's pride in her birth as well as bringing her some fame as one of the most clever and prolific needlewomen in Europe. Adelais had said it would be very easy to find a very suitable husband for their daughter Matilda. The parents admired the work and Adelais went to the wall on which hung that family tapestry. Baldwin laid his hand on Matilda's shoulder.

'It is beautiful, daughter. What a fine mingling of the blue and the white.'

Matilda smiled happily.

'If Judith leaves us shall you be able to finish it alone?' asked Baldwin.

'I shall not be going yet, Father,' said Judith.

'Not for a long time, I hope, my love,' Baldwin assured her.

'We must work hard,' added Matilda, 'for it may be my turn before long.'

'It will come I doubt not,' said the Count. 'And now, Judith, I wish you to come with me and your mother. I have something I wish to say to you.'

Judith rose with alacrity.

She will marry Tostig, thought Matilda, and she will go to England and then it will be my turn.

She went on stitching at her tapestry, taking special delight in that beautiful shade of blue which was just the colour of Brihtric's eyes.

* * *

Looking from a window she saw him crossing the courtyard.

She called to him, 'Brihtric, a merry good day to you.'

He looked up at her; the sun touched his fair hair making it almost lint white; he bowed his head in acknowledgement of a Princess's greetings.

'You have never seen my tapestry, Brihtric,' she said.

'It is a pleasure I hope to enjoy one day.'

'Why not this day?' she asked.

'My lady, I have business with the Count.'

'Will you refuse my invitation, Sir Brihtric?'

'Has your father given you permission to ask me, my lady?'

She tossed her head. Did he not know that she was considered somewhat wilful in the household? Did he not know that she acted as she wished and if her acts were not approved she smiled mischievously at her father and was forgiven?

Evidently he did not for he considered it not in

108

accordance with the behaviour required of an ambassador to visit a Count's daughter at her request.

She would show him otherwise.

'Brihtric, I insist that you come and see my tapestry.'

He hesitated. How beautiful he was when he was uncertain.

'Come now,' she said.

He turned towards the door. He was coming. She glared at the attendants who were huddled together in a corner of the room, like crows she thought. She wanted to dismiss them, but perhaps that was going too far. They were looking shocked. What would the Lady Matilda do next, they were pondering in their silly old heads. They should know by now that the Lady Matilda did what she wished no matter how strange people might think it.

At the door stood her beautiful Saxon.

'Enter Brihtric Meaw,' she said. 'I hear they call you Snow because you are so fair.'

He bowed. He was so gracious; his voice was like music; she loved to hear him say 'my lady Matilda'.

'Come, my lord, and see the tapestry which has been admired by many. I shall be pleased indeed if you add your admiration to it.'

'I believe I could not fail to do that ... when I recall what I have heard of your talents.'

'Then come and see for yourself.' She took his hand. Oh, you old crows, why are you watching? Like vultures waiting for the death of virtue! I would it could be so. But how cautious was the Saxon! He was as amazed at her behaviour as were the crows.

She led him to the wall. 'There you see my noble ancestry.'

'It is indeed impressive.'

'Here is your King Alfred whom you call the Great. You see I have his blood in my veins, so I am partly Saxon.'

'That is why you are so kind to us.'

'I have a fondness for Saxons. There is so much I admire in them. And I like well to hear of your country. It is enjoying a period of peace now, I believe.'

'It has long been awaited and hoped for.'

'And now under your saint of a King you are all content.'

'The King is indeed a saint.'

'I know. He is called the Confessor as you are called Snow. Does it describe him as your name describes you?'

'He is indeed of a saintly disposition.'

'I hear his poor wife is not allowed to live with him.'

'My King is not a man to break his vows.'

'Even though he has a beautiful wife? Is she beautiful?'

'She is beautiful.'

'Are all Saxons beautiful?' Her voice and her eyes caressed him and he shifted uneasily.

'No, my lady,' he said.

She laughed at him. 'I could find it in my heart to disagree with you.'

He turned back to the tapestry. 'It is most exquisitely worked.'

'So you add your praise to others.'

'Whole-heartedly.'

'I treasure your Saxon praise. Look, here is the marriage of my grandfather with the sister of Robert of Normandy. So you see I have Saxon blood and Norman blood, Flemish and French. A fine mixture, do you think?'

'A *royal* mixture,' he answered.

'Tell me of yourself, Brihtric.'

'I? I am indeed humble compared with you, my lady. My father is Algar and he is the Lord of Honour of Gloucester.'

'And does he own great lands?'

'He owns lands, small in comparison with your father's possessions.'

'You are over-modest. I did hear that your great Earl Godwin was the son of a cowherd. Is that true?'

'It is not mentioned.'

'Nay, the Earl would see to that. But he grew to be a very powerful man. Now his son Tostig may well marry my sister Judith and is it not true that his daughter Editha is that poor neglected wife of your Edward the Confessor himself?'

'This is so, my lady.'

'Then does it not show that it is not necessary to be royal to begin with? A clever man may become royal ... or beget royal children. Remember the cowherd's son begat a daughter who is now the Queen of England.'

'My lady is well acquainted with the tangled skeins of royalty.'

'Indeed I am. So, son of Algar, Lord of Honour of Gloucester, I tell you, do not be too humble.'

She laughed at him and he flushed faintly. How

beautiful his skin was when he flushed. It was like rose petals, delicate and soft. She wanted to kiss his cheek and make him flush the deeper.

'My lady, I must to your father. There are matters to discuss.'

'This coming marriage?' she asked.

'Your father will acquaint me with his wishes when I present myself to him.'

'Go then,' she said. 'Later I will show you more tapestry, for I see you are very interested in it.'

He bowed and went out.

She smiled as the door shut on him.

The crows were regarding her with shocked amazement.

'And why,' she demanded, 'are you staring at me? Why are you not working? Let me see your work. It is disgraceful! Look at those stitches! You have been staring around at what does not concern you. You lazy creatures. I should have you whipped.'

The women lowered their eyes and stitched. How like the Lady Matilda, when caught at some misdeed, to turn the tables and find fault with others.

* * *

She found her father alone and going to him put an arm about his neck and laid her cheek against his.

'Dearest and best of fathers,' she said.

'What does my daughter want of me that she discovers she loves me so much?'

'Father, you are unkind!'

'Never to my Matilda.'

'Then why should you say I want something because I tell you how dear you are to me?'

'Forgive me. Then you want nothing of me.'

'Only to talk with you ... one of our cosy talks with no one to overhear us.'

'Then let us enjoy that.'

'Is Judith to marry Tostig?'

'It seems likely.'

'And you have given your consent?'

'If Judith agrees, yes.'

'How many royal fathers would give their daughters the opportunity to decide. Only the best in the world.'

111

'My dearest daughter, I want my children to be happy.'

'So if Judith wished to marry someone humble you would allow her to?'

'One can hardly call the son of Earl Godwin humble.'

'But if he were. If it would break her heart not to marry some humble gentleman, would you withhold your consent?'

'Do you imagine that I would allow my daughter's heart to be broken?'

She tightened her arms about his neck and kissed him.

'There! Am I not proved right! You love your family beyond aught else.'

'I fear I do.'

'It is no wonder that they love you too. You have made me very happy, Father.'

'Tell me what it is you have in mind.'

'Just to be happy, Father.'

'You know, do you not, daughter, that Judith is not the only one whose hand is sought.'

'Mine too, Father?'

'Yes, and we shall have to think about a husband for you.'

'I shall make my own choice.'

'I doubt it not.'

She hesitated. No, she would not tell him yet. First she would speak to Brihtric.

* * *

It was not easy to speak to him alone. Always she seemed to be surrounded by attendants from whom it was difficult to escape. She could of course order them to leave her, but they would hang around, waiting at the door. Even she could not easily dispense with the habits of a lifetime.

She chose a time when she could evade them and made her way to the apartment which was set aside for ambassadors in the palace.

By good fortune she found him alone in his study. She tapped at the door. He looked astonished as she entered.

He rose to his feet flushing. She held out her hand; he took it and bowed over it.

'Pray be seated, Brihtric,' she commanded. 'And I will too.'

He brought a stool for her and she sat on it opposite him,

112

smiling, her eyes dancing with amusement because he looked so startled.

'You find me strange, Brihtric.'

'I did not expect you to come here.'

'I act unexpectedly at times. You will grow accustomed to that. Everyone does.'

'I?' he asked raising his eyebrows; he looked as though he would like to run away.

'Do you like being an ambassador, Brihtric?'

'I do,' he said.

'And particularly in Flanders?'

'My stay here has been very pleasant.'

'And do you wish to return to your Gloucester?'

'It is always pleasant to go home, my lady.'

'If you went home you would say good-bye to my father and mother...to me. Would that please you, Brihtric?'

'Nay, I should be sad to go.'

Her smile was revealing. 'That gives me great pleasure, Brihtric. You would be sad to leave us.'

'One becomes attached to places...to people, after a stay—even a brief one.'

'You must not be sad. An alternative would be never to leave us.'

'I am at the call of my King,' he answered.

'Even that need not recall you.'

'I do not understand.'

'Brihtric, you are very handsome.'

'My lady is kind.'

'Nay, I am not always so. And it is not kind merely to state a truth. You are aware that I think you goodly to look upon. Are you aware that I like you, Brihtric?'

'You have shown me a kind interest...'

'That I like you very much.'

He flushed painfully.

'You could not speak to me as I can to you...until you have my permission of course. It would be impertinent for an ambassador to speak thus to a princess. That is what you feel, is it not? That is why when I tell you you are handsome, you do not reply by telling me how beautiful you find me.'

'It would seem unnecessary to say so. All the world knows it to be so.'

'All the world, yes, but you, Brihtric, it is you I wish to know about.'

113

'Assuredly I find you beautiful.'

She smiled happily. 'Now I will say to you what you dare not say to me. My sister is to marry a Saxon. I have a mind to do the same. Her husband will be Tostig. Why should mine not be Brihtric?'

He had risen. Alarm showed clearly in his face.

She stood up and going close to him laid her hand on his arm.

'Do not be afraid, Brihtric. I promise you I can prepare my father. If I tell him I will die if I am not allowed to marry you, I shall marry you. You need have no fear. You may trust me. My father will give his consent.'

He withdrew from her, his face frozen in horror. She took him gently by the arm and shook him.

'You are astounded by such great good fortune. Dear, dear Brihtric, you must not be. You may trust me. I will arrange this. Come, enjoy your good fortune.'

He stammered: 'My lady...my lady Matilda, it cannot be.'

'Cannot be? Oh, you fear too much. I tell you it shall be. I say it shall be. I have what I want to have.'

'Let me tell you...You are a princess...I am but the son of a humble lord of no great account...'

She stood on tiptoe and tried to kiss his lips but he stepped back hastily.

'It is impossible,' he said.

'I will arrange it. Have no fear. My father will give his consent.'

'Even if he did, I could not marry you.'

'You could not marry me if my father gave his consent! Why not?'

'Because...because I am betrothed.'

'In your Gloucester?'

He nodded.

'It can be overcome. It can be broken off. That shall not stop us.'

'My lady Matilda, this cannot be.'

She stared at him, sudden anger blazing in her eyes.

'You are a coward,' she said.

'No, my lady.'

'You are afraid.'

'I am not afraid. I merely tell you that I can marry only the lady to whom I am betrothed.'

'You cannot wish that now.'

114

'My lady, forgive me. I wish it and I am pledged.'

He bowed and because she was so dumbfounded, he was able to make for the door. He had gone.

Matilda stood looking at the closed door. All her planning had been in vain. She had to face the incredible fact that he did not want her.

*　*　*

She had never been so angry, so bitterly humiliated in her life. She had offered her hand to this Saxon and he had refused it. It was shameful. How could she have humbled herself so? Because she loved him. Because she knew that of all men she wanted him for her husband. And he had refused her—not because he feared he would be asking too much but because he was betrothed and he was determined to marry the woman of his choice. He was as determined as she had been.

She had noticed the firm set of his lips. He was only an ambassador and she was a princess but he would marry where he pleased.

What could she do? Whom could she turn to for sympathy? To Judith? To her mother? They would reproach her. How could she so demean herself? It was not for her to *ask* a man to marry her. It was for some important ruler to beg for her hand.

And a Saxon ambassador of no importance in royal circles had refused her.

Never, never would she forget the humiliation.

*　*　*

Only her pride sustained her. She would have liked to hide herself away but that would only arouse comment. No one must guess how she had humiliated herself. If Brihtric dared to tell anyone she would have him killed; she herself would kill him. She hated the thought of that betrothed of his kissing that fair skin. It maddened her; she wanted to have him dragged before her father; she wanted him punished. But how could this be done? They would have to know the reason.

Her father misconstrued her state.

'My dearest Matilda,' he said, 'you are wishing that you were to have a husband. It is natural. Judith is to marry.

115

Why not you? I will tell you something. I heard William of Normandy is putting out hints that he is considering asking for your hand.'

'William of Normandy! Normandy is in a sorry state, I believe.'

'There has been rebellion in Normandy ever since the death of the Duke's father. William was but a minor when the ducal cloak was placed on his shoulders. There is always danger when a ruler is too young to rule.'

'He would marry me, I daresay, because if he did he would have you for an ally.'

'A reasonable conclusion. I could not go against my own daughter, could I?'

'Nor would you ever, Father.'

'Nay, you know that well.'

'This William knows it too. Hence he asks for my hand.'

'It is the case with royal marriages. You know that well.'

'Is it true that my Uncle Henry of France, who recently helped him, is now ready to turn against him?'

'It may be so.'

'And if he did what would happen then to my lord Duke?'

'I feel he would not be subdued. By all accounts he is a strong man. I have made some enquiries about him. He is a young man of great vitality.'

'The father of many bastards, I'll warrant.'

'I have heard of none. So seriously does he take his duties that his time has been spent in learning how to govern.'

'He sounds a paragon of virtue.'

'Hardly that. He was ruthless at Alençon.'

'What happened there?'

'The people of the town displeased him. They referred to his origins. His mother was a tanner's daughter. He cut off the hands and feet of his prisoners and threw them over the walls into the city.'

'And you would give your daughter to such a man?'

'If she wished to go to him. Remember he was greatly provoked. He has a reputation for normally being just and has been over-lenient to his cousin who has betrayed him.'

'Should I, a princess, a niece of the King of France, marry the son of tanners?'

'He is the son of the Duke of Normandy who held that title before him. Think about this for I am certain that soon we shall have a visit from the Duke's ambassadors.'

'There is no harm in considering the matter,' she said.

116

Indeed there was not. It took her mind off the memory of her humiliation.

* * *

She thought about William, Duke of Normandy. He would be some twenty years of age. He needed a bride such as she was. He needed her for several reasons. For one, there were many who sought her and it would be to his credit to be the one to succeed. He needed her father's help against his enemies. He needed a wife with royal blood in her veins to make up for that which had come to him through the tanner.

I have no doubt, she thought, that this William is a very clever fellow.

What a fool Brihtric had been! He had turned away from her who was sought by the great men of Europe. How dared he—the little Saxon fool.

When she thought of him she wanted to hurt someone as he had hurt her. What was the use of trying to forget that humiliating scene? She could not. How dared he! When she had expected him to fall on his knees in gratitude he had become frightened and simpered about his betrothed.

She hated him. She hated the world. She hated all suitors.

She was in such a mood when the ambassadors of the Duke of Normandy arrived at the Court.

Count Baldwin listened sympathetically to their request.

He told them that if his wife agreed to the match he would have no objection. Since Adelais was a daughter of a King of France she was of higher rank even than her husband and it was natural that her consent should also be given.

Adelais declared that she would have no objection to a match between her daughter and William of Normandy.

'There remains but my daughter herself,' said Baldwin with a smile. 'I will send for her and you shall hear her answer.'

In her chamber Matilda was looking out disconsolately on the drawbridge. She had seen the arrival of the ambassadors from Normandy and she guessed on what mission they came.

William of Normandy, she thought, who needs my father's help and my royal blood and will therefore marry me. And Brihtric did not need me at all so he refused me.

She dreamed of Brihtric—all her love turned to hatred. How could any man have humiliated her so deeply. No matter how she tried to forget she could not do so.

The lackey arrived with the message that her father wished her to come to the great hall.

She went down, hatred in her heart not only for Brihtric but also for this William of Normandy who was only asking for her hand because he needed her father's help.

Her father greeted her, taking her hand and leading her to the men who stood looking at her. She was beautiful she knew, in her blue gown with the long hanging sleeves and her hair in two thick ropes, one arranged as though carelessly over one shoulder, the other hanging down her back. She hoped they would take home to their master a good account of her physical perfections.

'This is my daughter Matilda,' said the Count.

The men bowed low; she stood smiling at them.

'These knights are from the Court of Duke William of Normandy,' said her father. 'Duke William has sent them to ask for your hand in marriage.'

She drew herself up to her full height and feigned astonishment.

'*My* hand?'

'Why yes,' said Baldwin with a smile. Matilda was acting as she often did. She knew full well that William was going to ask for her hand.

Her lips curled slightly. She was thinking of him at Alençon—this little ruler of whom her father seemed to think so highly. How infuriated he had been when the citizens had jeered at his birth. It was not so much that he had descended from tanners as that he was a bastard. She turned to her father and said: 'You cannot think that I, a granddaughter of the King of France, would marry a bastard.'

There was silence in the hall. She saw the faces of the ambassadors. Her father's look of horror; her mother's astonishment.

She had not felt nearly so happy since her humiliation. She found great joy in hurting someone else as she had been hurt and she could not resist savouring her triumph. 'I would rather become a nun than give myself to a bastard.'

118

And with an intoxicating triumph in her heart she bowed to her father, mother and the ambassadors and turning, walked haughtily away.

*　*　*

Baldwin was concerned; he and Adelais reproved their daughter.

'How could you have spoken so?' demanded Baldwin. 'Do you not know that your exact words will be repeated to the Duke of Normandy?'

'It is as well that he understood my feelings. Perhaps he will now look elsewhere to prop up his crumbling realm.'

'Do you realize that had he been in a position to make war and we in a state of weakness, words such as that could have been disastrous for us?'

'But, Father, he is not in a state to make war. It is because he is weak that he wants the daughter of a strong man.'

'You are too proud, Matilda,' said her mother.

'You can say that—you the daughter of a King! Would you have me marry the bastard who though he may be the Duke could so easily be displaced by someone who has greater claim to Normandy?'

'He will always be a Duke,' said Adelais. 'He has been crowned as such. Your father has a high opinion of his qualities.'

'The qualities of a bastard!'

'It was not kind of you to stress that. Had you wished to refuse him you could have given some other reason.'

'Mother, have you not always told me that I should tell the truth?'

'Sometimes, my child,' said Baldwin, 'it is politic to veil the truth. You will learn this.'

'I am sure,' added her mother, 'that you have won the enmity of a man who could well be of great importance.'

Matilda faced them boldly. 'I have said what I have said. He will know now that he must take his suit elsewhere.'

Adelais looked at Baldwin. She was implying: You have been too lenient with your children. You have over-indulged them.

Baldwin was ready to concede this; but he loved his beautiful daughter too much to punish her. She was bold and wilful; and he thought he had never seen anyone as

119

lovely as Matilda with her flashing eyes and the faint colour in her cheeks angrily tugging at one of her flaxen plaits as though she thought it the hair on the head of the despised Duke of Normandy.

She would make a fine wife for a man who knew how to tame her; and they did say that the young Duke of Normandy was a man who always got his way. So it was a pity she had so bluntly refused him.

* * *

During the next week Matilda thought less of Brihtric. He avoided her as she did him, so she had not seen him. She did think a great deal about the Duke of Normandy though and imagined the scene when his ambassadors returned to him with the story of what they had been told at the Court of Flanders.

How furious he would be and powerless to vent his fury on any but his messengers! She had learned a little of him. He was a great fighter; they said that he excelled others in the field. He was in truth a leader of men. And women? she had asked. How many had he made sport with? How many had he taken from his captured towns? How many bastards—like himself—had he scattered about his dominion? No one could tell her.

'William of Normandy has had no time for women,' she had heard. 'In his youth he was under the close surveillance of tutors and when he came of age he was too busy defending his realm.'

'He will be an oaf, ill-mannered, gauche, inexperienced. As if I would want such a man!' she retorted.

She thought viciously of Brihtric. 'I have had enough of ill-mannered oafs.'

It was a week or so after she had delivered her reply. She teased her father about it. 'What, no declaration of war yet from Normandy?'

He shook his head over her.

'It was most unkind, Matilda.'

'It is the language such as he understands.'

'How can you know this?'

'Because he must be an ill-mannered oaf. How can a prince be made out of a tanner's grandson?'

Baldwin knew it was no use reasoning with Matilda when she was in such a mood.

She was going to hear Mass in the Cathedral. When she

rode out into the streets people came out to watch her pass. She enjoyed startling them with her beauty and her fine garments.

Before she left her women were commanded to take very special care of her toilette. She wore a rich white gown decorated with jewels. She was very proud of her long thick hair and this was made into two long plaits and on her head was a circlet of pearls.

How soothing to her vanity to ride through the streets, to listen to the gasps of admiration. 'Oh, how beautiful she is!' Proudly she sat on her saddle with its gold and silver decorations—a gift from her father.

There was a commotion ahead of her. She was annoyed. Who had dared distract the people's attention from the Princess Matilda?

Then she heard the shout: 'It is the Duke. The Duke of Normandy.'

She pulled up her horse. Her women fell in behind her. Her heart was beating wildly. It was a mistake. He could not have come to Lille. He would not dare!

But she was wrong. A man was riding towards her. There was no mistaking him for a person of very high rank; it was in the very manner in which he sat his horse. He looked magnificent, being very tall with dark hair and his firm, rather prognathous jaw. His eyes were cold and murderous as they looked straight at her.

'You are the Lady Matilda?' he asked.

She lifted her head high. 'I know not who you are. How dare...'

'I am William of Normandy,' he said, leaping from his horse, and seizing her by her plaits pulled her to the ground.

There was a shriek from the women; but they did not attempt to dismount.

Keeping hold of her plaits he dragged her into the gutter. Her beautiful gown was spattered by the mud of the street. He had not finished with her then. She lay there looking up at him.

'I received your reply,' he said. 'This is mine.'

He bent over her and slapped her face; he kicked her, and as though not content with that he hit her many times.

She lay bruised and almost fainting in the gutter. No one attempted to stop him. They stood in awed and fearful silence while they allowed him to mount his horse and ride away.

Only then did they attend to Matilda.

A litter was improvised and she was carried back to the palace.

* * *

Her women bathed her wounds. Her mother brought special unguents and ointments. Her father paced up and down the apartment. Judith was filled with consternation.

'By my faith,' cried Baldwin, 'I will find this fellow. I will hunt him to the ends of the earth. I will not rest until I have his head.'

Matilda opened her eyes and said nothing.

'How could it have happened,' asked her mother. 'There you were in a crowded street, surrounded by your attendants and our people, and this scoundrel comes along...and is allowed to maltreat you. How could it have happened? What was everyone doing?'

'None dared do anything,' said Matilda.

Her father came to her bed and touched her forehead.

'God's Faith, look at these bruises! My poor, poor child. Would I had that devil here.'

'Father, have they not told you who he was?'

'They know?'

'They do know and they are afraid to tell. They are afraid, even when he is not here. They must have heard as I did. The man who attacked me was the Duke of Normandy.'

'My God!' cried Baldwin.

'He made no attempt to disguise himself. He said to me, "I am William of Normandy. I received your answer. Here is mine."'

'My dear child! I knew some disaster would befall us as soon as I heard you say what you did.'

'He is a proud man,' said Matilda, a strange smile on her bruised lips, 'and I have learned that one thing he cannot endure and that it is to be called a bastard.'

She laughed aloud.

'You can laugh...after such a thing! My child, are you feeling...yourself?'

Her parents whispered together. They thought she was hysterical. She knew it, but it was far from the case.

'I will make a potion for you, Matilda,' said Adelais. 'I will make it myself. It will soothe you and make you sleep. You poor child, this has been a terrible experience.'

122

'If that fellow is looking for my help,' muttered Baldwin, 'he will look in vain. I will join his enemies. I will do all I can for those who want to take his dukedom from him. I'll not rest until I have had my revenge on this man who has dared to ride into my town and ill-treat my daughter.'

'Father,' said Matilda weakly, 'I should like to sleep.'

'Yes, my dearest,' said Baldwin. He kissed her forehead. The bruise on her arm; the swollen cheek so infuriated him that he was considering getting together an army and marching on Normandy.

Matilda closed her eyes.

'Let her rest,' whispered Adelais. 'Sleep will be the best for her now.'

They instructed one of her women to sit quietly in a corner and watch and to report immediately if she did not rest.

* * *

She closed her eyes and thought of it. She could see him so clearly. What powerful shoulders! How tall he had been! What courage! He might have been set upon. Not he! 'Stand aside,' he had said in a voice accustomed to command and the cowards had stood aside. They dared do naught else. 'I received your answer, and I have brought you mine.' How furious he must have been when his ambassadors had returned. So angry that he must have begun to make his plans there and then as to how he could be revenged on Matilda.

Not on her father, as some men might have decided, but on her. Her father had been willing for the match, so had her mother; she was the one who had declared she would rather be a nun then marry a bastard.

Her shaft had gone home. She had ample proof of that. So he had ridden to Lille and without an escort! He had no need of escorts. He had faced her alone. He had dragged her from her horse by her thick plaits. Had he thought her beautiful seated on her magnificent horse in her glittering gown?

She could see him now standing over her, his eyes blazing with fury. What a man! To ride alone into her father's stronghold and attack his daughter! What would have happened if those bystanders had had any spirit; they

123

could have taken him easily. But they did not. 'Stand aside,' he said and they stood aside. They knew instinctively that there was a man they dared not disobey.

What a man! What a great man!

She thought of Brihtric, nicknamed Snow because of his beautiful fair skin.

Bah! One could scarce call him a man when compared with the fierce bastard of Normandy.

* * *

She examined her bruises; she was quite pleased with them. How he had tugged her hair. Had he admired it? He must have noticed how long and golden it was. When she allowed it to escape from its plaits it hung round her like a cape. He must have been aware of it when he had pulled her from her horse by it.

What impertinence! What courage! To ride straight to her father's domain, alone!

She could not forget it. The knowledge filled her with a delicious sense of excitement.

Her parents came to her chamber, their eyes full of concern.

'And how are you, my love?' Baldwin asked. 'Your bruises are terrible. Are you still sore?'

'A little, Father.'

'My brave child!'

'Fancy, Father, he rode into your town without escort and no one moved to help me.'

'They should be flogged,' he said.

'They were powerless. Remember he is the Duke of Normandy.'

'I would wring his ducal neck.'

Matilda laughed.

'Father, I have made up my mind.'

'What do you mean, Matilda?'

'I will marry the Duke of Normandy.'

'My dear child, do you feel well?'

'But, Father, what a man he is. If you could have seen him standing there. Everyone was afraid of him ... except myself. I wasn't afraid. I was just excited ... excited because there is such a man in the world and I am going to marry him.'

'This man maltreated you.'

'He threw me into the gutter, he seized me by my hair. I believe he took great delight in ruining my gown and bruising my skin.'

'Are you sure you are feeling well, dear?' asked Adelais.

'Never better.'

'What! Bruised as you are.'

'They are honourable bruises. A kind of battle scar.' Matilda laughed gleefully. 'This is the only man I would marry. At last I have a man. He takes what he wants. He is unafraid. He rode right into the heart of your town alone and attacked me.'

'The child is not well,' said Adelais. 'This has upset her too much. Look-you, daughter, I will send you a posset.'

'Send rather your messengers to the Duke of Normandy. Tell him I have changed my mind. Bastard he may be, but he is the man for me. I will take him for my husband, Father, and I will take none other.'

It was some time before she could make them believe she was in earnest, but finally she convinced them. She displayed her bruises as though she were proud of them.

Life was no longer dull. Let Judith have her Saxon. What did she want with snivelling Saxons? She had found a man and life would be exciting for she would be a match for him.

At length she prevailed on her father to send messengers to Rouen.

Matilda of Flanders had changed her mind. She was not averse to a match with William of Normandy. She asked that he visit her without delay.

A Promise and a Wedding

In the castle of Rouen William was talking to his mother.

'Why did I do it?' he was saying. 'It was unworthy of a knight. I should be robbed of my golden spurs. I have lost her for ever and my good name from now on.'

'She behaved ill to you, William,' Arlette soothed.

'You would always take my side, Mother.'

'I should hope so. Who could you trust to do that if not your own mother? Oh, William, I am in some measure to blame. I loved your father and he loved me. There was no other woman in his life after I came. But marriage was impossible between us. You understand that. Hence you could not be his legitimate son and I your mother.'

He took her hands and kissed them. 'I would not have any other for mother,' he said.

'Even though it has meant you must suffer this slur?'

'Even so,' he said.

'William you are over-sensitive. Many of your illustrious ancestors were the fruit of unmarried love. Why should you care?'

'I want everything to be right for me, Mother.'

'Ah, my son. Is it ever for any of us?'

'And when I hear that word my gorge rises, my temper flares and I do terrible things. Alençon haunts me. The faces of the onlookers, Mother. It was terrible. And I responsible. I shan't forget Alençon in a hurry. And then Matilda. God's splendour, Mother, she is a beautiful woman. She compares with you.'

Arlette laughed. 'I am old now and growing over-plump.'

'It becomes you. You are as beautiful as ever.'

126

'Tell me of Matilda.'

'Long, thick fair hair that seems to shine in the sun; a proud face, the face of a princess...a legitimate princess who knows herself loved and sought after and therefore puts a high price on herself. She was on a horse and her saddle was decorated with gold and silver. Her gown was white ornamented with jewels and she was the most beautiful creature I ever saw...save you.'

'She was more beautiful than I. She had the beauty of a princess. And you threw her into the mud.'

'My fury possessed me. It was the greater because of her beauty. If she had been some plain little hunchback I would have forgiven her, but not that proud beauty. I thought: There is one I would have as my bride. And having seen her I fancy no other. She would bear me many sons—proud and royal, worthy of their ancestors. I wanted this woman, Mother, and because she had called me "Bastard", my fury blinded me to everything but revenge.'

'She might have been killed.'

'Nay, I would not kill a woman. I think of her. I have thought of none since. I have even thought of going to war with Flanders, taking this woman, and forcing her to marry me.'

'You have never cared for women, William. That seemed strange since you are your father's son.'

'Oh I have thought of them, now and then. But as I wanted perfection in my realm so did I want this in my wife, and never saw a woman whom I wished to bear my sons until I set eyes on Matilda of Flanders.'

'There are other women in the world—fine princesses who can bring you as much good as this one.'

'I want this one, Mother.'

'Then you should never have beaten her and thrown her in the mud. That will never be forgiven.' Her brows were drawn together in a frown. 'Herlwin said that the King of France is not so friendly as he was.'

'It's true. He was never a very trusted friend.'

'But he looked after you so well when you were a child.'

'True too, but I never trusted him.'

'And if Baldwin of Flanders should join forces with him?'

'Then we should be facing desperate odds. But fear not. I can command my armies. I am a better soldier than the King of France or the Count of Flanders.'

She shivered. 'Trouble! Always trouble. Oh, William, if you had but ignored this girl!'

'I cannot afford to ignore anyone who calls me a bastard. I want all to know that it will go ill with any who do, be they rebel citizens or marriageable young women.'

'I hear sound of arrival.'

She rose and went to the window.

'It is so,' she said. 'Is that not the Flemish livery?'

He was beside her.

'God's Splendour,' he said, 'they come from Flanders.'

He went down to the hall. More insults? he wondered. Or was this some ultimatum from the Count?

He received the messengers. He took the despatches handed to him.

'The Princess Matilda of Flanders has consented to your proposal. She adds a wish that you will call at Lille and this time come to the palace.'

He stared at it.

He could not believe it. Was it a trap?

But a wild excitement took possession of him. He was going to see the beautiful Matilda again.

* * *

He did not wait. With a small escort he left Rouen that day. Matilda, who had been watching, saw his approach and went down to the courtyard because she wanted to be the first to greet him. This was unconventional, of course, but he would have to understand from the beginning that the rules which others must obey did not apply to her. She acted as she wished.

He leaped from his horse and one of his men took it.

He is even more commanding than I imagined, she thought with pleasure, and her smile was radiant as she stood before him.

He took her hand and kissed it.

Her eyes were mischievous. 'A different greeting, my lord of Normandy, from when we last met.'

'You have forgiven my conduct.'

She liked the way he stated it. Not humbly supplicating her forgiveness but making it seem natural that she should.

'I was amused,' she replied. 'I have had suitors but you are the first who threw me into the mud and set upon me.'

'I have the devil's temper,' he said.

128

'Has he one? If it is like yours I should like to see it aroused.'

Her father came into the courtyard. He looked astonished and she knew he was asking himself what Matilda would do next.

'I have been told that we have visitors,' said the Count.

'Father, this is my future husband, William Duke of Normandy.'

She was amused to see the cold expression on her father's usually benign face.

'So you have come, my lord Duke,' he said. 'My daughter's decision has surprised me.'

'It surprised me no less,' replied William.

'I must present you to my wife,' said the Count.

And they went into the palace, the Count leading William, Matilda falling behind them.

How straight he was. How nobly he walked!

Dear God, she thought, I can love this man.

* * *

He was treated to the hospitality of the palace, although he was aware that her parents eyed him with some misgiving. Nor could he blame them. What had possessed him to drag this beautiful girl into the mud? And what possessed her to have forgiven him so easily for doing so?

The Count of Flanders had had him conducted to his bedchamber—which was the greatest honour. He would share his bed that night which meant that he was being accorded the utmost friendliness. He was to be a member of the family and the Count was to be his father.

He bathed from head to foot and donned his crimson velvet robe and mantle which was the insignia of his rank; on his head was placed the ducal crown and his shoes were purple.

Now he looked magnificent. Surely his father himself had never appeared more handsome? He was pleased with his splendour because he had donned it for the purpose of charming Matilda.

Down in the great hall the trestles were put up and there was the savoury smell of roasting meats.

She was there with her father and she had changed her gown too; she wore white—as she had when he had first seen her; there were ornaments at her neck and bracelets at her wrists; the hanging sleeves reached to the floor and she wore her hair loose about her shoulders.

Ceremoniously Baldwin took her hand and placed it in that of William and she led him to the table.

He could see nothing but Matilda, nor it seemed could she see anything but him. She loved him—not only for his boldness and his virile good looks but because he had wiped away the painful humiliation of that scene with Brihtric. That affair seemed comic now. How could she ever have admired the Saxon when there were men such as this one in the world? She had hated him when she thought of him and despised him but now William of Normandy clearly desired what Brihtric had turned from.

William could not stop looking at her.

'I trust you find me to your liking?' she asked.

'I never saw any so beautiful...save my mother.'

'Your mother. Am I then like a mother!'

'Not yet,' he said, 'but pray God you soon will be.'

'You go fast, my lord Duke.'

'It has been my usual pace all my life.'

'So your mother was beautiful then?'

'She *is* beautiful. She was reckoned the most beautiful woman in Normandy. Anyone would tell you that. Nor do reports lie.'

'Is it true that your father saw her washing clothes in a stream?'

'Ay, 'tis true.'

'And the result...was you, my lord.'

'I see you know a great deal about me.'

'Should not one learn all one can about the man one is to marry?'

'You knew a great deal about me when you decided that you would not have me. What made you change your mind?'

'When I saw you.'

'On that shameful occasion.'

'That was when I made up my mind.'

'I thought you would hate me for that.'

'I did—so much that it turned into love.'

'You are a strange woman, Matilda.'

'So my father thinks, yet he loves me dearly.'

'As I do.'

'So soon?'

'Ay, so soon?'

'Do you usually love so quickly?'

'I have never loved before.'

'You have the right answers for one unskilled in the art of making love.'

'It is because I speak from the heart which all lovers should.'

'Then you are indeed eager to marry me.'

'I would I could this night.'

'It will take a little longer than that, my lord.'

'I fear so. But now I have seen you, held your hand, witnessed your beauty, I shall not rest until you are my wife.'

'Nor I until you are my husband.'

'I did not think I should so soon succeed with you. I had thought you would be bashful, reluctant.'

'You did not know Matilda, but you will learn, my lord, that she rarely does what is expected of her.'

'I can see my life with her is going to give me great joy.'

She put her hand on his.

'I plight my troth with you, William of Normandy. I will bear your children. I will go with you throughout your life.'

'The happiest Norman this day is its Duke,' he answered.

Baldwin, watching his daughter, even knowing her as he did, was quite bewildered. But then when had he ever understood Matilda? He only wished her to be happy and he had come to the conclusion that Matilda needed a strong man.

She had got one. That much was certain.

What a night that was! The feasting, the drinking, the telling of sagas. William told those which his mother had told him and the company thrilled to the story of how Ragnar slew the dragon and how Sigurd awoke Brynhilde.

There was the music of psalteries and flutes to enchant the company and when William retired to the bed he shared with his host he felt bemused, yet he looked forward to the future with a delight he had never known before.

* * *

He could not dally in Flanders. He must return to Normandy to make arrangements for his marriage.

His mother was waiting for him in the castle of Rouen when he returned. She was down in the courtyard even before he dismounted.

'I have suffered such anxieties,' she told him. 'I was convinced it was a trap. As soon as you left I wanted to send Herlwin after you to bid you return and not enter Lille without troops. But he said you would have none of that.'

'He was right and your fears were groundless. Mother, you remember how it was when you came to my father. So it is now for me. Matilda has promised to marry me.'

'Then it was true ... indeed true.'

'She is so beautiful, Mother, and of a spirit that inspires me.'

'I trust there is no treachery.'

'I'd swear not from Matilda. She is the wife for me. None other would satisfy me.'

'She was gracious to you?'

'She loves me, Mother, even as I love her.'

'But it is such a short time ago that you trampled her in the mud. Can she love you after that?'

'Because of it, it seems.'

'It is incredible.'

'That is what is so exciting about Matilda. One can never be sure what she will do.'

Arlette looked worried but William was so exultant, so unusually gay that she allowed herself to be persuaded that all was well.

'Now, there is much to do. I shall inform my people that I am about to marry and then we shall go ahead with our preparations.'

He was merry in the castle that night. Everyone was talking about the change in the Duke and saying that they had been thinking for a year or more that it was time he married.

A few days later the mood changed.

That harbinger of evil, Archbishop Mauger, arrived at the castle and sought an immediate audience with the Duke.

William received him not very willingly. His uncle had always repelled him.

'You have come to talk about my proposed marriage I doubt not,' said William.

Mauger inclined his head in assent. 'This marriage cannot take place,' he said.

132

'Not take place! Are you mad? I have affianced myself to Matilda of Flanders and she has pledged herself to me.'

'The Pope will not permit it.'

'And why not indeed?'

'You are cousins.'

'Nonsense!'

'Six times removed, it is true, but the Pope considers the relationship too close.'

'You may tell the Pope to think again.'

'It is no use, my lord. The Pope will not agree to the marriage.'

'Then perforce he must disagree. Six times removed! A distant ancestor of Matilda's was a Norman and married into Flanders, and therefore we are too close to marry! I will not listen to such nonsense.'

'I have the Pope's answer here.'

'Then you may send it back to him and tell him I'll have none of it.'

'My lord, would you suffer excommunication?'

'Yes,' shouted William.

'And eternal damnation?'

'Yes...for Matilda.'

'You are losing your temper, my lord, as you did so often in the schoolroom.'

'I lose my temper with fools and scoundrels,' said William significantly.

'You cannot go against the decision of His Holiness.'

'I can go against all those who oppose my wishes,' growled William.

'My lord!'

'Leave me,' said William.

Mauger went out, a slight smile lifting one corner of his mouth.

Why do I tolerate that man? William asked himself. Did I not always know that he was my enemy? He is a sorcerer who delights in conjuring up mischief. He is clever, learned and my Archbishop, but I have always hated him. And what is the meaning of this?

He thought he knew. The King of France did not wish for the marriage. He had always wanted to take back Normandy. He resented that all those years ago Rollo had demanded the land and received it. He wanted to be the King of France who restored Normandy to the French crown. And if William married into Flanders the rich and powerful Baldwin would certainly become his ally.

The Pope was on the side of the King of France and William's enemies. For this reason they sought to stop the marriage through this absurd suggestion of consanguinity.

And Matilda? Matilda would doubtless have heard of the Pope's decision. He was afraid. He did not know her well enough to assess her reaction. Quickly she had decided she would have him for her husband. Could she as quickly decide against it? One thing he had learned about Matilda. The decision would lie with her, not with her father.

He must see her without delay. He set out for Lille.

* * *

She was delighted to see him.

She embraced him. How exciting she was, how unexpected. No coy looks from under golden lashes, no reluctance. That was not Matilda's way.

'I could not wait to inform your father of my arrival,' he said.

'Nay. It is enough that you have come.'

'I have had disquieting news from the Pope.'

'The old fool!' said Matilda. 'He is saying that we are cousins. Six times removed! Have you ever heard such nonsense?'

'I feared you might not see it as such.'

'You feared! And I thought I was to marry a man who knew no fear!'

'The only fear he knows is that he might lose you.'

'Come, my lord, you know full well what you would do if I showed signs of taking heed of this fool's pronouncement.'

'Carry you off by force.'

'It is what I would expect of you.'

'So we go ahead with our marriage plans even though this may mean excommunication for us both?'

'Even so, my lord.'

'You are the most wonderful woman in the world.'

'Remember that only the most wonderful man in the world is worthy of me.'

William rode back to Rouen.

'To the devil with the Pope,' he said to his mother. 'To the devil with the King of France. To the devil with Mauger and all my enemies. What care I for them when I have Matilda?'

*   *   *

The Pope's threat of excommunication was recognized for what it was by the Duke's enemies.

To have made the very distant connection of Matilda and William the reason for it was seen as the insubstantial pretext it was. What it did mean was that William's enemies were men of influence and that these men did not wish to see his position strengthened by alliance with Flanders.

It was the signal for revolt throughout Normandy. William must perforce, if he were going to keep a firm grip on his ducal crown, indulge in lengthy conflicts. Instead of marriage there must be battle and months had to be spent besieging the castles of those who rose against him.

His ancestors had scattered their illegitimate offspring rather liberally throughout the Duchy and the opinion of the descendants of these men was if one bastard could wear the ducal crown why not another?

One of these was William Busac, whose grandfather had been Richard the Fearless and because of the connection was in possession of a fine castle and lands. He led a revolt which resulted in a siege of his castle and this kept William occupied for months when he would have preferred to make arrangements for his marriage. Much as he longed to make Matilda his wife he could not do this if, by neglecting to protect his possessions, he had become a Duke without lands.

To add to his difficulties, the Pope had threatened to excommunicate Baldwin if he allowed his daughter to marry the Duke of Normandy.

*   *   *

Even Matilda could not persuade her father to allow the marriage to be celebrated with the threat of excommunication hanging over him. She might storm and rage but all he would do was shake his head sadly.

'We must find a way out of this,' he said. 'But we must wait...wait until we have.'

Matilda fumed, but in any case she knew that William was fiercely engaged in defending his dukedom, and all she could do was wait. Strangely enough she found consolation

135

in her needlework. It soothed her to work her stitches depicting the scenes from her life.

She was at her work one day, her ears strained for arrivals because she always hoped that William would come unexpectedly, when there was a shout from below and hurrying down the stone stairs to the hall she saw that a party of travellers had arrived.

To her amazement there was Judith with her husband Tostig and an older man of commanding appearance.

Matilda called to her father and they ran down to the courtyard.

Judith threw herself sobbing into her father's arms.

'There there, my love,' said Baldwin. 'There has been trouble, has there not, and you and Tostig have come to me for refuge? You did right to come home, my love.'

'Father, we had perforce to flee. This is my father-in-law, the Earl of Godwin.'

Matilda studied this man, whose name was well known throughout the whole of Flanders. The Earl of Godwin, son of a cowherd who had become a kingmaker, and who, she had heard, was King of England in all but name.

'Welcome,' said Baldwin, and he took them into the palace.

Chambers were prepared; the scullions were set to prepare meat. The visitors must be refreshed before they told their story.

*　　*　　*

Matilda was excited. She was exhilarated by drama and such was her nature that she preferred even tragic happenings, no matter what they might involve, to the boring routine of the day. Chafing as she was against the delay of her marriage, she thrilled to the story her sister had to unfold.

There was one fact which she stored away in her mind. William had said to her: 'It may well be, Matilda, that I shall make you not only Duchess of Normandy but also Queen of England!'

Queen of England! Ever since she had thought a great deal about that. She imagined Brihtric's thoughts when he realized that the woman he had insulted was his Queen. Beware, little Saxon, she said to herself. I shall not forget that day if you do.

136

The fact that she now laughed to scorn that girl who had thought she could marry the feeble Saxon and delighted in the fact that her affianced husband was a mighty man who would have been debarred from her had Brihtric accepted her proposal and her father indulged her wishes in it, did not make her forget the humiliation he had caused her; and the thought of being his Queen gave a delightful satisfaction.

Why should William not be King of England? He was connected with the family through Emma of Normandy, and Edward the Confessor was fond of him and had made this suggestion.

Matilda knew who would stand in the way: this man Godwin.

And here he was at the Court of Flanders. Life was exciting even though the rebels and his dukedom and the Pope were keeping her and William apart.

She learned as everyone in the palace did that Godwin had quarrelled with Edward and that his cause was just—as told by Godwin. But she believed that in women's gossip it might be easier to get at the root of the matter.

She said it should be her task to care for her sister and they would go to the sewing room and find solace, as they always had, in their tapestry.

She dismissed their women; they would sort out their skeins themselves and she would tell Judith about the forces which were keeping her and William apart and Judith would tell her about affairs in England.

Tostig was a good husband, but inclined to be wild.

'I like him,' said Matilda. 'Nor would you want a dullard for a husband, Judith. My Lord Godwin must have been a fine man when he was younger.'

'He is said to be the cleverest man in England.'

'Not clever enough to stop himself being exiled by old Edward! Tell me about Edward, Judith. What a strange man! Is it true that he has never taken his wife to his bed?'

'True indeed. He made a vow of celibacy.'

'She is your sister-in-law, this Editha.'

'Yes.'

'And what manner of woman?'

'Beautiful, learned and good.'

Matilda grimaced. 'I would never allow a husband to treat me as Edward treats her.'

'You would, perforce, if your husband were Edward.

137

Now she is in disgrace and has been sent to a monastery.'

'There she will learn to be as pious as her husband. William knew this Edward years ago when he was a boy.'

'Yes, Edward was many years in Normandy. Therein lies the heart of the trouble. Edward is more Norman than English. The fashions have become Norman. They never wear the long Saxon cloaks now; it is always the short Norman mantle with the wide sleeves. They say that if you wish to ask a favour of Edward you must ask it in the Norman tongue. It is spoken at Court. It is the fashionable language.'

'I thought King Edward did not care for fashion.'

'Nor does he. He will have nothing finer than lambskin to line his coats. My father-in-law and Tostig line theirs with sable, beaver and fox. He said it is well for such people who are skilled in the artifices of the world to wear the skins of cunning animals but he is a plain and artless man.'

'He is too pious to be a good king.'

'The people think highly of his saintliness.'

'Bah, Saxons!' said Matilda, thinking of Brihtric. 'Now tell me of this quarrel between your father-in-law and the King.'

'Although the King is admired for his saintliness there are many who deplore his preference for Normans. Why, Matilda, many of the high offices of the land are in Norman hands.'

'Which does not please Father Godwin.'

'It was my father-in-law who sent for Edward. His support made him King.'

'And now there has been this quarrel.'

'Of course many of the lords are jealous of my father-in-law. And because the King has no children he will have no son to follow him.'

'Who will do that?' asked Matilda quietly.

'Clearly it should be one of my father-in-law's sons.'

'Tostig, for instance.'

'Why not?'

'So, my sister, you fancy yourself Queen of England?'

'Tostig would be a good king, such as the country needs.'

'A country always needs a good strong king...and queen.'

But not you, Judith, she thought. My William, not your Tostig, should be king of that land and I its queen, not you.

She must curb her tongue. She must discover all and

138

betray nothing. Thus she could best serve William and herself.

'Tell me again of this quarrel.'

'You have heard of it already.'

'Not the intimate details. And, Judith, you tell the story to me far better than your father-in-law does to our father.'

'It is the fault of those Normans. You know it was when Eustace of Boulogne visited England with his wife.'

'Who was Edward's sister, was she not?'

'Yes. He landed at Dover and thereupon behaved as though he were the feudal lord. He and his followers went through the town, deciding where they would lodge and forced their way into the chosen houses and insisted that the owners therein treat them as honoured guests.'

'When they had no will to!'

'Why should they behave as servingmen and women to the intruders who ordered their servants to cook for them, who turned the masters of the houses from their beds and took their pleasure from their wives and daughters? Would you expect the English to stand aside and suffer that?'

'Indeed not.'

'And as you can imagine it was not long before the intruders were attacked, many killed and a battle broke out in the streets of Dover. The citizens were victorious and nineteen of the intruders were killed and many more wounded. Count Eustace escaped and went with all speed to Gloucester where Edward was staying, leading his monastic life, and there told him a false tale of how the men of Dover had risen against the visitors.'

'Which he believed.'

'He would always believe a Norman rather than an Englishman.'

'And he ordered Earl Godwin to take troops to Dover to teach the citizens a lesson. Is that so?'

'It is, and Earl Godwin refused to take up arms against his own countrymen.'

'Moreover,' put in Matilda, 'he was already complaining about the King's preference for Normans.'

'Rightly so,' said Judith warmly. 'He told the King that he would protect his fellow countrymen against foreigners, not chastise them for defending their rights.'

'And the King?'

'He had other matters to occupy his mind at that time. There was trouble on the Welsh border. Therefore he could

139

but fall in with Earl Godwin's wishes.'

'For which the people of Dover were grateful.'

'They are loyal to the Earl and they know the King to be a weak man.'

'Yet he is here now...in exile.'

'Earl Godwin has explained what happened. A few years after the citizens of Dover had taken up arms against Eustace and his men, the latter came back and behaved in exactly the same way. The King believed the story Eustace told him and this time ordered Earl Godwin to take his soldiers into the town and punish the people.'

'And again he refused.'

'Rightly so,' said Judith hotly. 'Should he raise his arms against his own people in favour of Normans?'

'It was his King's wish that he should.'

'You are being perverse, Matilda. Because you have affianced yourself to a Norman you are like King Edward. You wish to hear no ill of them.'

'It is not so. But should not subjects obey their kings?'

'Earl Godwin is no ordinary subject.'

'Nay, so I learn. But tell me more.'

'Instead of attacking Dover, Earl Godwin raised an army and marched on Gloucester where the King was; his intention being to warn the King that he would not allow the Normans to ravage our citizens' homes. Edward called in two of our greatest earls, Leofric and Siward, and they sided with him against Earl Godwin.'

'Why should they do this?' asked Matilda.

'Because they are jealous of Godwin. They would like to be in his place.'

'They would not wish it now,' said Matilda with a touch of malice.

'It is a tragedy,' declared Judith. 'We have been betrayed. The country was on the point of civil war and do you doubt who would have been the victor if it had come to this?'

'Your Godwin, I doubt not.'

'But it was decided to take the matter before the Witan. Edward meanwhile was amassing an army and he had put Normans in charge of it. It was clear that his attack was going to be aimed at us and our family. Our property was confiscated and our only hope was to escape. Naturally I came home.'

'And brought your new family with you. My poor Judith, I am sorry for you.'

'And I for you, Matilda. I hear they will never allow your marriage to take place. Perhaps it is as well. A Norman, Matilda! Think what the Normans have done to us. You should be thankful that the Pope has intervened.'

Matilda was about to tell her sister that no one was going to stop her marriage to William of Normandy and that neither he nor she were the sort of people to allow others to dictate their actions. When they made up their minds they wanted something, they were going to have it.

But looking at her sister and thinking of all she had told her and of her involvement with the Godwins, who, Matilda knew, had their eyes on the throne of England, she decided that discretion was more becoming and remained silently plying her needle.

* * *

William rode to Lille. The manner in which he visited his betrothed was unorthodox, but Baldwin had grown accustomed to that.

Matilda was so happy after one of his visits that she would be contented for days after; and as, poor child, she was being denied what he knew she earnestly wanted, her father felt a certain amount of licence must be allowed.

William sent a message to Matilda that he would soon be with her and in view of the fact that there were visitors at the palace he wished to see her alone.

This appealed to Matilda and she was waiting for him.

'Come,' she said. 'None know you are here. Has something happened?'

'Something of the utmost importance. Edward has invited me to visit England.'

She caught her breath. 'It is because Godwin and his family are here.'

She delighted him. There was so little he had to explain to her. She followed his train of thought; and she was for him as no one except his mother had ever been before.

'Why does he wish to see you? Do you think it is for the same reason as I think?'

'He is getting old,' said William.

'And he has no successor. He loves the Normans. They

141

say he is more Norman than English.'

'It is what I think.'

'If he made you his successor would the English accept you?'

'They would be obliged to, if I took the crown.'

'You must go without delay, William.'

'Would I could take you with me.'

'You will one day. You will take me as your Queen.'

'I swear it. And when I return from England, Matilda, we will be married. No matter what obstacles are put in our way.'

'I swear it with you, William of Normandy,' she said; and she added: 'King of England.'

* * *

How different was this old man from the beautiful fair-haired blue-eyed young one whom William had known. Edward had aged beyond his years. His hair was truly white now; his beautiful blue eyes misty; his garments were plain and the thin ascetic mien of a monk had become accentuated.

He embraced William warmly and told him how he would never forget the hospitality he had enjoyed from his father.

'Those were happy days when Alfred and I lived in Jumièges among the monks.'

'It was there that your taste for the monastic life was formed,' said William.

He was surprised at the spartan manner in which Edward lived, although he had heard much of his habits. He ate sparingly—certainly not a Norman custom—and he spent a great deal of time at prayer.

William told him that while he was in England he wanted to see something of the country.

'We shall arrange for you to make a tour,' said Edward.

He took him to his private chamber in the monastery at Gloucester where he had asked William to join him. It resembled a cell in simplicity.

He cannot have many years to live, thought William speculatively.

'You would have been happier to stay at Jumièges I believe,' he said.

'Ah, that may well be so,' Edward replied. 'In the days

142

when Alfred and I were there together, my life was one of contentment.'

'Although you were exiles from your native land.'

'Normandy had become home to us. We were so young when we were taken there and could remember little of England.'

'I see much that is Norman here.'

'They blame me for being too Norman in my tastes. Poor simple folk, I only introduce Norman customs when they are better than the Saxon ones.'

'This man Godwin is in Flanders.'

'I know. A traitor. Long may he stay there.'

'Are the people with him?'

'He has a following. He and his sons. Harold is the most dangerous. He is in Ireland now. They say he is gathering an army there and will come here and bring back his father.'

'You hate Godwin,' said William.

'I am a Christian and hate no man. I have tried to forget that he was behind the murder of my brother Alfred, but I find it difficult.'

'They are ambitious, this family.'

'They want the crown.'

'Who would you nominate as your successor? The sons of this man? Harold? Tostig?'

'Never.'

'Could they say they had a claim?'

'Doubtless they could. His daughter is my wife.'

'Whom you have put from you?'

'She was never my wife and now she is in a monastery. I have never taken a wife nor any woman. Godwin insisted on the marriage but he could not make me consummate it.'

'He says that he brought you to England, that he made you King, that you could not have come without his support.'

'I suppose that is true. But power such as that man has is corrupting, particularly when he was not born to it.'

'He is formidable. Are his sons equally so?'

'Harold is strong, a serious young man, ambitious like his father. Tostig is too wild; so is Sweyn who is in exile. He is a man who would never be accepted. He has been twice exiled. Previously because on his return from an expedition into Wales he passed a convent and sent for the Abbess. He thought it amusing to violate her and he lingered with her

143

for some time before sending her back to her convent. Such lewd behaviour I would not tolerate so I sent him away. His father, of course, used his influence to have him brought back but no sooner was he back than he killed his cousin and then even his father did not attempt to plead for him.'

'So it is Harold and Tostig whom Godwin will try to put on the throne.'

'Harold, I think. The eldest son, a man of courage, of action and beloved by the people. But you will understand, William, that I have no wish to see the son of my brother's murderer on the throne.'

'I see it, Edward. But what will you do?'

Edward turned his misty eyes on William. 'I would like to see Normandy and England under one strong ruler.'

William felt the faint colour rising in his cheeks.

'I would bring strong rule to this country,' he said.

'I know it. I have heard of all the dangers that have beset you in Normandy and I have applauded the manner in which you are succeeding. Yours was a difficult part, William. Duke when an infant. What dangers you have come safely through and I hear that you have not frittered away your strength in debauchery. Yes, William, I have had this in mind for a long time. Because of your strength, and the virtuous life you have led, I wish the next King of England to be you.'

* * *

He could scarcely wait to get back to tell Matilda, but first he wished to see something of this land which he was now determined one day to rule.

He begged that he might explore the country incognito, taking with him a small band of men who would look like a group of ordinary travellers.

He was excited by what he saw. Here was good fertile land; here were forests in which deer and boar lurked. He hunted a little and was delighted with what he found. He discovered that the many excellent laws introduced by Alfred the Great still remained. The monasteries which his pagan ancestors had destroyed had been rebuilt; the roads, many of them which had been built by the Romans, were good; and there was, for the traveller, the occasional house which was given the Saxon name of *inn*. There were other places where one could refresh oneself and these had the

144

name of *gest-hus* or *gest-bur* and in many of them they kept a chamber in which a number of people might rest for the night; they were placed at points on the road where they could be easily found. The ruling body was the Witenagemot; this was as the name implied in the Saxon language: the meeting of the knowing. It had supreme authority because it was made up of various witans from all over the country. It met once a year—or twice if the need arose. William decided that to a king such as Edward this was admirable. A ruler such as he was himself would prefer to have no restrictions.

As Edward had introduced so much that was Norman into the country, the people's manner of eating and enjoying their leisure was very similar to that which he had always known.

During the journey through the English countryside he conceived a great love for it and the desire to rule it obsessed him.

He was torn between a wish to linger and to go back to Matilda to tell her what he had seen and heard.

* * *

Flushed with the triumph of his visit to England William decided that Pope or no Pope he would wait no longer for Matilda. He rode to Lille and there he was joyfully received by her. He told her immediately what Edward had said to him.

'He has promised you the crown,' she said. 'He must make it clear that it is to be yours.'

'He will do that. It is for him to name his successor. But I may have to fight for it. I have seen much of these Saxons. They are a stubborn band and I believe could be good fighters. I heard nothing but praise from them for Godwin's son Harold.'

'When they know you, my love, they will have nothing but praise for you.'

'They will first have to know me.'

'How long can Edward live?'

He laughed. 'You go too fast. First Edward must die and there is the most important event of all which must take place—our marriage.'

'And the Pope's threats?'

'We will set them aside.'

145

'You mean that, William?'

'I mean I will wait no longer, come what may.'

She threw back her head and laughed.

'Why have we waited so long, William?'

'Because I could not ask you to marry me if I were without a land to rule and there were so many trying to wrest it from me. Only the defence of my land prevented our marrying. Then I took my trip to England.'

'Which I urged you to do. That time was not wasted, William. Did you not come back with Edward's promise—to make William of Normandy King of England. Oh, William, the future is ours. But first I must tell you what has happened here. Godwin has left for England. Edward has received him but is sending his son Wulfnoth and his nephew Haakon to Normandy as hostages for Godwin's good behaviour. I have heard through Judith that his son Harold has raised an army in Ireland. He will meet his father on English soil and then the Godwins will resume their old position in the country.'

'But I am to have the hostages. I'll guard them well. It's ill news, Matilda, that Godwin is back. But never fear, when the time comes I shall be ready for him and his sons. But that is for the future. Now without delay, our marriage shall take place. Lead me to your father. I will tell him that I will wait no longer.'

'I will come with you,' said Matilda gleefully, 'and add my voice to yours. Come, my William. The waiting is over.'

* * *

Who but William and Matilda would have dared marry with the threat of the Pope's displeasure hanging over them?

It was the month of May and the wedding ceremony was to take place in the first city of Normandy. Rouen was gay on that day. Banners fluttered everywhere; the bells rang out and the people thronged the streets.

All the chiefs, knights and barons were present. Arlette, the happy mother, was there with the members of her family, all men of substance now; Matilda's parents rode with her. She was very beautiful in her white gown, decorated with tiny pictures etched in gold thread and bordered with gold and precious stones. On her head was a glittering circlet of gems.

The people gasped in admiration no less for William than for his bride. He had always carried himself with dignity but on this day in his mantle of spun gold and his tunic of glittering gems he looked like a god, and the people of Normandy were proud of him.

There was one notable absence. Archbishop Mauger, who would in the natural course of the events have officiated, was not present. But it had not been difficult to find a priest to be his substitute. The ceremony took place in the porch where all might witness it and hear the firm responses of the bride and groom. The ring was on Matilda's finger. She was now the wife of William of Normandy.

They had been married in the eyes of the people and then it was time for them to celebrate mass, so they walked over the flower-strewn nave to the altar.

The ceremony over, there was feasting and revelry. This continued with games and dancing far into the evening; but the hour had come for which the bridal pair had long been impatient.

In the bedchamber the scent of flowers filled the air; they had been strewn on the floor as they had been in the church. Matilda's ladies came to her, undressed and prepared her for the wedding night.

Matilda was no reluctant bride. Joyously she awaited William.

Lanfranc Goes to Rome

THESE were the happiest days William had ever known. He threw aside his restraint; he forgot he was the Duke of Normandy. Thus, he thought, must my father have felt when my mother came to him and he loved her from then on to the end of his life.

So did he love Matilda. Her ready wit, her fearlessness, her strong nature and determination to have her way, delighted him. She resembled him in many ways. She excited him—not only physically but mentally. Here was a woman who would understand immediately his aims and desires—and help him to achieve them.

She had changed his life. He could now laugh at his anger when people had insulted him because of his birth. He cared nothing for that. Let them insult him all they wished. Nothing could undermine his confidence any more.

Papers were brought to him to sign. He penned a signature he had never used before. 'William the Bastard.'

He looked at the words and laughed aloud. He was proud of them. Yes, he, the bastard, the result of love such as he now knew to be all transcending. Better the son of such parents than the offspring of two who had been put together because their union meant the sealing of a treaty. To be born of love was nothing to be ashamed of; and to be ashamed was an insult not only to himself but also to his mother—the one he loved best in the world next to Matilda, who had never had aught but his good at heart.

He, the bastard, was a duke of Normandy (he believed in his heart that he would one day be King of England); he was married to one of the noblest Princesses in Europe and she had married him for love, not because she had been forced to do so. He was in love with her and she with him, with William the Bastard.

He was a great ruler and a happy husband. Bastardy had not prevented his becoming that. It was not a title to hide away. It was one to be proud of. He would flaunt it. He should be known from now on as William the Bastard.

* * *

Within a month Matilda was pregnant. She was overcome with joy.

Had she not always known it would be thus? She was married to the most important man in Europe—or so she insisted—and she was considering the future. Poor Judith, married to Tostig who believed he might have a hope of the crown of England. Ha! with William there to take it! And now their union was to be fruitful. They would have a son. Yes of course they would have a son. How could William and Matilda do aught else?

Very soon after their wedding news came of the death of Godwin. On his return to England he was joined by his son Harold and the Saxons, still smarting from Edward's favouritism towards the Norman population, flocked to his banner. Harold was their hero. He was not only brave but handsome in the Saxon manner and he had many loyal supporters. Edward's horror of civil war induced him to make a speedy peace and reinstate Godwin. Now the tables were turning and many Normans were arriving in Normandy to live in exile for it was clear that their enemy Godwin was back as strong as he ever was.

William, deep in the happiness of his honeymoon, refused to be perturbed by these events. Clearly if Godwin had remained an exile his chances would have been the greater; but he was not a man to flinch before difficulties and when the time came he would be ready.

He was not sure that Godwin's death was good news, for this meant that Harold, the idol of the Saxons, was now at the head of the Godwin family. He had become governor of Wessex, Sussex, Kent and Essex. Soon after Godwin died, Siward, the Earl of Northumbria, died too. Siward had been a man of great power in the north. He it was who had helped Malcom of Scotland to his throne after the usurpation of MacBeth. On Siward's death Tostig was then given the earldom of Northumbria, thus ensuring the important counties of England were in the hands of the Godwin family.

This was dangerous, William conceded. But the manner of the old Earl's death reflected no credit on him and would be remembered against them, for Godwin had died suddenly as though struck down by God for his misdeeds and it was generally believed that this was what had happened.

He and Edward were dining together when one of the servants carrying two large tankards, slipped and seemed as though he would throw the contents of the tankards across the board. One leg appeared to have doubled under him, but with the other he restored his balance. Such an odd and skilful piece of contortion did it seem that it set the company laughing.

Godwin said: 'It is well the fellow has two legs. They are like two brothers. When one is in difficulty, the other comes to his aid.'

This seemed like a reference to his sons who, he was implying, would come to the help of each other if any one of them was attacked.

Edward, who had never ceased to mourn his brother Alfred and constantly brooded on the terrible manner in which he had died when, it was said, with Godwin's connivance his eyes were put out, retorted: 'I think constantly of my brother and I pray that God may one day avenge him.'

Godwin turned a shade paler but assumed an air of innocence. He could not ignore the King's remark for the look which accompanied it was significant.

'Why do you look at me thus when you speak of your brother?' he asked. 'If I had aught to do with his death, may God stop me from swallowing this morsel.'

With that he took a piece of bread, chewed it and attempted to swallow it, but as he did so he began to choke: his face was suffused with violent colour and in a few moments he was dead.

An awed silence fell on the company. Many believed that they had just witnessed the vengeance of God, and Godwin had been struck down for the part he had played in the murder of Alfred Atheling.

Harold might persuade the country that the Earl was

ageing; he had recently suffered exile; he had been failing in health for some time. Had they not seen men before struck down at the board? And if it were true that God was wreaking his vengeance why should he have waited all these years for it when He could have put it into effect years ago?

But no matter what he said, people still believed that the Earl of Godwin died because he had asked God to strike him down if he were guilty of the murder of Prince Alfred, and this was God's answer.

*   *   *

The blissful days of the honeymoon were not allowed to continue.

At the instigation of Archbishop Mauger a declaration was read in all the churches throughout Normandy to the effect that the Duke and his Duchess were excommunicated because they had disobeyed the command of the Pope and married when forbidden to do so.

'To the devil with the Pope,' said William. 'I'd not go back on what I've done for all the Popes or any man in Christendom.'

Matilda was in agreement with him and they continued their idyll until the news was brought to them that William's uncle, the Count of Arques, his grandfather's illegitimate son who was therefore his uncle, had set himself up as the Duke of Normandy. He had extended his estates and fortified his castle.

'By God's Splendour,' cried William, 'I'll teach the fellow a lesson. He is going to take me away from you and that I find as hard to forgive as his treachery.'

He left Matilda to pray for him and begin embroidering garments for her baby. Finding solace as ever in the needle, she turned to it now.

Rarely had William shown his military genius so clearly.

Spurred on by his desire to return to Matilda, he laid siege to his uncle's castle, preparing to starve him and his followers out as he had done on other notable occasions, when news was brought to him that the King of France was coming to the aid of the Count of Arques; he had sworn to rescue him from his besieged castle and set him up as his vassal to work for him. In exchange he should be given the title of Duke of Normandy in the place of his nephew who was a bastard just as he was.

With all the skill at his command William contrived to lay an ambush which he commanded having left a garrison at the castle to hold the siege, and thus was able to cut down the French contingent before it arrived. Henry's best men were killed and he himself was obliged to return to France.

William wrote frequently to Matilda giving her details of what was happening. It was a condition she had insisted on. He was glad of it; it kept them in touch; moreover her advice was valuable. So deeply had she his affairs at heart that he always gave heed to what she had to say and delighted in her counsel.

She was not a soft woman but when the siege was finally broken and his starving uncle came to kneel before him and crave forgiveness, he gave it on Matilda's advice.

'He is your uncle,' she said. 'It is never wise to revenge oneself on blood relations. Let him go and he will think very carefully before he enters into a conspiracy again. He might even become your loyal subject.'

He agreed with her and the Count was allowed to keep his lands on which William had cast covetous eyes. But Matilda was right and what he needed more than anything was peace in Normandy. If the opporturnity to go to England were to come, Matilda had stressed, how could he go and leave Normandy at war within itself? His first task was to unite Normandy and let the world know of the strength of its Duke. Only the strong could afford to be merciful.

But the King of France had his honour to avenge. He could not pass over the loss of some of his finest soldiers. Moreover William was too strong a ruler to please him. What he wanted was a dependent vassal.

He declared war on William and very soon William had a new battle on his hands.

*   *   *

'Must there always be war to separate us?' he said to Matilda during one of his brief visits to her. 'When I was a boy I used to think old Mauger cast a spell upon me so that I

152

could not do my lessons. Now I think he has laid another spell upon me. He dabbles in black arts, you know. He is not a true Christian.'

'And he is your Archbishop of Rouen!'

'He has held the post for so long. Remember he is my father's brother.'

'Bastard!' growled Matilda.

'And not the only one,' said William, 'as you once reminded me.'

'Your bastardy is a credit to you. His a disgrace.'

'And why the difference?'

'Because you are my love, and my husband, and everything that is yours is precious to me.'

It was illogical reasoning but pleasant to hear.

'I never was happy until I knew you,' he told her.

'Wait till I show you your son. Then you will know the greatest happiness.'

'I long to see him.'

'As I do, you can well imagine. He is a lively fellow and heavy to carry.'

'That shows he will be a true son of his father.'

And very soon after that the child was born. As Matilda had prophesied *her* first-born could not be anything but a boy, and a boy this was. He was as lusty as his father would wish and it was true that William had never known such a proud and happy moment as when he stood looking down at Matilda with their child in his arms.

'Let us call him Robert after my father,' he said.

'Robert the Magnificent,' murmured Matilda. 'This one will be magnificent, I promise you.'

He bent and kissed her. 'And you are a woman who always keeps her promises. How I curse the King of France for taking me away from you and my son.'

'Despatch him quickly and come back to us,' said Matilda.

'You may rest assured that the moment I have done so I shall be with you.'

*   *   *

It was a mighty force that came against him and at the head of it was the King of France.

William was not deterred; he could beat the French at

any time, he was sure; but he must not allow himself to underestimate the enemy, and he knew that he had a major war ahead of him.

He was surrounded by enemies and the fact of his excommunication had given them fresh hope and fresh reason to displace him.

Often he thought of Edward in England and wondered how such a feeble king who could never be a warrior was able to live more peacefully than he. Always at the back of his mind was the thought that one day the call would come. And how could he go to England while Normandy was in turmoil?

He must get this excommunication lifted. When Pope Leo died suddenly his hopes were raised—until his successor pronounced his agreement with the excommunication.

Sometimes he was indeed sure that Mauger had set a spell on him.

One day wearily returning to his camp he came upon a man riding a lame horse. He recognized him as Lanfranc with whom he had long been acquainted and who had until recently been the Prior of the Abbey of Bec. Lanfranc was a man whom he had liked until he placed himself firmly on the side of the Pope and denounced the marriage because it was going against the Holy Father's commands.

He had been angry, particularly as he had admired Lanfranc, and to find him among his enemies had so incensed him that he had told him to get out of Normandy.

Lanfranc had come to Normandy from Pavia and because he was a great scholar he had been given the Abbey; William had been good to him and, finding him ungrateful, in a sudden burst of anger he exiled him.

At that time, feeling weary of battle, longing for his home, he was far from pleased to see the Prior.

He called to him: 'Hey, Prior. What do you here? Did I not order you from the land?'

'My lord,' answered Lanfranc, 'you did so.'

'Then, pray, why are you still here?'

'As you see, my lord, my horse is lame. You have many fine horses in your company. If you will but give me one of them you will be rid of me the sooner.'

William smiled. He had always liked the man and he felt his good-humour returning.

He said: 'I had not wished you to leave, Lanfranc, had you remained my friend.'

154

'I have never been aught but a friend to you, my lord.'

'You have sided with the Pope against me.'

'I have said that if the Pope forbids the marriage, then marriage there should not be.'

'God's Splendour,' cried William, 'is that not what I say? You are no friend to me.'

'Not so, my lord. If the Pope could be persuaded to give his consent, then would I support your marriage with all my heart.'

'You seek to play tricks with words. Is that not what all my enemies would say?'

'Your enemies rejoice in what you have done. I, your friend, deplore it. As your friend I would I might go to Rome and persuade the Pope that there is no valid reason why your marriage should not have taken place.'

'I see that you blindly obey the Pope even if it goes against reason and the wishes of your Seigneur.'

'That is my duty as a man of the Church, my lord, and my duty must be done.'

William narrowed his eyes.

'A horse shall be brought for you and you shall return to my camp. I have decided I do not wish you to leave...in exile. What you may do is make arrangements to go to the Pope and explain to him the folly of this ban.'

Lanfranc seemed well pleased.

'I believe I have the right explanations in my mind,' he said.

'Then go at once. For the sooner the ban is lifted the sooner my enemies will have one reason less to attack me.'

As a result Lanfranc left without delay to put the case of William and Matilda before the Pope.

*   *   *

The wars continued. His life was spent between the battlefield and the castle and his great joys were the days when he could be with Matilda.

Robert, their first-born, was flourishing and Matilda was pregnant again. In due course she gave birth to a daughter, Cecily; the pattern of life did not change. The war continued. As soon as one enemy was overcome another would rise.

Matilda gave birth to another daughter, Adelisa, and then a son Richard, and still the war went on.

William's family was growing; he longed to be able to

155

spend more time with them; he wanted to make Normandy prosperous; he wanted to indulge his passion for building which would enrich and beautify the countryside; but there must be continual war and devastation.

By the end of the decade, the pattern began to change. Henry of France, whom William had beaten back to his frontiers, died, and his successor, his son Philip, who was only seven years old, was placed under the care of Baldwin of Flanders. William naturally approved of having the young King in hands friendly to himself and when in France there was a rebellion againt the young monarch, he went into battle which resulted in his forcing the French nobles to swear allegiance to their young King and his guardian Baldwin.

Most important of all, Lanfranc returned from Rome with the Pope's decision that on certain conditions the excommunication would be rescinded.

Matilda and William were to set aside a sum of money to feed and clothe one hundred poor people; they were to build two abbeys—William's was to be for monks and Matilda's for nuns. If they did this God would forgive their disobedience to Holy Church and they would be taken back into the fold.

This was no hardship. Cheerfully Matilda set about founding Holy Trinity for nuns while William endowed St Stephens and as a reward for his good work set Lanfranc in charge of it.

Matilda was gleeful. She was pleased with a life which William, her children and her interest in affairs made exciting.

William's devotion had not diminished; he was that unusual husband, a faithful one. It was well for him that he was, she told him, for she would not endure infidelity.

'If you took a mistress there would be trouble,' she warned him. Not that he needed the warning. He was content with Matilda and too concerned with his ambitions to think over much of women. Matilda supplied all he needed in that direction.

'You would poison her, doubtless,' he said.

'Either you or her,' she answered almost casually.

He laughed at her, for the idea was absurd. They were as one; one life; one ambition. To keep the Duchy of Normandy under control so that when the call came to take England they would be ready.

It was rarely that a great commander could discuss his affairs with a woman; but Matilda was no ordinary woman. She must know all his plans. She was his helpmeet. Often she gave voice to what was uppermost in his mind at that time so that it was almost as though they could communicate by means other than words. It was so in the case of Mauger.

'Now,' she said, 'there is an opportunity of ridding yourself of Mauger.'

He nodded.

'He worships the old gods. Yet he is your Archbishop. I have made some enquiries. It is true that he practises sorcery. If there was a trial, evidence against him could be produced. I know that.'

He nodded.

In a few weeks after that conversation Mauger was brought before his judges. How right Matilda had proved to be. It was discovered that he had numerous children whom he had favoured with benefices; he had sold preferments and robbed the church. Moreover it was proved that during the lavish banquets he gave, which often ended in sexual orgies, he had boasted that at his command he had a familiar, who could not be seen but who could be heard to converse with him. He called this spirit Thoret and declared he was an offspring of the god Thor. At his banquets the Archbishop and Thoret were said to have held amusing but rather lewd dialogues.

Matilda and William awaited the outcome of this trial; there were some who felt wary of condemning Mauger too harshly for his reputation as a sorcerer inspired them with fear and as he was in communication with Thoret he could certainly have special powers to cast spells.

Matilda soothed William's fears in that respect. 'He has a gift of throwing his voice,' she said. 'He can keep his lips still and make the voice appear to come not from his mouth.'

The result of the trial was that Mauger was dispossessed of his lands and exiled to Guernsey where he went with his wife, his son and his mistresses, there to end his days in the enjoyment of the lusts of the flesh.

'This is the end of trouble in that quarter,' said William.

'Did I not tell you so,' asked Matilda.

Yes indeed they were one. She was for William and her family against the rest of the world.

157

She it was who suggested that little Robert should be espoused to Marguerite, the young sister of the Count of Maine. Her reason was that Maine, one of the vassal states, had long been turbulent and caused William trouble, and she believed that if the families were united there would be friendship between them. She had a stronger motive. The Count of Maine was young but ailing and without heirs. If he died the estates would pass to his sister and if that sister were married to Robert, they would be in the hands of William and his family.

There was no objection to the marriage and little Marguerite came to Rouen to be brought up under guardians chosen by Matilda, there to await the day when Robert would be of an age to marry.

It so happened the Count did die, but Count Walter of Mantes, who was married to Biota, an aunt of the dead Count of Maine, declared that his wife had the greater claim.

Here was another cause for war, but William, heavily engaged elsewhere, sent troops to wrest Maine from Walter and this was one of the rare occasions when there was not an easy victory

The Count drove William's force out of Maine and set up his own victorious standard.

William was incensed. He could not endure failure. He discussed the matter with Matilda. She was astute. He could rely on her. His mother had supported him in all he did but simply out of love, loyalty and maternal pride. Not that Matilda was not loving and did not give her absolute devotion. She did—but she had something else to offer. She had an understanding of affairs which Arlette could never have; she was far-seeing, shrewd and never over-scrupulous where the good of William and Normandy were concerned.

'Invite the Count here to talk terms over with you,' she suggested, and there was a veiled look in her eyes.

William accepted her advice and the Count came with his Countess.

They dined with William and Matilda and the position of Maine was discussed. William expressed his desire to be just and to find some amicable way of settling the difference.

The Count was agreeably surprised.

But that night both he and his wife died in their beds.

158

Matilda smiled secretively when the news was brought to her.

* * *

That was not the end of trouble; but William was beginning to be feared throughout Normandy. It was believed that he could not lose a battle and if he did, as in the case of Walter of Mantes, evil forces worked for him.

He had overcome the excommunication. Archbishop Mauger had died shortly after being exiled by him. When out sailing between Guernsey and Normandy he had feasted too well and when the boat was brought ashore undid his belt to give his swollen stomach some comfort. This released his hose which fell to his knees, and thus encumbered he fell into the sea and although it was low water he, being much the worse for drink, was unable to arise and so he drowned.

'A fitting end,' said William.

'No more to fear from that one,' added Matilda.

When Arlette became ill and sent for her son, he lost no time in going to her bedside.

She lay back, pale but still beautiful, and he kissed her tenderly.

'My William,' she said. 'I am proud of you.'

'And I of you,' he assured her.

'Of the tanner's daughter?' she asked with a smile.

'You know I would not change her for the greatest Princess in Christendom,' he answered earnestly.

'Bless you, William. What a happy day it was for me when I washed my clothes in the stream and your father rode by.'

'You have had a happy life, Mother?'

She nodded. 'And you have been a source of greater happiness than any. I have seen you grow in power and I remember always my dream.'

'It has not been fulfilled yet, Mother.'

'It will be. I promise you.'

'You saw the branches stretching out beyond Normandy, beyond the sea. You saw them over England, Mother.'

'My son will leave his mark on the world. I have always known it. William, my well-beloved son, will you do something for me?'

159

'It is done,' he said.

'Your sister and your half-brothers, Odo and Robert ...will you care for them?'

'With all my heart. Fear not, Mother. They shall have high places in the land.'

'I knew you would do this for me and remember always that I bore them even as I did you.'

'I will remember, Mother.'

'Shed no tears for me, William. I bless you. May you be as happy in your family as I have been in mine. I am sorry that you are a bastard. But it could be nothing else.'

'Set aside your sorrow. Know that I have come to be proud of the name. You know I use it on all my documents.'

'William the Bastard! You have made it a title of honour. Good-bye, my dearest. My love for you has been great.'

'I know it,' he answered.

She was buried with all honours and her body was laid in the abbey at Grestain which she had founded.

William kept his promise. Odo became the Bishop of Bayeux and Robert was Count of Mortain. His sister Adeliz was married to a Count.

The years were passing.

Another boy was born to them. This was William, after his father. The family was growing; it was beginning to be realized that William the Bastard, with Matilda of Flanders beside him, was one of the most powerful men of Europe.

Adelisa in Love

It was a year he would never forget. He was no longer young, being thirty-eight years of age. It had been a hard life mostly spent in fighting. He often said it was small wonder he was a great soldier since he had spent most of his life following that profession and there had been little time for anything else.

Often he talked to Matilda of how he would like to see the Duchy develop. There were so many better ways of living than fighting. He wanted to improve the farming lands; he wanted to set up glassworks; he admired fine works of gold or silver and wished to help the creators of these, but his greatest enthusiasm was for architecture.

'Do you know, Matilda,' he often said, 'when I have to burn some grand castle I feel a pang of sorrow. I would like to see fine castles, cathedrals, dwellings, all over the land.'

'And all in your possession, my lord,' Matilda reminded him.

''Tis so. My mother used to say that once I had acquired something I never wished to let it go.'

'And why should you, if it were hard-won?'

'Matilda, has it ever struck you how alike we think, we two?'

'Why should we not think alike? We are working towards the same goal.'

''Twas a happy day for me when I gave vent to my ill-humour and rolled you in the mud.'

'And showed me a strong man. None but a strong man would have done for me.'

He, who was never demonstrative with any but her, took her hand and kissed it.

'You have given me so much happiness in my home and my family.'

He liked to talk about their sons. Richard was his favourite, Robert hers.

There was, however, a little discord between them over Robert. Her first-born, her darling. Was he beginning to mean more to her than William himself? Richard of course was a good boy. He learned his lessons and was a credit to his tutors; he rode well; he was of a sweet and docile temper; he was handsome too, more like his father in looks than either Robert or little William.

The girls did not count in the same way as the boys. William had fiercely wanted boys and she had wanted them because she must show William that never could he be disappointed in her. Cecilia, Adelisa, Constance and Adela—four charming girls who stood in great awe of their father and of whom he was very fond, although he was not the man to show this. Cecilia was devout and Adelisa loved stories of romance; the others were too young as yet to show much preference for anything.

Of the boys they talked constantly.

Richard was the safest topic, for William could not find fault with him; but Robert who was now twelve years old was already showing signs of rebellion. He had all the spirit of his parents but he was more reckless than William had ever been and was constantly boasting of what he would inherit, and that he was going to be Duke of Normandy—which was rather irritating to his father.

'Remember, boy,' William reminded him. 'I am not yet in the tomb.'

Robert was good looking with his light chestnut-coloured hair and blue eyes, but he was short of leg, a fact which did not please William. He admired tall men like himself and Robert's legs were so short in comparison with the rest of his body that William knew he would never have the look of a Viking. He was a Fleming, not a Norman.

'And what is wrong with that?' demanded Matilda.

'It is becoming in a woman to be small and dainty,' said William. 'I would have liked him to have the height I expect of my son. Nay, Matilda, you have given me a Robin Curthose for a first-born.'

Matilda was not pleased. Height was not everything she would have him know; and the Flemings were none the worse if they were on average shorter than the Normans.

162

They might banter but resentment was growing in her towards William. Their first big disagreement was over their first-born.

As for Robert he was inclined to be saucy. 'Never fear my father's anger, Mother,' he said. 'He cannot change me for Richard though I fancy he would like to. I am the first-born.'

'He could dispossess you,' she reminded him. 'We shall have to take care of that.'

Already, though he was but twelve years old, she was siding with him.

Robert strutted in the children's apartments. He was good-tempered when not crossed and indulgent to his sisters. They were often visited by the Saxons, Wulfnoth and Haakon, who had come to Normandy as hostages when Godwin had gone back.

William had been discussing these two boys with Matilda.

'I have often thought,' he said, 'that on the death of Godwin there is no real purpose in our holding them. At least I can see a purpose but Harold I should have thought would have asked for their return by now.'

'Doubtless that man is so full of his own affairs that he has no time to think of a young brother and a cousin. How much longer can Edward live?'

'Not long surely. And then...'

They smiled at each other.

'Kind of England,' she said.

'And Queen.'

'While yet Duke of Normandy,' she added.

'I have a fancy for the place. I would fortify it. I would put it in order. Edward has been too weak.'

'I think of Harold. Now he will be making himself liked and winning the people to his side.'

'I have spent most of my life fighting for what I must hold. Do you think I shall hesitate to go on doing so?'

'I have the utmost faith in your power to take all that you want.'

'Did I not get you?'

'I trust England will fall as willingly into your hands as your wife did.'

They had their tender moments but he did suspect her of hiding Robert's misdemeanours from him and she thought him over-harsh with her favourite.

163

*   *   *

In their bedchamber little Adelisa was telling the younger ones the story of how Ragnar slew the dragon.

Grandmother Arlette had told it to her as *her* grandmother had told her. 'That,' had said Grandmother Arlette, 'is how the great stories of our heritage are handed down to us.'

The little girls listened attentively; William, whom they called Rufus, partly to distinguish him from their father and partly because he had a thatch of wiry red hair and very rosy cheeks, said he would rather have been the dragon than Ragnar. 'I wish I could breathe fire. I'd breathe it all over you and burn you up.'

Adelisa was shocked. 'But, Rufus, the dragon was bad. Ragnar was good and it was good really slaying evil.'

'I don't care,' declared Rufus. 'I'm a dragon. I'm breathing fire. You're all burnt up.' Adelisa went on with the story. They were used to Rufus so they ignored him.

'He was beautiful,' she said. 'He had long golden hair and rings on his fingers and bracelets on his arms. He was strong and brave.'

'Our father is strong and brave but he doesn't have rings and bracelets.'

They all laughed at the idea of their father in rings and bracelets.

'He has a gold crown for his head,' said Adelisa. 'I've seen it.'

'I've seen it,' boasted Rufus. 'I've worn it.'

'You must not tell lies,' said Adelisa. 'You will go to hell if you do.'

Rufus considered going to hell and decided he would like the adventure.

He went on: 'And his mantle. I've worn them. I've sat on a throne and...'

'Rufus is lying again,' said Adelisa sadly.

Rufus pulled her hair, and the little girls looked frightened.

'I'll tie you up by your plaits and leave you hanging,' said Rufus. 'Yes, I will. Right till you die.'

'You would be punished,' said little Constance.

'I'll hang you up too.'

'Don't let him, Adelisa. Don't let him,' screamed Constance.

164

Rufus crept stealthily towards her and she screamed with terror. Rufus liked to frighten his sisters; he had a violent temper too and would lie on the floor and kick if displeased. Only the thoughts of his father's displeasure and stern punishment was able to deter him.

Fortunately Richard heard the screams of his sisters and came in.

Richard was tall, with his mother's good looks and his father's physique, but the temperament of neither. He was gentle and kind and the little girls adored him.

Constance ran to him and flung herself against him.

'Now, Rufus,' said Richard, 'what is this?'

'Silly girls,' said Rufus. 'Only a game.'

'You shouldn't frighten them.'

'They shouldn't be frightened.'

'It is your duty to look after them. Did you not know that, Rufus?'

'I won't,' declared Rufus.

'Then you will never be a pupil in chivalry.'

'I don't want to.'

'Then you will never win your golden spurs.'

'Oh yes I will. I'll win thousands and thousands ...'

'He won't, will he?' said Adelisa clinging to her brother's hand and looking up at him adoringly. Richard was like a knight from the old romantic stories which Grandmother Arlette used to tell. Beautiful, kind and coming to the rescue of ladies in distress. How she wished that Grandmother Arlette had not died; she had loved her dearly, more so than she did her other grandmother who was so important, being the daughter of a King. Daughters of tanners it seemed were more beautiful and more kind and loving. Richard reminded her in a way of Grandmother Arlette. Yes, although he was a man and tall he had a look of her.

'I fear he won't unless he mends his ways,' said Richard. Then he turned his beautiful smile on Rufus. 'But I think he will. For he is a very clever little boy, our Rufus, and he will do what is best for himself.'

A slow smile spread across the rosy face of Rufus. He liked to hear that description of himself and of course he knew that he must win his spurs and that a knight did not torment little girls even though they were his sisters.

As he had done so many times before, Richard was restoring order in the nursery. He was about to continue with the lesson when the sounds of arrival below could be

165

distinctly heard. The children all ran to the window and clustered round it.

A man had ridden into the courtyard; his horse was steaming and had clearly ridden far.

The rider leaped from the saddle and, as a groom took his horse, he said in a loud and commanding voice: 'Take me to the Duke.'

* * *

William and Matilda bent over the chessboard. It was a game William enjoyed in his rare leisure moments. Nothing could thrill him as hunting did and when he was not engaged on state matters and the defending of his realm he indulged this pleasure with all the enthusiasm of which he was capable; but there were times when it was not possible to hunt; then he liked to sit down at the chessboard. The game with its implications of warlike strategies appealed to him and from his early days he had enjoyed putting his wits against a worthy apponent.

On this occasion as he sat over the board one of the servants came running in from the courtyard.

'My lord Duke, a messenger from Ponthieu. He asked immediate audience. He says it is news of the utmost importance.'

'Bring him in,' said William.

The messenger came; he bowed hastily and said: 'My Lord, Harold, Earl of Wessex, has landed in Normandy.'

'By God's Splendour,' cried the Duke.

'He is the prisoner of Count Guy. It seems he was shipwrecked off the coast of Ponthieu and the Count is now holding him for a ransom.'

'Harold, Earl of Wessex...here in Normandy!'

Matilda had risen, her eyes brilliant.

'He must be brought to me without delay,' said William.

The messenger hesitated and the Duke went on: 'Come, tell me. Do not fear. What has your master said?'

'He is holding the Earl of Wessex for a ransom.'

William laughed, a harsh laugh which his subjects and his children had learned to dread.

'A ransom, eh? The Count of Ponthieu was never a good vassal of mine. The Earl of Wessex here in Normandy and ⸱⸱⸱ prisoner by one of my vassals.' He looked at Matilda. ⸱⸱⸱ es were veiled. 'I will have a message for you to take

166

to your master,' went on William. 'You have ridden far and need refreshment. You shall be given this and a fresh horse.'

When the man had gone William cried: 'What great good fortune!'

'You must bring him here. We must entertain him. We must keep him here until we have his promise not to oppose you.'

'You speak my thoughts.'

They smiled at each other.

'How did he come to be shipwrecked off our coast?'

'I would guess,' said William, 'that he was on a voyage to your father.'

'For what purpose?'

'It may have been to negotiate with me through him for the return of Wulfnoth and Haakon. Edward must be growing feeble and Harold wants no hostages here.'

'So he would wish my father to bargain with you?'

'It seems reasonable. Don't forget your father is the father-in-law of his brother, Tostig. I wish that marriage had never taken place.'

'Well,' said Matilda, 'we have him here. The first step is to bring him to you. Let him be your *guest* '

'As soon as the messenger is refreshed he shall ride back to Ponthieu with my orders.'

'I never trusted Guy of Ponthieu.'

'Not I. But since he rebelled against me and I forced him to swear fealty he can do nothing but obey.'

'If he does not,' added Matilda, 'methinks it could go ill with him.'

'Let us hope he realizes that as well as you do.'

The messenger, refreshed, rode back with William's orders that Earl Harold was to be brought with all speed to Rouen where he would be the guest of the Duke of Normandy.

It seemed however that Guy of Ponthieu had not learned his lesson. The messenger came back with yet another communication. The Counts of Ponthieu had always considered that what was thrown up on the shores of their estates belonged to them. The Count realized that this particular piece of flotsam was somewhat valuable and in view of this he was asking a large ranson. Whether this was paid to him by Harold's family or the Duke of Normandy mattered not to him. All he asked was his dues.

Such a reply was enough to infuriate William. He was ready to march on Ponthieu. It was Matilda who restrained him.

She signed to him to dismiss the messenger and, knowing that her opinion was always worth considering, William did so.

'Harold must believe himself to be a *guest*,' she insisted. 'If you are ready to go to battle to take possession of him he will realize how eager you are to have him here and that he is more prisoner than guest. Nay, he must come here and we will show him friendship. We must have banquets and sports for him and while he is here we will discover what is happening in England—how long Edward is likely to live and how much support Harold has in England. You might even persuade him to be your vassal.'

'Persuade him?'

'Gently at first. I can be very persuasive.'

'I shall settle Ponthieu in my own way.'

'I pray you, don't have fighting over this matter—only as a last resource. Threaten Ponthieu but at the same time give him an opportunity of extricating himself gracefully. Offer him a choice. If he insists on holding Harold you will burn down his castle, take from him what he has and punish him with death. Let him give up Harold and you will reward him. You will pay the ransom and you might even give him certain lands in addition to what he holds already. This is the way to do it. You may be sure he is trembling in his shoes now, having incurred your wrath. He will think he has come out of the matter most happily.'

'There is wisdom in this,' said William, realizing that Matilda was right.

In a very short time a message came from Ponthieu. Earl Harold had been released and the Count with Harold and his retinue was setting out to meet the Duke.

Unable to curb his impatience William rode out with a glittering cavalcade to meet Harold.

In a field of Picardy they came face to face. William was somewhat dismayed by the sight of a man who for some time had been very often in his thoughts. He had expected a replica of Alfred and Edward Atheling. Far from it. This man was every inch—and there were a good many inches for Harold was almost as tall as William—a warrior. That ' as extremely handsome there was no denying. His was nd of face which demanded attention and held it. His

168

golden hair glistened in the sun; his eyes were deep blue, his features finely cut; his entire bearing charming. He must be some forty years of age, William calculated, but he looked younger than William. He lacked William's bulk, being very slender. William, although not exactly fat, was showing signs of a corpulence to come. His robe was embroidered. William thought grimly, Matilda will be interested in that. The Saxons were noted for their needlework. On Harold's wrists were gold bracelets and there were rings on his fingers. Noticing these ornaments William reminded himself that Harold was a seasoned warrior for all his finery.

'Well met,' said William. 'And welcome to Normandy.'

Harold thanked the Duke for his hospitality.

William threw a glance at the Count of Ponthieu, and said: 'We must make up for your harsh reception.'

He had since heard that Guy de Ponthieu had kept Harold in a dungeon. Well, as Matilda said, perhaps that was not such a bad thing for now he would the greater appreciate the kind hospitality of the Duke.

'I am glad to find the Duke more chivalrous than his vassals,' said Harold.

William cast a cold look at Guy and invited Harold to ride beside him.

'The Duchess was horrified when she heard of your treatment,' William told him. 'Pray do not judge Normandy by some of our churls.'

'Such rustics, alas, exist in all countries,' replied Harold. 'It could well have happened that had you, my lord, been washed up on our shores, some lout might have imprisoned you in a dungeon.'

'Happily we may dismiss that unfortunate beginning of your visit from our minds. We shall have much to talk of. Recently your King gave me great hospitality in his country; now I am going to endeavour to do the same for you in mine. Let us spur our horses. The Duchess will be impatiently awaiting our arrival.'

* * *

Something exciting was happening. Adelisa knew it. The smell of roasting venison filled the castle. It often did but there was a difference today. There was such a bustle everywhere, and Father had ridden off with a band of important people and Mother was excitedly awaiting his return.

Important visitors there often were but this was something even more.

Adelisa loved to watch from a window the comings and goings to the castle. Sometimes a messenger came, travel-stained, his horse sweating. That meant important news. There had been such a coming a few days ago and now whatever was going to happen was a result of it.

Constance and Adela kept asking questions. Cecilia, who was a little self-righteous, thought they should wait until they were told what was happening and not watch from windows and listen at doors. Adelisa supposed she was right but the temptation to discover was too great to be resisted.

'There will be feasting today,' said Adelisa; 'and then the minstels will play and there will be stories told down there. How I wish that I could be there.'

It was difficult to settle to lessons. Even the familiar stories which she liked to hear over and over had little charm for her. There was too much excitement in the air.

'There is something special about this visit,' said Adelisa. 'I know it.'

'You will have to wait and see,' said Cecilia, 'and I shall pray that the visitor will be someone good and not someone who is going to plague our father so that he has to ride away to punish people.'

'Listen,' said Adelisa. 'They are coming.'

That exciting sound of horses' hoofs? The trumpet calls! This meant important arrivals. The grooms were waiting to receive the horses. Their mother was waiting in a low-cut gown that flowed gracefully to her feet; one thick golden plait over her left shoulder, the other hanging down her back, a veil covering her head and a glittering ornament holding it in place. And then their father rode into the courtyard with their guest. Adelisa gasped. Never had she even seen such a beautiful being. Thus had she imagined the gods and heroes who had figured in her stories.

This man who rode beside her father was not so much a prince as a god. The sun made a golden halo of his hair; he was so beautifully clad in his embroidered robe; tall, slender, smiling.

He must be one of the heroes stepped out of her stories but never had she imagined one as beautiful as this.

Adelisa was bewitched.

                              *   *   *

She crept out of bed and hoped her sisters would not
hear. She must peer down into the hall where they would be
feasting. She must see him, hear him. He had spoken to her
father. His voice matched the rest of him. It was soft and
musical. How undistinguished everyone was compared
with him, even her own father of whom everyone was in
awe. They were earthly; he was heavenly. Could he be
really flesh and blood? Could there be such beauty on the
earth?

Her parents were excited by him. She had never seen
them so pleased with any of their guests. She was glad. It
would be unfitting for anyone not to pay him the homage
his beauty demanded.

She retreated up the stone stair which circled as it
ascended. She dared not be seen. She dreaded her father's
anger as they all did, even Rufus, although he pretended
not to; and even Robert, although he pretended even more.
Richard of course would never incur it.

Now even if she could not see she could listen and
perhaps from the sound of voices identify that sweet one.

She crept back to bed and dreamed of him.

She could not attend to her lessons. Whenever he rode
out, as he did often with her father, she was at the window.

Once her mother found her there. Her shoulder was
caught in a firm grip. Adelisa was as much afraid of her
mother as she was of her father. She was unsure of her,
even more than of her father. His anger was terrible and
fierce and punishments were meted out for disobedience
and wrong conduct but the children were aware of why they
displeased him and they could avoid that displeasure.
Their mother was not so easy to understand.

Now she said: 'Ha! what do you here? You are always
prying at our guest.'

A hot blush crept into Adelisa's cheeks. Then she had
been observed!

Matilda caught her ear and pinched it.

'It would seem to me that you have a high fancy for Earl
Harold.'

'I . . . I thought him good to look upon.'

'You are not alone in that, child. He is one of the
handsomest men most of us have ever seen. Your father is
very happy to have him with us.'

Adelisa looked pleased.

                                171

'Why, he has bemused you! You have begun early, my daughter, in giving your affections to men.'

'Only to this one, Mother."

That made Matilda laugh and again Adelisa was not sure whether she had pleased her mother or whether she was in disgrace.

'He is a mighty man in his own country, Adelisa.'

'It is clear,' said Adelisa, unable to stop herself. 'It is only necessary to look at him to see that he is ...'

'A great lord,' supplied Matilda, 'in fact a king.'

'Is he a king?' asked Adelisa excitedly.

'I believe he imagines himself to be ... almost that.' She laughed again. 'Why, Adelisa, I believe that if he offered to ride away with you on his charger you would go. You would leave us all for him.'

Adelisa was distressed and feared that her mother was really angry. The thought of this god riding off with her on a charger was intoxicating bliss; but of course a good daughter should not wish to leave her family.

Matilda pinched the ear a little harder.

''Tis natural,' she said. 'These people are attractive.' A faraway look came into her eyes and it was replaced suddenly by a look of fierce anger. 'They set a high price on themselves, Adelisa, but never forget you are the daughter of the Duke and Duchess of Normandy.'

Her mother left her. There were no threats as to what would happen if she were caught spying again; there was no reproach because she had implied she would willingly ride away with him on his charger.

She was free to indulge her imagination and Harold, Earl of Wessex, continued to fill her thoughts.

*   *   *

In spite of his easy manners, Harold was far from happy. It was an ill fortune which had thrown him up on the coast of Normandy. He did not trust Norman William and he well knew what his ultimate aim was. Harold had set out for the Court of Flanders, there to negotiate for the return of his brother and nephew. How unpredictable were the storms about the coast of England! If he had known he would find himself in Rouen, the honoured guest, which meant the prisoner, of the Duke of Normandy, he would never have set out.

His dignity had been outraged by his treatment at the hands of Guy of Ponthieu and considerably restored by William the Duke; but he knew that although he was accorded the respect by the latter which had been denied him by the former, his position at Rouen was no less hazardous than it had been at Ponthieu.

The fact was that he was the leading earl of England and that Englishmen were looking upon him as their future king and that William of Normandy believed that crown would be his by right on the death of Edward. The lavish hospitality, the friendly smiles of the Duke and his wife did not deceive him at all. He was wary, waiting for the outcome of this visit and wishing with all his heart that he was on the high seas bound for home.

Edith had tried to persuade him not to come. The mother of his children, Edith Swanneshals, which meant 'Edith of the Swan neck', had been faithful to him for many years and she was his wife in everything but name. No woman could have been more faithful and more beloved; their sons and daughters were his beloved family and he could rely on them all, Godwin, Edmund, Magnus, and his girls Gunhild and Gytha and even the young baby boy little Ulf. The longing to be with Edith and his family was great. When Edward died and he had the crown, Edith would be as his Queen and Godwin should follow him to the throne. That was his dream; but this ambitious and powerful Duke dreamed also. And what went on in that subtle mind while William behaved as though he were an honoured guest?

And Matilda? She was even more of an enigma. The Duke often left him with his wife. Why? Was he hoping he would indulge in some indiscretion? He could not understand what these two were planning although he knew that their ultimate motive was to rob him of the crown of England.

This he was determined they should not do. Before he had died so suddenly at the King's table his father Earl Godwin had said to him: 'Harold my son, I have been King of England in all but name. But you shall wear the crown. This is what I have striven for beyond aught else. My son to be King of England.'

He *would* be King of England and no one must be allowed to stop him. His brother Tostig had always been jealous of him. He would have to watch Tostig, for where he was there would be trouble; but the people wanted him for

King and when Edward died—which must surely be soon—he was going to rule England.

But in the meantime he was a prisoner in the hands of the Duke of Normandy and his first concern was to extricate himself from the friendly but firm hands of the Duke and return to England where he must be ready when the moment arrived.

The Duke wished to show him Normandy; they hunted together; in the castle they talked of their battles and they worked them out on the table. Harold showing how he had defeated the Welsh, William giving an account of his battles against the French. Pleasant days and companionable evenings, but Harold was restive and uneasy, and most of all perhaps when he was left with Matilda. William retired early. He was a man who was wide awake at dawn when most other men were drowsing in their beds, but at an early hour in the evening he would wish to sleep. Harold would be invited to sit with Matilda and those evening sessions were a mystery to him. She would sit opposite him, leaning forward to show finely formed breasts, her long hair often released from its plaits. She was an attractive woman and he was as susceptible as most; he was yearning for the swan-necked Edith and he knew of course that there was some deep-rooted and detrimental motive in Matilda's mind.

Matilda enjoyed these sessions. She was attracted by Saxons. They had a quality which appealed to her. He reminded her in a way of Brihtric. Not only was there a similarity in these Saxons but they were both reluctant to accept the friendship she was offering; and while they acknowledged her to be an attractive woman they both made it clear that their affections were not free.

Not that she wished to indulge in any entanglement with Harold. She grew cold at the thought of William's anger. Moreover what if there was a child? How could a bastard be introduced into the family of Normandy? No, she had William's interests at heart and this man was vital to them. She was as interested in his downfall as William was, but that did not prevent her enjoying the intrigue she was building up between them.

She was attracted to his undeniable good looks and his fair beauty did appeal to her. The soft-voiced Saxon tongue was musical; the Normans did in truth seem rough by comparison. She hated the Saxons too because they would

174

always remind her of that humiliating interview with Brihtric. After all these years she could remember it vividly when anything happened to recall it. And this man with his fair looks and soft voice reminded her of Brihtric.

Now as she bent towards him she said: 'How glad I am that you stay and keep me company.'

'It is a great pleasure,' replied Harold.

'You Saxons have such beautiful manners.'

'I am glad we please you, my lady.'

'I cannot tell you how happy we were when we heard you were in Normandy.'

The lifting of the eyebrows, the lilt in the voice—there was something mischievously malicious about them.

'They will be expecting me to return ere long,' he said tentatively.

'Oh, my lord Earl, we are going to protest about that. Having you here pleases us so much. We shall not let you go easily. Depend upon that.'

Said in a friendly voice but the note of mockery was there. Nay, he thought, you will hold me prisoner here and when shall I ever get away?

'I wish you could have seen William's face when he heard that you were in Normandy. Rarely have I seen him express such pleasure.'

'He is a good host.'

'And you are the perfect guest to stay up and entertain the wife of a sleepy husband. Tell me about England. I love to hear of it. It seems so close to us. I wonder if I shall go there one day? How I should enjoy that.'

'You and the Duke must be my guests as I have been yours.'

She nodded slowly.

'I should like our families to be joined. We have come to love you, Earl Harold. Have you noticed I have daughters?'

'I have indeed remarked your fine family.'

'There is nothing like healthy sons and daughters to delight the heart,' she said. 'I remarked to William that I would like to see our families united. He agreed with me. My little daughter Adelisa—oh a child, no more—has fallen deeply in love with you. Oh, but we all have. Yet Adelisa has done so with a candid charm which the young possess. The child thinks you are like a god.'

'I have noticed her. She is a delightful girl.'

'I am glad you think thus highly of her. She will swoon

with delight when she hears. Would it not be agreeable if our family ties were strengthened by this visit of yours?'

'I am many, many years older than your charming daughter.'

'You are a young man. I never saw any to compare in strength and health with you—except perhaps William. But then a wife would think thus in her husband's favour, would she not?'

'I am sure you are devoted to his interests.'

She leaned forward, smiling at him seductively. 'I trust I am his good wife. You have no wife, Earl Harold. No consolation can compare with the pleasures of family life.'

'I know it,' he answered thinking of Edith and the children and the solace he found with them when he was weary.

'My husband would be so happy if you agreed to a betrothal between yourself and Adelisa. I think only then would he be reconciled to losing you because he would know that in truth he was only saying a temporary farewell.'

So it is an ultimatum, thought Harold. Submit to a betrothal and you may go home.

He was excited. Could that really be the implication? If he agreed to take Adelisa would they release him? It might be that William had no designs on the crown of England for himself but was seeking a peaceful compromise by making his daughter Queen of England when the time came.

If this was so there was no reason why he should not be betrothed to Adelisa. Betrothals were not binding; and if by submitting to William's proposal he could get home, then submit he must.

No one at home would consider binding any promise he had made under duress. Nor would he.

* * *

Harold rode beside William into the forest, their falcons on their wrists, the company behind them. Harold enjoyed the exercise as much as William did but he had learned that he must be on guard in the company of the Duke even when they were on some pleasure jaunt. William often chose such times to put a question the answer to which needed a great deal of care.

As they rode through the forest William said: 'The Duchess tells me that you find our daughter charming.'

176

'I find the entire family charming,' replied Harold cautiously.

'But in particular the little Adelisa, my favourite daughter.'

Was that true, or had the child become his favourite because he had seen her as a good bargaining counter?

'A charming child.'

'Children grow up, my lord Earl. And how quickly! Girls are soon marriageable. I should put no obstacle to the marriage.'

'I fear she might.'

'The Duchess tells me you have bewitched her.'

'The Duchess is gracious.'

'She speaks truth. You have an unmarried sister. I would like to see her married to one of our Norman barons. Give her to the one I shall choose and in return you shall have Adelisa. Come, my lord, what say you?'

'I should need to discuss this with my family.'

'My lord, I know well that you are the head of that family. You do not ask your family what you should do any more than I do. Come, tell me you think the plan a good one and we will settle this matter as early as may be. I dare swear it would be necessary for you to go to England to make preparations for these marriages. Well, that is not a bad idea.'

Take Adelisa then in exchange for freedom. What could he say?

William went on: 'I would be generous with you, my lord Earl. I will not deny that you have captivated us all with your gracious manners. My wife finds you enchanting; you have bewitched my daughter; and I feel that you are a man whom I could trust. There are few in the world, alas. It is good when one finds one.'

'You are determined to be gracious to me.'

William leaned forward. 'And will be more so. King Edward is ailing, is he not?'

'He has never been strong.'

'But of late he grows more feeble. It will not be long before he will be in his tomb. That makes me grievous sad for I love the man. Did you know, Harold, that we saw much of each other when I was a boy?'

'I knew that he spent many years at the Court of Normandy.'

'Happy years for Edward. He was grateful to my father

177

and then to me. He is more Norman than English.'

'A fact which does not please the English.'

'But they learned to think highly of him. They think him a saint. Edward the Confessor! Why I hear that he has virtue in his hands and in touching his subjects heals them.'

'He is greatly revered.'

'I was in England not long ago.'

'I remember it well.'

'Then King Edward told me that when he died he would name me as his successor.'

There! It was out. Harold hoped that his expression did not betray him. His indignation was such as to make him choke. He had known this from the moment he had been brought into the presence of the Duke of Normandy but this was the first time it had been put into words.

Harold heard himself speaking and was not quite sure what he said. It was something like: 'The English would not wish for a Norman king.'

'But you are a power in the land. You are well loved, people respect you. They must always respect the wishes of their king. Edward has named me as his successor. Harold, I swear to you that if you will do all in your power to help me to the throne, there is nothing you may not ask me for.'

Harold was silent, and William pretended to take this silence as agreement.

'As soon as Edward dies I shall land in England,' went on William. 'Take Dover Castle and have it ready to deliver into my hands. Do this. Serve me and I promise you shall regret nothing. Your brother and nephew shall return to England. You shall be as my son, for you shall have my daughter.'

Still Harold did not speak. William did not look at him. He acted as though the matter was settled and turned his attention to his falcon.

*   *   *

In the schoolroom there was constant talk of the visitor. None of the children had ever seen anyone quite like him and they knew that their parents were more excited about Earl Harold than they had ever been over any other visitor.

Robert, who rarely spoke to his little sisters, was now boasting about how he acted as page to the guest. This was indeed a sign of growing up. He stood behind his chair and

178

waited on him. Robert as the Duke's heir had been given this task which showed how important the visitor was.

Adelisa could not stop plying Robert with questions. What did he say? What did he eat? Had he told any stories? Had he laughed or sung?

Robert replied that the visitor was different from anyone else who had come to the castle.

'He is more handsome,' said Adelisa.

Robert conceded that. He smiled little, said Robert. He seemed sad, but he was kind to Robert.

'He is always kind,' said Adelisa with conviction.

Richard said that he fancied Lord Harold was longing for his own home.

'How could he be,' demanded Adelisa, 'when we all wish him to stay here?'

'With the greatest ease,' replied Richard with a smile.

Robert and Richard exchanged knowledgeable looks which were infuriating. They implied they knew something which was not for little girls' ears.

Eagerly she gleaned all the information she could and on one memorable day she was dressed in a gown much more beautiful than any she had ever possessed before.

Her mother came to her chamber where the maids were braiding her hair. She smiled and said: 'You look well today, daughter.'

Adelisa smoothed the folds of her gown. 'It is beautiful, my lady,' she answered.

Matilda turned round and examined her critically.

'It's a pity you're so young,' she said. 'Why couldn't you have been born four years earlier?'

'That was a matter for you and my father to decide,' replied Adelisa demurely.

'Ah, so you can speak up for yourself. Come with me. You are to be presented to Earl Harold.'

Adelisa blushed with confusion.

'Oh come,' said Matilda, 'he is but a man. You will have to stop thinking of him as some divine being.'

She gripped her daughter firmly by the arm.

'Now we shall see whether you have learned your lessons. You will curtsy to the Earl and answer the questions he puts to you; and if you do not behave in a becoming manner in every way I myself will whip you.'

'I will do my best,' murmured Adelisa.

'I wish him to find you charming. If he does not, remember, it will be the worse for you.'

'I will try to please him.'

'If you show him you regard him as one of your grandmother Arlette's heroes you will doubtless do that.'

Matilda laughed as though something very amusing had been said and they went into the hall where Harold sat with William.

Harold rose as Adelisa entered.

'My daughter,' said William.

Harold bowed and smiled kindly. Adelisa curtsied with as much grace as she could.

'Our daughter is so overcome by the honour you do her that she is a little shy,' said Matilda.

Harold took her hand and for a few ecstatic moments the most beautiful blue eyes she had ever seen met hers in grave concern.

'You must not be afraid of me,' he said.

'No, my lord,' she breathed.

'For you and I are friends.'

She smiled and all her adoration was in that smile.

'She is by no means ignorant,' said Matilda. 'The Duke has always set a high value on education even for girls. Her Latin is good. Quote some Latin verses, Adelisa, so that Earl Harold may see that you are no dullard.'

Harold held up his hand and said kindly, 'There is no need. I see the intelligence shines from her bright eyes.'

'The Duchess and I will finish our game of chess while you converse together,' said William; and he and Matilda retired to an end of the hall, leaving Adelisa and Harold together.

'They want us to like each other,' said Harold.

'Oh but...I *do*.'

He smiled. 'You are a sweet little girl. I find you charming.'

She thought: I did not know there was such happiness in the world. She closed her eyes. Let this moment go on and on for ever, she prayed.

When she opened her eyes he was smiling at her.

'You are but a child,' he said. 'There are many years before you will be grown up.'

'I am ten years old,' she told him proudly.

He put out a hand and touched her golden hair.

'I am an old man.'

She was indignant. 'Nay,' she said, 'such as you are could never be old.'

'Alas, it is a fate which must overtake us all.'

She shook her head. The gods were never old—they lived for thousands of years and were always strong and beautiful.

He thought her enchanting; nor could he be blind to the adoration she was offering him. Poor little girl. As much a pawn as one of those pieces her father was moving across his chessboard.

'Methinks I shall soon be in my native land.'

'It is England, is it not?'

He nodded. 'It is a beautiful land and I love it.'

'It must be the most beautiful land in the world.'

'To me, yes—as Normandy is to you. It is always so where our native land is concerned.'

'I should like to go to your land.'

'The Duke and Duchess want you to do that.'

She clasped her hands.

'They want us to marry. What would you think of that?'

'Oh!' she said and was silent.

'Of what are you thinking?' he asked.

'That I shall die of happiness.'

He talked then of England, the beautiful land of green fields, of monasteries, golden sands and silver seas, and he spoke as one spoke as a lover.

'One day,' she said, 'you will take me there with you.'

'And if I did?' he asked.

'That would be the happiest day of my life.'

The chess game was over; William and his Duchess came to them as they sat at the table.

'You may go, Adelisa,' said Matilda, and the child rose and curtsied to Harold and then to her parents.

She went to her chamber; she lay on her bag of straw and she saw nothing but the blue eyes, the glittering person of the man she was to marry.

She was as one bewitched. She did not hear when her brothers or sisters spoke to her. She was living in one of the legends which had enchanted her childhood; and the hero of that legend was far more beautiful, far more brave than any other had ever been.

* * *

She had grown up suddenly. She was no longer a child of the schoolroom. She might join the company at the feast.

181

Harold sat on a chair especially placed for him. Robert stood behind it. He was not pleased that he must stand and wait while his younger sister sat. He must hold the dish for Harold; and when the eating was over he must bring the bowl in which the guest washed his hands; he it was who must fill the horn from which Harold would drink, making sure not to dip his fingers into the great wassailing bowl.

And she, little Adelisa, was allowed to share Harold's dish; they drank from the same horn. He smiled at her; he was so gentle and kind although she knew that he was a mighty warrior. Loving him was painful; her heart seemed too big for her body; her eyes often filled with tears, so that she saw his beauty through a mist.

He smiled at her as though he understood and he said she must have the tenderest pieces of the meat because she was of tender years; he would not allow her to drink too frequently, for he said, 'You are too young for over-much wine.' And always he spoke with a gentleness which moved her and yet hurt because she loved him so much.

It was a very important occasion because they had special meats; there were peacocks, swans and pies; and she was aware too that her father and mother were trying to show Harold how grandly they lived.

But he was sad. She knew that, and she wished that she knew too how to make him happy.

* * *

William discussed his plan with Matilda.

'The time has come for the final scene in the drama of Harold's visit to Normandy.'

'All has gone well so far,' agreed Matilda. 'He is betrothed to Adelisa whose devotion he has won; all he has to do now is return to England, send his sister to Normandy and prepare the people to accept you when the time comes.'

'The last is the most difficult to achieve and that is what I am planning now. We are going to Bayeux.'

'I always loved Bayeux,' said Matilda.

'And there he is going to swear in such a way that he will never dare to go against his word.'

'But can you make him swear?'

'What else can he do? He is our prisoner. Perhaps it was as well Guy of Ponthieu gave him a taste of the dungeons. He will not wish to spend the rest of his life here—in exile,

182

when exciting matters are about to break in England.'

'Good luck go with you.'

'We shall all go to Bayeux to witness the scene.'

'That will delight your daughter.'

'At least Adelisa is happy with the arrangement.'

'It would break the child's heart if you took her Saxon from her now.'

'These Saxons are not without their attractions.'

'The men are handsome. I wonder if the women are equally so. In which case I must perforce keep a wary eye on my lord.'

William laughed at her. 'Have you ever had to do that?'

'Oh, you have mingled only with Norman women till this time and been too busy fighting your wars.'

'Rest assured I shall doubtless be busy in England, and as soon as I have put myself on the throne I shall send for you to join me.'

'I shall be there. I have a score to settle with the Saxons.'

'Why so?'

'For taking you from me. Which they will do, I doubt not, for the settling of yourself on the throne will take some time.'

'It may be not. If Harold prepares the land for me it should be an easy matter.'

'Do you think he will calmly hand over that which he wants for himself?'

'When he has given his sacred oath, yes. Remember Edward. He made an oath never to have sexual relations with a woman and he kept that vow even though he married.'

'That was because he did not want to. But, believe me, William, Harold wants that crown as much as you do.'

'Then it is time he swore his oath to give it up.'

That day William said to Harold: 'I want to show you my castle of Bayeux. We will ride there tomorrow. We can hunt on the way.'

Uneasily, at the head of the company, Duke William beside him, Harold rode to Bayeux.

* * *

In the great hall of Bayeux stood a large coffer over which had been laid a coverlet of cloth of gold.

William had commanded that all the nobles and knights

who had accompanied him to Bayeux, with those who lived within ten miles of the town, present themselves and assemble in the hall.

It was an impressive gathering.

When they were there he himself donned his ducal robes, including the circlet of gold which he wore on his head on state occasions, and seated himself on his throne.

He then sent for Harold.

As soon as Harold entered the hall he guessed what was about to happen and inwardly cursed the winds which had thrown him up on the coast of Normandy. He was going to be made to swear to marry Adelisa, he knew. How could he marry such a child? And how valid must an oath be considered which was taken under duress?

What would happen to him if he refused? He had heard stories of the ruthlessness of William of Normandy. He had assessed his character during his enforced stay here. A strong man, a ruthless man, a man who once he had made up his mind to do anything would allow nothing to deter him.

'Welcome, Earl Harold,' said the Duke, as Harold entered the hall.

'Welcome,' echoed the assembly, but the word had none of its usual kindly meaning. There was something sinister about it. Well come from their point of view perhaps, because it had placed him in their hands. And most untimely come for him since their gain must be his loss.

'You have given me certain promises,' went on William, 'and I have summoned this company hither that you may confirm them and swear on oath that which you and I have agreed upon. You will now place your hands above the gold cloth.'

For a moment Harold hesitated. He wanted to turn and run from that hall. It was impossible. He was surrounded. What would happen to him if he refused? The picture of a dungeon rose before his eyes; he thought of the terrible things that could happen to prisoners.

He raised his hands.

'You have promised to help me to the crown of England on the death of King Edward,' said William. 'Swear to it.'

Harold was silent and William said insistently: 'Swear!'

There was no help for it. He was trapped.

'I swear,' he said.

William smiled slowly. This was the important oath. He

184

went on: 'Swear that you will marry my daughter Adelisa.'

'I swear,' said Harold.

'Swear that you will send your sister to Normandy that I may wed her to one of my knights.'

'I swear,' said Harold.

William then signed to two of his men. They came forward and, taking the gold cloth in their hands, drew it off, disclosing a large coffer beneath it. When they opened the coffer Harold gave a gasp of horror for in it had been laid the holy relics of Normandy, the bones of long-dead saints.

It had been a sacred oath. Men tempted fate who lightly swore by such and broke their word.

He was trapped as he had guessed he was from the moment Guy de Ponthieu delivered him into the hands of William of Normandy.

'God aid!' cried William, and the words were echoed throughout the hall.

'Now, to the feast,' said William, his eyes gleaming with purpose. 'Come, Earl Harold, this day our frienship has been sealed.'

The board was loaded on that day. William was in excellent spirits. He was thanking the great good fortune which had washed up Harold on his shores. He had seen his change of colour when the sacred bones had been revealed. He would never dare break a vow which had been made in such circumstances.

Adelisa sat beside Harold. He was sad, she noticed, though as before he left the tenderest of the meat for her.

'I shall go to my home very soon now,' he said.

And she thought that was why he was sad.

* * *

A few days later a brilliant cavalcade left the castle; at the head of it rode the Duke of Normandy and beside him Earl Harold.

They were making for the coast where vessels would be waiting to take Earl Harold back to England.

From the turret Adelisa watched.

This was the saddest day she had ever known. He was going away and she would not see him for a long time. True, she was his affianced wife and her father had said that she would go to England in due course and marry him. But she was so young yet. How many years must she wait before she was his wife? Three perhaps. And who knew what could happen in three years?

How could she live for three years without seeing that beautiful face?

A terrible foreboding of evil had come to her. It was that she would never be happy again.

Her sister Cecilia came to her and stood beside her at the window.

'It is no use looking further,' she said. 'You can see nothing now.'

Adelisa turned to her pale-faced sister, who was so unlike the rest of the family, being quiet and serious, stern and critical.

Adelisa could not resist saying: 'Oh, Cecilia, I am so unhappy.'

'Because he has gone? How worldly you are, Adelisa!'

'Is it worldly to love?'

'To love anyone but God, the Virgin and the Holy Church, yes. You must pray to be delivered of your sins. Come, kneel with me.'

Adelisa shook her head. 'I can see only him,' she said.

'You pity yourself, Adelisa. Others have trouble. What of Earl Harold's brother Wulfnoth? He has lost his cousin Haakon who was with him since he was brought as hostage to Normandy and has now gone home. He will be sad too, for he has lost one he must have loved even as you have.'

'He lost his cousin, I have lost Earl Harold. Oh, Cecilia, did you ever see one so beautiful?'

'I am not concerned with the beauty of men, but of God.'

Adelisa went on: 'But he will come back to me. He has sworn an oath.'

'He will never dare break it,' said Cecilia, 'because he has sworn on the bones of dead saints. If he broke that vow a terrible fate would overtake him.'

'He would never break his vows,' said Adelisa proudly. 'He will come back to me.'

But she could not shake off the terrible foreboding of evil.

* * *

Each day Adelisa looked from the turret. A messenger would come from England to take her back with him. Often

186

when young girls were betrothed they went to the country of their future husbands. She thought of leaving her brothers and sisters, her father and mother, and was sad; but when she thought of the great joy of being with Harold how happy she was!

One day, he will come, she assured herself; she must believe it. It was the only way in which she could bear her life.

* * *

The Duke and the Duchess waited every day for the news of Edward's death.

'I must be ready as soon as the news comes through,' said William.

'And as soon as you are settled there I shall follow,' Matilda assured him.

When she reproved Adelisa she would say with a half smile: 'You will have to behave better when you are Earl Harold's Countess.'

That was the day Adelisa was living for and the stitches in her embroidery became smaller and neater because, as she told herself, none but the best of wives would be good enough for him.

There had been no word from Harold since his return.

'Doubtless,' said William, 'he is considering the vows he has made.'

'And doubtless wishing he had not made them,' added Matilda.

'He will know it is no use regretting what is done, though he will be cursing the day he was thrown up on our shores.'

'He has got himself a doting little wife for his adventure. I wonder how he has explained that to the swan-necked lady and her bastards. I'll swear he promised his sons by her that they should follow him to the throne, bastards though they may be.'

'It so happens that bastards sometimes inherit from their fathers.'

She laughed up at him. 'With what excellent results we have seen. When you sail for England I shall follow all with the greatest interest. l have decided that the only way I can possess my soul in quiet is to work in tapestry of all that happens. I have started it here in Bayeux, which is the proper place to work it I think, because it was here that

187

Harold swore his oath. I have had the shipwreck designed and his swearing of the oath and have started to work. It will keep me occupied; while you are doing great deeds I shall record them and in my own way contribute something.'

'You have contributed already, my love. I often feel that without you I should have been but a pale shadow of myself.'

'An admission, William of Normandy, of which I shall doubtless remind you from time to time.'

There came news from England.

There was trouble; and, as it had so often happened, this came through Tostig. Tostig was a man who could not be ignored; he was rebellious, hot-tempered but at the same time managed to be lovable. Matilda's sister Judith was his devoted wife; Tostig's own sister Editha, who was the Queen of England, loved him dearly and he was said to be her favourite brother; even the King, who appeared to have little deep feeling for any human being, favoured Tostig.

One who must regard him with some suspicion was Harold, for clearly an ambitious man such as Tostig would have his eye on all that Harold believed should be his.

Tostig would naturally be thinking of the crown of England.

He had ruled Northumberland for ten years; but he was not popular there. Tostig belonged to the south of England and northerners did not care for southerners. The north had felt more strongly the influence of the Danish invaders; the south was Saxon and Tostig was the grandson of a Saxon cowherd. This was held against him and his reaction was one of brutality. Determined to have his way, he was not a man to be crossed; he imposed heavy taxes on his people and they were constantly seeking a way of deposing him.

Tostig often absented himself from Northumberland and on one of these occasions rebellion broke out. The rebels were successful and declared Tostig an outlaw; they then invited Morcar, the younger brother of the Earl of Mercia, to become Earl of Northumberland.

Tostig immediately appealed to the King who hated being involved in trouble and who promptly offered the matter to Earl Harold to set right.

Tostig was all for war with Mercia but Harold cautioned him and suggested that the differences between Morcar and Tostig be talked over at the Witan. The result of this was that Morcar was declared Earl of Northumberland and Tostig exiled.

'Traitor!' cried Tostig to his brother.

Harold wearily replied that this was the decision of the Witan and not his.

'You incited my people to revolt against me,' declared Tostig.

'Why should I?'

'You know,' cried Tostig; but he dared not say that he and his brother were quarrelling over the crown of England while King Edward still lived.

There was nothing Tostig could do. He was branded as an outlaw, so with Judith and his family he left for the Court of Flanders to take refuge with his father-in-law.

'So,' said William to Matilda, 'your father has guests once more.'

'I will ask Judith to come here,' replied Matilda. 'I may discover from her what is going on at the King's Court.'

'Here is a tangle,' said William. 'For Tostig will know that Harold has sworn to stand aside for me.'

'That makes three of you with your eyes on the crown,' said Matilda. 'And Tostig has not sworn on the relics' bones.'

'It is Harold whom I feared.'

'And do no longer.'

'I shall be watchful of that gentleman, never fear, until I am on the throne.'

* * *

The year 1066 was about to begin.

'Why,' said William, 'I remember the King of England told me that he was born at the turn of the century. He must be in his sixty-sixth year. He cannot live much longer.'

'Judith writes to me from Flanders,' said Matilda. 'She tells me that the King had always favoured her husband, and that the fact of his exile gave him great sorrow. He had aged in the last weeks before they left, according to Judith, and he was already an old man.'

'His death is imminent,' said William. 'I am certain of it.'

Christmas had passed and it was January. Winter was the time for the hunt. When the bushes were white with hoar frost the short days must be enjoyed to the full.

Waiting was tedious; there was nothing for breaking the tension like the joy of the hunt. Always it had been so with William; he liked to be in the midst of hunters with the dogs straining at their leashes, the horses pawing eagerly on the hard ground, the falcons waiting to pounce on their prey, to feel the keenness of the winter air—all this exhilarated him. For a few hours there was nothing but the hunting of the quarry. He ceased to think of what might be happening in King Edward's palace and whether Harold would attempt to break his vows.

The day before, one of his foresters had brought a bow to him, such a bow as he had not seen before.

'Only a man of great strength could bend such a bow, my lord. Thus have I made it for you.'

He took the bow. He bent it to the applause of those who stood round. He would try it out the next day.

Others tried the bow. It seemed it would bend for none but William. He was in a good mood.

So now he was trying his bow in the forest while his followers looked on with admiration. The hunt was about to begin.

Young Robert and Richard were of the party. Never did William look on his eldest son without deploring the shortness of his legs. It was even apparent when he was on horseback. He was small and would never look like the Normans who were noted for their height and their long legs.

'Let me try the bow, Father,' said Robert.

William handed it to him knowing full well that he could not bend it. It would teach him a lesson. He was a stripling yet and it would do him good to learn that he was not capable of doing what his father could.

'Ha, Robin Curthose,' said William, 'you are not yet of the age and strength to perform such a feat.'

Richard did not ask to try the bow. Wise Richard who was aware of his limitations. A good hunter though—both boys were that. They would not be his sons if they were not.

William took the bow and tried it again and again.

Those about him said: 'There is only one among us worthy of such a bow.'

Robert scowled. 'I'll do it,' he said. 'Not today but I'll do it.'

He galloped off a little sullenly but he was back almost at once.

190

'A messenger is coming,' he said. 'He is riding like the devil.'

William was tense, the bow forgotten, indifferent to the call of the hunt. A messenger. He knew before the man appeared that he came from England.

He had placed his spies about the English Court and knew what was happening there.

The messenger came into sight; he had clearly been riding hard. He came straight to the Duke and gave him a packet.

William broke the seals and as he read the colour flamed into his face; for a moment anger blinded him so that he could not read the page properly.

Edward had died on the fifth day of January and on that very day Earl Harold had been proclaimed King of England. There had been no opposition to this. The next day he had been crowned.

His oaths had been forgotten. By God's Splendour, thought the Duke, he will regret the day he took the crown.

'The hunt is off,' he cried.

He dug his spurs into his horse and without another word rode back to the castle.

A new hunt was on.

PART TWO

THE CONQUEROR

Harold and Edith
of the Swan's Neck

KING HAROLD OF ENGLAND sat at the feet of the woman he
had loved for many years. Edith Swanneshals was no
longer young but hers was a beauty which age could not
destroy; there was a calmness about her face and the grace
of that beautiful head on that long neck, which had given
the name by which she was known, was as remarkable at
this time as it had been when she was a young girl.

She had been faithful to Harold for many years and he to
her; and now only she could understand the agony of his
mind for she knew what had taken place in the hall of
Bayeux castle and how at night he would awake from
dreams in which the bones he had seen in the coffer rose up
and formed themselves into shapes which threatened him.

'The oath was not binding,' she said comfortingly. 'You
were forced to it. The saints will remember that. What right
had William of Normandy to make you swear away your
heritage and to deceive you into it, too? You did not know
until after you had sworn what the coffer contained.'

'But I swore,' said Harold. 'Oh, why did I get shipwrecked on his coast!'

''Tis done and naught can change it now,' said Edith.
'And you are the King. Did not Edward appoint you?'

There was comfort in remembering that death-bed
scene. Yes, it was to him that Edward had turned. Poor
Edward, was he beset by misgivings? Had he played the
saint better than he had the king? He was deeply disturbed;
he knew well the troubled state of the kingdom. He knew too
that one man and one alone would be accepted as the king,
and that man was Harold. Was he remembering the

promise he had made to William of Normandy—if such promise there had been? It seemed not, for on the point of death his eyes were on Harold.

Harold said to Edith: 'In his last moments he raised his hand and pointed to me and he said so that all present could hear: 'To thee I commend my kingdom.''

'It was his wish and a wise one,' said Edith. 'Who else is fit to govern?'

'William of Normandy?' whispered Harold.

'A Norman! The people will have none of him. Let him rule his own lands. He has a heavy task enough there by all accounts. That should occupy him.'

'You have never seen William of Normandy, Edith.'

'I pray God I never shall. Put him from your mind, Harold.'

'It is not easy to put such a man from one's mind.'

'I picture him,' said Edith. 'Tall, strong.'

Harold nodded.

'Ruthless and cruel. Determined to have his way. Never fear, Harold, we will stand against him.'

'He will come, I know it.'

'Let him come. We'll face it. But first you must rest. Come, let me help you to bed.'

He allowed her to take off his boots. He smiled at her. She comforted him. Then fleetingly he thought of the little Adelisa who had so adored him. He had mentioned the fact to Edith that William had made him promise to marry his daughter, but he had never told her what a pleasant little creature she was—a child of some ten or eleven winters. Her innocence had been charming.

He wondered what she had thought when she had heard that he was breaking his vow not only with regard to the throne of England but also to her.

* * *

By light of day Harold was able to cast off his fears. He was a natural leader who had many times led his armies to victory against great odds. Why should he fear the dead bones of saints and why, as Edith pointed out, should those saints be on the side of William of Normandy who had forced him to swear?

Harold was unanimously acclaimed King by his own

195

people. He was the one they wanted, not some stranger from over the seas.

He gave orders that a grave should be prepared before the altar of St Peter in Westminster Abbey which Edward had just rebuilt and had consecrated, and arranged for the burial to follow the day of the King's death.

It was the Feast of the Epiphany and at dawn the cortège moved from the palace to the Abbey. The coffin was carried by eight gentlemen of the King's household, followed by priests and Benedictine monks and the procession was led by the new king, Harold.

The bells were tolling and the people came from their houses whispering that this was the passing of a saint.

Harold praying for Edward's soul, wondered whether the news had yet reached William of Normandy.

* * *

Harold's first act as soon as the funeral was over was to call the Witan to ask for its support. This was given. He wished his coronation to take place without delay for only when a King was crowned was he recognized as the true sovereign.

Within a few days the ceremony took place, and Harold, the crown of office—a circlet of gold—on his head, walked to the altar where so recently Edward had been buried with royal pomp.

When the moment came for the Archbishop to ask the assembly whether they would accept him as their king, Harold listened eagerly. There was no questioning the enthusiasm of the response. The shout that went up in the Abbey proclaiming their loyalty was fervent enough to please even him.

He wished that William could have been there to hear it.

Harold swore the oath required of him. He would work with all his heart, body and soul for his people. The ceremonial axe was passed to him and the assembly prayed that he would hold the crown of the Angles and Saxons in all honour and govern his people in peace, or should war arise defend them with all his might.

The new King was then anointed and the crown placed on his head.

After the High Mass of consecration the company

repaired to the palace where a banquet awaited them. Harold the King took his place on the dais and Edith sat beside him.

He would have the whole world know that he regarded her as his Queen and he expected all to accept her as such.

The feasting was not as merry as was general on such occasions. The old King was so recently dead, and for Harold it seemed as though a shadowy figure presided over the hall: the irate figure of the Duke of Normandy rattling the bones of long-dead saints.

*   *   *

Harold was realizing that it was not only from Normandy that he must look for trouble. His brother Tostig had always been jealous of him. He had been a favourite of Edward's and had clearly hoped he might have been nominated for the crown. It irked him that he was the younger brother. The fact that he had been driven from Northumbria rankled. It seemed almost certain that he would come in arms against his brother.

The North of England which was Danish in outlook would not willingly accept a Saxon King, and Harold expected trouble from Edwin and Morcar. Trouble from the North; trouble from Normandy; and somewhere in between mischief-making Tostig. Tostig loved drama; he was a born adventurer; it was possible that even more than a crown he wanted an exciting life. It had been so when they were boys. Where Tostig was there was trouble. Brave, courageous, brilliant fighter that he was, he was unpredictable, without loyalty, swaying to whichever side would give the greater excitement which his adventurer's heart craved.

He was married to the sister of the Duchess of Normandy—an ill-conceived match.

Which way to turn? How could he be sure? There was only one thing of which he could be certain and that was that he must be ready to face attack from any direction.

The first threat came from the north. Edwin and Morcar were massing against him. He was ready; but what if while he were fighting in the north, William of Normandy landed in the south?

He called the Witan and put the case to them.

They were behind him to a man. They knew the threat

197

which hung over them from Normandy and were determined with him to have no Norman on the throne. William's reputation was well known. He was one of the most skilled generals in the world; he was ruthless and determined. Spies reported that already he was planning to attack. There must not be civil war in England.

There was a possibility that peace would be kept and Edwin and Morcar turned from enemies to allies. They had a sister.

'I know of her,' said Harold. 'She is the widow of the Welsh rebel chieftain whom I slew in the service of King Edward.'

'A widow, my lord.'

'What of this?' said Harold fearfully, half guessing.

'If you married her, you could win her brothers to your side. It is being said that this is a condition they are asking in return for peace.'

'Marriage!' whispered Harold.

'It is sometimes the duty of kings to marry where they have no will to,' was the answer.

'I must consider this.'

* * *

'Marry this woman,' he cried to Edith. 'The idea is repulsive to me. How can I marry the widow of a man whom I have slain?'

'She seems to be ready to forget that.'

'She! She will hate me. It is her ambitious brothers who would force the marriage.' He took Edith's hands and looked into her well-loved face. 'My only love, my queen,' he said. 'How could I marry this woman?'

'The Witan decided it is necessary.'

'Am I not the King?'

'Kings keep their crowns by the will of the people, Harold.'

'You, to urge me to this marriage!'

'It would be but for form. She would have the title of Queen and her brothers would be placated. It would make no difference to us.'

'That is something I would not tolerate.'

'Let me consider it then. What if Edwin and Morcar strike in the north?'

'Then I shall take an army and defeat them.'

'And William, knowing you are engaged in the north, chooses that moment to land.'

'You echo the Witan, Edith.'

'Because it is clear that this is what could happen. You must marry this woman, Harold.'

'I see that you are right,' he said. 'But what when she is here...in my palace...What then, Edith? What of you?'

One of Edith's great attractions was her placid temperament. It was never more evident than at this moment.

'That is a matter we must deal with when it comes,' she said. 'For the moment our great need is to turn your enemies of the north into your friends.'

The next day Harold announced that he would marry Aldgyth, widow of Gruffydd the King of Wales whom his armies had recently slain during the Welsh rebellion.

* * *

Delay was dangerous, it was decided. Edwin and Morcar hinted that they wanted immediate action. Harold had made promises to the Duke of Normandy which he had not kept. The Earls of the north wanted to see the promises made to them carried out.

In the midst of the preparations Harold's sister Elfgiva died. Some thought this an evil omen as Elfgiva was she who had been promised to Normandy. She was buried quietly lest the idea grow that her death could be construed as some sort of judgement that had grown out of the anger of saints whose bones had not been treated with due respect.

Without further delay Harold was married to Aldgyth.

* * *

There was no question of consummating the marriage. Aldgyth was well aware of his relationship with Edith, and she knew that he had married her because her brothers had demanded it.

But she was the Queen and her place was on the dais beside him. She would never forgive him for making her a widow for, although his may not have been the hand which had slain her husband, it was his men who had done so.

The marriage had been forced upon them both, and she,

no more than he, wished it to be anything but in name only.

She eyed the beautiful Edith Swanneshals with disdain, although she did feel a pang of envy for that incomparable beauty; and it had to be admitted that Harold with his fair good looks and Edith with her calm beauty were as handsome a pair as could be seen through the country.

As for Harold, the crown had brought him little joy. Often he brooded on how different everything might have been if he had never been shipwrecked on the coast of Normandy. If he had made no promises to William he would have been free to turn his attention to the north, and subdue Edwin and Morcar instead of having to placate them with his distasteful marriage.

There came news from William.

It was with trepidation that Harold broke the seals.

William wrote reasonably. He knew that Harold could not have forgotten any oath taken with such solemnity and sworn over the dead bones of saints. He understood how, on the death of Edward, he had been put into the position which he now held.

William was ready to forgive if Harold would immediately put right the wrong he had done. It could be simply arranged. He would send his sister to Normandy that the marriage William had arranged for her should take place; his own affianced bride Adelisa should come to him. He would fortify Dover castle on William's behalf and publicly renounce his crown.

On receipt of this command Harold cried out: 'I'll not be dictated to by the Norman bastard. What right has he to the throne of England? No greater one than mine and I have been elected by the Witan and I have their pledged support.'

He answered William somewhat jauntily, implying that he had no intention of complying with any of the demands save one. If William so wished he would send the dead body of his sister to Normandy.

He was now firm in his intention. He would fight to the death to hold what he had.

*   *   *

At the Easter celebration Harold appeared in public in his crown—a handsome figure of a man, kingly in his bearing. The people cheered him. How different from pallid Edward! He was a great commander, a just man; his love for Edith of the beautiful swan-neck pleased their romantic notions; his marriage with the less attractive Aldgyth showed them that he would put duty before pleasure.

They were pleased with their King, although rumours reached them that across the channel the fierce Duke of Normandy was seething with rage.

Then a terrible fear came to the nation for there appeared in the sky what many of them believed to be a sign of God's anger. A flaming body—as big as the moon—with a long tail appeared in the sky.

People stood about looking up at it, expecting the skies to open and God to appear in his wrath.

They were sure that God was angry.

Edward was dead and there was a new King of England—a King who had sworn away his kingdom on the bones of saintly men.

Was this why God was angry?

In the north it was seen. It was a warning, said the men of the north. Old men said that their grandfathers had seen it blazing in the sky and it was always followed by invasion. The Danes had come in their hordes and ravaged the homesteads; they had plundered the riches of the land and taken the women. It was a sign of God's anger.

It hung over Westminster, said some. It was God pointing to what had angered him. It was God's fingers, some said. It was a sword, said others.

It meant that there would be war and a disaster in the land.

The men of the north said it was a sign to them to rise for the comet hung over the north.

In the south they said it meant disaster for the King for it hung over the palace. In Normandy they were saying it was a good omen because it hung over Normandy and it was God showing the Duke the way.

Its presence was interpreted by people according to their mood and the fact that the Normans regarded it as a sign of God's approval and the English as a sign of his anger was an indication of the mood of the people.

At night as soon as darkness fell the comet blazed in the sky.

Harold and Edith watched it from the window.

'What does it mean?' asked Harold. 'What can it mean?'

'It *is* like a sword,' said Edith. 'It could mean that William will come and you will defeat him.'

How she comforted him! He smiled at her and thought of Aldgyth whom he had married; and he thought of his vow to William of Normandy and said in anguish: 'Oh God, what have I done?'

He looked at the comet. 'Go away,' he said. 'I beg of you go away.'

And after seven days and nights had come and gone the comet was no longer there. But men and women continued to talk of it.

Preparations

THE comet hung over the castle of Rouen.

'By God's Splendour,' cried the Duke, 'this is a sign. God is on our side. He has set a sword in the sky as sign. I am to go and take that which was vowed to me.'

Harold's insolent reply had come to him. His sister was dead, but he had married Aldgyth; and he had been crowned King of England.

He must show Harold that he, William, was not to be crossed and that he would not stand by while others took that which had been promised to him.

He shut himself into his chamber; he wanted no one to interrupt him; not even Matilda. She respected his mood for she knew that his head was full of plans.

He was going to cross the sea and conquer England but he needed ships and men; and he needed to know that the whole of Normandy stood with him.

He must state his case to a council of his vassals; he must tell them that he needed their help. They had sworn fealty; now was the time he could demand it.

To demand was not wise. There had been trouble enough in Normandy. What he needed was a united Normandy even as Harold needed a united England. Trouble on the home front could destroy them both.

He thought first of men whom he could trust. There was his Seneschal William Fitz-Osbern, son of that faithful man, who so many years ago had been done to death in the bed in which they had lain together. There were his two half-brothers, Arlette's sons by Herlwin, Robert, who was now Count of Mortain, and Odo who was the Bishop of Bayeux.

He summoned these three men to him and told them that he was determined to take England and he wanted every influential baron and knight in Normandy behind him.

'They will need to be persuaded,' said the Bishop.

'Persuaded to do their duty!'

'Ay, persuaded,' added Odo.

'They must be reminded of their oaths of fealty.'

'Which,' pointed out the Bishop, 'applied to the defence of Normandy.'

'Come,' said the Duke impatiently, 'are they such dullards that they cannot see what these could mean to them?'

The three men looked at each other and William said to Fitz-Osbern, 'I charge you with this duty. You will summon them all and make clear their duty to them.'

The Seneschal said he would do what was required of him.

'And with all speed,' added William. 'I grow impatient.'

Fitz-Osbern forthwith summoned a meeting of the barons. They knew for what purpose they had been called together. Harold of England had sworn a sacred oath to their Duke which he had flouted. He had promised to help him to the throne of England and had taken the crown for himself; he had agreed to marry the Duke's daughter and had now married another woman. The honour of Normandy was at stake.

'The honour of the Duke,' said one of the barons, 'which is not necessarily that of Normandy.'

'Are you such fools that you cannot see what great good this would bring to us?' demanded Fitz-Osbern. 'There would be lands and riches, for naturally the spoils of the conquered land would fall to those who had helped the Duke to obtain it.'

'Death could also be our reward,' said another.

The general opinion was: 'We have pledged to support the Duke in any attack on Normandy; we have taken no oath to conquer foreign lands.'

When the Duke heard this answer he was enraged. But he would not allow his temper to take charge of him. He needed all his astute statesmanship and nothing was achieved in anger that could not be better done through calm.

He visited his shipyards. He said that work must go on

apace. He was going to need ships and of the best within the next few months.

It was clever Odo who had the idea.

'Your vassals have refused to assist you in assembly. They stood together as one man. "No foreign adventure," they said. But if you were to ask them singly, would their answer be the same? Invite them to come to you, flatter them, tell them you need their help, tell them that you know them for the most reliable and worthy of your vassals. Say to each separately: "My friend I cannot do without help." Promise them spoils. They say the Saxon women are very fair. Try this, William. I think it would be more successful than asking for loyalty and service in an assembly.

William saw the wisdom of this.

It was surprising how successful Odo's strategy proved to be.

* * *

Matilda spent a great deal of her time at Bayeux working on her tapestry.

She delighted in it. There on her canvas blazed the comet. There was Harold taking his oath over the bones of the saints; there was Edward on his death-bed pointing to Harold. She brooded as she worked. She could not go into battle; all she could do was help her husband whenever possible and re-create the story in her stitches. She had caused a ship to be built which would be the first of the fleet which sailed to England. She had not told William yet; the ship was to be her gift to him; she was going to name her *Mora* and she should be a ship the like of which had never been seen before and have the honour of carrying William to England.

She laughed to herself when she thought of that mighty enterprise. He was going to conquer. She could not conceive otherwise. She would stay at home working her tapestry, acting as Regent here in Normandy while he went ahead with the conquest of that country.

She smiled secretly. Somewhere in England a man of her own age would be thinking of Normandy, perhaps of her. He would be saying: 'Matilda of Flanders will become Queen of England. Does she remember how I refused to marry her?'

No, Master Brihtric, I do not forget. Nor shall I ever

forget till I have taught you what it means to humiliate a Queen.

William was preoccupied with his advisers. She did not disturb him nor ask him anything he did not wish to tell. But he talked to her, though perhaps not as much as he once had. The children had in some measure come between them; it was Robert who had done this. Robert was critical of his father and criticism was something William had never liked, and that it should come from his own family was intolerable to him. Robert was reckless and mischievous. He liked to taunt his father just as far as he could without bringing his wrath down on his head. Matilda often laughed inwardly to hear the little shafts Robert sent in his father's direction.

'Such a pair as we are could never have expected a peaceful brood,' she often told herself and William.

William's reply was: 'I expect respect from all my vassals including my own son.'

Robert would not like to hear himself referred to as a vassal. He already fancied himself as Duke of Normandy.

He had said only the other day: 'Why, Mother, if my father conquered England he would be its King, would he not?'

'He would indeed.'

'Then he cannot be a King and a Duke, can he?'

'Your father could manage them both very comfortably I doubt not.'

'If he is a King, then I should be Duke of Normandy. He cannot govern two lands at the same time.'

'You might be considered over young to govern,' Matilda reminded him.

'At thirteen?'

'A great age my son!'

'You mock.'

'Only with love.'

'Mother, you would always be on my side?'

'Are you not my son?'

'But *he* is your husband.'

'You talk as though it must be a matter of taking sides.'

'So must it be ... in time.'

'Nay, you will work together.'

But she knew it would not be so and something in her mind exulted. She had always loved excitement and

206

conflict. Somewhere at the back of her mind she had been wondering for a long time whether her later years might not be enlivened by the pull of loyalties.

The two who touched her feelings more than any others: her admired husband, her beloved son! She would be interested to see which of them she loved the best. If it were a matter of taking sides, which would she take? Time would show her.

*　　*　　*

There was excitement at Bayeux. Tostig had arrived with Judith and their children. His eyes were alight with the desire for adventure.

Matilda received the family with delight. William guardedly.

Tostig was an attractive creature, Matilda decided. These Saxons often were. While he was closeted with William Judith talked to her, and Matilda had always got what she wanted from Judith.

'What does Tostig hope for?' she asked. 'The crown of England?'

Judith's eyelashes fluttered down and she hesitated just a second or so too long. Did not Matilda remember her gestures from their childhood?

'How could he be? That is for William,' said Judith.

'Indeed yes, sister. But that does not stop Tostig's hoping.'

'He has come to offer his help to William.'

Matilda nodded. She knew what was in Tostig's mind. Let William conquer England and then some sly piece of treachery and there would be Tostig waiting to snatch the crown.

'Against his own brother?' asked Matilda.

'Tostig has always hated Harold.'

'He has been jealous of his elder brother doubtless.'

'Harold was his father's favourite. Harold could do no wrong.'

'By all accounts he is the people's favourite. Poor Tostig was outlawed, was he not?'

'It was all due to that pair of traitors, Edwin and Morcar.'

'Who are now Harold's brothers-in-law. How complicated these family relations are! Well, Judith, life with Tostig must be enthralling. You can never be sure where you will be.'

'Tostig is a great man, Matilda,' said Judith earnestly. 'One day...'

Matilda held up her hand. Don't say it, Judith, she thought. You will regret it. In any case there is no need to say it. It is as clear to me as daylight. Tostig wants to be King of England; and that, my dear Judith, is a position which God has reserved for my William.

*   *   *

In the quiet of the bedchamber she talked to William. 'What of Tostig?'

'I don't trust him.'

Matilda drew a deep breath. 'I knew there was no need to warn you.'

'So you have sounded Judith?'

'Poor Judith, she is a devoted wife but scarcely a good strategist. I hope I shall do better for my husband when he leaves me for the conquest of England.'

He took her face in his hands, tender suddenly. 'My dearest love, I constantly ask myself what I should do without you.'

Nay, William, she thought, you have constantly asked yourself nothing these last weeks but how you can begin the conquest of England.

'You would miss me sorely, William,' she said, 'if I were not here. But here I am, your good and patient wife, stitching at her tapestry while she asks herself how she can serve you. I gathered today from Judith that, in spite of his desire to help you to the crown of England, he rather fancies wearing it on his own head.'

'I would not trust Tostig for one moment. He is as treacherous as his brother.'

'Poor Harold, he had little chance to be anything else.'

'He swore to me...'

'Under duress.'

'I believe you have a softness for the fellow.'

'Well, he is a very handsome man and one whom I began to regard as my new son, which he would have been had he taken Adelisa.'

'By God's Splendour how he has tricked me!'

208

As surely, she thought, as you tricked him, my lord.

'What shall you do about Tostig? I gather he has come to offer to fight beside you in the expedition.'

'I am giving him a few ships...nothing of great importance. If he can sail back and harry Harold in the north while we attack in the south, he could be useful.'

She nodded. 'I might have known you would do the wise thing.'

'Come, Matilda, do you fancy yourself as a general?'

'I fancy myself as anything that can serve my lord.'

He smiled at her and gently stroked her hair.

'May God bless you for ever,' he said, his voice tinged with tenderness and even a hint of passion.

But the tenderness was because he could rely on her and the passion was for the ships which were being built and which would carry him to England.

*　*　*

'Why are you always watching the turret?' Cecilia asked her sister. 'For whom are you looking?'

Adelisa turned her frightened gaze on her sister.

'There are always people coming. I wonder who will come next.'

'And you are looking for someone special?'

'I think there will be messages from England. There must.'

'Adelisa, what is wrong with you? You eat so little. You always look so lost and frightened.'

'What is happening, Cecilia, do you know? There is something going on. Our father is often angry. He is alone so much. He cuffed Robert the other day for no great reason. Robert is angry and sullen and said if he were old enough he would join the other side.'

'Robert should be whipped. You know what is happening, Adelisa. Harold the Saxon who came here has broken the vows he made to Father.'

'I don't believe it.'

'Of course he has. Everyone is talking of it.'

'It is a mistake.'

'A mistake! How can that be? Harold has flouted our father. Have you not seen the messengers? Do you not see the black mood our father is in? He will be so until he sails for England and takes the crown from Harold.'

209

'Harold is a king now,' said Adelisa softly.

'He has dared take the crown after promising it to our father.'

'The crown was his,' said Adelisa hotly.

'You had better not let our father hear you say that. It will be every bit as bad as Robert is when he says that he will be Duke of Normandy the moment our father is King of England.'

'I believe Harold will write to our father and explain that there has been a mistake.'

'You are so foolish, Adelisa.'

'I know Harold.'

'You! What did you know of the deceitful Saxon? You should pray more, pray that Father will punish him soon and take back the crown he has stolen.'

'He didn't steal it. It's a mistake. If he promised it to our father...'

'*If* he promised. He swore on holy relics. He will go to hell for that.'

'He will not go to hell. It is others who will go there.'

'Hush! Do you mean our father?'

'Of course I do not.'

'You cannot be the friend of them both.'

'I am Harold's friend,' said Adelisa boldly.

'Then you are a traitor to Normandy.'

'I am going to marry Harold. He is my betrothed. A woman must never be her husband's enemy.'

Cecilia said: 'Have they not told you then?'

'What should they tell me but that Harold has the crown which the King of England gave to him?'

'Have they not told you, Adelisa, that he has taken a wife?'

Adelisa turned pale. 'That is not true.'

'Yes, sister, it is true. He has married the sister of two of his troublesome earls because he was afraid they would make war on him if he did not.'

'How could he? He is to marry me.'

'He could break his vows to you as he has broken them to our father.'

'I don't believe it. I won't believe it.'

'You should pray to the Virgin, Adelisa. You should pray to be saved from your folly.'

'I won't believe it. I won't,' said Adelisa.

She ran from Cecilia and shut herself into the bed chamber she shared with her sisters. She threw herself down on her bag of straw and lay staring at the wall.

It could not be true, could it? He, that godlike creature, that incomparable man, could not break his word to her. He had been so kind to her; she remembered how he had made her have the tenderest pieces of meat; he knew that she loved him. He could not love her as she loved him. How could that be? She was but a young girl, not yet grown up, not beautiful as he was, not clever. She could only adore, but he had shown that he liked her adoration and she had been told she was to be his wife.

It was not true. Cecilia liked people to suffer. She thought it was good for them. Then they prayed and asked God for help and were supposed to be comforted.

But if she lost him, if it were indeed true that he had married someone else and forgotten his promise to her, then there was no comfort. All she would want to do then was to lie on her bed of straw, turn her face to the wall and die.

* * *

'My lady,' she said, 'may I have speech with you?'

Matilda looked at her daughter. How pale and thin the child was! A sudden pity touched her. Was it possible for a girl of such tender years to feel passionate love for a man who must be thirty years her senior? Matilda believed it was.

Poor child, she thought.

She laid aside her needle and drew Adelisa to her.

'What is it?' she said.

'Cecilia has told me that Harold is married.'

'It is true, child.'

The look of tragic horror smote Matilda. But no, she assured herself, children get over these things.

'I don't believe it,' said Adelisa.

'My dear child, he has broken his promises to your father.'

'He was forced to promise.'

'That's true. He was forced to promise to help your father to the crown and to marry you.'

'Then he did not want to do either.'

'Nay, my child, he did not. It was a matter of expediency for him. He promised because he was in your father's power and dared do no other.'

Adelisa did not speak. She could not. There was heavy

211

pain somewhere within her. There was nothing but this pain. She supposed it meant that her heart was breaking.

'Why, child, you are trembling,' said Matilda gently. 'And how thin you have grown. I will send something to make you sleep. Go to your chamber.'

Adelisa shook her head and Matilda drew her into her arms.

'You are but a child,' she said. 'You think you do not wish to go on living. But it will pass. There will come a day when we shall find you a finer husband than the Saxon deceiver could ever have been.'

Still Adelisa did not answer. There was nothing to do now. It was true that she had lost him.

She would die now of a broken heart.

* * *

It was July of that fateful year. The fleet was almost ready. The shipyards had been working day and night and William surveyed his growing fleet with pride and excitement. It was assembled in the estuary of the Dive and his troops were waiting to embark. As soon as a favourable wind arose they would set sail.

There was his pride, his own flagship, the *Mora*, which Matilda had had built in secret, a noble vessel at the prow of which was the figurehead of a leopard, the emblem of the dukes of Normandy. At the stern of the ship was the figure of a child in pure gold holding a horn in one hand and waving a pennant in the other. From the top mast floated a banner embroidered by Matilda with beautiful blue silk on a white background and in its centre a cross of gold.

'You have asked for my prayers,' she had said. 'These you know you have. But the *Mora* is the outward symbol of my devotion to you and your cause.'

'By God's Splendour,' replied the Duke, 'I will sail her to victory and I shall not rest until you are crowned Queen of England.'

'You will succeed,' she told him. 'I could find it in my heart to depict your victory on my tapestry before it has taken place.'

Even William was a little sobered then.

'It is a mighty undertaking,' he told her. 'We shall need all our skill and then with God's help we shall succeed.'

212

And now there was the impatience of waiting. Why did God not send the wind? A waiting army grows restive. William himself was tense; he must continually guard his temper. At times such as this it was more ready to flare up. He must be watchful for enemies. When he looked at those fine ships dancing on the water and could remind himself that many of them had been supplied by his faithful vassals, he could congratulate himself on being fortunate in his subjects.

But the traitors were always lurking. There were few whom a man in his position could trust. He thought of his cousin Guy and what a shattering revelation it had been to find that the companion of his childhood had sought to destroy him—and all because he wished to take William's crown. Men would sell their souls to the devil for a crown.

What of Saxon Harold who had vowed over the relics of dead saints and had broken that vow...all for the sake of a crown! And now he, William, was setting out on his perilous expedition and for that crown, a great crown this one. He would be a King of England; he would found a race of Kings. Richard his son would follow him for Robert should have Normandy. He frowned thinking of Robert. We shall have trouble with that boy, he thought. He has mischief in him. He has none of my qualities. If I did not know Matilda as I do, I would suspect he was not my son.

Richard would be a good and serious king. As soon as he was settled on the throne he would send for Richard. He should come to England and learn the ways of the English. They would accept him all the better for that. Rufus should come too. The girls he supposed would be found husbands. But that was for the future.

Would the wind never come?

He inspected his troops; he inspected his ships. He was aware of the respect of his soldiers and sailors. There was a legend growing around him. He was unbeatable. None could stand against him.

He must preserve that legend. Often what was in the minds of men won their battles more than what was in their hands.

Still, be wary of traitors. Be ever watchful. Remember Guy. Remember but recently Conan, Duke of Brittany. The traitor who had been ready to make war because he knew his Duke was about to engage on a mighty enterprise.

213

Conan's father had been a cousin of William's and like other members of the family believed he had more right to the crown of Normandy than its Duke.

He had said: 'Give me what should be mine by right—the Dukedom of Normandy—or instead of fighting with you for the crown of England I will fight against you for that of Normandy.'

War in Normandy at such a time was unthinkable and it had been necessary to resort to other means of removing an enemy than the sword.

Conan did not long survive that braggart statement. He died suddenly. William knew that a good servant of his—posing as a servant of the Duke of Brittany—had treated his riding gloves with a deadly poison.

Conan's successor had been a wise man. He had offered the Duke of Normandy help in his enterprise.

A happy solution, thought William; but yet another reminder that he must be constantly on the alert.

* * *

At Bayeux Matilda waited for the news that the expedition had sailed. She was uneasy, wondering what would happen if, by some mischance, William did not succeed. She thought of Harold who would be waiting for him when he landed. Beautiful Harold who had won the heart of little Adelisa—and others, she doubted not. They were handsome men, these Saxons. She herself was not indifferent to their charms. A little of the magic of Brihtric lingered on and she had seen something of it in Harold. Saxons, both.

One of these men—Harold or William—might well die in battle. She prayed for William's success of course but she could spare a thought for Harold because he was beautiful and his manners more gracious than those of the Normans, his voice more musical. It saddened her to think of such a handsome man dead or mutilated on the battlefield.

She sighed. Something must happen soon. Before the year was out great events would have taken place. Triumph or disaster. Victory or defeat. Who could say?

The children talked of the enterprise. Robert boasted of what he would do were he in charge of it. He would not have let the wind stop him. Richard said he was foolish and knew nothing of battle or the navigating of ships. But Robert went on boasting.

214

They had better take care, he said, because now father was going he was the Duke.

Richard did not attempt to argue. Richard never wanted to indulge in pointless arguments. Rufus would have been ready to challenge his brother, but Robert in spite of his short legs was bigger than he was.

They saw more of their mother than they did when their father was in the castle. She superintended their education and they were all aware of how she favoured Robert, he most of all for he took every advantage of it.

She had just granted a charter to La Trinité, the Abbey which she had built on the orders of the Pope to expiate her sin in marrying without his consent. There was to be a ceremony of consecration which she would attend with her family. The timing was right. It was good while William was on the brink of embarking to show her piety.

She had another idea. She sent for her daughter Cecilia.

'My daughter,' she said, 'you have long expressed a wish for convent life. Tell me truthfully, do you really wish to shut yourself away from the world?'

Cecilia answered earnestly: 'It is true, my lady. I have already vowed to myself that I wish to dedicate myself to God.

'Very worthy,' said Matilda. 'Tell me of Adelisa. She is very sad at this time.'

'She mourns for the Saxon still,' Cecilia's eyes were scornful. 'She still dreams of him, my lady.'

'Alas, poor child.'

'I have told her to pray.'

'Her affairs cannot be resolved as easily as yours, Cecilia. But it is of you I wish to speak. You know your father is going off on a great expedition which may well change all our lives.'

'I pray for him constantly.'

'Prayer is good but sometimes more than prayer is necessary. My Abbey of La Trinité is to be consecrated and if you have firmly decided to take the veil you can begin your novitiate without delay and it seems to me that there could not be a better time to start than now.'

Cecilia clasped her hands with pleasure and then feeling it might be sinful to be so pleased about something immediately looked serious.

I wish Adelisa's future could be solved so easily! thought Matilda.

So, while William waited for that fair wind, the Abbey of

La Trinité was consecrated. And what a good augury for William's success. His daughter preparing to take the veil. Surely God must be on his side.

* * *

Divine assistance was not readily given.

Oh, that elusive wind!

William chafed against delay. Everything was in order. Matilda would be Regent in his absence. The trusted Lanfranc who had done such good work at Rome and had risen in William's favour ever since, would watch over affairs during his absence.

William had applauded Matilda's suggestion that Cecilia should enter La Trinité and at the same time that Lanfranc should be appointed Abbot of St Stephen's at Caen. This would enable him to work closely with Matilda. With two such deputies William felt safer than he could with any others.

If only the wind would come!

William stood on the shore and invoked the heavens. How puny was man against the elements! There he was, a great soldier who had rarely been beaten in battle. Four hundred sailing vessels and a thousand transports were dancing on the waters, their sails slack, equipped for an expedition on which the mischievous sea would not allow them to embark.

William remembered that his father had once dreamed of conquering England and what had happened? He had set out in great spirits with a fair following wind; then suddenly the mood of the sea had changed and he had been blown back to where he started, his fleet disordered and many lives lost. Before he, William, could defeat Harold he must defeat the sea and as all wise men knew that was an impossible feat. Only if the sea was his ally could he win.

He had to sail across that water over more than twenty miles of treacherous sea that could smile and be gracious and suddenly change its mood. How quickly a wind could bring up to sweep an army to destruction! So his father had found.

'Oh God of battles,' he prayed, 'let this not happen to me. My father died on a pilgrimage, washed clean of his sins. My wife has founded a convent. I have given my daughter to your service. Remember this, O Lord, and calm the seas for me this day.'

But God remained indifferent to his pleas. As a general he knew the dangers of boredom in an army. The families of men who would sail had come to the shore to take their farewell of them. They should have sailed off days ago in a blaze of glory. Instead they waited, the soldiers in their camps, the beautiful ships tossed hither and thither straining at their anchors; and there was a murmuring in the camp.

Why does God not change the wind? Is it a sign that he is displeased with us? Can it be that he is on the side of the man who vowed away his kingdom on the bones of dead saints?

But the waiting went on and each day the tension mounted; each day the misgivings rose.

*   *   *

At last they sailed. There was a great tumult on the shore. The women who had said good-bye to their men were weeping; but even they felt the tension was over. The trumpets sounded; the sails were billowing in the breeze; the expedition had begun.

Alas for the mischievous wind and the unpredictable sea!

As the fleet kept close to the coast it was clear that it would be folly to venture out to sea for the violent wind had risen again and the grey waves dashed over the decks.

There was nothing to do but put back to harbour. They came in at Saint Valéry, there to continue the waiting.

The soldiers disembarked. They set up the camps once more. Depression was rife.

'The expedition is doomed,' it was whispered.

'It is unlucky to start out and turn back.'

'Remember what happened to the Duke's father? Didn't he attempt the same game?'

'This is a sign from Heaven.'

217

The Brothers

ALTHOUGH none chafed as bitterly against the delay as William, he was later to be thankful for the unpredictable winds of Heaven.

Tostig had quickly realized that William would be of no use to him. He was shrewd enough to know what was the Duke's mind. He had decided not to help William by attacking Harold...yet.

He made up his mind to go to Norway and put some suggestions before the King of that country. This was Harold Hardrada, one of the greatest fighters of the age. His skill in battle had been greatly aided by his enormous height. Even for a Viking he was tall, being six feet seven inches high. Battle was joy, fighting his reason for living, and although he was by no means young, being all of fifty years, he was still aching for a fight.

Trouble-maker Tostig was well received at his Court and the plan he had to lay before Harold Hardrada seemed a good one.

Tostig could testify that all was not well in England. Harold might be the choice of the south but it was another matter in the north. Why should not Harold Hardrada conquer the North and set himself up as King? It would be a short time before the whole of England was in his hands.

Harold Hardrada sat nodding his head and dreaming of battle and the rich spoils which were awaiting him.

He would accept Tostig's challenge.

At the beginning of September while William was waiting on the coast for the wind to change, Harold Hardrada set out. With him came his family, his treasure

218

and his warriors, all bent on plunder. Towards England the long ships sailed, their striped sails billowing in the wind and the shields that hung on the sides of the ships making the ocean gay with their colour.

Morcar of Northumbria, sighting the fleet, was filled with apprehension. He immediately sent an appeal for help to his brother Edwin of Mercia; and when the warriors landed they were waiting for them.

The very sight of the Norse giant was enough to strike terror into his enemies. There he was at the head of his army, brandishing his sword in his hand, his reputation as formidable as his size.

He ravaged the land, and Edwin and Morcar were soon in retreat. Hardrada and Tostig reached York which surrendered. With Edwin and Morcar defeated Hardrada was accepted as King. He was a Viking but there had been such kings before and one of the best of them King Canute himself.

The North would accept him. But there was still Harold to be defeated.

It was now the twenty-seventh of September.

*　　*　　*

The twenty-seventh of September! That day came in with a change of weather and while Hardrada was being proclaimed King in York, William's fleet at last set sail for England.

William had never been so elated in his life. He told himself that he was on the brink of his greatest adventure. Hardened warrior that he was, he could feel such an uplifting of his spirits that he was young again. Young in spirit, old in experience. What an irresistible combination.

He surveyed his fleet. Never had there been such ships. And his *Mora* was the pride of them all. Matilda's gift to him and Matilda was God's gift to him. There she sat at home with her tapestry, praying for him and longing for the day when she would join him.

He prayed: 'Oh God who has given me Matilda, give me England and with those two I will ask for nothing more.'

Night fell. The sea was eerie at night with the sound of the water dashing against the sides of the ships and the wind in the sails. How one listened to that kindly caress which could change suddenly to roar of anger or drop to nothing at all—either of which could ruin his plans.

From the *Mora* shone a large lantern. He had decided that his ship should carry such a light so that none should lose sight of him.

That night he was sleepless, his thoughts all for the morrow; and when the dawn rose to his dismay he could see none of his fleet.

He stared at the empty sea and thought that God had indeed forsaken him. What had become of those grand ships which had filled him with pride? Where were his soldiers whom he was to lead to victory?

One of his knights came to him and said: 'What has happened to the fleet, my lord? We are lost.'

'Nay,' said William, hiding his true feelings, 'we are so much fleeter than the rest. Remember we sail in the finest ship afloat. It is natural that we outstrip the others. Go and tell the cooks to prepare a meal and to bring some of our best wine. We are going to eat and drink and by the time we have done this you will see the fleet appearing on the horizon.'

He watched the preparation of the meal, every now and then turning his eyes to the horizon. Men on the verge of a great exercise must never be allowed to imagine for one moment that it was unlucky. They must believe that God was on their side against the enemy. They must be occupied and well fortified with food and drink, and the best thing to do in the circumstances was to make sure that they were fed.

He sat down with them and partook with a heartiness he did not feel; and as he ate his last mouthful he called one of the sailors to him and bade him go to the masthead and report what he saw.

'I see four ships,' was the sailor's reply.

Four out of hundreds! William feigned to look pleased.

He sat for a while and then sent the sailor again to climb to the top of the mast.

This time he returned jubilant. 'My lord, I see a forest of masts.'

William looked triumphantly round.

'The fleet is with us,' he said. 'God be thanked.'

And there they were sailing proudly towards him on a calm sea with the right amount of wind to carry the ships where they wished to go.

'No sign of an English ship,' said William. 'No sign of anything! But...yes. There! Land!'

A cheer went up. They had made the journey safely.

It was nine o'clock on the twenty-eighth day of September of the year 1066. William of Normandy had arrived at Pevensey Bay.

* * *

He stood on the *Mora* and watched the unloading of his ships. It was done quietly and expeditiously; and no one came to stop them or even to look at them. They could not have landed at a better spot. There was no hindrance whatsoever. They would be ready to go into battle as though they had never crossed the sea.

First his soldiers—archers and crossbowmen—waded ashore. Then the cavalry without their horses, which would be landed later. He had planned the operation with the utmost skill. He was determined that they should be short of nothing they needed. Nor did he wish his men to plunder as they went. He was to be the King of these people and he did not wish to alienate them at the beginning. His army would come equipped with what it needed as far as was possible. Hence he had brought his carpenters and ostlers and other workmen who would serve in any capacity which might be needed.

It was difficult getting the horses ashore, for the poor creatures were startled at having to swim the short distance between the ships and the land, but eventually the difficult operation was completed and the last man to come ashore was William himself.

As he stumbled up the sandy shore he tripped and fell.

There was a hushed silence which conveyed horror. Those watching knew that they were on the most dangerous enterprise of their lives and they could not resist seeing signs and portents in everything that happened.

William himself had his share of superstition. He wore about his neck at that moment—for he had donned it before leaving Normandy—a bag in which were some of those bones of holy men, the very same over which Harold had sworn to help him to the crown of England. Superstitious he might be but at the same time he was a practical man. He realized in those seconds as he lay sprawling on the sand that this fall could have cost him his victory. Not for one moment must these men of his have a doubt in their minds that he was the unconquerable leader.

221

He took two handfuls of sand and let it trickle through his fingers.

'Look ye,' he cried in a voice of thunder. 'I have taken England in both my hands. This is a sign from Heaven.'

A cheer went up.

He had turned their fear into elation.

* * *

William had planned to the smallest detail. On that morning at Pevensey he wished to make sure that in the event of having to retreat he would be able to save his ships and his men. He therefore hastily built a fortress which could be held while his men escaped to their ships if need be.

After a few days he decided to move to Hastings where his scouts had discovered he could easily set up his base.

Ships, men and stores were conveyed to this spot; and William then commanded that one of the wooden fortresses which he had brought with him be assembled.

Here meals could be cooked and councils of war could take place. When this had been done William chose twenty of his most trusted captains—among them his half-brother Robert of Mortain and William Fitz-Osbern—and they rode off to reconnoitre the land.

There was very little hostility. The inhabitants of Hastings had wisely realized that there was nothing they could do to turn the invader away and they quietly accepted their fate.

Impatiently William awaited the coming of Harold.

* * *

A few days passed. Some of his men who had been filtering into the villages brought news of a mighty battle which had been raging in the north. It was for this reason that there had been no army to meet them by that time.

Harold Hardrada and Tostig had landed and were in control of the North and King Harold had marched up there to meet them.

'We cannot know,' said William to his friends, 'whom we shall have to fight. It might be Harold of England or Harold of Norway.'

'Harold Hardrada is said to be the finest fighter in the world,' said Robert of Mortain. 'Six feet seven high.'

222

'Inches do not win battles,' replied William tersely. 'And I doubt not we can match his bravery. I would rather it were Harold of England. I wanted to settle my score with him.'

'I hope the sight of Harold Hardrada does not snatch our men's hearts from them. They say he is a fearsome spectacle at the head of an army.'

William smote the table with his fist. 'Be it Harold of England or Harold of Norway make no mistake he will go down before us. Oh God,' he cried, 'how long must I wait to do battle?'

*   *   *

At Stamford Bridge Harold was preparing to drive the invader from the north not knowing that there was another in the south.

He had said good-bye to Edith a short while ago and she had kissed him in her calm and tender way and had said she would pray for him.

She would, he knew; but what happened to him and to her would be in God's hands.

He had known no peace since the crown had been placed on his head. He wondered whether he ever would.

Even as he prepared to face the Norseman he was thinking of that other who came from Normandy—a Viking no less than Harold Hardrada—William, descendant of Rollo, who passionately wanted England and to whom he had vowed to relinquish it.

'I was forced,' he said, as he had said a hundred times to Edith. 'A vow which is forced from a man is not a true vow.'

But he would always remember that his vow had been broken and he would wonder at times like this when danger was close and death could be imminent whether he would be asked to pay for his sin.

And now he was going into battle against his own brother. How sad his mother would be, for she loved her sons. She had already lost Sweyn and now he with Gurth and Leofwine were going into battle against Tostig.

It was unfitting that brother should fight brother.

He sent for a messenger and told him that he wished him to take a letter for him which must be delivered to Tostig. Safe conduct would be granted him.

Then he sat down and wrote to Tostig, reminding him of their boyhood days, begging him to break with Harold

223

Hardrada. He would not ask him to come to his side and fight. That would be too quick a turnabout; but if he would retire from the battle and he, Harold, succeeded in driving out the invader, he would give Tostig the earldom of Northumbria and they could learn to be friends again.

Then he sat and waited for the reply.

It came.

There was only one thing Tostig wanted from Harold and that was that he should give up the crown. And what, he wanted to know, would Harold give to Harold Hardrada for all the trouble he had taken to come to England?

Harold's reply was terse. He would give him seven feet of England. For some men he would have offered six but because the Norseman was a big man he should be granted seven.

There was no help. Brother must fight brother.

So Harold rode out to the battle of Stamford Bridge.

* * *

Harold was an experienced general. He had learned his trade through experience even as William of Normandy had, and surveying the selected battlefield he realized at once that his great chance of winning would be to get control of the bridge before Hardrada and Tostig did. If he could do this and get his army across they could take their stand on the top of an incline which meant that the enemy would have to come to them uphill.

The sun had risen; it glinted on the shields of the Norsemen, rows and rows of them.

Harold and his men must break down the defence of these shields with sword and axe. Harold could not rid his mind of the fact that in the lines of the enemy was his brother Tostig.

All the day the battle raged. The enormous figure of Hardrada beneath the standard was an inspiration to his men and a fear to the enemy. But Harold's taking the bridge had been a major piece of strategy and in securing the advantageous position he was half-way to winning the day. The sun was hot and the Norsemen in their heavy armour suffered more from it than the lighter-clad Saxons.

By afternoon wedges had been driven through the rows of shields; and there was a cry of dismay as an arrow from a Saxon bow pierced Hardrada's throat.

Their leader dead—and because of his great height it was seen by many that he was no longer at his post—the Norseman knew the day was lost. A Saxon axe had been driven through Tostig's head. By the time the sun went down the battle was over.

Harold of England was the victor.

*   *   *

It was quiet now. The camp-fire threw a flickering light over the grim scene. Harold stared into the embers and thought: So I have lived through another day.

His brothers Gurth and Leofwine came to him and he grasped their hands.

'Thank God you came through safely,' he said. 'But we have lost a brother this day.'

'Let us not mourn,' replied Gurth. 'Had he lived there would have been more slaughter.'

'Poor Tostig. He dies on a battlefield as he would have wished—but fighting his own brother.'

'He always envied you, Harold. He would have gone on doing so had he lived. You would never have been safe from him. It had to be you or him. Come, you are a victor. This is a time for rejoicing.'

But Harold shook his head.

He lay sleepless through the night and in the morning sent men out to find Tostig's body and bring it to him that he might give it a decent burial. 'Bring, too, the King of Norway,' he said. 'I promised him seven feet of England soil and he shall have it.'

So they went out and although they could easily find the body of Hardrada they could not find that of Tostig.

'I shall go myself and search for him,' said Harold. 'I shall know my own brother.'

A battlefield was a terrible sight in the light of day. Among the mutilated bodies Harold searched for Tostig. It was not surprising that others had not been able to find him. Harold himself would not have been able to but for one small thing.

As he looked in vain among that mass of corpses he was thinking of Tostig as a boy, when they had played together, fighting their mock battles. They had not dreamed then that the day would come when they fought against each other in earnest and one should be killed.

225

Harold pictured Tostig clearly as he had been one day when they were in a forest together and came upon a stream. Tostig had thrown off his jerkin and plunged into the stream. A vivid picture came into Harold's mind. The laughing boy looking over his shoulder. 'Come on, Harold. Are you afraid of cold water?' And he had plunged in and they scuffled with each other in the water. Would he ever get out of his mind the memory of Tostig standing naked in the sun. Every detail seemed suddenly clear—the hair that curled about the nape of his neck, the odd-shaped wart between his shoulders.

The wart! There was no other such wart in such a place on any other body.

Frantically he searched and found it. There it was as it had looked that day in the forest stream.

He could not bear to look at that head which had been split by the axe of one of his own men.

He ordered that Tostig's body should be carried away and given decent burial.

As he stood by his brother's grave, remembering so much from their boyhood, a messenger arrived with urgent news.

William of Normandy had landed at Pevensey Bay and was now encamped at Hastings.

* * *

Harold conferred with his brothers Gurth and Leofwine.

'If I had not been at Stamford Bridge,' he said, 'I could have prevented the landing.'

'If Tostig had been with us instead of against us . . .' said Gurth angrily.

'He was never with me,' said Harold. 'He is dead now. Let us not speak of him. It is usual to say if this and if that. The situation is that William has landed and is now doubtless erecting his fortifications. What we have to decide is what we shall do.'

'The Army is depleted,' pointed out Gurth.

'It needs rest and reforming,' added Leofwine.

'The point is,' said Harold, 'should we stay here or march south?'

'If we stayed here, the Norman would be forced to march north to us,' said Gurth. 'An army which has had a long march to a battlefield is never as fresh as one which has rested there.'

'If I could stay here and muster an army, I would do so,' explained Harold. 'But could I? If I called men from all over England to arms, they would not heed me. All I could hope for is to march south and attempt to muster men to my banner as I go. I will send messages to Edwin and Morcar but I don't trust them. They may not want the Norman but they don't want me either. I must think of this. On it could depend the outcome of the battle.'

After a great deal of deliberation he came to the conclusion that his greatest hope of success was to march south.

Senlac

In his Norman camp William heard the news that Harold was coming.

The battle would not now be long delayed.

Harold, it was said, had defeated Harold Hardrada, a giant whom many had believed to be unbeatable. Harold was flushed with victory; he had slain his own brother Tostig, and now nothing could hold him back. He was coming to deal with the Norman who had dared invade his shores.

William pointed out to his captains, 'He and his army will be weary. He has fought a great battle at Stamford Bridge. Have no doubt he is a fine general. We shall not have an easy victory. But we are the stronger and we have right on our side. He will remember that he vowed on the bones of the saints and that memory will be with him throughout the day of battle.'

He decided that he would give Harold a last chance. He called one of the monks who had accompanied him on the voyage to England and said: 'Go to Harold. Tell him that my right to the throne of England is the true one. Edward the Confessor promised me the crown and he, Harold, vowed to help me to it.'

The reply came back. The oath had been forced from Harold and no oath taken in such circumstances could be regarded as valid.

'Go back to Normandy,' warned Harold. 'I will compensate you for the expense you have incurred and we will form an alliance of friendship. But if you insist on a battle, I am ready.'

He knew of course what William's reply would be.

*   *   *

In his tent William was preparing for the battle.

'Bring me my hauberk,' he said; and his servant brought it but in putting it on William turned it the wrong way round.

There was a hushed silence in the tent, for this was indeed an evil omen.

The Duke hastily turned the hauberk round and looked at the watching faces.

'Ha,' he said, 'so you will tell me now that this is a sign that I shall die in battle and this makes you fearful. Let me tell you this. I know that many among you—and brave men—would not dare go into battle on a day that had happened. But I never believed in omens and never will. I trust in God, for He does in all things to His pleasure and I commend myself to our Lady. The hauberk turned wrong and was righted by me. Well, if you want signs you can see one in this. The Duke has been turned even as the hauberk—turned from a Duke to a King.'

'He has no fear,' said those about him. 'He welcomes the battle.'

William mounted his horse, a present from the King of Spain, and never had a finer been seen. It served only one master and whither the Duke went there his horse would go with him, without fear while the Duke was on its back.

He surveyed his soldiers. A goodly band. Fresh and ready for the fight—the cavalry first and the foot-soldiers behind with their bows and arrows.

His confidence grew as the hour for battle drew near.

*   *   *

Friday, the 13th October, and Harold with his army had encamped about the heights of Senlac. William had left his camp at Hastings and was on the march.

The battle, said William, should take place the next day; and the night before should be spent in prayers for Divine help.

At the end of that day he had reached the field and sighted the English. Harold would be there close to the spot where his banner fluttered.

'Oh God,' prayed William, 'give me the victory and I will build an abbey on that very place.'

229

He knew that he faced a general as skilled—or almost—as himself; and it was generals who won battles. A good general with an inferior force could wring victory from a great army, ill-directed. But he had a great army; he was a great general; his men were not wearied by a battle so recently won, by a long march south. At his neck he wore the bag of relics. His men knew it; and they knew too that Harold had sworn away his kingdom on those very bones.

God must be on their side together with those saints whose bones had been treated so disrespectfully by Harold.

'We shall win,' declared William, and added: 'If it be God's will.'

* * *

It was nine o'clock of the next morning when the battle began.

It did not go as William had thought. The spears and javelins of the English were formidable and from their catapults they hurled sharp flints into the enemy's ranks.

William gave the order for the cavalry to charge but this did not achieve the success he had planned and the English wielding their axes clove many of the horsemen through the head. The rain of flinty stones had wounded many and as they were flung from some distance there was no immediate way of stopping them.

The first phase of the battle went to the English.

As the morning wore on, William was unhorsed; when his beautiful steed was killed beneath him. He went down but one of his men sprang forward to kill his would-be assassin.

The cry went up: 'The Duke is dead.'

The effect was immediate. The Normans believed they were beaten. Into their minds rushed the memory of William's fall as he had stepped ashore and the story of his putting on his hauberk back to front had been repeated throughout the camp.

With the English roar of triumph in their ears they began to retreat.

William however had found a new horse and was up again.

'You fools!' he cried. 'Do you want to be mown down? What will happen to you if you run? Where will you go? You face death if you retreat. Turn back and fight.'

He took off his helmet that they all might see him.

It was dangerous and an arrow could pierce his eye but it was better to risk that danger and to have the men know that he was alive, as vital as ever, and that they dared not turn and run while he was there to lead them.

The retreat was a blessing in disguise, for the English, believing they had won, had come down from the heights in pursuit. William realized his advantage at once. He gave the order to turn, and there were the English before them, vulnerable, called sharply to a halt in their rush to victory.

Savagely William led his men to mow them down. They were convinced now of the invincibility of their Duke. He could turn defeat into victory. They had to fight or face his wrath, and what could there be for them now, on foreign soil, if they did not fight?

The afternoon wore on; the position had been reversed. The English were becoming exhausted.

William called a halt to the battle and ordered his archers to shoot their arrows straight into the air. He could see that these would fall directly among the troops who were now holding the hilltop under the standard.

They obeyed, and it was one of these arrows which pierced the eye of Harold.

Gurth seeing his brother fall and knowing that Leofwine was dead also, galloped out with a little band into the heart of the Norman troops. He was going to kill William of Normandy, the usurper who had come here and killed two of his brothers.

So determined was he that he found the Duke—a not very difficult task because William was bareheaded. The onslaught was sudden and William's horse was killed under him.

William lifted his lance and ran it through Gurth's body.

Evening had come. Forays continued and outbreaks of fighting continued on the hill of Senlac and in the forest beyond; but the tragic battleground was covered with the bodies of the dead and the battle of Hastings had been won by William of Normandy.

*   *   *

With dawn came the sorrowing women to search among the dead for their own that they might take them away for burial.

231

Among them was the beautiful Edith of the swan-like neck. Quietly, with her despair clear in every gesture, she moved among the dead.

Others had tried to discover the body of the dead king without avail, but Edith found him.

She knelt down beside the body and unfastened the mail. Even as Harold had recognized Tostig by the wart between his shoulders, so did Edith by a birthmark on Harold's chest.

She laid her face against it and stayed there until monks who had been sent by Harold's mother to claim his body begged her to come away.

She rose and stood straight and stately among the dead; then she said to one of the soldiers whom she knew to be Norman: 'Take me to your master.'

He shook his head but she cried out: 'Take me to him or I will curse you in the name of the man you have slain.'

William received her in his tent. He had removed his armour and just risen from his knees when he had thanked God for the victory.

He looked imperiously at the beautiful woman so stricken in her grief, so careless of what happened to her. For what could it matter now that Harold was dead?

She hated this man, this Norman usurper who had come and taken Harold's life as well as his crown.

She said: 'I have come to demand the body of Harold.'

He looked at her intently. He sensed her sorrow and respected it, for he knew who she was. He had rarely seen such beauty and her long neck was remarkable. So this was the woman whom Harold had loved!

'None make demands of me,' he said. 'They may make requests.'

'I request you, then, to give me Harold's body that I may take it from this field of carnage and give it honourable burial.'

'Harold is a perjurer,' he said. 'He does not merit honourable burial.'

She looked at him with burning hatred in her eyes. Many will look at me thus, he thought, when I go about my new kingdom. I must be harsh with them, or they will think me weak and rise against me.

What if he gave this woman her lover's body? She would bury it with pomp; she would make a saint of him. Nay, he would bury Harold where he deserved, in an obscure grave.

232

There must be no shrine, no pilgrimages.

He had no illusions about the task before him. He had won merely the first battle; he had opened the door as it were. The great war was before him and he had an idea that he would go on fighting it for a very long time.

So, no weakness, no giving way.

'Have you no pity?' she asked.

'I am a just man,' he replied. 'I see no reason why a perjurer should be given an honourable burial.' He turned to the man who had been standing at the door of the tent. 'Take this woman away,' he said.

She went but before doing so gave him such a look of hatred that he was to remember for a long time. He respected her courage for he could have ordered her to her death. He understood her grief for she loved Harold and he thought that Harold had been fortunate to win the love of such a woman. He bore her no malice. This was an example of how he must rule his land. There would be no sentiment; nor did he want revenge. He would give harsh justice and if any failed to recognize him as their master they would be met with punishment and death. Yes, they should be robbed of their lands, their limbs and if need be their lives.

He would be a harsh master but a just one, he hoped.

*   *   *

There was another request. This time it came from Gytha, who was Harold's mother.

This woman, weeping bitterly, threw herself at his feet. The wife of Earl Godwin, a Danish Princess no less, and the mother of brave sons.

'This day,' she said, 'I have lost three sons. Harold the King and his brothers Gurth and Leofwine. My nephew Haakon whom you knew well is also dead. My son Tostig died but a short while ago. Have pity on me. Give me the bodies of my sons that I may bury them. It is all I ask of you.'

'You ask too much,' said William.

'I beg of you. Have you no feelings? Have you no pity?'

'I have no pity for perjurers.'

She wept; she entreated. But he was unmoved.

He is a hard man, thought those who looked on.

'I will give the weight of my son Harold's body in gold if you give me my sons.'

233

'All that you have could belong to me if I wished to take it,' William reminded her.

She lifted her face to his and he saw the hatred there.

I shall see it often in this land, thought William, so I must needs grow used to it.

'Take the woman away,' he said.

She cursed him as she went. Another brave woman! he thought. When I am crowned King of England, when I have subdued these people, Harold shall have a decent burial, but it shall be in my good time.

These people would learn fast enough what manner of man he was. They would learn that more than a new reign had begun. He had a kingdom to govern; he had long had plans for it. He would give good government but it might seem stern and often harsh.

He cared nothing for that. He was going to build a great country as he could not in Normandy. This country should be his and his sons would beget a royal race to rule it. So that in the years to come people would look back on that October day in the year 1066 and say: That was the day when England was born. There was the beginning of a new great age, and the father and creator of it all was William, bastard yes, and conqueror too.

PART THREE

THE KING

Matilda's Revenge

IT was Easter. Six months had passed since William had sailed for England; and his family now awaited his return to Normandy.

He had written to Matilda. 'These are a stubborn people. I am determined to subdue them. I am leaving them to my most trusted supporters for I must see you. I have been too long away.'

Matilda, delighted that he should feel the need of her, as she had of him, prepared a great welcome. She knew what had been happening in England for he had kept her well informed. She had heard of the difficulties he had had to encounter, the intransigence of the Saxon people, of his coronation at Westminster which had taken place on Christmas Day; and how he had ordered that there should be great celebrations and rejoicing in the cities of London and Westminster to celebrate the coronation of the new King on the birthday of Christ.

'We gave them such a spectacle as they had never seen before,' he wrote, 'and there is nothing the people like better than spectacles. We were acclaimed as we rode to Westminster, but alas, there was a rising of certain Saxons and I ordered the burning down of a number of houses to reward them. I must show a stern hand with these people. Well, I am coming to you, Matilda, for I have much to tell you, and I shall not be content until I have seen you crowned with me as sovereign of England.'

So they waited his coming.

'We must be at the shore to greet him,' Matilda told her family, 'so we will go to the coast.'

236

The family were excited. Robert now fourteen, impatiently waiting to be of age that he might take his inheritance. Richard handsome, tall and restrained in contrast to his brothers, for Rufus had never grown as tall as William would have liked. Adelisa had not lost her listlessness; she still mourned for Harold. The little girls were obedient and now showed signs of mingled pleasure and apprehension, for William had always inspired a certain admiration as well as fear in his children.

And how proud was Matilda to see the *Mora* approach the shore. Her ship! There never had been such a one. A true vessel for a conqueror.

He was the first to leap ashore, wading in to land where his children, standing a few paces behind Matilda, waited.

He seized his wife in his arms and kissed her.

'Matilda, my love! It has seemed such a long time.'

'I have followed your actions whenever possible. I have been there with you in my thoughts.'

'I shouldn't have left those rebels ... but I had to come back to you.'

She laughed triumphantly. What an admission from such a man.

'The children are here ... eager to greet you.'

He looked at them. Young Curthose had not grown at all, he noticed, nor had Rufus. Richard! There was a Norman if ever there was, a true descendant of Rollo!

Richard, by God's Splendour, should be King of England to follow him. Robert could have Normandy, the lesser prize.

And Rufus ... well, he would see about Rufus, but he was a younger brother.

What was wrong with Adelisa? The child was like a wraith.

'Here, daughter, what ails you? You are nothing but skin and bone.'

She lowered her eyes and did not answer.

Brooding for that traitor still! They would get a husband for her quickly.

And the little girls. He embraced them, but they were too young to interest him. Later he would make marriages for them. Marriageable daughters of kings made good bargaining counters.

But it was Matilda who claimed his interest.

'Come, let us leave here. There is much we have to speak of.'

* * *

He had much to show them too—rich treasure which he had brought with him. The spoils of war.

'These Saxons have some skills, Matilda. Look at this gold and silver plate. They surpass our workmen. They have a delicate touch which we lack. Look at these embroidered garments. You will be interested in those. Are they not fine?'

She agreed that they were.

'I shall make a great country of England, Matilda. But first I must subdue the rebels. They are not a meek people. They will not accept the fact that they were conquered. We shall have uprisings here, there...everywhere, and we have to be prepared. I intend to show them with fire and sword who is their master. It's the only way. They are stubborn and proud and they will rebel against me. How good it is to be in Normandy...with you and my family and the forest and good hunting.'

'Is there not hunting in England?'

'The forests are magnificent there, but this is my native land. I shall make England like it. I am going to insist that they speak Norman instead of Saxon.'

'Will that be easy?'

'For the young ones, yes, for the older ones more difficult. But there is much Danish in their tongue and you know ours is a mixture of Danish and French. There are words which are similar and our Normans do not find it difficult to make themselves understood. Now I want our people here to understand what a great victory this is, and I plan that you and I shall ride through Normandy to let them know that we are here, and although I am King of England I am still their Duke.'

Matilda, who had always enjoyed excitement, was pleased at the prospect. They discussed it at length.

A less satisfactory subject was the children.

'Robin Curthose was a little sullen I thought,' William remarked. 'He looked at me as though he were hoping I might not long delay my departure from this life.'

'You are hard on Robert.'

'As hard as you are soft.'

238

'He is your first-born. Remember how proud you were when you first saw him.'

'I did not know then how he would turn out.'

'But he is a brave boy.'

'A braggart. Too much ambition.'

'Can you blame him from inheriting such a quality from his father?'

'When I was his age I had inherited a dukedom and had perforce to keep it. He has not inherited a dukedom...yet, although it seems to me that he longs for one particular circumstance which would give it to him.'

'That is not true, William. He admires you so much.'

'He admires my possessions,' growled William. 'But let us talk of happier things. Richard is growing into a fine young Norman.'

'He'll be as tall as you are, William.'

'He has a good pair of Norman legs. How did Robert and Rufus mislay theirs?'

'Because you married a Flemish Princess who was not over tall but still to your liking.'

He gave her his tender smile and then went on: 'And our daughter? I was shocked to see her so. What ails the girl?'

'She took it into her head to regard Harold as a hero, the love of her life. I wish we had never affianced them.'

'We could not know then what a perjurer we should discover.'

'Now that he is dead and killed by you...'

'By God's Splendour,' cried William, 'to what have I come home! To a son who wants my dukedom and can scarce wait for me to relinquish my hold on it, and a daughter who blames me for the death of my enemies.'

'This is not true,' retorted Matilda. 'Robert takes his duty seriously and if he were of age you would make him Regent of Normandy. He longs for that day. As for Adelisa, Harold with his Saxon fair looks beguiled her, She is but a child and children set up their heroes and enshrine them in their hearts.'

'You are right, I doubt not. I will find a husband for Adelisa and set that matter to rights.'

'She is over young for marriage.'

'As yet. But she can go to some court where she will forget what has happened to her and be brought up with her future family. That will turn her mind from the false

239

Saxon. As for Robert, I can do nothing for him. He must perforce wait for the years to pass.'

* * *

The triumphant progress began. Everywhere they were acclaimed. Their Duke was now known as the Conqueror; he had set sail on an enterprise which many had believed would fail. Hadn't his father tried before him and not succeeded? And he had been Robert the Magnificent. But their Duke had succeeded and he was now more than a Duke. He was a King.

He had conferred with Lanfranc. He had plans, he told him, of bringing him to England. He did not trust their Archbishops, neither of Canterbury nor York. He wanted to replace them by Normans, and he had decided that Canterbury should be for Lanfranc. At the moment though he was needed in Normandy.

'When my son is of an age to be my Regent, then, Lanfranc, you must come to England.'

Lanfranc replied earnestly that his only object would be to serve his King as faithfully as he had served his Duke.

'Why,' laughed William, 'I deplore Curthose's lack of years even as he does himself.'

He could not endure the looks of Adelisa. She reminded him of that beautiful woman who had come to claim Harold's body and the look of hatred she had given him—cursing him no doubt in her thoughts. She had loved Harold as Adelisa had. What had these Saxons, he wondered, that women seemed to care for them. Even Matilda had enjoyed those late night talks with him for more than she had admitted.

The opportunity arose. He was no longer a Duke merely, he was a King and as such a greater power in the world. He would not have difficulty in finding matches for his children.

He heard that a bride was being sought for the King of Galicia. Adelisa was eleven years old...too young for marriage. But perhaps in two years, three certainly...and such marriages were made in advance.

He entered negotiations and to his delight they were received with enthusiasm.

'Send for our daughter, Matilda,' he said. 'I have news for her.'

She came and stood before her parents. She was more like a shadow than ever. Did she not eat? William wondered. She should be forced to. He would not tolerate disobedience in his children any more than he would in his subjects.

Matilda, who could on occasions be as harsh as he was, was gentler with her children. She seemed to be over-indulgent with this folly about Adelisa's love for a Saxon enemy.

Adelisa stood eyes downcast, looking meek; and, although he expected meekness, he did not admire it.

'Daughter, here is good news,' he said. 'You are to go to Galicia to finish your growing up in the court there. You are to have a bridegroom.'

Adelisa raised frightened eyes to her mother's face.

'It will be best for you,' said Matilda gently.

'No, *please* ...' began Adelisa.

'What nonsense is this?' cried William. 'You are fortunate. You will be Queen of Galicia. Does that not please you?' She was silent and he roared: 'Answer me.'

She said in a whisper: 'No, Father.'

'No!' he shouted. 'You say *no* to an offer like this!'

'I would rather go into a convent.'

'Convent! Your sister is in a convent. One daughter is enough for the Church. You will be pleased by your great good fortune or by God's Splendour ...'

Matilda raised a hand. 'Think about this, Adelisa,' she said. 'It is indeed a good match. You must remember that you are the daughter of a King and it is your duty to marry where your father chooses and in such a manner as will bring him good.'

Adelisa was silent.

'You will eat the food that is prepared for you,' cried William. 'What do you think the King of Galicia will say if we deliver a bag of bones to him?'

Still she did not answer. Matilda saw the blood flood William's face; he lifted his fist. She remembered that occasion when he had rolled her in the mud. She knew that temper. She had seen it repeated in Rufus.

She took charge of the situation.

'Adelisa needs to grow accustomed to the idea,' she said. 'I remember how I felt when my father told me I was asked for.'

241

She smiled at William; his temper cooled a little at this reference to his violent courtship.

Matilda did not add that her benign father would never have forced her. But it would not be so with William of Normandy, King of England, William before whose will all must bend...except Matilda, of course.

She saw though that this marriage could be good not only for Normandy but also for Adelisa.

She took her daughter's arm. 'I will talk to you, Adelisa,' she said; and smiling over her shoulder at him, led her daughter away.

* * *

Adelisa stared stonily before her.

'I can never marry anyone...now, my lady.'

'My dear daughter, you are but a child. You cannot go on mourning for this infant passion.'

'You do not understand.'

'I understand perfectly. This Saxon came and he was handsome and seemed kind, but all the time he was deceiving your father.'

'My father thinks he can rule everybody. He forced Harold to make his vow.'

'How could he force him to do such a thing?'

'He would have cast him into a dungeon, put out his eyes, cut off his hands and feet, perhaps poisoned him.'

'What are you saying?'

'These cruelties have been carried out.'

'By your father!'

'If not by his hand in his name. Harold swore because it was his duty to go back and take the crown which was his.'

'You talk like a traitor.'

'I am true to the man who would have been my husband.'

'He would never have been your husband. He had a mistress whom he is said to have loved. She is the most beautiful woman in England. She came to beg your father for his body...a body which she alone could recognize because she knew it so intimately.'

Adelisa covered her face with her hands and shivered.

'You know little of life, dear child,' said Matilda gently. 'You will learn. In time you will have children of your own, and children can become as dear to you—perhaps dearer—than the man who gives them to you. My daughter, you

242

must do as your father wishes. All must obey him. He had decreed that you shall go to Spain. Accept your fate, Adelisa, with a good grace, for you must accept it in any case. Try to eat the food I choose for you. Try to grow strong. Look to the future. Pray that you will be fruitful. Then you will love again.'

Matilda took her daughter's face in her hands and kissed her.

Adelisa put her arms round her mother and clung to her.

'You must not hate your father, Adelisa,' whispered Matilda. '"Honour your father and your mother." Remember that your father is a great leader, a great conqueror. In the defence of his possessions it is often necessary to kill and the methods cannot always be nice. Harold betrayed you. He loved his mistress. If he had married you it would only have been for form's sake. But he married another woman, the sister of his enemies, because he feared them. Remember this. Go to Spain and begin a new life.'

'I cannot do it.'

'Now lie down, I will send some good broth for you. Take the drink I send with it. It will make you sleep. Nay, I will bring it myself. And tomorrow you will feel better. You will see everything more clearly. There is a future for you, Adelisa, in Spain.'

Docilely Adelisa drank the broth and the potion and very soon after she was asleep.

Matilda returned to William. 'Our daughter will go to Spain,' she said.

'Indeed she shall.'

'It is better she should go my way than yours, William.'

'You are always over soft with your children, Matilda.'

'Over soft with those I love,' she answered, smiling at him; and she was triumphant, thinking how even now after fifteen years of marriage she could still direct him. No mean feat, she congratulated herself, with such a man.

*   *   *

Richard was the only one to whom Adelisa could explain. Her sisters were too young; Cecilia was in a convent and she would never have understood. She would have said Adelisa must pray and look for comfort in her devotions. Robert was too full of resentment against their father because he would not give him Normandy immediately. Rufus was too concerned with his own affairs to care for anyone else's; he was always with his dogs and horses, or fighting with Robert. He would have fought with Richard if Richard had allowed him.

But Richard was different from anyone else in the family. He was quiet and kind and he hated to make anyone unhappy. She was able to tell him.

'When I was affianced to Harold,' she said, 'I vowed I would marry no one else.'

Richard said gently: 'You were over young to make such a vow.'

'Nay, Richard, I made it and I meant it and I mean it now.'

He smiled at her gently: 'We have to do what is distasteful to us because we are the sons and daughters of a king.'

'I was happier as the daughter of a duke merely.'

'You were happy because Harold lived and you loved him. He is dead now. You must forget him. In Galicia you will find much to interest you. Perhaps your future husband will be kind and you will grow up together. He is more your own age.'

'Age is of no importance. You remember Harold, Richard. Was he not the most beautiful man you ever saw?'

'He was indeed handsome but he is dead now, Adelisa, and it seems he was never meant for you.'

'I have a feeling, Richard, that I shall keep my vow.'

'You dare not go against our father.'

'None dare do that, but God.'

'What do you mean, Adelisa?'

'We shall see, Richard, but it comforts me to talk to you. Sometimes I wonder what manner of king you will be, for kings have often to be cruel and I believe you would never be that.'

'My fate, like yours, Adelisa, is unknown, but whatever it may be, when it comes I must accept it . . . as you must.'

Yes, she was indeed comforted by Richard.

* * *

The triumphant journeys continued and so did the preparations for Adelisa's departure for Galicia.

William said: 'Last Christmas I was crowned King of England. This one I intend to celebrate in Normandy. We

244

shall have such feasting as never before. I want people here to understand what this conquest means to us...and to them.'

Alas, for his plans. Messages were constantly arriving from England. There were risings throughout the country. William himself was a kind of figure-head, a bogey; his absence gave the conquered people hope that they could rise up and drive the enemy back into the sea.

There had been a massacre of Normans throughout the land and this must have been carefully planned for the people rose in various places on precisely the same day and slew every Norman on whom they could lay their hands.

'There is no help for it,' said William. 'I must go back. As soon as possible you shall join me there, and then, Matilda, there shall be a coronation. I shall not be content until you are crowned Queen of England.'

So Adelisa sailed for Galicia and William once more set out in the *Mora* for England.

* * *

Soon after he had arrived in England William had crushed the revolt. The people who had boldly declared they would drive the Conqueror back into the sea on his return realized how rash they had been. His forceful energy and his passion for oganizing his affairs and his genius for ruling were strained to their utmost; but he was not the man to be defeated. He had come to the conclusion that softness did not pay with these people. There should be no forgiveness when they erred. He was going out to punish those who flouted his authority and the punishment would not be lenient.

He would burn down the house of any man who did not realize that he was the master. There was not time to teach these people that they must obey; it was a lesson they must already have mastered if they were to keep alive.

They would have to learn that great countries were not governed well except by a rod of iron. People must live in terror of him if that was the only manner in which he could extract complete and unquestioning obedience.

He thanked God that he had left Matilda in Normandy to look after his affairs. She was the one whom he could trust more than any other. Lanfranc was his man, he doubted it not, but from a wife one could hope for the ultimate devotion. He did with Matilda. How many times had he thanked God for Matilda. He did so now.

There were letters from her. He read carefully of state matters in Normandy before he turned to the private letter.

He sat with the letter before him for some time. The words danced on the parchment. Instead of them he saw the face of his sad little daughter.

'She set sail as we arranged she should,' wrote Matilda, 'but she never reached Galicia. She had vowed not to marry. I believe she willed herself to die.'

A flame of anger flashed into his eyes. She had willed herself to die when she could have brought great good to his house. He needed the King of Galicia as his friend. And she had died when on her way to make the alliance!

She *willed* to die. How could that be? How dared that be?

What a man suffered from his children! His daughter had flouted him by dying on her way to form an important alliance.

Poor child! He could not forget those great sorrowing eyes that looked too big in her little wasted face. Matilda was grieving for her, he could tell by the tone of her letter.

'Poor Adelisa,' she wrote, 'we should never have forced her. She had vowed to marry none but Harold the Saxon and you see, she did not.'

William thumped his right fist into the palm of his left hand.

He had more to think of than the whims of disobedient daughters.

* * *

'It has always been my wish that you should join me here,' wrote William. 'You know of my great desire to see you crowned Queen of England. Now the moment has come.'

He pictured her receiving that letter. How she liked excitement! She would stop brooding about Adelisa when she knew she was coming to England.

It was true that Matilda was delighted. She set about making preparations without delay. There was one other matter which pleased her.

'Our son Robert,' William had written, 'is young yet, but he should begin to realize his responsibilities. Leave him

246

behind and let him be a member of the council that he may learn something of government. I have a notion that this will please him.'

She went to Robert.

'My darling,' she said, 'I have good news for you. Your father is allowing you to take part in the government while I am in England.'

'I am Regent, then?'

'Nay, that is going a little far. You are but sixteen remember.'

'How can I forget? I am constantly told I am but a boy.'

'A situation which time will remedy each day.'

'I suppose I shall sit with the council as a matter of form.'

'You will sit so that you may learn how a Duchy is governed.'

'I know that,' cried Robert impatiently.

'You must remember that there is something in what your father says. You must not be so impatient, Robert.'

'So you are on his side...now.'

She laid her hand on his shoulder. 'You know I am always on yours.'

He looked at her slyly. 'One day,' he said. 'You may be asked to prove it.'

She refused to see the implication of that remark and left him to continue with her preparations.

The rest of the family were excited. It was good, for it took their minds off the news of Adelisa's death. The little girls were sad for they had loved their sister; Richard mourned her too. He said: 'I think she knew she was going to die.' Rufus was too full of his own affairs to think much about his sisters. He did not seem very moved by her loss.

It was exciting to leave in the *Mora* which had been sent back to Normandy to carry them over to England; and to arrive to find William waiting for them and to be accompanied to Westminster amid some pomp. That was gratifying.

Poor little Adelisa who had wanted to die when she might have been a Queen!

How Matilda enjoyed seeing the countryside—a beautiful country of green fields and thick forests it was; the people did not seem hostile; they came out to look at her as she rode by and it was clear that they admired her and her children. Richard appeared to charm them with his good

247

looks, and Rufus looked merry and friendly; as for the girls they enchanted the people.

William told her that the ceremony of coronation was to be at Winchester and it was to be a much grander occasion than his own which had taken place at Westminster on that Christmas Day.

'Your coming here will be a sign,' he told her. 'So will your coronation. It will show the people that we regard England as our home and that we have come to stay.'

So to Winchester they travelled and the ceremony on which William had lavished his love of planning and organization was a great success. Matilda was still young enough to look beautiful in her coronation robes and the presence of the children delighted the people.

William ordered that the bells should be rung all over the country and that there should be bonfires. There should be free wine in the streets and a tournament in which William and his knights would take part.

The people had never seen anything like it and expressed their delight in such pageantry. Moreover it was pleasant to see another side to William's character. The man whom they had considered to be a tyrant, was after all a good husband and father, proud of his family and happy to be in the midst of it.

* * *

Queen of England.

She was delighted with her title. And William had missed her. He was so happy to have her with him; to show her his new possession. And how proud he was. How full of plans. He seemed as young as he had when they had first married. In fact coming to England was for Matilda like those first days of their marriage. The separation had made them fonder.

William made it clear to everyone how dear she was to him by insisting that she be treated with the same respect that was accorded to him.

Often Matilda would see a Saxon face which reminded her of Brihtric. It was so long since she had seen him that perhaps she had imagined the beauty of those blue eyes and that fair skin.

Where was he now? What did he think when he realized that the woman he had spurned was now his Queen?

Her humiliation had not diminished. Even now she could remember everything they had said on that occasion.

She sent for one of her servants.

'There was a man I met once in my father's court of Flanders,' she said. 'He was the Ambassador from England. I have been wondering whether he is still alive and where he is. Go and discover whether a certain Brihtric Meaw, known as Snow, still lives. His father was the lord of honour of Gloucester so you should have little difficulty in discovering him.'

The servant went off to do her bidding and in a few weeks returned with the information that Brihtric still lived on his estates which he had inherited from his father and which were considerable.

Matilda thought of him a great deal. Was he as handsome as ever? Had he married? Had he ever boasted to his wife that Matilda of Flanders had so urgently desired to marry him that she had cast aside all convention and asked him to become her husband?

Was it possible that such a thing could be said of the Queen of England?

*   *   *

She had discovered that she was pregnant, a fact which delighted her.

'It must be a son,' she said. 'I want a son who is born on English soil. He will differ from the others because his parents will have been a King and Queen at the time of his conception.'

William smiled at her. Her fruitfulness delighted him. 'I too want a son,' he said.

'You are demanding,' she told him affectionately. 'Have I not already given you three?'

'A King needs sons,' was his reply. 'As many as he can get.'

'I should like to build a castle to celebrate my arrival here and the birth of our child and I should like to choose my spot.'

'Then you must do this.'

'I shall choose my land and take it.'

'No matter where and whose, it is yours.'

She was contented.

A few days later she wrote an order. She had chosen

lands in Gloucester. They were now in the possession of a certain Brihtric Meaw. As this man had committed a grave misdemeanour and was in the Queen's opinion known to be false, his lands were to be confiscated and given to the Queen and Brihtric was to be conveyed to prison in Winchester where he should remain until his innocence should be proved.

* * *

She sat in her chamber smiling secretly.

Would this be the moment when the guards arrived? Would he be seated in his dining hall, his wife beside him—that wife of his choice who was so much more desirable than a queen? Would he be startled when the messenger said, 'I arrest you Brihtric Meaw in the name of your Sovereign'?

He would be startled; he would stammer; he would demand to know on what charge he was being arrested.

My dear Brihtric, one does not ask kings and queens on what charge one is arrested. Suffice it that one has displeased.

And you displeased me, Brihtric. You refused me and never was I able to forget it. Ever since there have been moments when I have seen you as clearly as I did on that day and I remember the look in your eyes when I told you I loved you and would marry you.

Horror it was. You can never be forgiven for that. It is my turn now, Brihtric the Saxon. Who are you now? You will go to prison because I have the power to send you there. I will take your lands. What of your wife now? What will become of her? Do I care for that, Brihtric? Let her starve. Let her go to some other man. I shall forget because I have settled the score and that is the only way I can.

Her servant came back to her.

'How went it?' she asked.

'He is in prison.'

'And was he surprised?'

'Bewildered, my lady. He kept saying, "I have done nothing. How dare you."'

'But you dared in the name of the Queen and he *has* done something. He has been no friend to the Queen.'

She sat smiling for a long time, thinking of his beautiful blue eyes and his fair fair skin.

250

His eyes, even if they were still as beautiful, would grow dim in prison; his fair skin would doubtless ere long be blotched with disease.

At last Brihtric would learn how foolish he had been to humiliate Matilda of Flanders.

* * *

She had not realized his estate was so large. It included such places as Tewkesbury, Fairford, Whitenhurst and Thornbury. He had been a rich man, poor Brihtric!

She continued to think of him. She could not get him out of her mind.

Nor would she ever, she feared. She wished that she could go and see him and taunt him with what he had done. Had he guessed why he was there? Did he ever remember that scene in the Palace at Lille?

Foolish Brihtric! What had he missed!

And what she might have missed! William and Robert—those were the two who meant most. Not for the world would she have missed them; and deep in her heart she was glad that Brihtric had refused her. But he had humiliated her and she had greatly desired him; and that she could not forget.

He had been punished; he had lost his possessions; he was languishing in prison. But it was not enough.

There were many eager to do her bidding. She remembered how William had once disposed of those whom he wished removed. It was easier to make such an arrangement about a prisoner than the guests at one's table.

What a glorious possession was Power! It was for this that men went to war; it was for this that women worked in secret. Power to say 'This shall be done', and to know that it would be done.

All she had to do was send someone she could trust to find a means of bribing a jailer in the prison. It should not be difficult.

Nor was it.

A month after he was imprisoned in Winchester, Brihtric Meaw was found dead in his cell.

When she heard the news Matilda felt a little sad. 'He was such a handsome man,' she said. 'One of the most handsome I ever knew.'

Then she smiled her secret smile.

The matter of Brihtric Meaw which had overshadowed her thoughts for a long time, was closed.

The Jealous Couple

GREAT was the joy of William and Matilda when their child was born for, as they had hoped, it was a boy.

Their popularity increased. A son born on English soil was regarded as English and the people joined whole heartedly in the celebration. They called the boy Henry.

William realized that the coming of the family had changed to some extent the people's feelings for him. They seemed to regard him as more human, which was all for the good—his and theirs. He wanted to impress on them that he was harsh only when necessity demanded it. He was not a man who wanted to practise cruelty for cruelty's sake.

He was a ruler; he had lived through a hard life. He had seen death so often that he did not regard it with any great respect; and he knew that the only way to subdue rebellious subjects was with fear. He intended to be feared; his subjects must know that he was a man of his word and if they disobeyed him there would be no mercy. If they would submit, then he would turn his immense talents into giving them wealth and prosperity. He could see great prospects in his country, and he was determined to develop them. If any stood in his way they must expect to be denuded of their property, mutilated or killed, whatever the offence in his opinion merited.

He knew that those two troublesome earls, Edwin and Morcar, had been responsible for a great deal of discord in England. Had they been faithful to Harold, he, William, might not have succeeded in his conquest. He had known from the beginning that he must be watchful of these earls and had, when he arrived, promised Edwin one of his daughters.

The death of Adelisa had made him change his mind. He had lost one bargaining counter and did not wish to be reckless with what was left. So he now felt lukewarm about the alliance. He had other thoughts with which to occupy his mind.

His passion for building had always been strong and already there was evidence of it in England. He had met and admired Gundulph, the Bishop of Rochester, who in addition to his religious calling was an architect of great ability. He and William had much in common and William told Gundulph that he had the mind to build a tower which should stand on the Thames in London and he would like to start the planning without delay.

Gundulph was excited and together they discussed plans, after which Gundulph produced some drawings which delighted William and for some days he was absorbed as he could be by his architectural adventures, to the exclusion of all else.

Then suddenly there was trouble.

William was first aware that Edwin and Morcar had left the Court without asking his permission to do so.

He was disturbed. These two could be said to be the most popular men in the country and William was well aware of the rumblings of revolt against him beneath the show of outward obedience. He knew that many of his new subjects avoided meeting his eyes as he passed them; he knew that when he went by many turned and shook their fists at him and muttered curses under their breath.

His precarious safety in his own dukedom had warned him of how much more likely was revolt in a conquered land.

Edwin was one of those beautiful Saxons like Harold who had the power to win people to their sides because of great personal charm. William had none of this. He exuded power and strength; he excited fear in all, even his own family, but this was very different from the affection men like Harold and Edwin inspired—and all because of their pretty fair locks and their gentle voices, and their beautiful Saxon blue eyes.

So the two earls had removed themselves—then he must be wary.

How right he was! Edwin and Morcar were in the north

254

where they were conspiring with the King of Scotland to attack William and drive him back to Normandy; William determined to act without delay and with such severity that these people would think twice before rebelling again.

The first thing was to send his family back to Normandy.

'You must go,' he told Matilda. 'There are the children to think of.'

Matilda understood this, so she sailed back to Normandy, taking her sons and daughters with her.

William acted promptly. He instituted an order which was called the *couvre feu* and which the Saxons soon called the curfew. A bell was sounded at eight o'clock at night and at that hour all fires must be doused. This was because it was after dark that people assembled to discuss rebellion. If fires were extinguished people went to bed. It was a small precaution but one which William believed was necessary.

He then gathered an army and marched north.

There he gave the rebels an example of how terrible his vengeance could be. He, who was a parsimonious man, found it against his nature to destroy crops and grazing land; but this he did ruthlessly. Of what use a prosperous countryside if it did not belong to William? These people must be made to understand that in rebelling against him they courted terrible disaster.

The people of Yorkshire looking on their devastated countryside were filled with dismay; and when Earl Edwin was slain there was universal mourning throughout the nation.

But the people had learned a lesson.

They began to call the King, William the Conqueror. They hated him but they feared him, and they knew then that he had come to stay.

*　　*　　*

On his way south he passed through Gloucester. These were the lands which Matilda had been so eager to possess. He wondered why, without seeing them, she should have chosen them.

To whom had they belonged? A certain Brihtric who had been imprisoned, he discovered, for some misdemeanour of which no one seemed very certain.

So when Matilda had acquired the land Brihtric had

gone to prison. Perhaps he had opposed the gift. Small wonder he resisted when such fine estates were to pass from his hands.

His passion for detail would not allow him to dismiss the matter. He wanted to hear more of this man Brihtric. It was a pity he had died in prison or he would have questioned him himself.

He was surprised—and dismayed—to learn that Brihtric had been an ambassador at the Court of Flanders. He would have been there at the time he was courting Matilda.

Then Matilda would have known him. It was clear now that she was settling an old score.

He was amused. She could be secretive, his Matilda. He wondered in what way Brihtric had offended her.

It was no use. He must know. It was not difficult. He discovered that Brihtric had died rather mysteriously in his prison. A little questioning of his jailers, who were terrified to do anything but tell the truth, and he had the whole story.

Before Brihtric had died he had talked. There were two to whom he had spoken.

'She wanted to marry me,' he had said. 'She asked me. She, a Princess of Flanders. But I did not love her. I was betrothed. So...she hated me. But I would not have believed she would have so taken her revenge.'

'By God's Splendour,' muttered William.

* * *

So she had taken her revenge. All these years she had remembered. One did not take such revenge unless one felt strongly.

What was the fatal attraction of these Saxons? He remembered the face of the swan-necked Edith who had begged for her lover's body. Adelisa had drifted into death because she had not wished to live without Harold. And Matilda...his own Matilda...had desired a Saxon and for years when she was William's wife she had not forgotten him.

It was no passing fancy. That much was clear. One did not remember passing fancies for years. She had brooded on her loss. She had taken William because her Saxon would not have her.

Whom could one know? Whom could one trust? She had

256

been a faithful wife. He would swear to that. But had she been faithful in her thoughts? How often when they were together had she in her mind substituted him for Brihtric?

He was not a great lover, he knew that. He was a soldier. He had never philandered with women.

He remembered Osbern's telling him, 'Many rulers have frittered away their realms through their love of women. Beware. Marry, and find what you need in your wife. That is the way to make good strong sons, legitimate sons whose succession none can dispute.'

And so much had this Saxon been in her thoughts that one of her first acts on coming to England had been to take her revenge.

* * *

Fresh from devastating the North he rode through his dominions. He wanted the people to see him, to talk of the trail of devastation he had left in his wake. He wanted them to understand: This is the reward of all who defy me.

And as he rode he thought of Matilda, who all those years when they were together had thought of her Saxon. If this Saxon would have married her, she would have taken him. Why had she turned so quickly to William? From pique? To show the Saxon that there were some who wanted her?

So he, William the Conqueror, had taken second place to an insignificant Saxon.

He thought of the years of fidelity. It was not that he had any great inclination for other women; perhaps mildly now and then, but never had he indulged his whims. Nay, he had said, the bond between us two is sacred.

And all the time she had been thinking of the Saxon!

It was while he rested at Canterbury that he noticed the beautiful daughter of one of the canons of the Cathedral. She was young; she attracted him. This would be a kind of revenge. After this he would not say: I have been faithful to Matilda all these years.

The girl was not unwilling. Or perhaps she dared not be. He had a reputation for being a tyrant. It was quite a pleasant experience and yet it taught him that he was not by nature a philanderer.

He was first ruler, then a family man. He wanted no distractions from his armies and his state affairs. They

257

gave him all the excitement he needed.

But naturally this lapse, because it was so unusual, had been remarked on.

William was human after all.

* * *

The Governor of Winchester, Hugh Grantmesnil, was married to a woman who regarded herself as a great beauty, irresistible to men. When William had visited Winchester she had determined to attract him, for she thought how interesting it would be to become the King's mistress.

The fact that he had at that time shown no interest in women made him all the more desirable in her eyes.

So when William had gone to Winchester she had done everything in her power to attract him. As Governor her husband must entertain the King and she had had the honour of sitting beside him at table, while her husband stood behind him waiting on him.

She had dressed herself in a low-cut gown, heavily bordered with gold embroidery and which revealed her fine bosom. Her long fair hair was worn loose about her shoulders and she was indeed a beautiful woman.

William had taken no more notice of her than if she had been the chair on which he sat; he had been far more interested in the men's talk of rebuilding an abbey and he discussed the plans for the Tower of London all through the meal.

Lady Grantmesnil was furious. That man, he is no man, she declared to her servants; and from then on did everything she could do, but she had discovered long before that insidious gossip and scandal—even if it was not the truth—could cause trouble.

This William for all his arrogance was not very firmly on the throne. He had come to England, taken it from King Harold, but that did not necessarily mean it was his. He relied a great deal on the goodwill of the people and his supporters must be loyal. A people such as those of this land were not easy to subdue. There were going to be continual risings and who knew, one of these one day might push the new King into the sea.

Serve him right, thought Lady Grantmesnil. He deserved no more after refusing the considerable favours she had so blatantly offered.

What could she do? She could not raise an army. She could talk though. She was known throughout Winchester as possessing one of the most vicious tongues of the day.

She began by discussing the Norman knights who seemed to find the ladies of England very much to their taste. How amusing to think of those Norman wives sitting at home in their castles. No wonder their husbands did not want to return. Why should they? They were having a very happy time in England.

Messengers were constantly going back and forth between England and Normandy and it was not long before such news began to be circulated. The Norman ladies were incensed. They wrote urgent letters. Their husbands must return without delay, they wrote. Their estates needed them...and so did their wives.

The effect of this began to be seen.

Lady Grantmesnil was delighted every time she heard that some Norman knight had slipped back to Normandy.

When she heard of William's infidelity with the Canon's daughter she was incensed. So this simple little girl had achieved what she had failed to do!

It was unforgivable.

She wondered whether Queen Matilda was aware of her husband's infidelity.

'If she has not already heard,' vowed Lady Grantmesnil, 'she soon will.'

* * *

The letter was unsigned. The messenger said he did not know how it had found its way into his pack.

Matilda read it and a wild fury possessed her. He had sent her back because he had feared for her life, he had said. He had sent her back so that he could indulge his lust with this Canterbury girl.

She had been insulted. No sooner had she avenged one humiliation than another was heaped upon her.

And William too! She would have trusted him because he had never looked over much at women. She had believed he had been completely devoted to her.

Often he had told her that no one else had ever attracted him.

259

And had she not been faithful to him?

Theirs had been the perfect marriage until he had spoilt it through his lust for this woman.

What was she like? Young, she supposed. She had not borne children. A girl younger than his own daughters. It was shameful!

But she would be revenged. There were many who would be ready to carry out the wishes of the Queen of England. She had her friends everywhere. It was significant that they were her friends and not William's.

She wanted that girl dead; and she was going to have her dead. She wanted her face mutilated in the killing because that was the face which had attracted William.

* * *

Lady Grantmesnil was delighted with the effects of her whispering campaign.

Moreover the mother of Harold, who would never forget that awful moment when she had looked into the hard face of the Conqueror and begged for her son's body, delighted in circulating rumours about his misdeeds. It was true that William had since ordered that the body of Harold should be given decent burial in the church at Waltham and that there had been Normans in his funeral processions to do honour to him; and it was clear that he refused on the battlefield, not because he wished to deny the mother's request but because he did not want it to be presumed that Harold was a martyr. Once William was firmly on the throne he was ready to concede a King's burial.

But Gytha, his mother, never forgot nor forgave; so with delight she repeated rumours of his harshness and realizing that the desertion of the Normans who were filtering back to Normandy was disastrous to him, she made sure that the stories of the orgies attended by Normans in England went back to their wives.

When William heard that the young girl who temporarily had been his mistress had been murdered, he went to see her body. Her face had been horribly mutilated and he set up an enquiry to discover her murderer.

He did but he did not punish the man for he had learned on whose orders he had been acting.

So Matilda had discovered. And she would wonder why he, the faithful husband, had suddenly changed.

260

She should know.

What a woman she was! How fierce in her hatred! He had always known that she had a spirit to match his own.

He felt a horrible revulsion as he looked down on that once lovely face. Poor child. It was no fault of hers. He would reward her father. Not that that could compensate him.

He went away and thought of Matilda and wished she were with him.

How furious she must have been when she heard the rumours, how magnificent in her anger! Hurt, bewildered and furiously, murderously angry, because William who was hers had momentarily strayed.

* * *

His days were full. He had little time to brood on Matilda's deeds. Lanfranc had come to England and been made Archbishop of Canterbury; there was one friend in England then on whom he could rely.

Those were the fighting years. There was rebellion everywhere. These Saxons were a stubborn race.

There had appeared on the Isle of Ely a mysterious and romantic figure: Hereward the Wake. His estates had been taken from his family while he was away on the Continent and on learning of this he had come back and because he had succeeded in driving out the Norman to whom William had given his family's estates, a legend had grown up around him.

He had set up a banner to which men flocked; it had begun to be said that there was a mysticism about him and that Heaven had chosen him to drive out the Norman invader.

The marshy fen country which was often enveloped in mist was known as the Isle of Ely. The unwary traveller venturing into this strange place would find himself sinking into swamps and lakes which were often stagnant; it was dangerous country, the home of wild fowl whose cries, sounding weirdly through the mists, were said to be the voices of spirits.

Because of the nature of this part of the country it was not easy for the Normans to rout out the rebels and because Hereward continued to harass them, he became known as England's Darling and stories circulated about his daring

261

exploits. Legends grew up around his name and many adventures were attributed to him.

When a Danish force sailed up the Ouse, Hereward and his followers joined with it and together they raided the Abbey of Peterborough and stole its treasure, which Hereward rather naïvely believed he was saving from the Normans. The Danes were naturally delighted to gain so much for so little trouble but proved themselves false allies for, when William offered to leave them unmolested and allow them to keep all the spoils they had managed to amass during their stay if they would desert their friends of the Fen Country, gleefully they accepted and sailed off with the Peterborough treasure, leaving Hereward to his marshy Fens.

No one gained anything from this adventure as a storm destroyed most of the Danish fleet before it reached Denmark and although the treasure was saved it was lost in a fire which broke out when those who survived the expedition were celebrating their return.

William was determined to rout out Hereward. He was well aware that a legend could be more difficult to displace than an army. To burn down castles was nothing to William. To march at the head of an avenging army, to lay waste towns and villages—that was fighting he knew well. But to lead an army through the misty marshes was another matter.

Often his men were lost in the mists; some were sucked down into the marshes. They developed a horror of what they called the haunted country; and Hereward was allowed to live on in defiance of the King.

But William was not the man to be daunted. It was imperative that he drive Hereward from his stronghold and most important of all he must prove to the people that Hereward was a man no less; ay, and as a mere man could not hope to stand against the might of the Conqueror.

As he stood looking over those marshes and listening to the weird call of the wild fowl he realized that he could not take the place with land troops. He would have to build bridges over swamps; he would have to make firm roads. Once he had done this he would rout out Hereward the Wake.

His attention to detail was meticulous; but even he was disturbed by the strange atmosphere of that marshy wilderness. Yet he would allow nothing to stand in his way.

He commanded that a tower be built and in this he installed a witch whose duty it was to drive off the evil spirits.

In due course it was as he had known it would be. He conquered Ely as he had conquered all; Hereward fled the country and was heard of no more.

Even then there were fresh outbreaks of rebellion. The Scottish King marched into England; William met him and drove him back. So terrified was Malcolm when William the Conqueror set foot on his soil that he immediately swore to become his vassal.

William marched south, the triumphant conqueror. When men were tempted to rebel against him they would consider what had happened to those who had made the attempt.

The people of England were beginning to accept the fact that William was their King, that he was determined to remain so and that they would be well advised to accept his rule.

There was peace—if an uneasy one—in England. William had been fighting for four years. It had passed quickly for there had been so much to do—so much marching from place to place. He had fought Hereward in the Isle of Ely and marched up to Scotland to subdue Malcolm.

England was quieter; he could safely leave it for a while. He would go to Normandy, see his family.

'By God's Splendour,' he said, 'four years is a long time to stay away.'

Conflict in the Family

SHE was waiting for him, as eager as she had always been. Four years! he thought. And she was beautiful still.

She was smiling at him, unusually soft and tender, her eyes brimming over with her delight.

Of course she loved him. How foolish to doubt it!

'You have grown fat,' she cried. 'Too much good living in England.'

'There was no good living for me when you were not there.'

They were lovers. They would always be lovers.

* * *

But there were shadows between them.

He said to her: 'I know of this man Brihtric.'

'He whose estates I took?' she said lightly.

He caught her arm and swung her round to face him. She had forgotten how rough his gestures could be.

'What was he to you?' he demanded.

'He was a man whose estates I took.'

'And why?'

'Because I wanted them.'

'Because you wanted him and he would have none of you.'

She flushed scarlet. 'So you have set your spies on me. How dare you!'

'I dare as I will,' he answered. 'And if I wish to know aught of my wife I will know it.'

'And if I wish to know of my husband...'

264

'Doubtless you will know that too.'

'How much do I know?' she cried passionately. 'How much is there to know? I know of the whey-faced whore of Canterbury.'

He laughed at her, maddened by the thought of her desire for Brihtric, so strong that she, a Princess of Flanders, had asked him to marry her.

'A very respectable maiden,' he said, 'the daughter of a canon.'

'Respectable no longer after her lecherous King had passed that way.'

'Should you reproach me? What of you and your Saxon?'

'I took his lands. He took nothing from me.'

'You cared enough for him to have him murdered.'

She turned pale. 'Who has told you this?'

'I have made it my affair. Matilda, you are a dangerous woman.'

'Has it taken you all these years to find out that?'

'You took his lands. Why? You did not want him.'

'I am like you, my King, a lover of lands.'

'And of handsome Saxons.'

'Not such a lover of them as you are of Canterbury whores.'

'All these years you have been thinking of this Saxon. When we were together you thought of him. You preferred him but he would have none of you so William of Normandy would serve instead.'

She narrowed her eyes and said, 'Believe that if you will. And how often have you deceived me with your women?'

'You murdered him.'

'I was nowhere near his prison.'

'But you murdered him none the less. One does not have to be near a victim to be the one who will stand before God accused of murder.'

'You to talk of murder! How many men have you slain with your own hands? How many have been done to death through you... at your orders?'

'What I have done I have done for my country. What you have done has been done for your pride.'

'And when you cut off the hands and feet of the citizens of Alençon was that for your country? Nay, William of Normandy, King of England, William the Conqueror of all—or so you think... but you never shall be of me... Nay, William, that was for your pride. They called you Bastard.

265

They reminded you that your mother was the daughter of a tanner. That was why they lost their hands and feet. Oh, assuage your pride, do as you will, but pray do not take such a lofty attitude with me. I know you too well.'

'As I am beginning to know you. You had him murdered...that man whom you had loved. Matilda, I saw that girl afterwards...'

'And tell me, did you still desire her?'

He lifted his hand suddenly and smote her across the face.

She fell to the floor and lay there laughing at him. 'Come,' she said, 'beat me. It will not be the first time. Do you remember how you rolled me in the mud because I said I would not marry a bastard.'

'I would to God you never had.'

She was on her feet suddenly. 'You mean that?' she asked. 'William, do you mean that you wish you had never married me?'

She was clinging to him, her face upturned and suddenly his temper had disappeared. This was Matilda...his Matilda, the only person in the world for whom he truly cared.

His arms were round her and he was saying: 'No, never...never. Whatever you are...whatever I am...we were meant for each other.'

She was laughing now. 'No one else in the world would have done for me. Brihtric the Saxon! Bah, that puny lily-livered churl. Had I married him I would have murdered him for other reasons than I did when you came along. It was because he had insulted William's wife that he must die. The Queen of England, wife to William the Conqueror, could not allow him to live. Are you fool enough not to know that?'

He looked into her face at the red mark on her cheek which his hand had made. He kissed it.

'You are heavy-handed, William,' she said. 'But I like well that you have marked me with your hands. On that other occasion the bruises stayed for weeks and I would use no lotions, no unguents, to soothe them because they had been made by you.'

'I was maddened when I heard what you had done.'

'You cared so much about a miserable Saxon!'

'I thought only that you had wanted him.'

'I was a child, William. A foolish girl. Nay, I have never wanted any other but you since I set eyes on you. That is

266

why the news of your love for this girl maddened me.'

'"Twas not love. It was anger ... anger against you and Brihtric. You need not have treated her so cruelly.'

'She took you from me.'

'No one has ever done that. No one ever shall.'

'It seemed so. I shall never forget when I heard of it. I could think of nothing but revenge, and revenge I took.'

'On an innocent girl.'

'Pray cease to mourn for her or I shall believe that you truly loved her.'

'We should never have been separated.'

'For,' she added, 'clearly I cannot trust you.'

'You can always trust me as long as I know that you love me and that I am the only one for you as you are for me.'

And then it was between them as it had ever been.

* * *

He prayed that all would go well in England for he wanted to stay in Normandy. The differences between himself and Matilda had been wrought by their separation; they only had to meet face to face and all was well.

Now it seemed to him that they were happy as they had been in the very beginning of their marriage. Matilda was once more pregnant, and he was delighted.

Easter came and Cecilia was about to take the veil. It was some years since she had entered the convent and she had passed through her novitiate.

The great ceremony was attended by William and Matilda.

'It is good,' said William, 'to give a daughter to God.'

In the privacy of their chamber they talked of the children. Richard was in England.

'Lanfranc tells me he is a good student. He will make a good king to follow me,' said William.

'He will be less harsh.'

'Let us hope that by the time he comes to the throne I shall have made England so secure that there is no need of harshness. Robert shall have Normandy. His fingers itch for it now.'

'And Rufus? And Henry?'

'It seems to me that you have given me too many sons.'

'You have often said that a King could not have too many.'

'I doubt not we shall find possessions for them. And it is

267

well for Kings and rulers to have brothers. They should be more able to put their trust in brothers than in strangers.'

'Yet the trouble in Normandy has been with members of your blood. And in England had Tostig stood by Harold there could have been a different story.'

'I would wish my sons to be good brothers one to the other. Many of those who rose against me did so because I was a bastard. I saw their reasoning. Had my father married my mother and I been his legitimate son much less blood would have been shed over Normandy. And had Tostig been as good a brother to Harold as Gurth and Leofwine were, then Harold might still be King. So you see why my sons must have more wisdom than others have had. They must remember that united they will be strong, in discord they are weak.'

'I pray with you that there may never be discord between them.'

'I have decided Adela shall be given to the Count of Blois. He will be a good ally to Robert when he governs Normandy. I want to see the children settled in their niches, which I shall before I die.'

'I beg of you do not talk of dying. You are a young man yet.'

'When I am with you I feel so,' he answered. 'And now we have Cecilia, a holy nun. I trust she will remember to pray for the good of her family.'

'I am sure she will do that.'

'I have decided on Alan, Duke of Bretagne, for Constance. He has been a good ally and it will strengthen our friendship.'

'Soon they will all be settled,' sighed Matilda.

There was much to be done. Triumphant tours, matters of state, visits to his various castles—all this exhilarated him. He was particularly interested in the magnificent piece of tapestry which was not quite finished. It depicted the scene of William's conquest from the landing of Harold in Normandy to his fall at Hastings and was worked on a canvas which was sixty-seven yards in length though but nineteen inches wide.

He admired it and said that when it was completed it should be set up in the Cathedral of Bayeux and he would often come to look at it.

'Turold the dwarf has done his work well,' said Matilda. 'He is a fine artist but you should see him strut whenever the tapestry is mentioned. I have rewarded him.'

'Doubtless you will employ him to design more of your canvases.'

'Doubtless I shall for I could not find a better designer.'

William could not take his eyes from the work— everything was brought back so clearly. Harold being delivered into his hands, the blazing comet, the landing in England and the battle of Hastings.

It was a monument to his victory; it would live through the ages as surely as his great Tower of London which would be erected by the time he returned.

But he did not want to think of returning. For a period here he could perhaps forget rebellion. He wanted a little respite, to stay cosy in the heart of his family.

*   *   *

Matilda's child proved to be a girl. They called her Gundred.

'Perhaps 'tis as well,' said William. 'Had it been another boy what should we have given him? Daughters are good for marrying and making strong alliances.'

'Pray do not talk of my children as though they are pawns on your chessboard.'

He smiled at her. 'What a brood we have given ourselves, Matilda! I come to think that Richard is the best. He will make a good king of England. Lanfranc tells me that he has all the qualities.'

'You should not have favourites.'

'You to talk of favourites! What of Master Curthose? Is he not the darling of your heart?'

'He is my first-born and I beg of you do not call him by that name. He does not like it.'

'Then he must needs endure it. By God's Splendour, Matilda, I have had enough of his arrogance.'

'Since he is your son, what do you expect?'

'Come, let us talk of pleasanter matters. Henry will be for the church. I may take him back to England with me and put him in the charge of Lanfranc.'

'He astonishes his tutors, William.'

'Odd that we should have given birth to a scholar. Curthose will never be that.'

'He will be a fine general of his armies which is perhaps more useful.'

269

'I am weary of hearing you sing his praises. Rufus is growing up a brave fellow.'

'A shadow of yourself. The devil's temper and a passion for the hunt.'

'Oh come, I have other qualities, would you not say?'

'I doubt whether Rufus will ever be anything but a shadow of his father—nor will any of them,' said Matilda seriously.

He smiled at her tenderly and she said quickly, 'Robert is of a different nature completely.'

'Well, I must perforce make allowances for a mother's prejudices."

'Remember it,' she told him.

* * *

Robert was restive. He wished his father would go back to England. He hated William. From his childhood he had felt inadequate in his presence. 'Curthose', William had called him and given him the nickname he hated. Why should a man have to be tall to be a great one? Were inches of such importance? Rollo was too big for his horse, Richard the Fearless, Robert the Magnificent, William the Conqueror, to the devil with them all. So proud of their Viking ancestors. It was time they started to be themselves instead of shadows of the past. He was weary of the name of Rollo. He himself was half Flemish half Norman and he felt closer to the Flemings than the Normans, closer to his mother than to his father. His mother could be relied on; she was sympathetic and understanding. He knew she pleaded his cause with his father.

Here he was, nineteen years old. Old enough to be a ruler in his own right. He was to have Normandy. When? Was he to wait until his father died? By the look of him he had years left to him. And while he lived he, Robert, must be of no importance, except that he was the eldest son, but always in leading strings.

'The trouble with my father,' he had told his mother, 'is that he cannot bear to give up anything. He has to own everything within his reach and keep it.'

Matilda said: 'It has been hard-won.'

'He has Normandy and England. How can he govern both? When he is in England he needs rulers in Normandy and so in England. What way is that to go on? He has chosen England. He likes better to be a King than a Duke. Very well, he is the almighty one, the all-powerful one. Let him have England. But Normandy should be mine.'

'Do not let him hear you say that,' begged Matilda. 'He might even give it to Richard.'

'Richard is to be King of England.'

'Rufus, then.'

'Rufus. That red-faced fool.'

Matilda said: 'It ill-behoves you, my son, to jeer at his red face.'

'But my short legs may become a jest.'

"Twas no jest, Robert. 'Twas in the first place a term of endearment. Now, I beg of you, try to make peace with your father.'

'I make peace with him! Is he not the one who decides whether or not there shall be peace?'

'You know how upset I am when I see discord between you.'

'You think only of soothing him.'

'You know I think of you, too. Oh, Robert, for my sake, try not to anger him.'

Robert's anger evaporated as he looked at his mother. She was his friend, he knew. Her loyalties were torn between them both. He wondered whose side she would be on if it were necessary at some time to take sides.

It might well be, for he had no intention of going on in this way.

*　　*　　*

On a balcony high up in the castle Rufus and Henry were playing a dice game.

Henry, though years younger than Rufus, was so clever that mentally they were almost of an age; because of this his family were apt to forget his youth.

Rufus looked down suddenly and saw his brother Robert in the courtyard surrounded by his companions. These were young men whom he had chosen to favour deliberately because he knew his father did not like them. They were inclined to be dissolute, cynical young men who, knowing they would never find favour with William, sought to curry it with Robert and with him looked forward to the day when William returned to England.

Rufus, mischievous and hot-tempered, had his own

grievances. Robert was always complaining that his father delayed in passing the dukedom over to him. Richard was training to be King of England. But what of them...and Henry? What were they to have, with big brothers stepping in before them?

'Look at old Curthose strutting down there,' he said to Henry. 'He acts as though he is the Duke of Normandy, this his castle, and we his vassals.'

'It is because of his short legs,' said Henry. 'If they were longer he would not need to tell us that he is as good as...nay better than the rest of us.'

'And those friends of his. They look at me as though I am of no account. I'd remind them that I am the son of a King and a Duke even though I am not the eldest. Come, let's have some fun with them, Henry.'

Standing on the terrace was a jar of water which had been there for some time and was stagnant.

Rufus picked it up and carrying it to the edge of the balcony, tilted it forward so that the group of young men, in the centre of which was Robert, were sprinkled with it.

Rufus drew back and the two boys were convulsed with laughter for they could hear the angry exclamations from below.

'That,' said Rufus, 'will teach them a lesson. This is dirty water, Henry. Look at the green slime. Their fine robes will be thoroughly spoilt.'

This seemed a tremendous joke to the boys and boldly Rufus determined to repeat it. He perched the jar on the edge of the balustrade and tipped it over.

There was a cry from below.

'Look up there,' said a voice.

'By God,' cried Robert, 'it's those devils of brothers. I'll teach them a lesson.'

'Quick,' said Rufus. They ran into the chamber and drew the heavy bolt.

It was not long before there was a hammering on the door. 'Come out, you young varlets.'

'Go away and grow your legs, Curthose,' called Rufus.

'I'll kill you, you insolent young devil,' was the answer.

'Just try,' shouted Rufus.

Henry listened, applauding Rufus.

'Open this door,' cried Robert, who had been joined by his friends.

'Get out your battering ram,' shouted Rufus, and he and

Henry were hysterical with laughter.

'You are deliberately insulting me,' said Robert. 'You did it purposely. You think you will have your father on your side if you insult me. I'll not have it. I shall run you through with my sword, William Rufus. We'll see if your blood is as red as your hair.'

They were hammering on the door. It was heavy and Rufus regarded it complacently. But he was thinking that he could not stay here for ever and when he came out Robert would be waiting for him. Robert was impulsive; he had a quick temper. Most of them had in the family and he meant—at least at the moment—what he said about running him through.

The door shook.

He looked at Henry. 'They are battering it down.'

'It's like a siege,' said Henry excitedly. 'This is how it must be when your castle is being taken by the enemy.'

Rufus was really getting rather frightened. He looked about him. Could they escape by way of the balcony? The drop was too steep.

Henry was watching the door with a calm calculation which was typical of him.

'If only I had a sword, I'd fight him,' said Rufus.

The door creaked on its hinges. Then gave a groan and moved inwards.

There stood Robert, the green slime of the dirty water on his coat, his eyes blazing with fury. Seeing Rufus he drew his sword from its sheath.

'There you are, my brave Rufus. What say you now? Wait till I slit your throat with the point of this fine steel. Perhaps I will put out your eyes, how's that?'

'Go away,' said Rufus, backing to the wall.'

'And Henry,' mocked Robert. 'You are in this, you insolent young dog. Don't think you will escape me.'

Rufus ran for the door. He was on the balcony. Robert ignored Henry and went after him. Rufus was leaning against the balcony, his face more ruddy than usual, his red hair wild.

A thunderous voice from behind said: 'What means this?'

Their father was standing in the doorway. Robert turned to him, his sword raised. In a second William's sword was in his hand. The two young boys looked on in relief. They were safe now. Their father had come to their

273

rescue and Robert was the one who would be punished.

William stepped on to the balcony. Robert glowered at him. Their swords crossed for a few seconds while they looked into each other's face. Robert had forgotten his anger with his brothers in his hatred for his father.

With a gesture of contempt William sent Robert's sword hurtling from his hand. He still stood holding his own.

'So you would kill my sons, eh?' he said. 'They are of a size to make you brave. Come, let us see you fight now.'

'I...have no sword.'

'And why not? Were you not holding it in good fighting spirit when I came in?'

Robert could say nothing. His humiliation before the grinning Rufus was intolerable.

'Come,' said William. 'Pick up your sword. If you must fight. Then we will.'

Robert picked up his sword but in an instant William had once more sent it swirling from his hand.

'You have not yet learned to hold it. If I were you, I should learn how to handle a sword before I was so brave with it.'

With a cry of rage Robert sprang at his father's throat. With one hand William hurled him against the parapet. He approached him, sword in hand. Fortunately for Robert at that moment Matilda came running in.

'For the love of God,' she cried, 'what means this?'

William turned to her. 'Your son has been trying to kill his brothers.'

'They insulted me,' screamed Robert. 'They tried to humiliate me and my friends.'

'William,' said Matilda, 'I beg of you put away your sword.'

'I may need it,' said William, 'to protect myself against this son of yours. He is in a bloodthirsty mood and threatening to slay me as well as his brothers. Mind you, he is in less fighting mood now than when I entered. I don't think he was counting on me as an opponent. He likes better to try his skill with a sword on unarmed children.'

'William, please...'

Robert's face was dark with anger. He turned to Matilda. 'Those boys insulted me. They threw dirty water on me and my friends. I merely meant to teach them a lesson.'

'With a sword?' asked William.

'I was...but frightening them.'

'And were frightened in your turn, Master Curthose.'

274

What hatred blazed from the eyes of both! It alarmed Matilda.

'It is a storm over nothing,' she said. 'As for the boys they shall be punished. They must learn not to throw water on their elders. Now, Robin, my son, leave us.'

He was only too glad to get away from the scene of his humiliation. Matilda turned to the boys. 'Go to your chamber,' she said. 'You will be whipped soundly. You, Rufus, because you are the elder, and you, Henry, because you are old enough to know better.'

That left her with William.

'I'll kill that boy one day,' he said.

'He was angry because his fine clothes have been spoilt. It's a just cause for anger.'

'I believe he would have run Rufus through.'

'Rufus is an irritating boy. He never thinks of others, only his own fun and pleasure.'

'But he is his brother.'

'And you are their father. What do you want from your children, William? Meekness?'

'I expect good sense. Richard has it. Why not the others?'

'Richard is a saint, it seems.'

'I thank God he is my second boy that I may make him King of England. Robert would be useless. He would never rule well. He lets his emotions override his judgement and that is not good in a ruler. As for Rufus...'

'Oh come, William. Rufus is young yet; and Robert is chafing because he is a man now and has no position of his own. Once he has that you will see a change in him.'

'I want to see a change in him before I hasten to put power into his hands.'

Uneasy as she was, Matilda was thankful that she had arrived in time. Perhaps it was as well that William would soon go to England and Robert remain in Normandy.

If they were often together one would surely ere long do the other a mischief.

* * *

That day Robert left the castle taking with him his special friends.

He had no intention, he said, of staying under the same roof as his father. He was weary of being treated as though he were a child. He would like his father to know that he had *friends* . . . sympathetic friends.

There was something about that phrase which was ominous.

Matilda was in despair. There were two people only in the world whom she truly loved—William and Robert—and these two had chosen to hate each other.

She tried to reason with William.

'He is your son, William. Try to understand. He is no longer a boy. Naturally he resents being set aside.'

'He would have to show me that he is capable of rule before I give him the power he asks:'

'He will. I promise you, William.'

'Matilda, why are you so blind where he is concerned? I had always thought you were a discerning woman.'

'I am, William. I know my own son and I know my own husband. They are so much alike that they must of necessity have their differences. If he came back would you talk with him?'

'If he talked sense I would.'

'He will talk sense.'

'I like not his friends. Do you not see that he chooses them from the ranks of those whom I distrust?'

'If you would but try to understand him it would make me happy. This discord between you alarms me. He is young and I fear your enemies will take advantage of his youth.'

'And of his folly and his disloyalty, I doubt not.'

'William, I am going to beg him to come back to talk to you. Will you promise me that you will see him and for my sake try to come to some understanding?'

At length he let her persuade him. Matilda then set about begging her son to come back and attempt a reconciliation.

*   *   *

Robert came, but in no humble mood. William, eager to please Matilda and realizing that a son—and his eldest at that—roaming through Normandy would collect adherents and the outcome of that could be trouble, wished to bring about some sort of reasonable understanding.

Robert sensed this and misunderstood. He believed that his father could be forced into granting his request. He did not know the Conqueror.

276

'I have been promised Normandy,' he said. 'I am no longer a boy and I am weary of being treated as one. I demand my inheritance.'

'So you demand?' said William, dangerously quiet.

'Ay, I demand my rights.'

'And who has assigned these rights to you?'

'I am your eldest son.'

'A fact which has often seemed unfortunate to me.'

'I know you prefer Richard and that Rufus is your favourite. You would rather give Normandy even to Henry than to me. But you cannot. I am your first-born.'

'Do you imagine that I cannot do what I wish? What should have given you such a notion?'

'You have promised me...'

'I have promised nothing. You have been listening to evil counsellors, Master Curthose, and they have sought to seduce you from your duty. Do you remember the fate of Absalom? I would consider that if I were you.'

'I have not come here to listen to sermons,' retorted Robert. 'I had enough of those from my tutors. I came here to ask for my rights. I want my inheritance without delay.'

'Then know this,' cried William. 'It is not my custom to strip before I go to bed. As long as I live I have no intention of giving up Normandy. Nor will I divide it, for it is written: "Every kingdom that is divided against itself shall become desolate."'

'You have become very pious,' sneered Robert, 'in your efforts to explain your denial of my rights.'

'Forget not that you depend for what you call your rights on me. I won England with my good sword. The vicars of Christ placed the diadem of ancient kings on my brow and the sceptre in my hands; and if all the world were to come against me they would not compel me to give up my power to another.'

'You have promised me...'

'I have promised nothing. I will not endure that he who owed his existence to me should aspire to be my rival in my own dominions.'

'How will you prevent it?' asked Robert angrily.

'With my sword,' answered William, 'that same sword which has put down many a rebellion. And by God's Splendour so shall it do again...no matter in what quarter.'

'It would seem that I might find better justice from

277

strangers than from my father.'

'It is justice which irks you. Think you that I have seen that in you which would make me wish to give you part of my dominions?'

'If you will not keep your word it is better for me to leave Normandy.'

'I am sure we shall both be the happier for that.'

'I, by right its Duke, will not remain here as a subject.' Robert bowed briefly and left his father.

William sat down and stared ahead of him. Was this his first-born, this young man who stared at him with hatred in his eyes, who cared nothing for him only for what he could get?

He thought of the day he had been born and how proud he and Matilda had been, how they had prayed for a son, a son who would delight their days.

And God had given him Curthose!

* * *

Matilda was waiting for her son.

She seized him in her arms and held him tightly against her.

'How went it?'

'He is the most obstinate, arrogant swine...'

'Hush, Robin, you speak of your father.'

'So he kept reminding me. By God, how I hate him!'

'No, Robin, no.'

'It is no use saying No, Mother. The answer is Yes. He has always hated me and I've always hated him.'

'He is your father and a great man. Some say the greatest of our times.'

'He may say that. I say otherwise. It shall not always be as it is now.'

'But what said he? I see he has not promised to give you what you want.'

'He'll give nothing. He'll not strip till he goes to bed,' he said.

'But he will shortly be going to England. Surely...'

'You do not know him, Mother. He will cling to everything he has. Don't you know him for the most avaricious man alive?'

'He has always said that you are to have Normandy.'

278

'When he is dead. I shall be an old man by then...but I am determined not to wait.'

'What are you saying, Robin?'

'I am leaving here.'

'But where will you go?'

'Away from him. He must not think I have no friends. I have many who are weary of the Bastard's rule. Let him go to England. He is so proud of what he has won with his good sword, so pleased that the vicars of Christ have set the diadem on his head. But I shall not let him keep what is mine.'

'You must never take up arms against your father, Robin.'

'Oh, Mother, you talk foolishly. He is my enemy before he is my father.'

'Where shall you go?'

'I have not thought yet. But rest assured there are many who will be anxious to receive me.'

'His...enemies!'

'They will have to be if they are my friends.'

Matilda was silent. Then she said: 'Go to Flanders. My brother will receive you. He will look after you for my sake. You will need money. Wait awhile.'

She went away and came back with a bag into which she has hastily thrown some of her most valuable jewellery.

'Take this,' she said. 'Go now. Do not let your father see you before you go. I know his anger will be terrible. And, Robin, my son, keep me informed. Promise that you will let me know what is happening to you.'

He embraced her tenderly.

'May God's blessing be with you,' he said.

'And with you,' she answered.

* * *

She was at the turret window watching him ride away when William came to her. His face was suffused with blood and she guessed that he had been greatly provoked and was still angry.

'He has gone,' he announced.

'Who?' she answered.

'Curthose.'

'But he has only just arrived.' William must not guess

that Robert had been to her. That would only increase his anger.

'I had never thought to hear a son speak to me in such a way.'

'Oh, William, this makes me so unhappy.'

He put his arm about her. 'We shall have further trouble with that boy, Matilda.'

'I trust not.'

'He will be exploited by my enemies and he is such a fool...such a young, inexperienced fool.'

'When you were his age you had been Duke of Normandy many years. How many battles had you fought and won?'

'Therein lies the difference. He is a boy. I was a man. He is demanding from me what I fought all my life for. He would like it handed to him...just like that. By God, I could have killed him and enjoyed seeing him die.'

'I beg of you do not talk so.'

'You will have to realize the truth about him, Matilda. He is no friend to us. He is dissolute. I like not his friends. I like not his way of life. He is extravagant. He likes gaming and the company of loose women. He is no son of mine.'

'You ask too much of people, William. You cannot expect your sons to be as dedicated as you have always been. There was never one like you nor ever will be.'

He laid his arm about her shoulders. 'You have helped to make me what I am. In all my trials I think of you. And this is by no means the least of them. Our son, Matilda, to turn against us!'

'It is a childish rage.'

'Nay, I think not. We must be watchful of him. I know what he intends. To go among my enemies to stir up trouble. He will find some to support him, but not for long. He will not have the means to buy their support. He will soon find them false friends. I thank God that our first-born is a fool, Matilda. God will punish him, you will see. Come, there are pleasanter subjects. We will forget him until such a time I may find it necessary to teach him what it means to take up arms against me.'

Matilda shivered. She did not tell him that she had given their son a small fortune in jewels which would perhaps enable him to take up arms against his father.

How could she say: You are my husband and he is my son I am torn between you because I love you both.

280

* * *

William behaved as though he had forgotten the existence of Robert. He turned his attention to the marriages of his daughters. Alan of Bretagne had been accepted for Constance and Stephen of Blois for Adela. The celebrations were lavish and William was pleased with the alliances.

But he had been away too long, and matters of England needed his attention.

He was uneasy, thinking of Robert. Where was he? He could not be sure, but that it was somewhere where he was making mischief was almost certain.

There was one man whom he trusted completely and this was Roger de Beaumont.

Roger had been a close friend for many years. He was an able minister and a learned man; he had helped in the education of the children some years before and William knew that in a situation which might be delicate—if Robert decided to do something foolish—Roger would take a clear view and keep him informed.

He was closeted with Roger for some time before he left.

'The Queen is clever and shrewd,' he said, 'and a worthy regent but since my son has gone away with disloyal thoughts in his mind, an unpleasant situation could arise. I beg of you in my absence to keep a firm hold on affairs here.'

'You may trust me,' said Roger.

'I do with all my heart. I can go to England, where my presence is urgently needed, with an easy mind because I know that you are here.'

So William left for England taking Rufus with him. He left Henry, for he had not yet made his plans for his upbringing with Lanfranc, and Matilda had protested that she could not be deprived of all her children.

Death in the New Forest

How lonely it was without her family. Matilda was feeling tired and old. She needed the stimulation they could give her. Even the dramatic quarrels which had taken place between William and Robert stimulated her and suited her nature better than boredom.

It was all very well to sit over her tapestry recording great events. That was some consolation she admitted; but she was of a temper to prefer being at the heart of drama.

I am getting old, she sighed. She was nearly fifty, time perhaps that she ceased to look for adventure. She would never reach that stage.

Sometimes she almost wished there had been no conquest of England. Then there would not have been these long absences. The best times were when the children were babies and William was in Normandy.

Yet the dream of England had always been with them; but like so many dreams the anticipation was more exciting than the realization. What was the King of England but a man who must be continually on the alert, expecting disloyalty and rebellion from every quarter, hated by his subjects both here and in England? In England it was natural enough. The Saxons were not lightly accepting the Norman yoke. William's life was one long succession of battles to hold what he had taken. And here in Normandy there was trouble.

Someone was at her door. A messenger had arrived.

News from William? she wondered, her spirits rising. But it was not from William the messenger came, but from Robert.

He was in dire need and he was pleading with her for her help. She had given him a great deal when he left but that had gone now. It was necessary for him to live in the manner befitting his rank and as he had followers and some of them humble men of no substance they must come under his care.

She sent the messenger to be refreshed and lay back closing her eyes.

She could picture him so well. Robert, her beloved child. He had inherited his love of magnificence from his grandfather whose name he had taken, Robert the Magnificent. William did not understand his son. William was so austere. Yes, she would face the truth and say avaricious. He hated spending money on anything except that which would bring him more. Extravagant living had never attracted him. The only thing he spent money on was maintaining his troops, building castles, forming industries. There were times, such as his daughter's weddings, when he would cheerfully pay for lavish entertainments, but that was for a purpose, to let the people know that he approved of these marriages and the reason he would do this was because he had brought in powerful allies to be his daughter's husbands.

No, William could never understand one as gay and charming as Robert. Full of faults, perhaps, from William's standpoint, but what he could not understand was that some frailties were lovable whereas great strength of purpose could result in a coldness of manner which was quite the reverse.

Robin in difficulties! That must not be. He must understand that whenever he was in trouble the first one he must come to must be his mother.

She was rich in her own right. Some of William's cautiousness had rubbed off on her. She had coffers full of treasure.

Robin should not ask her in vain.

There was someone at the door begging admittance. It was Roger de Beaumont. She had once been rather fond of him but now she thought of him as the watchdog. William had sung his praises before he left. 'Always consult Roger. Rely on Roger. He is a good man.' There was no doubt of it.

She sighed.

'Well, Roger? What is it? I see you are concerned.'

'I like not the news I have. Lord Robert is stirring up

trouble throughout Normandy. I think he is attempting to raise an army and take the Dukedom.'

Matilda laughed in an attempt to hide her dismay.

'Oh come, Roger, how could this possibly be?'

'He is a reckless young man.'

'To take the Dukedom from his own father!'

'My lady, you know that is what he has threatened to do.'

'Threats mean nothing. As if he would ever take up arms against his father.'

'There is a messenger from him in the castle now.'

Matilda raised her eyebrows as though in surprise. How much did Roger de Beaumont know?

'I am holding him here.'

'Why so?'

'Because I think it not in the King's interest that his enemies should have free communication with the castle.'

'Perhaps you are wise,' said Matilda.

'I knew that you would agree with me.'

'I do not think for one moment that Robert would dream of taking up arms against his father, but William would applaud your decision, I am sure.'

Roger bowed and retired.

When Matilda was alone she sat pondering the situation. Of course he would take up arms against William. His friends—and he would have many—would advise him to do that. Her own brother had never liked William. Hatred for William had grown since he had become the King of England. When he was merely the Bastard Duke they had sneered at him because his mother was the daughter of a tanner; but now that he had earned the title of Conqueror they could not despise him and their envy and malice was intensified.

She knew this. She admired him more than any man she knew. She loved him; he was a part of her. She could not imagine life without him—nor, she knew, could he without her. But Robert was her son.

William did not share this love for her children which was hers. Or love for Robert that was. She did not feel so strongly about the others. Yet little Adelisa's death had moved her. Poor little girl who had loved the Saxon Harold and died, some said, of a broken heart. How different were their children from them. Adelisa had died for love; she, Matilda, had had murdered the man who had refused her. Robert yearned for his Dukedom and would doubtless fight for it. He was brave but too reckless. Deep in her heart she knew he would never get the better of his father.

And he was in difficulties. He needed help.

Sly Roger might well know that the messenger had brought a letter for her. He would guess what it contained; and for this reason he was holding the messenger captive in the castle.

She pictured Robert, perhaps suffering hardship, chafing against delay, asking himself: Has my mother turned against me?

What had she said before he went? 'Always come to me. Let me know where you are. I will help.'

She sent for a man who held a post in her household. Because she loved intrigue she had always kept certain agents whom she could call when she needed some private business transacted. She would send for them, secretly. She would meet them as if by chance when perhaps she was out riding or they called with travelling packs of goods—which was a favourite method, and perhaps, because of this, becoming suspect. Then she would tell them what she required of them.

One man whom she trusted particularly was Sampson. She arranged to meet this man now, for she had made up her mind that if her son was in need she could not fail him no matter what the consequences.

* * *

William was growing very corpulent. It was jokingly said that he grew more and more like Rollo every day and that soon it would not be possible to find a horse to hold him.

Since his quarrel with Robert he had grown morose. He had always been thus when parted from Matilda. While his grasping nature loved his possessions yet he grudged the need constantly to defend them.

Now he was in England, parted from Matilda, wondering what Robert was doing in Normandy. He had his sons Richard and Rufus with him; and he often wondered, what dark thoughts were going on in the mind of Rufus.

Rufus was clever in his way. He had a certain wit; but William did not care for the companions he chose. Unlike Robert he was not interested in extravagance and women. He surrounded himself with young men like himself. They might be effeminate. Rufus was certainly not. His great passion in life was the chase and in this he and his father at least had something in common. Even Richard enjoyed the chase. It was the great relaxation. To ride after the deer, the wild boar, the stag with the dogs yelping at the horses' feet was the complete joy. While he was thus engaged William could forget the disloyalties of his first-born; his dissatisfaction with Rufus, his longing to be home with Matilda. Nothing could soothe him as the chase.

It was said of him: 'The King loves all wild beasts as though he is their father.'

He was determined to preserve the forests. He had made new ones, in particular one in Hampshire which was called the New Forest. In order to make this humble people had been turned out of their homes.

The fact that the people of England had fought against him and that he had had to conquer them over many years had hardened him against them. Had they accepted him after the battle of Hastings he would have treated them more leniently. Much blood had been shed, much treasure wasted in the conquest of England and he grudged that.

He was hated. He was always the conqueror. Therefore he retaliated with harsh laws. Any man who killed a wild beast was punished by having his eyes put out. As many of the peasants had lived by what they could catch, this was a hard and cruel rule.

Because the people would not accept him he was determined to show them who was master. He displayed a blind indifference to their dislike. Let them beware. If they broke any of his laws, he would have no mercy.

His New Forest was his delight and he had special laws to protect the animals. If any man kept a dog within a certain radius of the forest that dog must have its hind leg clipped that it might not chase and possibly kill the precious hares. To hunt in the forest it was necessary to get the permission of the King. But the New Forest, which the King so loved, was regarded by the people with misgiving; it represented so much that was cruel and harsh.

There came a day when William went hunting in the New Forest with his sons Richard and Rufus.

Richard had gone off in one direction with Rufus, leaving William with his own party.

William gave himself to the joys of the chase and as he was contemplating one of the finest stags he had ever seen lying dead on the grass, a forester came galloping up with news that there had been an accident.

The hunters left the stag and rode off.

Richard was lying on the grass, bleeding to death. He had fallen from his horse and been gored by a stag.

By the time they could carry him from the forest he was dead.

* * *

A hush had fallen over the land. Richard, the King's son, who was destined to be King of England, had been killed in that forest, the construction and preservation of which had caused such misery to so many people.

'It is a curse on the King,' was the whispered comment.

People began to think of all those who had been turned out of their homes to make a happy hunting ground for the King; they thought of those poor men who had always hunted the wild boar and lived on its meat who, following their usual custom, had been caught by the King's foresters and now lived in sightless misery. They thought of all those who had not survived the King's savage punishment.

They thought of harsh rules, of taxes levied, of the curfew and all the harshness of a conqueror's rule, and they said: 'This is a judgement on the King.'

* * *

Matilda in Bayeux, heard the news.

Richard, the good one, the one they had trusted to be a credit to them, the son who lacked Robert's arrogance and the crudeness of Rufus, Richard, the one of whom they had been proud!

How William must be mourning. His son Richard whom he had loved best...to die. Robert working against him. Rufus? Who could be sure of Rufus? Henry, little more than a child. Richard, the flower of the flock, dead, killed by one of those stags for whose sake peasants had lost their eyes.

William should be with her now. They should be sharing this grief. She alone would know how to comfort him.

But even while he mourned he would be thinking of the effect this would have on the people. God was against him, they would be saying. One son a rebel, another slain by God's hand in that very forest of which he had been so proud.

287

She was right, William mourned deeply. There had been something saintly about Richard as there had about little Adelisa.

Were they too good for the world?

He had felt so happy in Richard. There was a son in whose hands he would most happily leave his crown.

Richard would not have been a harsh king. Nor had William wished him to be. The harsh laws had to be made by the man who had conquered the land. The people would have loved Richard.

And now what was left. Rufus. Rufus for King of England!

I must perforce make him into a King, thought William.

And he admitted to himself that that would not be an easy task.

A Dramatic Encounter

WILLIAM read the despatches in his hand. He could not believe it. It was not possible. Roger de Beaumont had made a terrible mistake. His anger rose up against the man. How dared he! He could not believe and yet...'

'I am greatly disturbed,' Roger had written. 'Robert has risen against your rule. This was expected and our defences are strong. What I feel it my duty to tell you is this: He has been receiving help which has enabled him to equip men to fight against you, and this aid has been supplied to him by the Queen.'

Matilda! She could not work against him. She could not side with his enemy!

Yet for Robert...

Nothing had ever touched him as deeply as this. The death of Richard, the death of Adelisa, the slurs he had suffered in his youth when he was called a bastard, the loss of good and faithful friends, none of these had ever touched him as deeply as the treachery of Matilda.

He would not believe it. He dared not believe it. If he had to accept this hideous accusation there would be great emptiness in his life from which he would never recover.

Matilda and he were as one person. He was not an affectionate man, but from the first days of his marriage with Matilda there had been one in his life who was as necessary to him as all his dominions. He could love possessions rather than people, the hunt rather than the company of men; he could be a ruler, a good one though a harsh one and he cared passionately for his kingdom and his dukedom; but he cared as passionately for Matilda.

And she had betrayed him. She had been forced to take sides and she had not chosen his.

Clearly he must return to Normandy.

* * *

The evidence was in his hands. He would trust no one with this but himself. He had captured her miserable agent. He had read the letters in Matilda's own hands. She had robbed her coffers for the sake of Robert; she had supplied him with money and jewels. She had enabled him to equip an army that he might stand against his father.

He rode to Rouen. She was not expecting him but her delight in his arrival was obvious.

He said: 'I must speak with you alone.'

She knew immediately that something was wrong.

'What ails you, William?' she asked.

'Trouble in my realm,' he said, keeping his eyes on her face as he thrust a letter into her hands. 'Your handwriting,' he added.

'Why yes.'

'So you are in league with my enemies.'

'I write to my son.'

'You...traitor!' he cried, and there was anguish in his voice. 'You deceived me. A woman who deceives her husband destroys her house. Oh, my wife, whom I have loved as my own life, where could you have found a husband as faithful as I have been, so devoted to you in my affection? Yet you have deceived me. You have joined my enemies against me. I have given you riches and treasure and these you have passed over to my enemies. You have squandered my wealth on those who work against me. I have confided my government to you, believing that I could not leave it in more faithful and loving hands. Yet in secret you have joined my enemies against me.'

Matilda faced him, her anger matching his. 'Should you be surprised at a mother's feelings for her son?'

'Yes. If that son be an enemy of her husband.'

'He is my son, my first-born son. I love him, William, even as I love you. You are rich and powerful. He is in need. I gave to him yes, and would give again. If I could give my life for him, most cheerfully I would do so. And for you. You know this well. You are my husband but he is my son.'

'You had to choose between us,' said William.

'Yes,' she said defiantly. 'I had to choose and because he was in need I chose him.'

'You chose him because you love him the better.'

She was silent.

A wave of such jealousy overtook him that he seized her by her plaits and threw her to the ground.

It was almost as though he were back in that street in Lille years ago when incensed because she, who was so beautiful, so royal and had declared that she would never marry a bastard, was for him the only woman he wanted. Now he was conscious of a fierce hatred that was born of love and was in some measure love. He was wounded as never before; he was hurt and angry; he was jealous of that short-legged boy whom he had never liked and who now had taken first place in Matilda's affections. He beat out his misery on her with heavy hands. He bruised her body as he had on that other occasion, but she was no longer young and she had borne many children.

'William,' she cried, 'you will kill me.'

'Ay,' he said, 'as you have killed my love for you. By God's Splendour, I have been foolish in my devotion for you. But it is over. You are my enemy. You, who were my wife and bore my children! I will be revenged on you ... and your agents. Your man Sampson shall not see his way to the enemy's camp ever again.'

'Nay, William, the fault ... if fault there be, is mine. He but obeyed orders.'

He smote her again and he saw that she had fainted.

'Oh God, Matilda,' he cried. 'Have I killed you, Matilda, my love?'

He lifted her tenderly and carried her to her bed.

He sat beside her until she recovered consciousness.

'Matilda,' he said, 'speak to me.'

'Oh, William,' she said, 'is it you?'

'I will send your servants. They will tend you but first I must speak to you.'

'Your hands have lost none of their heaviness,' she told him with a wry smile.

'How could you do this to me?'

'I can say no more than that I am a mother.'

He bent over her and kissed her.

'Whatever happened,' she said, 'whatever you did to me or I to you ... we are as one. We know that, William.'

''Tis true,' he said. 'Rest now.'

291

She did not rest. She sent for one of her most trusted servants.

'Sampson is on his way here with letters,' she said. 'He must not come. They are waiting for him. The King will put out his eyes. He must go to a monastery and ask for sanctuary. Tell him to do this on my orders.'

She lay in her bed waiting. William was no longer angry with her, it seemed, only hurt and deeply wounded. He was anxious now because of any harm he might have inflicted on her.

But he was waiting for the return of Sampson. There would be no mercy there. She knew William. When his violent temper was aroused it must be assuaged. He would wreak his revenge for her treachery on Sampson.

He came to her, his anger no longer blazing, but smouldering still.

He looked down at her sadly.

'Still unrepentant,' he said.

'Still always ready to help my son.'

'Against your husband?'

'Nay, I would die for them both.'

'Oh, Matilda,' he said, 'I would he had never been born. To think that my tall good son Richard should have met his death in my forest while Curthose lives.'

'What has happened,' replied Matilda, 'is God's will.'

She was weak and as the days passed it was clear that she was still suffering from William's onslaught. The beating had been less severe than that suffered in the streets of Lille but she was less able to bear it now. Then it had been an exhilaration; now it was humiliation. She knew—and surely he must know—nothing could be quite the same between them again. But they were too close not to be necessary to each other.

She was at her tapestry when he came to her and told her that Sampson had escaped to a monastery.

'He will stay there in sanctuary. Doubtless he will become a monk. So he keeps his eyes. He has you to thank for them.'

'If he had lost them he would have had me to blame.'

'But you saw that he found refuge, did you not? Your agents warned him. Is that not so?'

'That's so,' she said.

He laughed then. Then he embraced her. 'By God's Splendour,' he said, 'I must keep a firm hand on those who work against me.'

But he would never wholly trust her again. She knew it and it saddened her. When he left for England she was still Regent but there were those who were set to watch her.

He loved her, he needed her, but he no longer trusted her. She loved him, she needed him, but she would betray him for the sake of her own.

She could never admire Robert as she admired William. She knew that she had married the greatest man of his age and her love for her son did not blind her to his weakness. The arrogance, the love of power, the desire to be popular and appreciated, the fancy for finery, the preoccupation with women, choosing friends who flattered him, hating criticism, always looking for the slight—these were not the qualities which made a ruler. But he was her son and she loved him; she did not know why she must devote herself to him in preference to William, except that Robert was weak and William was strong.

Robert would never love her as William did. Yet William for all his strength needed her too.

She, a woman who admired strength and power must turn from William for Robert's sake. Why? Love was something too subtle for her understanding.

Gone were the happy years. Never again would she know them. Even when she had been separated from William she had had the excitement of waiting for his return. Every day she had looked for him and the overwhelming joy when he arrived had been an event outstanding in a lifetime of outstanding events.

Never again.

She feared his coming for that might mean that Robert was making an attack on one of his strongholds. He would come suspiciously, wondering how much of the treasure she had given had gone towards building up Robert's strength.

There was news and that from Robert. He was gathering adherents to his banner. There were always men to be jealous of William. He was a power in Europe. King of England and Duke of Normandy; there were many watchful eyes upon him.

The King of France, while not wishing to indulge in open warfare with William, would not be displeased to see strife in his kingdom. When Robert appealed to him for help he declared that it was a sad thing to see the heir of Normandy

293

dispossessed of his rights and roaming the countryside seeking supporters. He would therefore give him the castle of Gerberoi so that he might have headquarters in which to carry out his plans.

This was naturally construed as an act of friendship to Robert and as a result many Frenchmen flocked to his banner and perceiving this, those Normans who felt they had a grievance against William did not see why they should not join their fortunes with those of the heir. They had nothing to lose, for William would give them nothing and it seemed likely that Robert must inherit sooner or later, since William could not live for ever.

When this news reached William in England he was filled with wrath. He sent for Rufus who was constantly with him and who, now that he knew that he was to inherit England on the death of his father, was determined to please him.

Rufus was a good soldier who revelled in the hunt, even as William did, so that they had many a good excursion into the forest together. It seemed that this son was making up for the loss of Richard and the treachery of Robert. If he could have one good son he supposed he should consider himself lucky.

Rufus was ambitious. There was young Henry to consider of course, but he by this time was with Lanfranc and proving himself quite a scholar. Henry for the Church, then, for the archbishop's role was an important one as his Uncle Odo was proving in England now. (Sometimes he wondered whether the power he now had was changing Odo.) But it was as well to have one of the members of the family in the Church.

'Listen to this,' said William to his son. 'Curthose has set up his banner at Gerberoi. French and Normans are rallying to him. He plans to set himself up as Duke. What say you, my son?'

'I say this,' said Rufus. 'It is time we set out for Normandy to show him that we have other plans.'

Rufus's red face glowed with passion; the Conqueror looked at his son with approval. They were, as so often, of one mind.

*   *   *

Matilda took to her bed. She felt dizzy and sick. That it should have come to this—William and Robin fighting

294

against each other! It was for Robert she trembled. If they came face to face how would he fare in the hands of the old warrior? What hope would he have? In her mind's eye she saw the lance pierce his heart.

Who would have dreamed of this when he was a baby and they had both been so proud of him. If he had had long legs like Richard, if he had the Norman looks, would it have been different?

She tried to pray but if she prayed for Robert's safety might she not be praying for William's defeat? But William had never been defeated. In the countless battles in which he had taken part not one drop of his blood had ever been shed.

'Oh God,' she prayed, 'save my son.'

* * *

On the plain of Archembraye beside the castle of Gerberoi the battle raged fiercely. In William's heart there blazed a mounting anger. The fact that the man he had sired had dared take up arms against him and was leading this attack seemed to him incredible. It was like a bad dream.

'By God's Splendour,' he had vowed, 'I will show this Curthose what it means to take up arms against me.'

He did not believe the battle would last long. He despised Curthose. He had not the experience. He had nothing to commend him. It was true he had managed to gather together a formidable force and it was shocking to think that so many Normans had rallied to his banner. William himself was relying on some of his English troops whom he had brought with him. But he was the general and with him in charge a handful of men could make short work of a legion.

It was with some dismay that he discovered all was not going as he wished. What had happened? Had some sorcerer put a spell on him? Fleetingly he thought of Matilda—on her knees no doubt, praying for the success of her son.

He was attacked at the rear and he had not expected this. Suddenly the ranks of his troops seemed to disintegrate. He roared at them but they could not re-form.

A lance pierced his arm and he fell. The enemy was upon him. He, the Conqueror, had been unhorsed and was at their mercy.

He must get up. He must remount. He must be there to lead his troops.

He began to shout. 'Help me up. Get me on my horse. Don't you see who I am?'

A man was bending over him to strike. At the sound of his voice his assailant paused. He lifted his vizor and the man who was preparing to kill him was his own son Robert.

It was almost as though fate had contrived this dramatic moment. There lay the Conqueror defenceless on the ground and standing over him lance in hand ready to pierce him through the heart was his son.

Robert stammered: 'Father!'

'Yes, you traitor!' roared William. 'It is your father.'

Robert knelt down. 'Oh God, so it is indeed you.'

'Well, you have your lance. It is a fitting deed and one I would expect of you.'

But Robert laid down his lance.

'Let me set you on your horse,' he said.

'You are a fool,' retorted William. 'I am at your mercy. Slay me now and carry my head to your mother. Doubtless she will applaud you.'

'Father,' said Robert, 'forgive me.'

And with that he helped William to his feet and on to his horse.

He leaped on to his own and bareheaded so that all would know him, he led the wounded William out of the mêlée to safety.

* * *

William lay tossing on his bed. The wound in his arm was not serious. He heard with dismay that Rufus had been wounded also. Most disquieting of all, the day had gone to Robert by whose munificence his life had been saved.

Matilda nursed his wound and that of Rufus.

The wound to his body was not serious; it was that to his pride which was so hard to bear.

Matilda was exalted. Robert had saved his father's life. It was the answer to her prayer. All would be well now. All must be well.

She sat by his bed; she had scarcely left him since they had brought her to him.

Each day she said to him: 'You must ask Robert to come and see you now.'

But he turned his face to the wall.

She would not give up. Every day she raised the subject. It made her so happy, she said, that Robert had been the one to save his life.

'Ha,' he growled. 'Doubtless you will make a tapestry depicting your gallant son, his lance poised to murder his father.'

'It would be a good subject but I doubt you would like our little dwarf to design it for me. Nor would I wish to see you where you had been but once...at the mercy of another.'

He took her hand. 'It pleases you,' he said. 'Admit it. If one of us had to die you would liefer I were that one.'

'Nay,' she cried. 'If either of you had died that day my heart would be broken. Bruised it has been by this conflict between you. William, I grow old. See my hair is almost white. You remember how golden it used to be. And you have grown so fat that there is scarce a horse will hold you. We grow old. Let us have peace in the family if we cannot have it elsewhere.'

'You know what will happen. He will want Normandy.'

'And you will refuse it.'

'My mind is unchanged. I'll not strip now before I go to bed any more than I would then.'

'He will not ask for Normandy this time, William.'

'And why not? He was fighting for it a short time ago.'

'He will come here and ask your forgiveness. He will understand that it is easier for him than for you.'

'Easy for the victor of his petty battle.'

'Much easier. He saved your life, therefore he can come in humility. You were at his mercy, therefore your pride is great. But I do not wish him to come in humility or you to remain in your pride. I want you both to be friends for your love of me, for I grow old, William, and there cannot be many years left to me.'

'Don't talk so. Am I not older than you?'

'You are a man. You see yourself among the immortals. Oh, you are fat and you must now ride horses that can carry your weight and they are not so swift as others you have known. You have your kingdom to govern, your dukedom to hold. But I must sit at home and wait and that is hard for a woman such as I am. I want you and Robert reconciled. I want peace in our home. Please, William, see Robert for my sake and when he asks for your friendship and that the past be forgotten, give it and forget. Please, William.'

She stooped and kissed him.

And she knew that she had won.

In the castle of Rouen William awaited the coming of Robert.

He had written to him telling him to come that he might receive a full pardon for his rebellion. If he did so, William added, he would be ready to grant him everything that he could expect from the affection of a father.

With memories of that emotional encounter on the battlefield, Robert lost no time in journeying to Rouen. He came attended by only three servants to show that he put his entire trust in his father.

Matilda embraced him warily and even William received him with a show of affection.

Rufus, who was present, hid his sullen feelings. He was not pleased by the reconciliation and Robert's dramatic act, although if his father had been killed he realized it could have gone ill for him. Robert might well have kept him prisoner and taken England as well as Normandy. So as things had turned out it was as well but he did not like to see friendship between Robert and his father.

Still, there was nothing he could do about it but feign pleasure.

There was feasting in the great hall and Matilda seated with her husband on one side of her at the great table and her son on the other, declared that this was one of the happiest days of her life.

Those days at the castle with the feasting and hunting jaunts in the forest passed quickly and pleasantly. But the time must eventually come when William must return to that kingdom which demanded so much of his time to subdue and govern.

'I wish you to come with me, Robert,' he said. 'I have work for you to do. The King of Scotland is giving me trouble. I think you could help me there. You have proved yourself a good general.'

Robert, still living in the glow of that dramatic incident, declared his willingness to help his father defeat his enemies.

When Rufus and his father were alone together Rufus ventured: 'It is well my brother is accompanying us. I feel safer with him under our eyes.'

And William replied: 'I see we are of like mind.'

Odo Dreams of Greatness

BACK in England William put into progress a scheme which he had long had in mind. This was a survey which was to cover the whole of the country—not an acre of land was to be left out and there was to be a record of all cattle and such livestock. His idea was that because of the unrest in the country he needed money to maintain order and he would devise a means of taxation according to property owned.

He called this the Great Land Register but because the landowners saw this as another of the King's methods of taking their possessions from them it was called the Doomsday Book.

There was dissatisfaction with the Conqueror throughout the country but all but his greatest detractors were beginning to see that his harsh, but often just, rules had strengthened the land. Since his coming the country had become dotted with fine buildings; monasteries, churches and castles had grown up. He had brought in law and order, for so ruthless was the punishment accorded to offenders that few dared offend. The Danes appeared to be wary of raiding the coasts for fear of meeting the Conqueror whose reputation was well known. He had studied the laws of the country and kept the best and substituted the rest by those of Normandy. He had encouraged marriage between Normans and Saxons, for he had said that the surest way to a peaceful country was to destroy racial differences. He set up industries and rewarded those who worked hard. He introduced the laws of chivalry. He was rich, but did not indulge in personal extravagance. He owned many manor houses and castles; all the forests of England were his property and he would allow no one to hunt in them without his permission. This was his great passion and he, with Rufus, sought the consolation the hunt could give on every possible occasion.

Disappointed in Matilda and never trusting his eldest son, he turned more and more to Rufus. Rufus was at his conferences, and would ride beside him when there was any need to settle a rebellion; and of course they were constantly together in the hunt. He was seeking consolation in Rufus.

He often thought that he had only two sons left now—for he had never wholly forgiven Robert: Rufus and Henry. Of Henry he was proud, but Henry was a scholar—a proud bold youth but still a scholar. Lanfranc thought highly of him, so William was pleased, but his companion was Rufus; and he took pleasure in training him to step into his shoes.

* * *

Whenever possible he went back to Normandy. There he was shocked to see how Matilda had aged. Some of the spirit had gone out of her face that day when he had beaten her. He thought of this with remorse yet the memory of it sent the blood rushing to his head and his anger was so great that had either Matilda or Robert been with him he would have struck them again.

It was unwise to care too much for people. His relationship with Rufus was a sensible one. He had an affection for his son and would teach him all he would need to know, but if Rufus played the traitor he would put him aside as he had Robert and turn to Henry. It was only Matilda who was different.

But now she was gentle and loving. That was because Robert so far had behaved loyally. William knew that if his eldest son decided to rise once more against his father Matilda would betray him again as she had before. This knowledge had set a cancer in their relationship.

Families, he decided, were a mixed blessing; and there was yet another example of this. For some time he had been growing suspicious of his half-brother Odo. Their mother, Arlette (who was one other whom William had loved, but she had never done aught to harm him; there would never have been any disloyalty from her), had begged him on her death-bed to care for his young brothers, her children by Herlwin. Odo and Robert. Robert had been a loyal friend: William had given him the estates of Mortain; and Odo had become the Bishop of Bayeux.

After one of the northern revolts William had sent Odo to pass judgement on the rebels. This he had done with harshness that was remarkable even in Norman England; he had been universally detested and because of his mother's origins was known as the Tanner of the English.

Since then Odo had become ambitious. He was the brother of the King of England and Duke of Normandy: moreover William was illegitimate and their mother had been married when he, Odo, was born. It was true his father was not the Duke of Normandy so he did not aspire to the crown and the dukedom. But he was as avaricious as his brother William. He had begun to amass possessions; in his position of power he was able to extract bribes, and this he did.

He was a proud man. He could not be first in England or Normandy, he had always known that. But there were other fields. This idea came to him when he heard that an Italian soothsayer had prophesied that a Pope named Odo would follow Gregory VII. The Pope of Rome wielded as much power as any King. He knew then which way he was going.

He needed money, so he increased his extortions. He bought a palace in Rome. To make sure of his elections he must have the cardinals on his side so he sent them rich presents.

It was while William was in Normandy that Odo decided to leave for Rome. He gathered together a company of Normans who were dissatisfied with what they received from William and invited them to accompany him to Rome where, when he was Pope, he would make their fortunes. He had had a ship built and this he had loaded with treasure. It was at anchor off the Isle of Wight and he was almost ready to leave.

But William's spies outwitted him, and when the King was told of what was happening, he hastened to England and was in the Isle of Wight just before Odo's ship was due to set sail.

When William heard of Odo's pretensions to the Papal crown he jeered; but when he realized what treasure his half-brother had sent out of England his fury was great.

301

He ordered his arrest.

'I am a churchman,' retorted Odo. 'You cannot arrest me nor condemn me without the judgement of the Pope.'

William, who had been persuaded by Odo to bestow an English title on him that he might reap the monetary rewards which went with it, retorted: 'I am not arresting the Bishop of Bayeux but the Earl of Kent.'

Odo was trapped.

William himself conducted his trial after which Odo's wealth was confiscated and he was sent to prison in the dungeons of Rouen Castle.

William had stopped Odo's departure in time, but he was depressed.

He had never felt so lonely since before he had married Matilda.

Where could a man turn when his own family were so ready to betray him?

The Last Farewell

How dreary were the days at Rouen. Matilda fell to brooding on the past. She felt tired and weary.

Often she went to Bayeux Cathedral where her tapestry was on show. Studying it she could recall those events portrayed as they had happened; and she thought: If he had never conquered England we should have been together here. There would not have been these long separations. Robert would never have thought of taking Normandy if his father had not been King of England. I believe we should have had a happy life if a less glorious one.

She had changed. She longed for peace now. But what chance was there of achieving that happy state? At the moment there was an uneasy truce between Robert and William, though in England Robert had done well and proved himself a good general. He had founded a city in the north which he called New Castle Upon Tyne. But she knew them both well enough to realize that the friendship would not last. Robert had not given up his ambitions and William clung to his determination to concede nothing till death.

Each day she expected disaster. Every time a messenger came she feared to open the letter lest it contain bad news.

There was a tap on her door.

'My lady, a messenger.'

She closed her eyes. Not Robert, she prayed. Not further bad news from England.

But this was not from England. It was from Bretagne. Her daughter Constance was seriously ill and feared to be dying.

*   *   *

Is God taking His revenge on me? she wondered.

She thought of Brihtric in his cell. Did he ever understand why he had died? She thought of the girl whom William had briefly loved. Had he loved her? She would not believe that he had. Yet she had loved Brihtric...after a fashion...and had cared enough to murder him for refusing her. That girl had died too. Two deaths at her door.

Foolish! How many people died every day? Who at her Court or in Normandy or England was guiltless of having killed someone at some time? Death was no stranger in the world. It came swiftly, unexpectedly.

William had murdered many in his day yet God had given him the Conquest of England, but William had killed for state reasons, which was different she supposed. To kill for personal pride, was that a greater sin?

How sad to be old, for with the grey hairs came shadows from the past, to mock, to question. Soon it will be your turn, they said. Do your sins lie heavily upon you?

Robert and William in conflict, Richard and Adelisa dead...and now Constance dying.

She called her women to her and said: 'I will make a journey. I am going to pray at the shrine of St Eurole and beg of the saints to spare my daughter's life.'

*   *   *

She made the tedious journey to the Abbey of Ouche and there laid costly offerings at the shrine and on the altar.

She sat with the monks and dined in the refectory and begged them not to make any difference for her, for she came in all humility.

She prayed fervently for the forgiveness of her sins and a sign that she was forgiven would be the recovery of her daughter.

When she returned to Caen it was to find the news waiting for her that Constance was dead.

*   *   *

A great melancholy came to her. Her health began to deteriorate rapidly. She began to consult soothsayers so greatly did she long to hear that her son and husband were at peace.

304

There was little comfort for her.

Hearing that a German hermit could prophesy the future she sent gifts to him and begged him to tell her what the future hold for her.

His answer was not comforting. His visions had shown him a noble horse feeding in a rich pasture. Other animals approached but the horse would not allow them to encroach. In the vision the horse died and a silly steer came to take over the guardianship of the meadow; but he could not hold back the herd of marauders who trampled into the field, devoured the pasture and destroyed the land.

The interpretation was that the horse was William the Duke, King of England; the steer was Robert. Only the powerful horse could keep order. The vision showed what would happen if the horse was replaced by the steer.

'Illustrious lady,' wrote the hermit, 'do not rest in your endeavours to bring peace in Normandy. If you do not you will find misery and death for your Duke, and the ruin of your country.'

What have I done? Matilda asked herself. I have worked against him, the greatest man of his age, who is my life and my husband.

But Robert is my son.

Was ever a woman in such sad case?

She could not sleep. She wandered about the castle by night. Her women found her at the turret window watching for riders who would bring tidings which she feared would be evil.

They took her shivering to her bed.

Then one day when they went to awaken her they found her unable to rise.

They sent for William.

* * *

He sat by her bed and held her hand.

'William,' she said, 'how is it in England?'

'Well,' he told her, 'all is well.'

'And safe for you to leave and come to me?'

'I should have come in any case.'

'This is the last time, William.'

'Nay,' he said. 'You will get well.'

'You command it. Oh, William, God is one even you cannot command and Death an enemy you cannot overcome.'

He did not answer; she saw the tremor of his lips.
'William, beloved William,' she said, 'forgive me.'

'Forgive you for being my love, my life, the only one I
ever cared for or ever shall?'

'"Twas so, was it not? Am I forgiven my sins?'

'They *shall* be forgiven. We will make such offerings...'

'So you will command them in Heaven. My sins lie
heavy on me, William.'

'Nay, you have been a good woman...a good wife and
mother.'

'Sometimes it is difficult to be the two.'

'You did well,' he assured her.

'William...you and Robert...'

'He does well in England.'

'Let it remain so, then I shall die happy.'

He pressed her hand. 'Should you not rest, my love?'

'It makes no difference, William. This is the end for me.
You will miss me, William.'

'I beg of you...'

'I see tears in your eyes, William. They are the first you
ever shed...and for me.'

'For whom else should they be shed?'

'William, come close to me. Tell me it is the same as it
ever was...tell me nothing is changed.'

'I loved you through life and shall do so till death.'

A faint smile touched her lips so that she looked like the
old mischievous Matilda of her youth.

'No more beatings...no more loving...Oh, William!'

His emotion would not let him speak.

He sat by her bed holding her hand until she died.

Then he rose, strode away and none dared look at him.

He shut himself into his chamber and gave way to his
paroxysms of grief.

When he emerged he was the strong man again.
Whatever tragedy he had to face there was a Dukedom to
hold, a Kingdom to govern.

A Game of Chess

He was old and fat and weary of life without Matilda. His doctors warned him that he must eat less or his corpulence would be the death of him. He could still ride to the hunt but the fast steeds were no longer for him. He must judge a horse by its ability to carry him.

He had made England prosperous. His Doomsday Book was completed. The people might rail against this and what it meant to them but when a Danish invasion was threatened he explained to his people that for once it was better to buy off the Danes. Because of his wise government his exchequer was full and a settlement with the Danes, which would keep them out of the country, would be less costly than a war.

William had foreseen what would happen. The Danes fought among themselves for the gold he gave them. Their king and leader was killed and only half their number went back to Denmark. A wise move it was seen to be, for William had the means to fight and was never afraid of a battle; but on this occasion he had avoided bloodshed and in his own manner defeated the Danes.

'They'll never come back to England,' prophesied William, and he proved to be right.

*   *   *

There were occasions when he must take to his bed. His doctors ordered this. Then he must drink the potions they prescribed for him and eat frugally. After such treatment he found he had lost a little weight and therefore agreed with them, for his huge body was becoming a burden, and he was often out of breath.

He was still hunting frequently, usually with Rufus. Rufus was his great comfort now, although he enjoyed a discussion with Henry.

After his mother's death Robert made no pretence of friendship; he left his father and went back to Normandy. William expected trouble from him daily.

Often from his bed he thought over his life and assessed what he had done. He knew that he was the greatest ruler of his age. He had stern ideas and had put them into practice. He believed that England was a better country than it could have been under Harold. He had been fair to men who had obeyed him, and harsh with those who had not.

England was not the lawless place it had been when he came and conquered. Now it was said that a man could travel fearlessly on the lonely road with a purse of gold. No man dared slay another for that crime would be met with the direst punishment. William had abolished the death penalty. The putting out of eyes was a punishment often inflicted. A man should not have the comfort of dying, declared William, if he had broken his laws. He should live to suffer and be an example to others. William had always been a firm upholder of chastity. Any man who violated or attempted to violate a woman was punished by the cutting off of his sexual organs.

Such were his laws and from them he never diverged. He was determined to impose his will on the land and at last the people had come to realize that this could make life more comfortable for them in many respects.

His great weakness was his love of hunting and it was true that violating his beloved forests would rouse his anger to an extent far in excess of other crimes.

His thick dark hair had receded considerably and his enormous bulk encumbered him, but he still had that quality to command with a word and seated on his horse he looked indeed one of the finest figures of his day.

The change in him after Matilda's death was noticeable. He was morose, given to moods of fury; his temper was easily aroused. This he cooled by those jaunts in the forest.

He had subdued Wales, and the Scottish King was little more than a vassal. He had brought greatness to England.

Passionately devoted as he was to the country he had conquered, he was happiest in his native Normandy. There was always some reason for going. England he had conquered and somehow convinced the people that harsh as his rule was it was fundamentally good rule. But in Normandy there would be always trouble.

The French King was at heart an enemy; and, although he had not indulged in actual warfare, trouble was always about to break out.

That province of the Vexin was at the centre of trouble. When William's father had gone to the aid of the King of France this province had been given to Robert the Magnificent in gratitude for his services; but ever since, France had sought to take it back from Normandy. Previously there had been a treaty concerning this and this gave one section of it—that between the Epte and the Oise—to the French Counts of Mantes and the Normans held the land between the Epte and the Andelle. But the King of France to show his appreciation to Robert the Magnificent had agreed that Count Drogo of Mantes should be a vassal of Normandy. Some years before, the Count had died and the King of France had taken back Mantes, and from the castle the French began a series of raids into Norman territory.

William was at Rouen resting on his doctor's orders, and endeavouring at the same time to decrease his bulk.

Peace in England, he thought. I would there was peace in Normandy.

He thought of the stratagem he used with the Danes. That had surprised many, he was sure. He, William the Conqueror, who had never been defeated in battle, to buy off his enemies!

He laughed into his pillow.

A great general was first a strategist and that way had proved the right one. It had cost good gold, true, but how much more would a war have cost! And not a drop of English or Norman blood shed. What a stroke of genius to get Dane fighting Dane. They would never venture again to England.

And now the King of France. He would try to make some compromise with him ... at least until he was well enough to rise from his bed.

He had two good sons: Rufus and Henry, and they were here with him at the time.

He sent for them.

'Here is a mission for you both,' he said. 'You will have need of your diplomacy.'

The young men brightened a little. They found life a

little dull waiting on their father.

'Where, Father?' asked Rufus.

'To the Court of France.'

'To our enemies,' cried Henry.

'My son, you will learn that sometimes it is necessary to parley with our enemies.'

'I don't trust them,' said Henry.

'Do you think I do? Nay, go there, make yourself agreeable, discover the mood of the King of France. We will see if we can dispense with the costly business of war.'

He talked for a long time to his sons. He wondered about them when they were gone.

Rufus was rough but clever, in his way. Henry might be shrewd. He was a brilliant scholar. It would be amusing to report to Lanfranc whether Henry had been able to combine diplomacy with learning.

William settled down to await the outcome of what he called his embassy to France.

* * *

The King of France received the sons of the Duke of Normandy with a show of affection. The King's son, Prince Louis, a rather plump boy of fifteen, had been amused when he heard that William's sons were paying a visit. There was a theory in the French Court that the Normans were nothing more than pirates, rough in manner and ill-educated.

Louis, who was a very arrogant young man, was looking forward to having a little sport at the expense of Normans.

Rufus with his red face and ruddy locks was perhaps what they might have expected; Henry was a different type and, although his reputation as a scholar had preceded him, the young Prince of France refused to believe that, being a Norman, he could be anything but uneducated.

Philippe was extravagant in the extreme and after the almost parsimonious manner in which their father insisted his court should be run, the young men found that of the French very pleasant.

There was hunting, of course, at which Rufus excelled, and the young Princes gave quite good account of themselves at the joust.

Louis laughed at them in secret and said those were pastimes at which pirates might excel. He fancied himself

310

as a chess player and invited Henry to a game.

He did not realize that Henry had played chess with Lanfranc and his father and that he was of such a nature that he had quickly mastered the game. Slyly he had kept quiet about his skill and had rather mischievously allowed Louis to believe he was a novice.

Louis was fourteen; Henry nineteen; but as the young French boy said to his attendants, he would trounce him completely and then he could send the scholar back to Normandy to tell the tale. He had arranged that several of his friends should watch the game.

Rufus was among them, and knowing of his brother's skill at the game was prepared to enjoy himself.

Louis, very confident, sat down at the board. He won the advantage and started with white. He was smiling happily, confident in his supremacy.

Alas for Louis. They had made half a dozen moves when Henry had his knight. Nonplussed, Louis concentrated on the board.

'Ha!' cried Rufus. 'My Prince, you are about to lose a castle.'

Louis glowered. It was true. He was cornered. Angrily he moved and Henry took the castle. Louis' face grew dark and petulant while Henry sat calm and impassive. Those watching were silent with dismay because it was clear that Henry was a master of the board.

'Check,' challenged Henry.

'A thousand curses,' muttered Louis.

A few more moments passed and then came the inevitable checkmate. When Louis saw no way out and realized that he was beaten, his face puckered in anger.

He had been so certain that he would win; and here he was defeated and humiliated ... and by the son of the Duke of Normandy who should remember that even if he were the King of England, as Duke of Normandy he was a vassal of the King of France.

Louis had been over-indulged. He hated to be crossed and no one at Court ever dared do so. This fool of a Norman should have had the grace to let him win even if he was such a superior player.

In the sudden rage he picked up a handful of the chess men and threw them into Henry's face.

Henry laughed. 'That, monseigneur,' he said calmly, 'is not the way to play chess.'

311

'Silent...son of a bastard.'

Henry had heard from Lanfranc the truth about his father's birth; he knew how that word had haunted and disturbed his youth and how when he had married Matilda he had used it proudly to sign documents. But...this ill-tempered, ill-mannered little boy who thought he was so superior to Normans had used it in a derogatory form and Henry was not going to allow a fat, pimply, over-indulged coxcomb to utter a word against the greatest ruler in Europe.

Calmly he picked up the chessboard, scattering the rest of the pieces and brought it down on the Prince's head.

Louis screamed at him. 'How dare you...Norman vassal...how dare you touch the Prince of France.'

'How dare you speak disrespectfully of the King of England.'

'That...bastard...'

Henry rose. The Prince of France lay on the floor; Henry was on top of him, pummelling him while Louis screamed.

Those watching did not know what to do.

Louis screamed: 'Arrest him. Arrest this knave who has dared to insult France.'

Rufus was quick; he had seen the danger they were in.

'Come, Henry,' he said. 'Quick.'

Henry looked at his brother and saw the urgency in his face.

He rolled Louis across the floor into the group of watchers; then affecting to stroll he followed Rufus out of the room. They ran down the stone stairs into the courtyard and through the stables.

'Not a moment to lose,' panted Rufus. 'We could be held as hostages.'

They sprang on to two horses and galloped off.

Henry realized how quickly Rufus had acted, for as they passed through the castle gates they heard the alarms sounding throughout the castle.

'To Pontoise,' cried Rufus. 'A Norman town. We'll be safe there.'

They rode on and would not stop their sweating horses until they came to the friendly city. Rufus explained what had happened and commanded that a force of men be ready for him. Then he and Henry rode out with them and as they did so a small troop which the French King had sent out to bring the Princes back to him came galloping towards them. Rufus and Henry sprang out of their ambush with the men of Pontoise. There was a fight in which the French were outnumbered and to Rufus's great glee they were soon retreating.

Rufus led the troop after them right back to the gates of the castle; then they returned, burning the village on the way to let the French know that it was a victory for Normandy.

* * *

When they presented themselves to William he had already heard the tale. He laughed heartily. He was proud of them. Rufus had acted as he would have done in his youth and he was glad Henry had won the game of chess.

'It's the end of the peace talks, though,' he said. 'Now we must prepare for war.'

Furious at the insult he and his son had received at the hands of the Princes of Normandy the King of France gave vent to insults.

'So the Duke of Normandy lies abed to rid himself of his fat!' he said. He described with some wit, what it must be like in the Ducal castle with the great man lying in his bed with a swollen belly.

'By the Holy Mother of God,' he went on, 'the King of England takes longer over his lying in than do the women of France.'

This jest was repeated throughout the Court and it was not long before it reached William's ears.

William was furious. That the young King whom he had helped to his throne should so speak of him now that he was an old man, was unforgivable.

He would see whether there was anything womanish about William the Conqueror.

'When I go to my churching,' was his answer, 'I will make the King of France an offering of a hundred thousand candles that will set his country ablaze.'

It was war.

313

One Hundred Thousand Candles

RUFUS came to him.

'Father, let me take on this in your name. You should not leave your bed.'

'What say you?' cried William raising himself to glare at his son.

'I can command your troops. I am your son. It is for me to fight this battle.'

'The King of France and you would make me an old man. Nay. Let me tell you this: today I feel as young as I ever did. I am going to take Mantes. I am going to burn it to the ground. I am going to teach the King of France to choose his jests most carefully.'

Rufus could see that there was no dissuading him. It was useless to point out to him that he was no longer young and agile; that the only horse which could carry him was no longer of the calibre he was accustomed to taking into battle.

William rose from his bed and when they helped him into his armour he cried: 'I feel better than I have since the Queen died. I feel as I did when I was a young man going into battle.'

His attendants looked at him in astonishment.

It was true that on his horse he was magnificent. He looked invincible—William the Conqueror.

*　　*　　*

Mantes was blazing.

One hundred thousand candles burning for the King of

France. This would teach him what an adversary he had in the King of England.

The lust for battle was with William. He had been inactive too long. He must listen to his doctors; he just rid himself of this unwanted flesh. Then he would be as a young man again.

How fiercely the town burned! Spars of flaming wood were flying through the air. One almost hit his horse. The creature shied and in doing so trod on a burning ember.

It reared and William's enormous body was thrown against the heavy pommel of his saddle. He cried out in sudden agony. The horse moved sideways and William slid to the ground.

*　*　*

They took him to the castle of Rouen. He was in great pain from an internal injury and he knew his end was near. His physicians, skilled men though they were, could do nothing for him.

His agony was prolonged but he did not complain. For six weeks he lay in misery but this gave him the time his orderly mind needed to set his affairs in order.

He had great need of forgiveness, he said, for he had been guilty of much wrongdoing. But he had been thrust into office at too early an age. He had escaped death too often as a boy to have much fear of it. He had seen his best friends killed for their loyalty to him.

He commanded that his notaries be sent to him that they might prepare his behests. First he wished a sum of money to be set aside for rebuilding the churches he had burned at Mantes. More sums were allocated to monasteries, convents and churches. Nor did he forget the poor—both of England and Normandy.

His two sons were at his bedside. Robert was not there. Who could say where Robert was? Living in the castle of one of his father's enemies doubtless, awaiting the moment when he would rise and snatch that dukedom which had been the cause of the dissension between them.

It was William's wish that all those whom he had imprisoned should be set free with the exception of Bishop Odo. 'For,' he said, 'he was my brother and he owed all to me, yet he worked against me for his own gain. Let him remain in his dungeon.'

315

But his other half-brother, Robert of Mortain, fell to his knees at the bedside and implored William to reconsider his decision.

'He has sinned,' said Robert of Mortain, 'but he is our brother. For the sake of the mother who bore us all, do not, when you are on the point of facing your Maker, deny this act of mercy.'

William could not, in face of such pleading, refuse to be lenient; so Odo was freed on his brother's request.

'Though,' said William, 'this man will do no good wherever he is and it is weak of me to give in to you.'

Then he called his sons to come closer.

'My son Robert,' he said, 'has been a traitor to me. Yet I promised him the Duchy of Normandy and shall not break my promise. He will not rule well. He is selfish, arrogant and lacks the qualities of a ruler. Yet he is my first-born, greatly loved of his mother, and I gave him my promise. To you, my son William ... to you, Rufus, I leave the crown of England. And Henry, where is Henry? Ah, my son Henry. I have no land to leave you for your elder brothers have it. But I will give you five thousand pounds of silver.'

Henry looked dismayed. It was hard to understand that Robert, who had been his father's enemy, should have Normandy and he, who had striven to be a good son, no land at all.

'What shall I do with the money if I have no land?' asked Henry.

'Come close to me, Henry,' said William. 'Be content and trust in the Lord. Wait. I tell you Robert will have Normandy and William England. But in time you will have all my possessions and you will be greater in power and wealth than either of your brothers.'

There was hushed silence in the chamber. It was as though a prophet had spoken.

*   *   *

Death was elusive and the pain was great.

He lay on his bed waiting for the end. He was not always lucid in his mind, which ranged back over the past.

Once he thought he lay in bed with a brave man who had guarded him and that he awoke and found a bloodstained corpse beside him. Often he believed Matilda was with him. Then a smile of tenderness would curve his lips.

But again and again he was brought back to the chamber of death by the violence of his pain.

Through a haze he saw Rufus.

'What do you here?' he cried. 'You should be claiming your kingdom.'

His mind wandered again. I have lived a long time, he thought. It is nearly sixty years. I have achieved much and men will remember me. I shall stand beside my ancestors. 'Rolo,' men will say, 'Richard the Fearless, William the Conqueror; and in the halls of Valhalla they would not be ashamed of me.'

But he was a Christian and he could hear the bells of Rouen.

Soon they would be tolling for him.

'I commend myself to Holy Mary, Mother of God,' he said, 'that by her prayers she may reconcile me with her Son, Our Lord Jesus Christ.'

It was the 9th of September of the year 1087, twenty-one years since he had landed at Pevensey Bay.

My life is ebbing fast, he told himself. The pain is nearly over. This is farewell to my power, to my conquests, to all earthly glories. Soon I shall be with God...and Matilda.

BIBLIOGRAPHY

Aubrey, William Hickman Smith	*The National and Domestic History of England*
Barlow, Frank	*William I and the Norman Conquest*
Brooke, Christopher	*From Alfred to Henry III*
Brown, R. Allen	*The Normans and the Norman Conquest*
Compton, Piers	*Harold the King*
Coryn, M.	*The Acquirer, Life of William the Conqueror*
Davis, H.W.C.	*England under the Normans and Angevins*
Delarue-Mardrus, Lucie. Translated by Colin Shepherd	*William the Conqueror*
Evans, R.B.D. Wilson	*King William the Conqueror*
Guizot, M. Translated by Robert Black	*History of France*
Linklater, Eric	*The Conquest of England*
Lloyd, Allan	*The Year of the Conquest*
Loyn, H.R.	*Anglo-Saxon England and the Norman Conquest*
Lytton, Lord	*Harold*
Matthew, D.T.M.	*The Norman Conquest*
Page, R.I.	*Life in Anglo-Saxon England*
Poole, A.L.	*From Doomsday Book to Magna Carta*
Slocombe, George	*William the Conqueror*
Stenton, F.M.	*Anglo-Saxon England*
Stenton, F.M.	*William the Conqueror*

Stephen, Sir Leslie and	The Dictionary of National
Lee, Sir Sidney	Biography
(edited by)	
Strickland, Agnes	Lives of the Queens of England :

GREAT ROMANTIC NOVELS

SISTERS AND STRANGERS   PB 04445 $2.50
by Helen Van Slyke

Three women—three sisters each grown into an independent lifestyle—now are three strangers who reunite to find that their intimate feelings and perilous fates are entwined.

THE SUMMER OF THE SPANISH WOMAN

CB 23809 $2.50

by Catherine Gaskin

A young, fervent Irish beauty is alone. The only man she ever loved is lost as is the ancient family estate. She flees to Spain. There she unexpectedly discovers the simmering secrets of her wretched past...meets the Spanish Woman...and plots revenge.

THE CURSE OF THE KINGS   CB 23284 $1.95
by Victoria Holt

This is Victoria Holt's most exotic novel! It is a story of romance when Judith marries Tybalt, the young archeologist, and they set out to explore the Pharaoh's tombs on their honeymoon. But the tombs are cursed...two archeologists have already died mysteriously.

8000